THE HIERARCH WARS

THE HIERARCH WARS SERIES
BOOK ONE

M.J. BADAL

This is a work of fiction. Names, characters, places, and incidents are either products of the author's imagination or used fictitiously. Any resemblance to actual persons, living or dead, or actual events is purely coincidental.

First edition

Published by Moon Bean Publishing, LLC

ISBN: 979-8-9948495-2-1 (ebook)

ISBN: 979-8-9948495-0-7 (paperback)

ISBN: 979-8-9948495-1-4 (hardcover)

I did it, Papa.

Lumesphere

SIRENYA
ISLAND
BLUEGILL
ISLAND
CASPER
ISAND
EVERETT
ISLAND
ALIF
ISLAND
AKHAD
ISLAND
N
W
E
S
AELTHEON

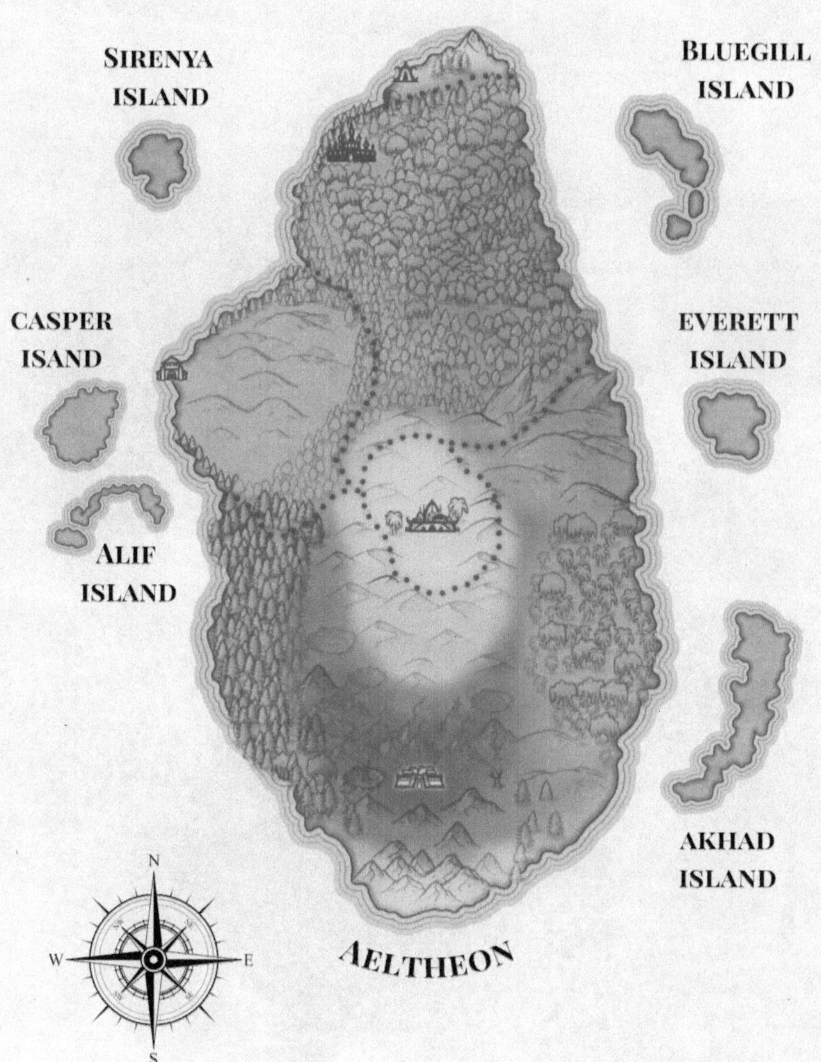

Aeltheon

REYLAND
Reyani Temple
Crystal Court
VIRENNA
THERIBANE
Veyn Manor
RUITHEON
Aurethium
ZAROKAN
Infernal Citadel

ONE

Evalene Lovejoy sat cross-legged on a granite bench, a half-eaten apple in one hand and a small, weathered journal in the other. The sky above the cloister's open roof had begun to pale—a dusty blue-gray that came just before the sun outshone the stars. Water droplets from last night's rain clung to unkempt vines, and the air carried a chill that seeped through her wool coat.

She shivered, but she didn't mind. Nestled deep within the heart of the Reyani Temple, the cloister was her favorite place to steal a quiet moment and breathe in the scent of nearby pine forests.

A spectral white orb hovered above her shoulder. The light spirit brushed lovingly against her cheek, then drifted back to its place over the journal, casting a warm glow across the open pages.

Evalene flipped to the final page and bit into her apple.

The journal was old—its leather spine cracked and its pages browned with age. It had belonged to Linius Wells, a former Shaman King, and contained handwritten accounts of his expeditions. She traced a finger over the final paragraph.

After years of looking for answers about our ancestors, my journey must come to an end. The dangers of Hollowrift cannot be taken lightly, and though I feel immense guilt over the lives lost, our expeditions have not been in vain. I have learned from my mistakes and enacted laws to prohibit Witch-kind from traversing through Hollowrift, for beyond the portal lies a world of death and darkness.

It is no place for the living.

Evalene had read this entry before. Several times, in fact, and she could recite it from memory alone.

Wells's adventures were morbid, but they were equally fascinating. He wrote about Hollowrift's shifting landscapes and creatures that prowled its darkness. His words were laced with apparent fear, yet she couldn't help but marvel at the boldness it must have taken to embark on such journeys.

Evalene smoothed a crease in the page and wondered if any of his adventurous spirit had carried into her. After all, she was one of his later reincarnations. Perhaps some of Wells's courage still lived within her, urging her toward a journey beyond the temple walls.

She'd have to ask the Spirit Matron about it. Though, knowing the temple's head keeper, she'd likely receive a lecture rather than a straightforward answer.

"Evy! There you are!"

The voice echoed from the hall across the cloister. Evy startled, and the apple slipped from her hand. She frowned, watching it roll away.

Irma hurried into the cloister, dark curls bouncing with each step. The handmaid's round, freckled face was flushed as she stopped in front of Evy.

"If you weren't going to be in your room this morning," Irma said, pressing a hand to her chest, "you could have at least left a note. I walked into an empty room and immediately thought, 'Oh, Gods. The Shaman Queen finally did it. She ran away. Under *my* watch.'" She clutched her apron. "My heart nearly stopped. I thought the Spirit Sisters were going to skin me alive."

Evy closed the journal and tucked it into her coat pocket. "Run away? Where would I even go?"

Her mind briefly drifted to her parents' farmstead on the outskirts of Reyland. The low stone cottage. The smell of her mother's fresh-baked bread cooling on the windowsill. If she ever tried to run away, that was the only place she would go.

She shook the thought away, feeling both foolish and guilty. If she ran to her parents' house, the Spirit Matron and Sisters would find her within the hour and drag her back to the temple. Besides, what reason did she have to run? Her place was at the temple. This was where she belonged until she died and the next Shaman was born to replace her.

A slow smirk spread across Irma's face. "I thought maybe you'd finally worked up the courage to run away and elope with Aeric."

Evy's cheeks caught on fire. She had been enduring this particular brand of teasing since they were girls—since the day a young Irma had spotted Aeric visiting from the kitchen doorway and made it her life's mission to make Evy squirm about it.

"Don't be ridiculous."

"I'm just saying—"

"Stop it, Irma."

Irma raised her palms in surrender. "Fine, fine." She swallowed whatever joke she had been about to make and gave Evy a once-over.

Her expression dropped, amusement curdling into horror.

"You're a mess!" Irma plucked a small green leaf from Evy's hair. "I can't let you walk into the Bonding Rites looking like this."

Beyond the courtyard walls, the sky had transformed. The

light spirit beside Evy dimmed, sensing the redundancy of its glow against the growing sunlight.

Evy's eyes widened. "I thought I had more time."

Irma grabbed her hand. "You don't."

They sprinted toward her chambers, their footsteps echoing off the stone as they cut through the corridors. By the time they arrived, Evy was already fumbling with the buttons on her coat. Irma closed the door behind them, and Evy tugged her nightgown over her head, the cold air biting at her skin.

Irma crossed to the fireplace and flicked her wrist. A tiny orange wisp bloomed at her fingertip and darted forward in a streak of gold. The fire spirit sank into the logs, and flames leaped to life, warmth spilling into the room.

"The Bonding Rites are at the end of every season," Irma said. "You do remember that's *today*, don't you?"

Evy busied herself with her stockings.

She *had* forgotten. How had she let herself forget? It was still so cold that it didn't feel like the end of spring yet.

Irma flung open the armoire doors and rifled through Evy's robes.

"If I could perform the Bonding Rites for you, I would," she said, then held up a simple white dress. "But alas, that's a task reserved for the Shaman, in case you forgot that too."

"I couldn't forget even if I wanted to." Evy took the dress and pulled it over her head. "The Spirit Sisters recited my duties to me before I could form full sentences."

Irma reached back in and plucked a set of deep-violet ceremonial robes embroidered with gold thread. She walked over and held them open for Evy. "Gods, I can't imagine being raised in this temple by the Spirit Sisters." She shivered. "Poor thing."

"It wasn't that bad," Evy said, stepping into the robes. "They were kind to me. And I still got to visit my parents once in a while."

"They were kind because they thought they were raising Goddess Reya incarnate," Irma said with an incredulous scoff.

Evy sighed but didn't argue. There was no winning that particular debate with Irma, mostly because she knew it was likely true. And because of what it meant. Being raised as a vessel of a deity left little room to be a girl, which was what Evy truly felt she was.

Every time frustration stirred over the unfairness of it all, a pang of guilt followed. She was Reya's vessel. There was no room for fairness.

Irma tied a brown belt around the ensemble, tugged it snug, then stepped back to assess her work. She grabbed a comb from the vanity and gestured for Evy to sit.

"Hold still." Her fingers moved swiftly, combing out tangles. Then, she weaved an intricate braid while leaving a few snowy tendrils to frame Evy's face. The pale strands were vivid against her tawny skin, like the season's first frost streaking across golden autumn grass.

"Oh, before I forget!" Irma bounced with sudden excitement. "I heard a rumor that a courier rode in from Ruitheon. An Elf, and a handsome one, from what the girls are saying."

Evy's brows lifted. An official courier sent directly from the capital?

"He hasn't made it to the temple yet—though I assume he eventually will—but the other servant girls are loitering outside, pretending to look busy just to catch a glimpse."

"I can imagine." Evy smirked. "We don't get many visitors to this domain. Definitely not many handsome ones."

"What do you think he's here for? That's more than a week of travel just to deliver a message."

Evy considered. It had to be information sensitive enough to warrant an official courier rather than the regular post. "If I had to guess, he's probably here to announce that Thylarion Veyn is dead."

"The Hierarch?" Irma's hands paused. "I was wondering when he'd finally kick the bucket. Do you think the courier is here to name his replacement?"

Evy shook her head. "I don't think so, not if he only just died. I'd imagine the Hierarch Wars would take at least a month or two to conclude before we'd know the successor." She met Irma's gaze in the mirror. "But let's be honest. It'll be another member of the Veyn family."

"The Shifters always seem to find a way." Irma tugged a little too hard on a knot in Evy's hair. "The Elementals and Ethereals never really stood a chance against them."

"Ow— Irma!"

"Sorry." She winced, then worked more carefully. "So why bother telling *us* if everything's already set in motion?"

"Probably just a courtesy," Evy said as she brushed Irma's hand away to work through the knot herself. She bit the inside of her cheek. What else would it be? It's not like the Witches had anything to do with it.

Irma swatted her hand away. "Seriously, Evy, did you intentionally tie these knots in your hair?" She took the clump and worked through it gently. "Anyway, I think we should have some kind of say in how mana is governed. Having a little more power flowing through Reyland would be nice."

"I agree, but I didn't make Aeltheon's rules."

"Yes, but can't you say something about it?"

"It's not like I can waltz into Ruitheon and demand an audience with the Council. Even I can't leave the Reylandic borders without a permit."

"But you're a *queen*. How can you stand the disrespect?"

Outside of this domain, she was barely seen as a queen—she knew that without ever stepping foot out of Reyland. To ask for respect would be like asking a wolf to honor the sheep. "Maybe we should feel lucky to have a land of our own."

"Do you really believe that?"

Evy pondered for a moment, then shrugged.

"Still," Irma said as she pinned a few loose strands into place, "an Elf riding all the way from the capital just to tell us some old Shifter's dead? That has to mean something."

She was right. It *was* odd that the Council would bother sending an official courier to inform Reyland of anything. But Evy didn't like the way Irma spoke of the dead.

She shot her a warning look, mouth half open to scold her maid, but the deep clang of the bell echoed through the temple halls.

Evy leaped from her seat and scurried for the door. "We'll talk more later. Thank you, Irma!"

"Wait— What about breakfast?" Irma shouted after her. "I don't want you fainting during the Bonding Rites!"

Evy rounded the corner as Irma's groan echoed behind her.

TWO

Before entering the Sanctum, Evy took a moment to compose herself, straightening her robes while catching her breath. A warm stream of light filtered through the window and struck her face as the sun crested over the hill. She was right on time.

But running across the temple had left her heart pounding against her chest. She couldn't go in like this. She drew in slow breaths, then looked up at the wooden doors of the Sanctum, where a mural had been painted in vivid strokes.

Reya stood at the center with her silver hair shining like starlight, her arms open and raised at her sides. Radiant energy trailed from the Goddess of Spirits' hands, connecting her to a circle of kneeling Witches, young and old.

Behind Reya stood another celestial figure—Rui, her mother and the Goddess of Mana. She embraced Reya, her eyes shut, savoring the closeness of her child. Cerulean strands of hair spilled downward, weaving through the painted ground like a coursing river.

Evy lingered on those blue strands.

Mana.

Without it, no one in Lumesphere could wield magic. Not the Shifters. Not the Ethereals. Not the Elementals. Not even the Witches.

It was Rui's gift to the entire realm. The method in which Witches had to access it should not make them lesser. How could the realm not see? The Witches were part of this world too. Yet they were kept at the edge of the continent, penned where the mana intentionally ran thinnest.

The sharp clearing of a throat jolted Evy from her thoughts.

A Spirit Sister stood beside her, watching with quiet expectation. The woman wore a heavy robe, its hood pulled up to shadow her face. Only the faint curve of her lips was visible beneath the fabric.

"Your Majesty." The Spirit Sister's tone was polite but edged with impatience. "If you would please, the families are waiting."

Evy exhaled and gave one last glance at the mural before nodding. The Spirit Sister pulled open the heavy wooden doors, revealing the chamber beyond.

Colored light streamed through the tall stained glass windows, scattering mosaics of violet and sapphire across the polished stone floor.

Evy crossed the threshold, the prismatic glow washing over her as she stepped into the Sanctum's sacred space.

Inside, the Spirit Sisters glided through the chamber, their copper thuribles swinging in slow arcs. The scent of lavender and sage drifted through the air, thin curls of smoke rising toward the domed ceiling.

At the heart of the chamber, Witch families stood gathered before a circular stone platform. Parents clutched their children's hands. The little ones, no older than three to five years, shifted nervously, their wide eyes darting around the vast chamber. Some sagged against their parents, heavy with sleep, unaccustomed to such early mornings.

The murmur hushed as Evy stepped through the towering

doors. Instinctively, she straightened her back and lifted her chin. The families dropped to one knee, bowing their heads.

"Your Majesty," they rang in unison.

A stout, elderly woman wearing a hooded lavender robe stepped forward, ringing a small silver bell. The Spirit Matron turned to Evy, her stern demeanor obscured beneath a gossamer veil.

"The Sanctum has been cleansed, Your Majesty. The dark spirits will be kept at bay."

Evy offered a nod of gratitude.

The Matron faced the gathered assembly. "Today, our blessed Shaman Queen will perform the sacred ritual that grants our young their power through spirit."

At her signal, the Spirit Sisters stepped forward, forming a crescent as the Matron continued.

"But first, we give thanks to our generous Goddess, who took pity on the Forgotten Folk." The Matron's voice swelled. "When Reya saw that our ancestors were left behind, unable to use the gift of mana, she offered them the ability to bond with spirits."

The Spirit Matron took Evy's hand and gently guided her to the center of the crescent. "This gift from Reya transformed the Forgotten Folk into Witches, forever marking our people as her children. And now our holy vessel—our Shaman—shall perform the rites in our Goddess's honor."

Evy squared her shoulders and approached the waiting families. Then she knelt to meet the children at eye level.

"Do you know what's going to happen today?" Evy asked, scanning their eager faces.

"No!" the children chorused in unison.

The parents exchanged amused glances.

"Well," Evy said, "today is a very special day."

A few of the children gasped, turning to their friends, eyes wide with excitement.

"Today, you're going to bond with spirits! That means you'll get to use magic just like your mamas and papas!"

The children squealed and bounced, their joy echoing through the chamber. The Spirit Sisters didn't need to cleanse the Sanctum. The children's laughter alone could banish any residual darkness.

"Now listen carefully." Evy put a finger to her lips. "I'm going to open a gate and let the spirits come through. They'll take a look at all of you, and if they feel connected to your soul, they'll tell me who they want to bond with."

She rose. "Some of you might receive one spirit, and some a few. It all depends on what the spirits decide. Are you ready?"

"Yes!" the children cheered.

Evy stepped onto the platform.

The Spirit Sisters moved through the gathering, guiding the families into an orderly line. As Evy prepared to begin the ritual, her gaze swept over the chamber until it landed on an unexpected figure.

Aeric?

Near the back of the room, leaning against a stone pillar, was Aeric Whitlock. Arms crossed over his chest, he watched her with a familiar mix of warmth and mischief.

Evy narrowed her gaze in a silent, pointed question: *What are you doing here?*

Aeric scratched at his tousled auburn hair, then shrugged. His lips quirked into a roguish smile.

Evy shook her head, though heat gathered in her face.

The chamber had fallen into expectant silence, the children standing in a neat row, patiently waiting.

Evy closed her eyes and focused. The temperature in the chamber fluctuated. She exhaled slowly, attuning herself to the presence surrounding her.

When she opened her eyes, the chamber remained still, but to her sight alone, it thrummed with motion.

Spirits invisible to all but the Shaman drifted around her in a spectral dance. They glowed in different shades, their forms shifting between light and shadow. Their energy brushed affectionately against her skin.

She stretched out her hands, welcoming her bound spirits and letting their vibrations thread through her.

She envisioned a gate waiting in an unseen plane.

A shadowed realm suspended between worlds.

It was a passageway—a liminal threshold where spirits and souls drifted. Where the expeditions in Linius Wells's journal took place.

The vision bled into her spirits, and they whispered for her command.

"Open the door to Hollowrift."

Thin blue strands of glowing mana gathered in the cracks beneath her feet and surged upward, rising inside her like a swelling tide.

The spirits pressed closer, siphoning energy from her body. Countless overlapping voices crowded her thoughts as they all reached for the unseen door.

"Open." The command rang out, louder this time. The spirits answered, moving through their bond to draw in mana and shape it to her will. Her vision blurred at the edges. Her knees locked. She pressed her fingers together to keep them from shaking.

A violent gust of wind tore through the room, spiraling outward in a sudden rush. The sconces flickered wildly. Parents hushed their children, murmuring reassurances.

Before Evy, a gleaming strand of silver sliced through the air, stretching as tall as the chamber itself.

The space trembled.

Slowly, the line split apart, widening like the slow unfurling of a scroll. An endless black chasm swirled within its borders. It shifted and warped until the void gave way to more.

She still couldn't control where the gate would lead, and with each opening, Hollowrift revealed a different view. This time, a meadow emerged from the darkness. Wind swayed the tall grass, and the landscape appeared bleached of color.

Evy's words carried through the chamber. "Come forward, spirits, and forge the sacred bond with a child of Reya. Let spirit and soul intertwine."

The chamber remained silent. Everyone was still. For a moment, it appeared as if nothing was happening.

Until beyond the gate, luminous figures emerged from the darkness.

Wisps of light drifted in, shifting in myriad colors. They hovered near the threshold, pulsing. Slowly, the first spirits floated in.

The spirits moved, studying the children. Some hovered near one child, then zipped away to another, whispering words in soft, musical tones only Evy could hear.

This one. Yes, this one.

They were assessing who they would bond with for life.

A few of the spirits didn't drift toward the children at all. They circled around Evy, brushing against her hands, her shoulders, her neck. Their whispers layered over one another in soft, eager voices.

You. We choose you.

Evy gently nudged them away with her will. *Not me. You're here for them.*

The spirits paused before reluctantly floating toward the waiting children.

It happened every time. The spirits couldn't help it. To them, she was Reya. She was their Goddess.

Evy felt a sudden pressure behind her eyes. She wasn't a Goddess, but the spirits didn't know that. They couldn't sense her mortal limitations—that every bond added another voice to contain, more pressure straining against the dam.

Evy looked at the crowd ahead of her.

The gathered families couldn't see the spirits, but they could feel the electric hum of their energy. Evy forced herself to smile at the parents through her discomfort. "The bonding ceremony may now begin. Who's first?"

A tall, broad-shouldered man stepped forward from the gathered families, a small boy cradled in his arms. The man's dark hair was cropped short, and his bright green eyes had the sharp vigilance of a soldier. Leo Warring, captain of the Bound Blades—Reyland's border guards and peacekeeping force.

"Captain Warring, how is your wife?"

Leo bowed. "Your Majesty. She's well, thank you. Due very soon."

"That's wonderful news," Evy said. "I suppose I'll see you back here in a few years for your second child's Bonding Rites."

"Yes, I imagine so." Leo chuckled. He set his son down in front of Evy.

She crouched. "And what's your name?"

The little boy puffed out his chest. "I'm Eno! I'm three!" He proudly held up two fingers.

"Enolios, say 'Your Majesty' when you address the queen," his father prompted.

"Your Majy!" Eno beamed up at her.

Evy patted his head before straightening and surveyed the spirits drifting through the chamber. "Are there any spirits here who'd like to bond with Enolios Warring?"

A white wisp darted forward, flitting excitedly over Eno's head before returning to hover beside Evy.

"Ah! A light spirit has chosen you, little one. They are strong protectors who will shield you from the forces of darkness. May I take your hand so I can complete the bond?"

Eno looked up at his father, who nodded. The child placed his hand in Evy's.

She extended her other hand toward the spirit and cradled

the glowing wisp between her fingers. She closed her eyes and reached inward, summoning Reya's essence as she began the ritual.

"I bind you, spirit, to your chosen, forever entwined with his soul."

A pulse of energy thrummed through Evy's fingertips, an invisible thread weaving between the spirit and Eno. When she opened her eyes, the wisp flared brightly before flowing into the child's chest.

Eno gasped, his tiny body jolting at the sensation. His hands clenched into fists, and his bright green eyes widened with wonder.

A second wisp drifted forward, shifting between hues of earthy green and warm brown.

Evy's brows lifted. "It appears a strong earth spirit has chosen you as well." She turned to the wisp, giving it permission to bond. With her concentration split, the gate strained, threatening to shut if she didn't focus harder. A bead of sweat slid down her temple as the spirit settled within the child's heart.

Just as Evy was about to release his hand, a speck of molten orange and red darted toward Eno, circling his head in quick, excited spirals.

"It seems another spirit would like to bond with your son."

Leo, who possessed two spirits of his own, broke into a wide, proud grin.

The moment a child was chosen by their spirits shaped the entire course of their future. It determined their affinities, their careers. Even their identities.

Most Witches bonded with one spirit during their Rites, two at most. Being chosen by three meant Eno possessed a natural affinity for magic.

Evy squinted at the restless spirit. "This one is fire, and a very energetic one at that."

She completed the third bond, feeling flames thread into

Eno's being. As soon as she finished the ritual, Eno let out a triumphant "Woo-hoo!" and sprinted across the chamber, arms flailing with newfound energy.

A Spirit Sister hurried after him, trying to tame the boy.

The sight made Evy laugh. "He's going to make a formidable soldier one day, Captain Warring. When the time comes, bring his Bound Blades application straight to me. I'll make him my personal guard."

Leo inclined his head, brimming with gratitude. "Thank you for the honor, Your Majesty." Then, he hesitated, gaze narrowing as it flicked toward the gate to Hollowrift.

"Is everything alright?" Evy asked, half expecting to see a creature emerging from the portal.

Leo's voice dropped. "I don't mean to cause any concern, but there have been troubling reports along the outskirts of the village."

Evy's expression tightened. "What kind of reports?"

"Bodies found outside their graves," Leo said slowly. "Three so far."

Evy frowned. "Grave robbing?"

"That was my first thought." Leo shook his head. "But the earth wasn't disturbed from above. It was pushed outward from below. As though the bodies had clawed their way out themselves." He rubbed his chin. "It seems like the start of Draemor activity."

Evy's eyes widened. *Draemor? In Reyland?*

Leo cut in. "Don't worry, Your Majesty. I've already brought this matter to the Magister, and we're investigating if it's merely some natural phenomenon. Perhaps pressure from a geyser near the graves."

His attention navigated toward the open portal again. "Being near the gate simply made me uneasy."

"The Sanctum is warded, Captain Warring." She gestured toward the sconces lining the walls, each filled with the faint glow of light spirits. "No Draemor could come within a mile of this temple, let alone through that gate."

Leo gave a short nod, though the tension around his mouth didn't fully ease. He bade her farewell, then collected his son and hoisted the squirming child onto his shoulders.

Evy turned back to the gathered families patiently awaiting their turn. Hope lit their faces, anticipation bright in their expressions. None were aware of her conversation with Leo Warring.

She forced a small smile.

"Alright. Who's next?"

THREE

With a slow exhale, Evy released the strain at her wrist and let the portal close. While she felt the exhaustion deep in her bones, she never let it show in front of anyone. Performing the Bonding Rites always drained her. At least every child had bonded with a spirit today—none would have to return next season. Perhaps that meant fewer children would come at the next Rites. A welcome reprieve, if it were true.

Most of the families gathered their children and filed out of the Sanctum. A few remained near the stone platform, kneeling in hushed prayer to Reya.

Evy slipped out of the chamber and wove through the halls until she reached the cloister. Her stomach let out a protesting growl. She had skipped breakfast and should have gone straight to the refectory for lunch, but her mind was just as hungry for a moment of peace and stillness.

She sank onto the granite bench and sighed. The splash of the fountain and the soft chirping of birds offered a gentle serenity.

A sudden flash of light zipped past her.

She scanned the garden and found a bright blue wisp hovering in the air.

"Oh, hello," she said to the water spirit. "You were supposed to return to Hollowrift. Did you get left behind?"

The spirit floated up to Evy's face and brushed against her cheek.

"You want to bond with me?"

The spirit bounced in place, and she extended her hand. The water spirit landed in her palm and dissolved into her skin. She felt its small voice whisper in the back of her mind. Another voice. How many could she contain?

Though she feared she might be nearing an undefined limit, she rarely had the heart to refuse them.

Unlike other Witches, Evy's connection to Reya kept her open to bonds, her soul a constant conduit for spirits. As a result, she was bonded to over a hundred of them.

Once, when Evy voiced concern about the number, the Spirit Matron had dismissed it as *"typical for a Shaman."* And that was that.

She flexed her fingers as the water spirit's energy folded into her, ready to carry out her will.

"Found you."

Evy jumped but relaxed the moment she saw him.

"Whitlock."

"Lovejoy." Aeric approached with a wide grin.

"What brings you here?"

He sat beside her, and without thinking, she edged away. She cringed at her reaction.

"How could I miss the Bonding Rites? Such a moving ceremony."

He was still in his work clothes: a beige shirt with rolled-up sleeves, revealing strong, sun-bronzed forearms. The scent of salt and sea clung to him, and a few fishing lures peeked from the pocket of his dark green vest. He looked like he belonged on the docks, not here in the temple.

"I do this four times a year, Aeric. It's hardly an event to miss work over."

"Okay, fine," he admitted. "I came to see you."

"Really?" Her voice cracked. She frowned and cleared her throat.

Aeric leaned a little closer. His blue-gray eyes were like storm clouds rolling over a summer sky. "And I was hoping I could walk you home this afternoon. To see your parents, of course."

Evy caught the faintest glimpse of a dimple in his right cheek. Had he always had that dimple?

Her heart stumbled. They'd been friends for as long as she could remember, but lately, being around him felt different.

As he'd grown, Aeric developed sharp, handsome features she found hard to ignore. His shoulders had broadened to the point where her arms no longer reached fully around him. His laughter had deepened, often replaying in her mind.

She could still remember the first time they met, two small children with scraped knees and muddy hands, playing by the riverbank while their parents talked.

Somewhere along the way, he had grown taller and stronger, becoming a man who left her conflicted about her own emotions.

The Shaman took no vows of solitude like the Spirit Sisters and the Spirit Matron. There was no law etched in ancient scripture forbidding the Shaman from loving someone. But the expectation lived in the spaces between their teachings—in the way the Matron spoke of Evy's devotion to Reyland, to the Witches, and to her role as Reya's chosen vessel. Her obligations left no room for anything else.

Every hour Evy spent thinking about Aeric was an hour she wasn't giving to her people.

And she thought about him quite often.

"Oh, right. My parents. I was planning to head to the village to see them anyway," she said, desperately hoping her voice wouldn't expose the flutter in her chest. "But won't Yorik be angry you're skipping work?"

"My brother will understand if I miss a few hours. The fish aren't going anywhere."

Aeric's fingers brushed hers before he gently took her hand.

"I never get to see you, Evy."

For a second, neither of them moved. Evy was painfully aware of how his fingers fit between hers, how warm his calloused palm was. Then Aeric seemed to realize what he was doing and let go.

He cleared his throat and scratched the back of his neck.

Evy's cheeks were burning like fire. "I-I, um."

Aeric let out a nervous breath of laughter. "I was already heading toward our neighborhood. Yorik told me he'd handle the fish on his own and gave me the rest of the day off."

"What a good brother."

"Yeah, I suppose." His usual confidence softened, and for a moment, he almost looked like a boy again. She smiled. He was still Aeric, still one of her best friends, even if her heart hadn't quite gotten the message.

Though, if she were being honest, she wasn't sure she wanted it to. The flutter in her chest made her feel like a normal girl. Just a seventeen-year-old Witch with awkward feelings she didn't know what to do with.

"Alright," she said at last, then pushed herself off the bench and looped her arm through his. The warmth of his skin beneath her touch made her pulse stutter.

"I'm honored," Aeric said. His bicep tightened subtly.

"I should point out," Evy said, "that the fish are, in fact, going somewhere."

Aeric raised his brow. "What?"

"Earlier, you said the fish aren't going anywhere," Evy said. "They're literally swimming away. Shouldn't a fisherman know that?"

Aeric huffed. "You've always been smug, you know that? Ever since we were kids."

"Oh? I don't remember that at all. You must be making it up."

"Making it up? When we were ten, I tried to show you how to tie a proper fishing knot, and you—"

"Tied it better than you?"

"See?" Aeric groaned. "This is exactly what I mean."

Evy nudged him with her shoulder.

Aeric nudged her back. "Anyway, shall we get going?"

"Lead the way, Whitlock."

As they turned to leave, a tall woman stepped into the cloister, her steel-gray hair meticulously braided and wrapped around her head.

"There you are." Fine lines surrounded her deep brown eyes. Dark violet robes trailed behind her, and a stiff collar framed her long neck.

Evy straightened and released Aeric's arm.

"Your Majesty." Magister Orianna Gale bowed. "May I have a word?"

It wasn't like Orianna to seek her out unless it was urgent. Her conversation with Leo came back to her. "Is this about the grave robbers?"

Aeric snapped his head toward Evy. His brows knit together, mouth parting. Evy patted his arm in reassurance.

"Oh, no." Orianna shook her head. "A courier came from Ruitheon today."

"I'm aware," Evy replied. Though, if she were being honest, she had forgotten entirely through the rush of the morning.

"He was here to deliver a letter," Orianna continued. "I had him bring it straight to me, since you were occupied with the Rites this morning."

"What did it say? I assume it announced the death of the Hierarch."

"It did."

"Not surprising. Was that all, then?" Evy asked.

"It also announced that the Hierarch Wars will begin next month to determine the next Hierarch."

"I appreciate the courtesy, but I'm not sure why an official courier had to come all this way just to tell us that. News would've reached us eventually," Evy said as she linked her arm through Aeric's again. He had gone stiff. Not that she could blame him. Next to Evy, Orianna held the most power in Reyland. While Evy oversaw the spiritual and ritualistic responsibilities, Orianna managed much of the governance and legislative affairs.

"If that's all, Magister, I was hoping to spend the rest of the afternoon visiting my parents."

"Before you go, there's more. The letter contained additional news." Orianna's eyes darkened. "Of utmost importance."

A long pause followed. Her gaze dropped to the floor.

"The suspense is killing me, Orianna. What is it?"

"It's about Reyland's participation in the Hierarch Wars."

Evy released Aeric's arm. "What do you mean?"

Orianna opened her mouth to speak, but at the sound of Aeric shifting, her expression hardened. She turned her gaze on him, signaling a demand for his departure.

"Perhaps we can discuss this further in the study?"

Aeric hesitated, silently asking if she wanted him to stay. She did.

"I think it's best if you go ahead without me, Aeric. The Magister and I have a lot to discuss."

He patted her shoulder. "I'll see you later, then?"

She nodded. "I still plan to visit home."

Aeric left the cloister. She had been so close to a normal afternoon. A walk through the village. Her parents' kitchen.

Aeric's arm warm against hers, butterflies tangling in her stomach.

She composed herself, then gestured for Orianna to lead the way.

FOUR

The study was quiet, save for the distant whisper of wind against the temple walls. Lantern light danced across shelves filled with ancient tomes, and the scents of parchment and candle wax filled the air.

Orianna stood near the shelves, her robes swaying along the stone floor as she carefully selected a scroll. She unfurled it across a wooden table, revealing a map of Aeltheon.

"Please, sit." She gestured to the chair across from her.

Evy obeyed. "What did you mean by 'participation'? I assume Reyland won't be entering the trials."

Orianna set her elbows on the table and leaned forward until she was eye level with Evy. "That's exactly what it means."

Evy studied Orianna's face, searching for any trace of jest. "Is this real?"

"See for yourself." Orianna slid a letter across the table. The Council of Aeltheon's seal had already been broken.

Evy picked it up. Her eyes found the header, and she read.

To the ruling body of Reyland,

The Council of Aeltheon delivers this message by decree of our benevolent Goddess Rui, giver of mana and sustainer of our realm, Lumesphere.

Upon the death of a Hierarch, the domains of Aeltheon must compete in the Hierarch Wars, the sacred trials that determine Rui's next chosen leader.

As tradition mandates, the domains of Zarokan, Virenna, and Theribane must each send forth an Ascendant to represent their domain.

Nothing seemed out of the ordinary so far. Reyland wasn't mentioned in the list of domains required to send an Ascendant, as expected.

As a contributing domain of Aeltheon, Reyland is hereby recognized by the Council as a full participant in the Hierarch Wars.

Evy's fingers tightened around the parchment. "Full participant?" She read the line again, then once more before moving on.

An Ascendant from Reyland must report to Ruitheon before the month's end to stand among the contenders and compete for the right to the Hierarch's throne.

By divine mandate and Council authority,

Arch Councilor Lawrence Daryn

"But I don't understand... Why now?" Evy placed the letter on the table, her voice coming out quieter than intended. "The Council never acknowledged Reyland before, and now we're suddenly required to participate?"

Orianna pursed her lips before responding. "The Council's decision to include Reyland in the Hierarch Wars could not have been made lightly."

Evy folded her hands in her lap to keep them from clenching.

"You do see this for what it is, don't you, Evy?" Orianna leaned in. "We've been given a rare privilege."

"Do you truly believe that?"

"Yes, I do," Orianna said. "It's a chance to prove we belong, so we won't be sidelined or treated as outsiders any longer."

Evy's heart raced as she tried to make sense of it all. "There has to be a catch. Why the sudden change of heart from the Council?"

Orianna didn't answer right away, but the sideways glance said enough.

"It was my doing." She paused again. "I negotiated terms with the Council. And it came at a cost."

Orianna chewed her bottom lip.

She was nervous, Evy thought. *As she should be.*

Then she immediately felt ashamed—though the venom still burned within. There had always been trust between them, an agreement that neither would move without the other knowing. Orianna had gone to the Council behind her back and kept it secret until now.

Orianna knew it would sting Evy. And it did. It stung because Evy would have been grateful for any kind of warning —any notice that would have allowed her to prepare.

She swallowed her discomfort and forced herself to believe Orianna had her reasons.

"What did it take?"

Orianna remained silent.

"You can tell me," Evy said softly.

At last Orianna spoke. "I brokered a deal with Kaelen Reed."

Evy stiffened. "The First Councilor of Reyland?"

"He was a colleague of mine when I studied in Ruitheon."

Evy knew Orianna had studied at the College of Ruitheon—the first Witch ever permitted to leave Reyland and become a scholar in the capital city.

It was part of what made her such a powerful figure at home. The people of Reyland had elected her Magister because she was brilliant, respected, and unusually well-versed in Aeltheon's politics.

Accomplishments few Witches could claim.

But she had never graduated, and because of that, she rarely spoke of those years. In fact, she tended to avoid the topic entirely.

Hearing her speak so casually about someone from her days in Ruitheon, someone who now held real influence on the Council, surprised Evy.

Her words came out slowly. "You knew Councilor Reed personally?"

"I debated alongside him in Ruitheon's lecture halls. We didn't always agree, but he respected my intellect. I respected him in return."

Evy frowned. "Do you trust him?"

"I don't trust any member of the Council," Orianna said. "But I understand him. He values reason and practicality over sentiment. That's why Thylarion Veyn personally requested him to be on his Council."

She gave a dry chuckle. "Even old Thylarion knew he couldn't fill the Council solely with corrupt Shifters. He needed someone with a brain to help him govern."

"But he made him the Councilor of *Reyland*." Evy let out a short scoff. "Even though he's an Ethereal. I'm sure he would've preferred to represent Virenna instead."

Orianna shrugged. "Maybe. But it all worked in our favor because I was able to easily reach him and get him to agree to my terms."

"What did you promise him?"

"I offered a service." Orianna hesitated. "Perhaps it'll be easier to explain if I show you."

Orianna turned the map of Aeltheon toward her. The continent was divided into four domains—Reyland, Virenna, Theribane, and Zarokan—with Ruitheon, the capital, nestled at the center.

"These," she continued, tracing a slender finger over several dark marks on the parchment, "are Hollowrift portals."

Evy leaned in to study the map. "I never realized there were so many. Are they spreading?"

"Yes," Orianna said. "More are slowly appearing across Aeltheon, some near major settlements. And you know what happens if a portal goes unchecked."

Evy's throat tightened. Though rare, the Draemor could slip through the portals, bringing with them pure chaos. Born of malice, drawn to suffering, sustained by destruction—the thought of them roaming the realm filled her with dread.

"A Hierarch could close the portals. They could draw enough mana from the Heart to do it."

Orianna's lips pressed into a thin line. "One would think, but politics and governing the mana flow preoccupy our Hierarchs."

Evy's hands curled into fists. "What of those going through hardship because of the Draemor?"

"Historically, the Hierarch never cared." Orianna shook her head. "Councilor Reed, however, does. To Kaelen, unchecked portals drain resources. To him, it isn't fiscally sound. He needed a solution. I gave him one."

Evy exhaled, bracing for the inevitable. She had sensed it the moment Orianna mentioned the unchecked portals. "Let me guess. Me."

Orianna met her gaze. "You."

Evy stifled a groan.

Orianna went on. "Other than the Hierarch, only a Shaman can close portals, and you've already done so near Reyland's borders. I merely provided the idea, and Kaelen took it from there. He initiated the negotiations, then used your abilities as leverage to secure the Council's votes in Reyland's favor."

Orianna's implied request finally bore down on her. If she agreed to this, there would be little rest. When she wasn't fulfilling her duties in Reyland, she'd be traveling across

Aeltheon, sealing rifts before they could let Draemor into the land.

It would be grueling work, but she supposed she could manage it.

“That was the deal, then.” Evy’s voice barely rose above a whisper. “The Witches get to enter the Hierarch Wars in exchange for portal-sealing services.”

Orianna reached across the table, her grip firm on Evy’s fingers. “I know this is a heavy burden, but Evy, listen to me. This is for the good of Reyland. This could open doors for our people that have always been closed. *Please,* tell me you understand.”

Orianna’s careful scrutiny made it feel like a test of whether she truly understood her duty as Shaman Queen. Orianna had known her all her life. She likely already knew what Evy would say.

And she was right.

Because what choice did Evy have? This was what it meant to be Shaman Queen. Orianna knew that. She had used it to her advantage, and Evy played right into her hands. Orianna knew Evy could never refuse her duty to her people. After all, the Magister herself had helped instill that belief in her since she was a child.

Evy freed herself from Orianna’s grip and pressed her palms flat against the table to keep them still.

“Okay. If you really believe this will help Reyland, I’ll lend my power to the Council.”

“Thank you, Evy.” Orianna reached out again and gently squeezed her hands. “You’re doing the domain a great service.”

Her grip suddenly tightened as Evy tried to pull back.

“But that leaves one question,” Orianna said as she leaned in. “Who do we send as our Ascendant?”

FIVE

Evy had been so consumed by Orianna's deal that she nearly forgot about the Hierarch Wars entirely.

"Do you have anyone in mind?" she asked.

"It should be someone who can represent us in the best light," Orianna said. "Someone with strength, poise, and intelligence. Someone Aeltheon cannot ignore."

"You?"

Orianna shook her head. "I would volunteer, but I'm bonded to only a single light spirit. I wouldn't be the best example of strength."

"How strong do you have to be?"

"Well, the trials can be dangerous. There have been Ascendants who were maimed. Or worse. Some have died. And those who survive but fail to win..." She looked down. "They're never quite the same."

Evy felt surmounting dread gathering in her stomach. She was going to have to send someone into this. A Witch. One of her own people. "Never the same *how?*"

Orianna leaned back in her chair, considering.

"The trials vary each cycle, but the themes remain the same," she explained. "The first, the Trial of Wit, is usually harmless. Puzzles, perhaps a labyrinth to test your mind."

"Seems simple enough, I suppose."

"Evy, I've taught you better than to underestimate," Orianna scolded. "It may not be physically harmful, but it'll challenge you all the same. There will be tricks at every turn designed to throw you off course."

Evy chewed her lip in an attempt to control her scowl. "And the second and third trials?"

"The second, the Trial of Strength, is far more perilous. It might involve a brutal obstacle course. Sometimes it's combat against your rivals… or worse."

Evy's fingers curled into fists in her lap. Combat against Ascendants. Against domains that had been preparing their champions for generations. Whoever she sent would be walking into a fight they'd had no time to train for.

Orianna's voice dropped to a hush. "But it's the third trial, the Trial of Resilience, that takes the greatest toll. Few emerge untouched."

Evy's mouth went dry. "What does the final trial entail?"

"It tests both mental and physical endurance against the darkness." Orianna's gaze narrowed. "It requires the Ascendants to enter the Blighted Caves and find their way out. The Draemor imprisoned there will attack with everything they have."

Evy sank so far into her chair she thought it might swallow her whole. "They expect the Ascendants to walk through a prison full of Draemor and *survive*?"

Orianna's expression hardened. "There are no safeguards in these trials, Evy. It's dangerous. And then there's the matter of the Procession, the tour of Aeltheon the Ascendants undertake after the first trial."

"A tour doesn't sound very difficult."

"It may sound like a reprieve," Orianna said, "but it isn't."

She rose from her chair and paced slowly behind Evy. "In fact, it may be just as important as the trials themselves. All eyes will be judging the Ascendants, a trial in itself. That's why the best are chosen. The way the realm views a domain rests on the one who represents it."

Evy shuddered at the thought of sending a Witch to compete. "What if we don't want to send an Ascendant?"

"Now that Reyland is counted among the contenders, we *must* send an Ascendant or face the consequences."

"What could they possibly do? They already keep us at the continent's edge."

"They could cut off our mana completely." Orianna's tone became grave. "They've done it before to Casper Island."

"Casper Island," Evy echoed, the name haunting like a ghost on her lips.

It had once been a thriving Outer Island. Then the Council severed its mana as punishment for rebellion. Now it sat abandoned, a phantom of its former glory.

"A new Hierarch will be crowned, with or without us," Orianna continued. "And if we refuse to engage, the Council will retaliate."

Evy's mind leaped to a vision of the future, one that mirrored Casper Island's fate. Witches unable to wield magic at all. Crops withering in infertile soil. The land turning barren. Children suffering from starvation.

"We all answer to the Hierarch and the Council," Orianna said. "Their word overrules all local laws, reaches farther than any domain's border. You may be Shaman Queen of Reyland, and I may serve as Magister, but it won't matter. Not when they control the flow of power across the realm."

"Even if I agree to close the portals without sending an Ascendant?" Evy asked. "I assumed they'd like that notion—"

"That is *not* an option." Orianna's hand slammed against the table. The jarring crack caused Evy to flinch. "We mustn't embarrass ourselves by squandering this opportunity."

Evy's mouth parted. She had never seen Orianna's composure fracture like that before. And though she was still apprehensive, she decided to continue with caution.

"If there's truly no choice, then who do we send?" Evy asked. "What Witch would take these risks willingly?"

"It must be someone who won't just survive." Orianna eased back into her seat. "Someone who can show the realm what Witches are capable of."

Evy nodded. "Maybe someone from the Bound Blades. They're trained, disciplined."

Her thoughts drifted to Leo Warring. But how could she ask that of him, knowing his wife was about to give birth? It was an impossible choice.

She suddenly became aware of Orianna's close scrutiny.

"At just seventeen," Orianna said, "you're our Queen, our Shaman, and without question the strongest Witch in Reyland."

Evy stared at the ceiling. She really didn't like where this was headed.

"I know I've already asked so much of you," Orianna said gently. "I've considered every option. Every name. But there's only one the realm will truly pay attention to."

She met Evy's eyes. The room seemed to shrink. Evy knew what was coming. She knew what Orianna would say. And like before, Orianna knew how Evy would answer.

"Evy... I believe it must be you."

SIX

Yorik Whitlock stood beneath the shadow of an ancient tree, deep in the heart of Reyland's woods. Though it was midday, the dense canopy swallowed the sunlight, draping the forest in an eerie twilight.

Then the whispers slithered in. The voice was not his own and spoke only to him.

He's coming.

Behind him, a dozen figures stood in silence, their torches illuminated against the darkness. Heavy red hoods obscured their faces, revealing only the faint outlines of their mouths. None of them spoke, yet the whispers persisted, circling Yorik like a predator stalking its prey.

He's almost here.

Yorik attuned himself to the presence at the edges of his mind. It was there, pressing closer and stretching toward him.

Everything is going to change.

The whisper curled around him. He welcomed it, inhaling deeply.

Yes. Let us in.

A rustle broke the stillness behind him, footsteps shifting restlessly.

"Be patient," he commanded. At once, the figures behind him stilled. "He'll be here soon."

Suddenly, a sharp gust cut through the trees, stirring the torches and making Yorik's black cloak billow.

The prophecy came to him last night. A voice had whispered that there would be news that would set the wheels of fate in motion.

The voice rang out again.

It's time.

On cue, footsteps rustled along the path ahead. Aeric emerged from behind a tree, a twig stuck in his unkempt hair. Yorik welcomed him with a grin, and his younger brother managed a weak smile in return.

Aeric scanned the hooded figures. "Ah. I see you've gathered your secret club again."

Yorik's mouth pressed into a thin line. "Not a club, little brother. A movement. New Acolytes continue to join us. Perhaps one day we'll expand beyond Reyland's borders."

Aeric snorted though his smile didn't quite reach his eyes.

At seventeen, his face still held a boyish softness, his wide eyes untouched by time's consequences. Yorik, eight years his senior, had the hardened features of a man shaped by time: high cheekbones, a strong jawline, and a faint scar tracing the edge of his brow. They were different, yet unmistakably brothers with the same wild auburn hair, the same blue-gray eyes.

"Well?" Yorik asked. "Was I right? Did something happen at the temple?"

Aeric's fingers twitched at his sides. He shifted his weight and exhaled before muttering, "You were right."

Murmurs rippled behind Yorik.

He stepped closer. "What happened?"

"I don't want to involve Evy in this. You know how I feel—" He stopped as Yorik locked his gaze on him.

"I'll ask again—what happened?"

Aeric looked down at his hands. "I went to see Evy after the Bonding Rites today, like you told me."

"Continue."

Aeric hesitated, then forced the words out. "A courier came from Ruitheon. Thylarion Veyn is dead, and the Hierarch Wars—they're starting soon. And from what I've heard, the Witches are part of it this time. That's all I got. Orianna kicked me out before I could hear the rest."

Yorik paused, frozen in place.

The voices he heard had not lied, after all.

"And the Shaman Queen will be part of it," Yorik said under his breath.

The frenzied voices surged in Yorik's mind.

The Shaman Queen will venture to Ruitheon as Reyland's Ascendant.

"They've shown me." His voice dropped to a whisper. "Evalene—*your* Evy—will be sent to Ruitheon. She's going to represent Reyland in the Hierarch Wars."

Aeric froze briefly before speaking again.

But Yorik couldn't hear him over the voices.

Doors will now open for you.

It is time.

The words tore through Yorik's mind, sending a thrill curling down his spine. A wide grin stretched across his face.

He leaned in close to his brother. "They told me. And they never lie. It's time. It's finally time."

"You're not making any sense. Who told you?" Aeric asked, then stumbled back a step.

Yorik followed, closing the distance. He leaned in and breathed against Aeric's ear.

"The Gods."

Then he turned to the hooded figures before him and spread his arms. "As I prophesied, today marks the beginning of our destiny as the Chaosbound!"

Cheers erupted from the gathered Acolytes, their voices rising into the night like a ritualistic chant. All except for Aeric, who stood apart, head bowed, fists clenched at his sides.

The voice whispered again, a thread of shadow weaving through his thoughts.

We must cleanse the world.

Yorik lifted his chin and spoke with absolute conviction. "As the Herald of Chaos, it is my duty to lead you, to guide my Acolytes through our sacred mission."

Plunge the world into darkness.

"Lumesphere is rotting. Its foundation is built on corruption, its leaders drunk on power. The Gods have chosen *us* to heal it."

Envelop the world in chaos.

"But to heal, we must first purge the infection at its source. Mana. It disguises itself as strength, yet it festers like a disease, feeding the imbalance, breeding oppression."

Embrace the chaos.

"If we are to cleanse the world, if we are to rid it of its sickness, then we must cut it out at the root. We must sever mana from this realm forever."

Rise from its ashes.

"The Chaosbound have been given a divine task. It is we who will bring true justice. We who will burn away the decay."

Heal the world of its sickness.

"And to do that, we must destroy the relic that binds mana to this world. The source of its corruption." Yorik's voice sharpened like a blade. "We must destroy the Heart."

Through chaos, you will find justice.

"When we shatter the Heart, the realm will descend into chaos. And we will embrace it."

Through chaos, you will find peace.

"For only through destruction can the world be remade. The weak will fall. The strong will rise. And in the end, we alone will shape what comes next. A new order, free from the tyranny of mana."

The crowd stirred, their whispers feverish.

"Rid Lumesphere of mana?" Aeric scoffed. "If you haven't noticed, Yorik, even we Witches need it. Spirit magic still depends on the land's energy."

Yorik lowered his arms.

"We, the Chaosbound, don't need mana."

"What do you mean?"

Yorik took a step back and raised his arms.

The ground trembled.

A black, swirling pool of shadow formed at his feet, tendrils writhing from its depths. A guttural, unnatural moan carried through the air as the wind picked up, shrieking through the trees.

Aeric staggered back as a dark figure rose from the abyss, its shape shifting like living smoke. Hollow eyes, glowing with eerie yellow light, locked onto him. The creature's mouth stretched wide in a silent wail, its body trembling with agony.

Aeric gasped. "What is that?" He stumbled and fell to the ground, eyes wide with horror.

Yorik raised a hand, and at once, the figure stilled.

"I think a better question is *who* is that?"

"What?" Aeric's voice trembled. "Are you saying that *thing* was once a person?"

"Not just any person." Yorik let out a soft laugh. "You know him, little brother. Though you were very young the last time you saw him."

Aeric placed a hand to his mouth. "No." His voice cracked. "No, it can't be."

Yorik nodded slowly, confirming the assumption. "Our

dearly departed father, Marlin Whitlock. The bastard finally reunited with his beloved sons."

Aeric's fists clenched at his sides. "This is—this is wrong."

Yorik said nothing at first. The shadow—the tormented shape of the man who had once been their father—trembled, its moans of agony barely human.

He stared at it—at *him*—waiting for emotions long buried to surface. Not grief. He could never grieve a man like his father. Relief, perhaps. Or maybe satisfaction. The kind he had imagined so many times as a boy, lying awake in the dark, listening to his mother's muffled sobs through the walls.

His hand quivered as he searched for whatever stirred inside him.

There was only a hollowness.

And he realized consuming this man's soul would not fill the void he had carved into Yorik's childhood.

He steadied his hand. "He was a useless waste of space in life. At least now, he can serve a better purpose."

A terrible, wrenching scream filled the space.

The shadowy form of Marlin Whitlock contorted in agony before dissolving into dark vapor. The mist curled and twisted, then streamed toward Yorik's outstretched palm. With a final, shuddering gasp, the last remnants of their father vanished into Yorik's grasp.

Aeric stared. "Gods above."

Yorik flexed his fingers, then without hesitation, aimed his palm at a tree.

A bolt of black energy erupted from his hand and struck the trunk with devastating force. The tree splintered. Fragments and charred bark exploded into the air, its remains collapsing in a heap.

Yorik suddenly doubled over, a harsh coughing fit racking his frame. When he pulled his hand away from his mouth, it was streaked with blood.

"You have to see what this is doing to you." Aeric started to reach for him but stopped short. "This kind of magic… It can't be any good. It's tainting you."

Yorik turned to face him. "'Tainting' me?" He let out a disbelieving laugh.

"No, Aeric. This is a gift. I don't need spirits. I don't need mana. I am not *tainted*." He inhaled. "I am evolved."

He gestured toward the Acolytes. "We all are."

The hooded figures raised their hands in unison. Dark tendrils of shadow spiraled from their palms, and from each one, writhing shapes of tortured souls emerged.

Aeric's face was drained of color. The forest filled with the low, agonized wails of the dead.

"Gods," Aeric said. "Oh, Gods. Evy said something about grave robbers." He swallowed. "That was you, wasn't it?"

"My Acolytes needed practice. And those bodies came from the graves of criminals. I simply gave them a better purpose in the afterlife."

"Practice?" Aeric's lips curled in disgust. "Practice for what?"

"For what's to come." Yorik's gaze softened, almost tender. "Be part of the new world with us. Let me perform the Shadow Rites on you, brother. I'll free you from those feeble spirits and give you the power to command souls."

He brushed a finger against Aeric's cheek. "Let me awaken you."

Aeric recoiled. "Yorik, you're my brother. I love you, but I can't—" He gagged and turned away to retch on the forest floor.

"You're not ready. That's fine. In fact, it's perfect." Yorik folded his hands behind his back as he stepped closer. "You still have a part to play in all of this."

Aeric wiped his mouth, glaring at him. "What do you mean?"

"You must stay close to the Shaman Queen. Keep in touch with her while she's in Ruitheon. She will be our key."

"Absolutely not. I want no part of this."

"I'd carry out the task myself, but if I or one of the Acolytes gets too close, she might sense that something is..." Yorik trailed off, considering his words, "*off* about us."

Aeric's expression darkened. "I won't hurt Evy."

Yorik sighed and placed a hand on his brother's shoulder.

"Aeric, you won't be hurting her. When our plans succeed, you and Evy will finally be free. She won't have to bear the burden of being the Shaman Queen in our new world. She can just be yours. *Only* yours."

Aeric clenched his jaw.

"I promise, little brother, Evy won't get hurt." His grip tightened on Aeric's shoulder. "Trust me, I'm doing this for you and for our mother. I live to give you both a better world."

For a long moment, Aeric said nothing. Then, finally, he nodded. "As long as Evy doesn't get hurt."

"She won't."

Aeric's gaze narrowed. "How will you destroy the Heart?"

Yorik didn't respond right away.

Visions started to surge through him. Three offerings—ingredients—each torn from the blood of the strong. He saw them drawn together, their essence twisting, reshaping him.

Making him lethal. Unstoppable.

Forging him into his final evolution.

The vision shifted.

He saw himself tearing the Heart apart in a blinding rupture. The ground split open as mana was stripped from the land, the world collapsing inward. Civilization fell to ash and fire.

And from the ruins, the Chaosbound rose. Ready to rebuild the world in their image.

A utopia.

The Gods had shared their instructions with him.

And now, the path was clear.

They whispered their final command:

Bless the dawn with blood.

SEVEN

"You're making the right choice," Orianna said, gently squeezing her shoulder. "Not just for our domain, but for the future of Witches."

Evy felt drained beyond words. The Bonding Rites had already left her tired that morning, but everything afterward had piled weight on her shoulders like never before. Now, standing at the temple gates, she felt she might crumple beneath it. But Orianna stood beside her, and Evy drew on the last of her strength.

"I hope you're right."

What choice did Evy truly have but to accept Orianna's proposition? How could she ask another Witch to face the realm's prejudice and peril when she herself had the power and duty to stand in their place?

"I am." Orianna leaned down to meet her eyes. "I trained you for this."

"You trained me for the *Hierarch Wars*?"

Orianna hesitated. "Yes. All the lessons, the sleepless nights, the trials you endured—they weren't just to prepare you as Shaman Queen. I pushed you to become more."

"And here I thought being Shaman Queen was the hard part." Evy frowned. How long had Orianna been planning this? "I really hope I can live up to your expectations."

"You will. You're ready." Orianna pulled her into a firm embrace.

"Do you think I'm strong enough to win?"

Orianna drew back. "There's no doubt about your strength. But you need to understand, the Hierarch Wars will be rigged. One way or another, the Council will attempt to ensure a Shifter victory."

"Then how do I beat a rigged system?" Evy asked.

"You don't," Orianna said plainly. "I don't want you to."

Evy paused. "You don't *want* me to win?"

"No. Though I'm afraid you could." Orianna seemed to search for the right words. "I want you to *compete* in the Hierarch Wars. Don't try to win."

Evy waited for more. For clarification. For context. For anything that would make sense of the command.

When nothing came, she turned inward for an obvious detail she might have missed.

"I'm afraid I don't understand."

"The realm isn't ready for stark change," Orianna said, her voice lowering. "They've let us sit at the table, but they're not prepared to see a Witch wearing the Hierarch's crown."

She drew Evy closer. "If you show them your full power, if you come too close to taking it all, they'll panic. You'll be deemed dangerous, and they'll slam the door shut behind you. Maybe even bolt it." Her voice dropped to a near whisper. "But if you show them you belong, if you play this right by keeping up just enough, it could change everything. We might finally be trusted as a race. Maybe even open the path for Witches to have a seat on the Council."

Evy's shoulders sagged, suddenly as heavy as lead. "If I'm

strong enough to win, why should I hold back? Couldn't I force the change as Hierarch?"

"No." Orianna carried a sudden edge of impatience. "Because this isn't just about you. It's about every Witch who comes after you."

She pulled Evy in by the shoulders. "If we push too far, too fast, it could cost us everything. The world doesn't change overnight. It changes slowly. One step at a time."

Orianna went on. "We're not asking for a throne today. We're asking to be seen as part of this realm, not as a threat to it. And if that takes time, then we take the time."

"So you want me to give them a good show?" Evy failed to conceal the tremble in her voice.

Orianna offered a faint smile, but it quickly faded when Evy didn't return it. She sighed.

"Perhaps it would help you to know why I never graduated from the College of Ruitheon."

Evy looked up, wide-eyed.

Like everyone else, Evy had assumed it came down to homesickness, not fitting in among the scholars, or struggling under the weight of academic pressure outside Reyland. No one dared ask. No one wanted to wound her pride. And Orianna avoided the topic like the plague.

"I never left willingly, Evy. I was expelled."

"What?" Evy gasped. "Why?"

"Because I was studying a way to empower Witches. And they didn't like that."

Expelled for empowering Witches? Evy had to be missing an important part of the story.

"What kind of study would justify expulsion?" she asked.

Orianna shook her head. "It doesn't matter. What matters is *why* they expelled me. Because they didn't want Witches gaining power. Do you understand that?"

"I—" Evy searched for her words. She didn't understand. Not at all. "Is there something you're not telling me, Orianna?"

"Earlier, you said you trusted me." Orianna's attention dropped to the floor. "Will you trust me on this?"

A Spirit Sister passed by, startling Orianna. She bowed as she carried a jug of water in her arms. Orianna and Evy both gave the Sister a nod before she trotted off.

Evy studied her mentor—the slight tremble in her features, the faint glaze behind her eyes. This pain ran deeper than Evy had realized.

She decided not to press.

"I trust you."

"Then don't give them a reason to expel you too."

Evy felt the fire within her dim, the last of her energy fading with it. All she wanted now was the comfort of home.

She offered Orianna a small nod, then stepped away, waving a farewell.

The crunch of stone beneath her boots filled the silence as she walked the gravel path alone. She kept her chin level until she was certain no one was watching.

She stopped halfway and tilted her head to the sky, taming her erratic thoughts. She focused on the streaks of pink-and-white clouds overhead.

Evy's breath curled in the cool air. She forced a smile, grateful she was shivering from the cold, not from the frustration rising inside her.

The Magister had been in Ruitheon. Having faced its prejudice and threats herself, she would not ask Evy to restrain herself without reason.

And yet, knowing she was being asked to shrink into something the realm could tolerate—perhaps it was more than the damp air that made her shudder.

Evy squared her shoulders before continuing down the path.

As she entered the town of Moonveil, the late afternoon's

golden light glimmered across the dirt road. The briny scent of sea spray drifted in from the coastal fjords, mingling with the smell of seared fish. Smoke curled from rooftops, and somewhere deeper in town, a blacksmith's hammer rang steadily against iron.

People took notice as she walked—conversations dipped, heads turned. A fisherman mid-meal at a stall met her gaze and tipped his hat. A group of women gossiping outside a doorway paused long enough to curtsey before dissolving back into their chatter.

Evy returned each greeting with a nod and studied their faces. These were the people she would walk this impossible line for. The people Orianna said she could change the future for. It meant Evy would need to step into the most important competition in Lumesphere, show the realm what the Witches were capable of, then stop short of the finish line.

For them, she would do it.

But she thought of standing before these faces when it was over—of coming back home having let the crown slip through her fingers, of the immediate change she could have brought to Reyland. Could she bear to look at these faces again?

Ahead, a food stall crackled with meat and vegetable skewers. The rich aroma curled through the crisp air, and her stomach growled. She hadn't realized how long it had been since she'd eaten.

She handed over a few copper pieces with a soft "thank you" and accepted a skewer, the charred stick seeping with heat. She bit into the meat, tender and flowing with savory juices.

She took another bite and kept walking, the chatter of townsfolk fading into a hum behind her.

The path wound toward the farm villages, and the taste of grilled meat lingered as Evy's thoughts drifted. Orianna had once shared that many in the College of Ruitheon believed the

Forgotten Folk had crossed over from Gaiasphere, a theory not limited to the capital, but common throughout the realm.

Gaiasphere was a realm of myth and legend, a place where magic and mana didn't exist. How could scholars believe an entire people had braved the lethal landscape of Hollowrift and simply appeared in Lumesphere?

Yet that fiction had hardened into fact. It was how they explained why Witches couldn't control mana directly.

How can we trust mana-deprived outsiders to govern mana?

An all-purpose excuse for locking Witches out of power. Never mind that Witches *could* channel mana, just like all Aeltheans, and felt its loss just as keenly. The only difference was, they couldn't shape mana into magic. It was as if a circuit had broken somewhere in the process, requiring spirits to act on their will.

When Evy arrived in Ruitheon, she would have to walk a fine, impossible line. She would need to challenge their prejudice without overpowering them and show her strength without revealing the full weight of it.

And that, somehow, felt far harder than winning the Hierarch Wars.

EIGHT

The village soon gave way to open countryside, where the damp earth and wild heather filled the air. Rolling hills stretched into vast farmlands, framed by jagged cliffs that plunged into the endless sea.

Rye and barley fields swayed in the breeze, their stalks catching the fading sunlight. Along the horizon, dark pine forests loomed, an inky mass against the sky.

In the distance, a herd of shaggy-haired goats picked their way along a rocky hillside.

Generations of Witches shaped this beautiful, untamed land, coaxing life from its stubborn soil. But the farms here were smaller than those in Aeltheon's richer domains. Their pastures were more rugged and harvests more modest.

Reyland had never known abundance, but they had learned resilience.

Beneath the soft grass and packed earth, faint traces of mana pulsed through the soil, struggling to hold their form.

She passed a group of farmers tending their fields. One older woman swept her palm over the soil, her hands faintly aglow.

An earth spirit drifted between the crops, pulsing with warm brown-and-green light. It seeped into the ground, urging the roots to stretch deeper.

The farmer sighed. Without enough mana beneath her, the spell strained her to the bone.

"Good evening, Your Majesty." The woman started to push herself upright, knees shaking.

Evy motioned for her to stay seated. "Do you need any help?" she asked, voice carrying over the field.

"I'm ever so thankful, but my son should be coming by soon to help fertilize the rest of the crops. Thank you kindly, Your Majesty."

Evy couldn't help but feel relieved. The Bonding Rites had already taken so much out of her, she wasn't sure she had the strength to spare for the farmer. She continued on her path.

As she walked, she was overcome with sudden loneliness.

Aeric should have been there, walking alongside her.

Her gaze drifted toward the distant hills where their families' lands stretched side by side. The Lovejoy farm and the Whitlock homestead had always been neighbors.

Growing up, whenever Evy visited her family, Aeric had always been there, waiting with them, greeting her with a quiet smile. He was as much a part of home as the land itself.

Was he home now?

She hoped so. She longed for his company—needed it desperately.

As Evy crested the last hill, her parents' home came into view, a modest stone cottage nestled against the sloping farmland. Smoke curled from the chimney, carrying the rich scent of rabbit stew and fresh herbs.

She inhaled, savoring the aroma. It had been months since she'd last been home. Between her duties at the Reyani Temple and the expectations placed upon her as Shaman Queen, time with her parents had become rare and precious.

She missed it more than she let herself admit. Everything felt simpler here. She wondered, sometimes, what it might have been like to grow up just a farmer's daughter.

The rhythmic *thunk* of someone splitting wood echoed through the quiet countryside. Near the side of the house, Cyril Lovejoy stood at a well-worn chopping block. The evening breeze tousled his salt-and-pepper hair, and his weathered hands gripped the handle of an axe.

At the sound of Evy's footsteps, her father straightened and set the axe aside. A warm smile broke across his face, deepening the folds around his crystal-blue eyes.

"There's my girl."

She barely had time to return his smile before he pulled her into an embrace.

"Mara!" her father called toward the cottage. "She's home!"

The front door creaked open, and Mara Lovejoy stepped out, wiping her hands on her apron. Her snowy-white hair was braided over one shoulder, and her deep bronze skin glistened in the fading light.

"You're late," her mother said, though there was no scolding behind the words. The two women wrapped their arms around each other, and Evy let the pressure of the day momentarily melt away.

"I had a few things to take care of," Evy said, resting her head against her mother's shoulder for just a second longer. Her gaze shifted toward the empty path leading to the Whitlock homestead.

Her father noticed. "Looking for Aeric?"

"I was kind of hoping he'd be here already."

Her mother shook her head. "I went over to check on them earlier. Aeric wasn't home."

Evy nodded, though she was admittedly disappointed.

"Come inside," her mother said, giving her a gentle nudge. "Dinner's ready. I made your favorite stew and fresh bread."

Inside, the cottage was warm and inviting, a welcome

contrast to the Reyani Temple's cold halls. Simple clay plates and cups sat neatly arranged on the wooden table.

Evy took her seat and exhaled. "I have to tell you something." Her fingers traced the rim of her plate.

Her father clapped a hand on her back. "Are you finally getting married?" he asked. "Is that why you wanted Aeric here?"

Evy felt the blood rise to her cheeks. "What? No!"

Her mother ladled steaming stew from the cauldron. "Oh, leave her alone, Cyril. She'll give us grandbabies when she's ready." She winked at Evy and set a bowl in front of her.

Evy groaned.

"As I was saying"—she set her hands on her lap to keep them from shaking—"an official courier from Ruitheon arrived today. Thylarion Veyn is dead."

Her mother set a loaf of bread on the table. "And so the Hierarch Wars begin again, and we get another Veyn successor."

"I was starting to think old Thylarion Veyn would outlive me," her father said as he tore off a piece of bread and dipped it into his stew.

Evy paused, searching for the right words.

"This time, Reyland was invited to compete in the Hierarch Wars." She tried to meet their gazes but couldn't find the courage. "The Council voted to allow Witches to enter an Ascendant."

Her parents both stilled.

"What does that mean?" her mother asked, setting down a mug.

"I'm going to represent Reyland in the Hierarch Wars. I leave for Ruitheon in a week."

No one spoke. Only the crackling of the hearth filled the space.

Her father crossed his arms and leaned back in his chair. "Tell us everything. From the beginning."

So she did. She told them about the letter, Orianna's deal with Kaelen Reed, the portal-sealing, the politics, how she had volunteered as Reyland's Ascendant because she couldn't bring herself to ask another Witch to carry that weight—all of it.

Her parents listened, their mouths set in a tight line. When she finished, they exchanged a glance.

Her mother let out a slow, shaky breath.

"I knew this day would come. The way the Magister spoke of your destiny, I knew she had grand plans for you. Plans that stretched far beyond Reyland."

Her father rubbed a hand over his face. "The Hierarch Wars—" He shook his head. "I won't lie and say it doesn't scare me. But if anyone can face it, it's you, Evy."

Her mother nodded. "We believe in you. Just like we always have."

Evy wasn't sure what she had expected from her parents—fear, anger, maybe even a plea to turn away from this path.

But there was none of that.

Only unwavering trust.

But instead of easing her heart, it only tightened the pressure around it.

"Do you remember the day we found out who you were?" her mother asked.

Evy shook her head. "I was too little."

"Of course." Her mother laughed, the sound bittersweet. "You weren't even three yet. The previous Shaman King had been dead for years, and everyone was waiting, anxious for a sign of the next reincarnation."

"Ah, I remember this story," her father said, threading his fingers behind his head. "No one knew where Reya would place her blessing, but the first sign is always the same—the ability to see what others cannot. That year, my mother, your grandmother, had passed. It was hard on all of us." His voice softened. "Then, one morning, Mara called for me. She'd found you sitting in the middle of the floor, babbling away like you were having a conversation."

He paused for a brief moment.

"But there was no one there."

"And that's when you realized?" Evy asked.

"Not at first," her mother said as she pulled Evy's head to her chest. "I thought you were just talking to yourself, like toddlers do. But when I asked who you were speaking to, you gave me the brightest little grin and said, 'Gramma!'"

Evy lifted her head, her eyes widening.

Years into her training, the Spirit Matron had once told her that some Shamans were born hearing and seeing the souls of the dead. The ability dimmed as they grew older and focused on spirit communion, but it never vanished completely. With practice, a Shaman could learn to reach for both.

Evy hadn't realized she'd once had that ability herself.

Her father nodded. "Clear as day. You told us she was 'going bye-bye' through what you called 'the black door.'" His voice was thick with emotion. "Must have been Hollowrift. No child could've known those things. You were too young to grasp death's meaning."

"We took you to the Reyani Temple the very next day," her mother continued. "The Spirit Matron performed a few tests, asked you to describe things only a Shaman could see. And it was true. You were Reya's chosen."

Evy knew this tale, yet never so completely. She had never imagined her parents' experience of raising a child one day, only to be told the next that she was destined for something greater.

That she would never truly be their child again.

Her mother reached across the table, wrapping Evy's hands in her own. "I felt proud of you that day. But I was also heartbroken."

Evy's chest tightened. "Because you had to let me go."

Her mother nodded. "I only had my baby with me for a little

over two years. I wanted to keep you here, raise you myself, teach you about the world. But you were the Shaman Queen. That meant you didn't just belong to us. You belonged to Reyland, to all the Witches." She fought to keep her voice composed. "It was the greatest honor and the hardest thing we've ever done."

Evy squeezed her mother's hands. Nothing she could do would give them back the years they had lost. But she hoped they knew she had never stopped loving them. Never stopped longing for home.

"And now," her mother continued, her voice cracking with restrained sorrow, "it feels like we're letting you go all over again. Even when you come back from Ruitheon, you'll be traveling all over Aeltheon to close portals. Will we be able to see you again…" She trailed off as a few tears slipped down her face.

Evy felt her own lip tremble.

Her father took his wife's hand and offered a soft smile. "We don't regret any of it, you know."

Her mother nodded, brushing a stray tear from her face. "That's right. We don't regret it, Evy, because even as a baby, we could tell you were special. Like you could take on the world."

Her father leaned forward and pulled Evy in. "And look at you now, you've grown into a strong young woman. Stronger than both of us. Stronger than all the Witches combined. And I think Magister Orianna's right. You *are* the most worthy to be our Ascendant."

Her mother wrapped her arms around them both and gently stroked Evy's hair.

"Show them who we are, Evy."

NINE

As she did every night when she was home, Evy sat in the field just beyond her family's cottage.

Her fingers sank into the cool earth as she watched the stars twinkle in the night sky.

The wind stirred the tall grass around her, whispering against her skin, and for a moment, she simply listened to the rustling fields, the distant crash of waves against the cliffs, the crickets' soft chirping.

She exhaled slowly, unraveling from her conversation with her parents. Their untempered faith in her was a strange balance of comfort and tension.

A soft crunch of footsteps pulled her from her thoughts. Aeric appeared beside her.

"You're up late," he said, a small, lopsided grin tugging at his lips.

She had been hoping he'd find her.

"So are you."

Aeric lowered himself beside her and rested his arms on his knees.

She studied him in the quiet. Beneath his usual warmth, he

seemed uneasy—his attention far away. Evy placed a hand on his shoulder. "Are you okay?"

His face looked drawn, and beads of sweat formed on his temples.

"Shouldn't I be asking *you* that?" Aeric tore absently at the grass between them. "Ever since you took on all your Shaman Queen duties, I feel like you're always working. Nonstop."

She let out a soft huff. He didn't even know half of it. Didn't know she was about to leave for Ruitheon. That she'd been chosen as a symbol of Reyland, set to face trials that could very well kill her.

But she didn't want to shatter the moment of peace. Not yet.

So they sat in silence, letting the wind speak for them as it whistled gently through the fields.

"How's your mother?" Evy asked after a few minutes, breaking the stillness.

"The same."

Evy frowned. "The same" meant "not good" with Lydia Whitlock.

"She hardly gets out of bed anymore," Aeric admitted. "Some days, she doesn't even speak."

Evy had tried to heal Lydia before, but the wound beneath her skull had been too deep, calcified by time.

"I wish there was something I could do," she said.

"You and me both."

Evy hesitated before asking, "And Yorik?"

Aeric stiffened.

"It feels like years since I last saw him. Is he doing alright?"

Aeric rubbed the back of his neck. "He's just been busy."

"Has he?"

"You know how it is," he said, forcing a small shrug. "With our father gone, someone has to provide. He's been working nonstop, trying to keep food on the table."

"I suppose that makes sense. Tell him I said hello if you see him."

Aeric offered a smile, but it didn't quite reach his eyes. "Yeah. Of course."

Evy nudged him. "Word around the Moonveil fish market is he's the most dashing fisherman in town. I'm surprised he hasn't been swept up and married to a pretty Witch."

"Why?" His grin widened. "Are you interested?"

Evy shoved him hard, and he rebounded, nudging her back with his elbow.

"You know I'm not," she said. "I'm just saying, you should've been an uncle by now."

They exchanged glances, then laughed.

A moment passed before Aeric's smile faded. "You never answered my question from before."

"What question?"

"Are you alright?"

Evy paused to truly consider, then shook her head. "No."

"Did anything else happen?"

Aeric's voice held a nervous quiver. He had been there when Orianna announced the Hierarch Wars in the cloister, and he was probably dying to know what was going on.

So Evy reiterated everything she had learned after he'd left. Aeric's frown deepened with every word.

When she finished, neither of them spoke.

"Say something," Evy finally said.

"Why does it have to be you?" He exhaled sharply through his nose. "I'll go. Send me instead. You have enough to deal with here."

"No, it should be me."

"Then take me with you." His words came quickly. "I can protect you or at least try."

Evy offered a sad smile.

"As much as I'd love that, I only have permits to leave

Reyland for myself and three staff members. Orianna already sorted it all out."

"And after the trials, you'll be all over the world, doing a job the Hierarch should be doing." Aeric pressed his fist into the ground. "You're doing too much."

Evy rested her head on her knees, unwilling to meet his eyes.

"I'm just doing my duty."

"Yorik was right," he muttered under his breath, so soft she almost missed it. "I'll never have you to myself."

Her head snapped up. Have her to himself?

But before she could question, Aeric pushed on. "You've never left Reyland before. Aren't you scared?"

She shrugged, then leaned into him, feeling the warmth of his broad shoulder against her temple. "I leave in a week, and I keep telling myself I'm ready. That I understand the importance of my destiny. And I do— I do understand it. But I have to admit, that doesn't stop it all from bearing down on me." Words she'd never said out loud before. "I'm afraid one day the pressure will crush me."

He brushed his cheek against her hair.

"You may have Reya's essence within you or whatever," he said, "but I know who you truly are."

Evy let out a soft laugh. "Yeah? And who is that?"

She lifted her head from his shoulder. There was something sad about the way he looked at her—his brows furrowed, the corners of his mouth turned down.

"You're a Witch like the rest of us."

Aeric gave a faint, crooked smile. "You're the girl I met when we were four, when you were visiting your parents from the temple, and they thought you'd have fun playing with the neighbor boy. And the moment I laid eyes on you, I swear my life changed. It became brighter.

"You're the girl who brought me to your parents' house for

dinner because Yorik was away working and my mother was too sick to make me food." His eyes glistened.

"You're just a girl, Evy," he continued. "And you're allowed to feel nervous. Scared. Sad. Just like the rest of us."

Evy's lips parted, but no words came.

"You're not just the Shaman Queen. You're not just the Ascendant of Reyland. You're Evy—*my* Evy."

She interlaced her fingers with Aeric's, his warmth enveloping her and anchoring her to reality. If only she could be just *his* Evy. But that wasn't her fate.

Evy's heart hammered. "Aeric, I—"

His fingers tensed around hers. His expression shifted, intensity raging behind his stormy-gray eyes; feral and fierce, yet desperate all at once.

For a moment, neither of them moved.

Then Aeric cupped her face with one hand, their foreheads resting together. His hair brushed her skin as his lips hovered near hers.

Her heart must have stopped.

But he pulled back just as quickly, face flushed. Only then did she realize she'd been holding her breath.

"You're leaving soon."

Part of her wanted to grab the back of his head and pull him in—finish what he'd wanted to start. But even she had limits to her courage.

Evy sighed. "I'll be back before you know it."

His grip tightened.

"Promise." It wasn't a question.

A small, bittersweet smile formed on her lips. "I can't stay away from home for long."

Aeric let out a quiet breath of laughter.

"Good."

Above them, the stars blinked in the clear night sky. The

scent of sea air and damp earth drifted on the breeze, wrapping around them like a shawl.

Beside her, Aeric lifted his hand. A soft glow sparked to life in his palm. Then, with a simple motion, he released it into the air.

Light and fire burst forth, hundreds of glowing embers rising like fireflies. The embers swirled above them, drifting higher and higher until they disappeared into the stars.

Evy gasped at the display, then rested her head on Aeric's shoulder, willing herself to believe this would still be waiting for her when the trials were over.

TEN

A full seven days had passed since Evy left Reyland, and she still hadn't gotten used to how different the world looked beyond its borders.

Morning light filtered through the dense forest canopy, dappling the winding dirt road in scattered sunshine. Towering silver-barked trees stretched toward the sky, their blossoms shedding glittering petals that drifted down like rain. On the mossy ground, clusters of glowing toadstools pulsed with soft luminescence. Tiny motes of sparkling dust drifted lazily on the breeze, traces left behind by a winged creature of the Ethereal race.

When her journey first began, the sight of Virenna's dreamy landscape had taken Evy's breath away.

The main road to Ruitheon cut through the forests of Virenna. She had expected to be on it for well over a week, but the weather had been fair, and on the nights the coachman felt confident enough to ride through the dark, they had made remarkable time. But most nights, her party camped beneath the stars. Other times, they found shelter in roadside inns. She had grown used to the sweetness of flowers and honey in the air, replacing the familiar scents of salt and pine from Reyland's coastal fjords.

Homesickness struck each dawn, when she missed the soft melodies of Reylandic birds drifting through the cloister during her morning reading sessions. Yet even then, her heart beat with exhilaration. She had never imagined stepping beyond Reyland's borders. And now she was crossing the realm.

Perhaps Linius Wells's adventurous soul had carried into her present life after all.

That morning, Evy stood outside the quaint wooden inn where she'd spent the previous night. Moss and tiny white flowers blanketed its sloping roof, making the structure blend seamlessly into the woodland.

"Irma, let's go!" Evy called as her maid finished purchasing recipes from the innkeeper.

"These are my best," the stout Goblin said, his voice a low gargle. His pale green skin creased as he smiled, sharp, pointed teeth jutting in haphazard rows. "No offense, but you Reylandic folk could stand to season your food better."

Irma tucked the pages away. "Thank you, and no offense taken." She walked over to the carriage, grinning. "I can't wait to give these to the Spirit Sisters. Maybe we'll finally eat something other than onion-and-potato soup."

"I thought you liked that soup. You're the one who begs them to make it nearly every night."

Irma crinkled her nose. "That's true. Very true. But the minced meat pies here changed my life."

They climbed into the carriage. The coachman whistled, urging the horse forward, and the inn faded into the distance.

Evy craned her neck out the window for a final glimpse. That inn was their last stop in Virenna before reaching Ruitheon. Their journey through the enchanted forests of the Ethereal domain had been surprisingly pleasant. They had mostly been left alone while they traveled, though one night, they woke to find their rucksacks rummaged through by Pixies.

Virenna maintained a somewhat friendly relationship with its northern neighbor, Reyland, mostly because their histories were interwoven.

As the Witch population grew and settled in the northernmost region of Virenna, the Ethereals gifted the land to the Witches, under the condition that they would not expand beyond their borders.

Was the gesture entirely altruistic? Not quite.

It was the reason why permits to leave Reyland were introduced in the first place. And in truth, the Ethereals saw Witches as outsiders, as did the rest of Aeltheon, and had little desire to claim responsibility for them.

But regardless of intent, the act had been generous and gave the Witches a place to call their own.

The constant beat of hooves sounded beside the carriage. Leo Warring, who came along to serve as her personal guard, kept watch on the dense thicket of trees for any sign of danger.

Evy pursed her lips. When she learned Leo would be escorting her, she tried to refuse, knowing his wife was due so soon. She pictured the vivacious little boy he had brought into the temple that day—would his wife be able to manage him in her condition? But Orianna had assured her Leo insisted, understanding the honor and privilege of guarding the Shaman Queen. Though what Leo needed to guard her from, she still wasn't sure.

"Evy?" Irma said, jarring her from her thoughts. Her handmaid held out Virennese honey cakes. "Can we eat these now?"

Evy took one. "Save some for the coachman and Captain Warring." She smirked.

They ate in comfortable silence, the sweetness of honey clinging to Evy's tongue. The steady rhythm of the carriage, the gentle rocking over uneven terrain, soon lulled her into sleep.

Evy awoke to a hand shaking her knee. The carriage was bathed in the warm glow of deep orange light.

"What time is it?" Her voice was thick with sleep.

"Close to sunset," Irma said. "But, Evy, look outside! We're in Ruitheon!"

Evy shook off the last remnants of sleep and turned toward the window.

The world outside had transformed.

Gone were the dense green canopies of Virenna's forests. In their place stretched an endless expanse of golden dunes, rolling in vast, wind-carved ridges. The air itself shimmered, heat rising from the sand in waves.

"If we're already on the desert outskirts, we should reach the city in no time." Evy checked her map.

Beads of sweat formed on her temple as the arid heat enveloped her. It was nothing like the crisp, briny cold of Reyland's northern shores. Here, the air was thin, entirely lacking moisture.

Even the wind moved differently, a slow, dragging force that churned up swirls of sand with every gust.

Evy studied her map and traced a line along their journey all the way back to Reyland. She turned to peer through the back window. The Virennese forest was a distant smudge, and beyond it, the pine forests and shores she had grown up in.

How far they had traveled from home.

She began to feel the tether that bound her to the temple, to Aeric, to her parents, to Orianna, stretching thinner the farther they ventured.

Irma shrugged off her shawl, her eyes wide as she took in the unfamiliar landscape. "It's so—"

"Dry," Evy finished. "And lonely."

The only signs of life were towering, long-limbed creatures moving gracefully across the dunes—Sand Striders, insect-like beasts with sleek, scaled bodies and spindly legs built for traversing the shifting terrain. Their riders sat high upon their backs, draped in flowing cloth, faces covered against the biting wind.

And then, in the distance, emerging from the sands like a mirage, was the capital city of Aeltheon.

As the carriage rumbled forward, a deep pulse thrummed beneath Evy's feet.

She stiffened. Despite the wooden floor of the carriage, she could feel a heavy, rhythmic vibration deep within the earth.

Curious, she peered outside.

Thick strands of azure light wove through the ground.

The mana grid was alive, stretching in brilliant, glowing veins beneath the sand and stone road, winding in an intricate web.

Evy brought a hand to her mouth.

In Reyland, its presence had been fragile cracks of light. In Virenna, it had flowed stronger, weaving through the forests like rivers.

But here, it pulsed with a magnitude of power.

The grid was so concentrated that the energy didn't just stay in the ground; it rose in soft, rippling waves, sending faint turquoise mist into the air.

And the spirits felt the power.

The wisps whizzed through the carriage, moving faster, more erratically. Their energy was overflowing.

It was the most active Evy had ever seen them.

The spirits typically inhabited the edge of her thoughts, soft whispers she could tune out if she chose not to dwell on them.

But now their voices tumbled over each other in a manic frenzy, exhilarated by the energy:

I want to fly and touch the sun!

Cast a spell and see us soar, Evy!

Tell Irma to light the carriage on fire. It'll be fun.

Evy crinkled her nose at the fire spirit's request.

Across from her, Irma flexed her fingers, examining her hands with a puzzled expression. Outside, Leo shifted in his saddle and rolled his shoulders.

It was undeniable. They could sense the difference in energy too.

It was like being kept in darkness your whole life, only to be suddenly submerged in sunshine.

The rhythmic clip of hooves continued as Ruitheon's towering white walls loomed ahead. When they reached the gates, they slowed to a stop, and a line of guards stepped forward, their gold cloaks shifting in the breeze. One of them approached the window.

Evy reached for the letter from the Council and handed it over. The guard examined the wax seal, then gave a curt nod.

With a heavy groan of metal, the iron gates yawned open.

The carriage rolled forward, passing beneath the archway and into the city.

Everything gleamed. Immaculate white-stone buildings ascended into the clouds above, their facades adorned with intricate gold filigree. Tall, fluted columns lined the streets, supporting arched walkways and elegant balconies. The roads were paved with polished marble, so pristine the evening sun reflected across them, making them appear washed in molten gold.

At the heart of the boulevard, a grand waterway stretched ahead, its surface a perfect mirror of the sky. Crystal-clear fountains rose from the center, mana-infused water swirling in mesmerizing patterns before cascading into the aqueducts below.

"Evy, look at this place." Irma gripped her arm.

Evy was too busy taking in the sheer scale of it all.

Well-dressed scholars and citizens of various races strolled in flowing garments, their chins lifted in self-importance.

Merchants in silk robes tended ornate market stalls, their wares glinting in the sun.

While the carriage moved through the streets, a few citizens turned to watch. Some only glanced before returning to their conversations. Others halted, their stares sharpened the moment they spotted Evy and Irma through the window.

Whispers passed between lips. A woman eyed her coldly before turning away.

Had it really been that simple to spot the outsiders among them?

Evy's first instinct was to shrink back from the window. To pull the curtain shut and disappear into the safety of the carriage.

Instead, she straightened her spine and lifted her chin, just as Orianna had taught her. She must present herself as the queen she was.

As the carriage continued to wind, Evy's fingers grazed the edge of the Council's letter, still tucked in her lap.

Below the summons to the Hierarch Wars, a formal decree informed her that the Council had secured a townhouse in the city for her lodgings.

"That's surprisingly generous." Orianna's voice still echoed in her mind. *"It would have cost us a fortune to secure our own lodgings, so someone must have pushed for this."*

Evy had guessed Kaelen Reed, but Orianna doubted it. If not him, then who?

As they halted before the townhouse, Evy pushed aside her unease and studied the structure before her.

By Ruitheon's standards, it was simple—a modest, two-story dwelling of smooth white stone. Its columns were unembellished, its facade plain against the grandeur surrounding it.

But in Reyland? This would have been a palace.

Marble pillars framed a shaded entrance, the floors inside as luminous as polished pearl. Wide windows welcomed the sun's golden rays, filling a space even larger than the Sanctum in the Reyani Temple.

Evy barely had time to take it in before Irma hurried past her, stepping inside—only to freeze. She dropped the bags of clothes. "This is ours?"

Evy stepped in after her. "For now."

Irma pressed a hand to the smooth stone wall. "We've been here five seconds, and I already feel spoiled."

Evy couldn't help but chuckle. It was more than she had expected. They had even provided a stable for the horses.

The marble beneath her feet was worth more than most homes in Moonveil. She thought of the farmer she had passed on her way to her parents' house. The old woman whose knees trembled from the effort of coaxing life from mana-starved soil. What could that woman do with even a fraction of the power that flowed freely beneath this city?

How was she meant to stand in the heart of the realm, the birthplace of power, and not fight for it? Not try to win the Hierarch Wars and share that power with the Witches?

"Show them who we are," her mother had said.

But how much of herself could she truly show?

ELEVEN

Evy stood before the mirror as Irma draped a heavy violet robe over her shoulders. The fabric pooled around her, embroidered with intricate golden patterns that glinted in the morning light. She hadn't slept a wink. The air was too dry, and the plush, silken threads of the bed were too soft against her skin. She took another sip of black tea, hoping it would stave off the exhaustion.

She had hoped arriving ahead of schedule would buy her time to settle before the Council summoned her. It hadn't. The notice had been waiting on her desk before she'd even unpacked.

"Well, you sure look royal," Irma said, tightening a bronze belt at Evy's waist. "But thick wool and desert sun don't make the best pairing, in my humble opinion."

Evy couldn't agree more. But Orianna had insisted she present herself as majestically as possible when meeting the Council for the first time. These were the finest robes she owned.

"I'll be alright." She adjusted her sleeves, studying her reflection. Kohl darkened the outline of her eyes, making the icy blue of her irises sparkle like diamonds.

Evy was commanded to *look* powerful, but not to be *too* powerful. She wondered if it was possible to hold both truths in the same body.

"Fine. Just don't expect me to rescue you when you faint in the heat." Irma brushed dust from Evy's shoulders. "Mostly because I'd be right beside you on the ground."

Evy raised her fingers, and a soft blue glow curled from their tips. A water spirit materialized and whispered a gentle greeting in her ear. The orb circled her before sinking into the fabric of her robes. The violet cloth thrummed, and a refreshing chill brushed against her skin before the glow faded.

Irma ran her fingers over the sleeves. "What did you do?" Her eyes widened. "My word, it's cool to the touch. Will it stay like this all day?"

"I'm not sure," Evy replied. "With how dense the mana is here, I'll have to see."

"Very impressive. You'll have to do that for me so I can brave the markets later." Irma smiled. "You look ready to me, Your Majesty."

Evy made her way down the stairs and into the courtyard, where her carriage awaited. She stepped inside and settled into the seat as the coachman whistled, urging the horses forward.

Leo Warring rode on horseback alongside the carriage, scanning the streets ahead.

Ruitheon unfolded before them. Scholars hurried along marble pathways with arms full of scrolls, their robes billowing as they vanished into nearby academic buildings.

They passed a marketplace alive with commotion. Merchants tended their stalls, voices colliding as they bartered their goods.

But Evy barely took it all in.

Her focus was ahead where, rising above the skyline, the Aurethium came into view.

A fortress of white marble, crowned with a brilliant golden dome. Its spiraling ivory towers stretched skyward, piercing the blue expanse.

Beyond the thick metal gates, an extravagant courtyard sprawled before the palace. Pools and cascading fountains glittered under the dappled sun, shaded by swaying palm trees. Bright pink lotuses drifted atop the water, their delicate petals inviting the occasional dragonfly to rest.

The mana grid was as visible as the ground itself, a vast web converging at the palace. Thick bands of turquoise light rippled outward, spreading through the city and beyond.

And within its depths, hidden from the world, lay the Heart, the artifact that dictated the very balance of mana throughout Lumesphere.

Two guards in golden cloaks stood at either side of the gates, lifting a hand for the carriage to halt.

Evy retrieved her summons and handed it to Leo, who dismounted and strode forward, presenting the parchment to the guards. One of them took it and scanned the wax seal before turning and disappearing beyond the gates.

A moment later, the heavy doors groaned as they swung open.

The carriage rolled forward, passing beneath the grand archway and into the courtyard beyond.

The carriage slowed once more before coming to a complete stop. Leo opened the door and extended a hand, helping Evy down as she stepped out.

The scent of roses tickled her nose. Clusters of the deep red blooms were carefully arranged in the manicured gardens, their vibrant petals shifting in the morning breeze.

Evy let the tranquility of the garden settle her nerves.

Then she set her sights on the figure standing at the grand archway leading into the Aurethium.

The man was as tall and broad as Leo, if not larger. Draped in a long black robe, gold-and-sapphire embroidery curled along the fabric. A hood shielded most of his face from the sun, but beneath its shadow, Evy glimpsed slicked-back silver hair.

Even from a distance, his scowl was unmistakable. His neatly trimmed white beard couldn't soften the deep-set frown lines etched into his face.

A guard stepped forward and addressed Evy.

"Milady," he said, inclining his head. "I am instructed to guide you to the doors to the Aurethium. Only you may enter. Your party must remain behind."

Leo's stance shifted immediately. His broad shoulders squared, arms crossing over his chest.

"It's *Your Majesty,* not *milady.*" Leo's glare could have shaken a mountain to its core.

The guard flinched but held his ground.

Evy placed a hand on Leo's arm before he could escalate the tension further. "I'll be fine, Captain Warring. Thank you for escorting me this far."

She didn't need a scuffle at the gates of the most powerful institution in the realm.

Leo hesitated, then stepped back.

For a split second, Evy forgot how to walk. This was her journey—and she had believed she was ready to face it alone—but her legs were rooted beneath her.

A hand squeezed her shoulder. She turned to find Leo offering a firm nod of reassurance.

Right, Evy thought to herself. *A queen would not falter.*

She willed her legs to obey and followed the guard toward the entrance of the Aurethium.

And then, she was face-to-face with the man in the black robe.

He towered over her, his presence as imposing as the marble archway ahead.

Piercing gray eyes measured her with cold scrutiny.

"Evalene Lovejoy of Reyland?"

He didn't address her as a queen. To him, she was just a girl from Reyland. She lifted her chin, refusing to shrink.

"That's correct."

"I am Arch Councilor Lawrence Daryn." He paused, lips pursed. "I'm here to greet you and"—his scowl deepened—"*welcome* you to the Aurethium."

She knew that name.

Orianna had warned her.

"Keep an eye on that one, Evy. As the First Councilor of Theribane, Lawrence will not be your friend. And as the Arch Councilor, he won't make the effort to be."

Her mentor's voice echoed in her mind.

"The Daryn family is deeply tied to the Veyn family. They've prospered the most under their reign," Orianna had continued. *"Lawrence isn't just loyal to their rule, he is notoriously opposed to Witches. He's spent years spearheading anti-Witch propaganda in Ruitheon, pushing for decrees that would strip Reyland of its independence."*

And now, here he stood, the man who had spent years trying to erase her people's freedom.

She met his eyes and forced herself to stay composed. But inside, she braced herself.

"Let us go inside." He turned on his heel and walked.

Evy hurried after him, stepping beyond the soaring archway and into the Aurethium's grand halls.

The moment she crossed the threshold, the shift in atmosphere was almost tangible. It was a world of solemn majesty and power enclosed within white walls.

The ceiling rose into an impossibly high, elegant marble dome veined with gold. Sunlight streamed through the vaulted arched windows and beamed across the polished floors. Lanterns of crystal and sapphire hung from delicate gilded chains, while burning incense, rich and heady, drifted through the corridors and curled into the magically cooled air.

The hallway they entered was lined with statues, each sculpted from white stone and gold, their forms unmistakable—the Goddess Rui.

Artists captured her likeness in many poses. Some statues towered in gold, her sapphire eyes cast downward. Others showed her lifting her hands in blessing, long robes pooling at her feet.

They were so lifelike, Evy had to resist the urge to kneel in their presence.

As they walked deeper inside, Evy became increasingly aware of the figures in black robes standing quietly within the hallways.

Councilors.

Some gathered near the statues, others along the columned paths, their hushed conversations falling into silence as she passed.

They regarded her impassively, mouths drawn in a straight line.

Evy didn't need to guess their allegiances. Like Lawrence, most bore the sharp, refined features of Shifter heritage. They were likely loyal to the Veyn family and the rule that had secured their power for centuries.

Evy had expected open disdain as she walked by them.

But their silence was worse.

It felt as though they were waiting for her to make a spectacle, to stumble, to embarrass herself, to prove them right. That she was wild. Uncivilized. Out of place.

She straightened her spine, suddenly conscious of her posture.

Lawrence led her through a labyrinth of vast corridors until they finally arrived at a spacious, occupied lounge.

Tall, arched windows overlooking a courtyard filtered a gentle glow into the room. The floor, polished black marble streaked with silver, complemented the royal blue tapestries adorning the walls.

Before Evy could fully take in her surroundings, a lean figure in a black robe stepped forward. His pale hair was pulled tight behind his head, a striking contrast to the deep umber of his skin. His frosty-blue eyes held no hostility. Youthful, angular features, and the pointed tips of his ears marked him unmistakably as an Ethereal. An Elf.

"Thank you, Arch Councilor," he said. "I can take it from here."

Lawrence's mouth tightened. "You waste no time, Reed."

Kaelen Reed merely offered a polite, practiced smile. "Neither do you."

Lawrence gave a curt nod and turned without another word.

Kaelen clasped his hands behind his back.

"Welcome to the Aurethium, Your Majesty."

TWELVE

Kaelen led Evy farther into the lounge, inquiring about her journey. "You had no issues finding the road here, I trust?"

The way he spoke was calculated and efficient. Unlike Lawrence's cold hostility, Kaelen's tone carried no malice. But there was no warmth in it either.

"Yes." Evy tried to match his brevity.

Kaelen gestured toward a blue velvet armchair near one of the lounge's windows. "Please, sit. You've had a long journey."

Evy hesitated for only a moment before lowering herself into the seat. The cushions were softer than she expected, and as she leaned back, she realized how much tension she had been holding on her shoulders.

Kaelen remained standing, hands clasped behind his back.

Evy turned to him. "I wanted to thank you."

He tilted his head.

"For your efforts in Reyland's participation in the Hierarch Wars," she said. "I know it couldn't have been easy, and I appreciate it."

"Think nothing of it. It is our duty to protect the realm. Yours and mine both."

It was a reminder of the price Reyland had paid to be here.

Of the price *she* had paid.

"How is Magister Gale?" Kaelen asked.

It was subtle, but his voice softened at the mention of Orianna.

Orianna had studied with Kaelen. It occurred to Evy that they might have even been close.

"She's doing well."

"She's had no issues in her role as Magister, I presume?"

An odd question. "No. She's doing quite well."

Kaelen hummed in response. Evy wondered if he still worried for Orianna after her expulsion. He'd likely witnessed the fallout firsthand, saw how it wounded her pride.

He tapped the armrest of her chair. "We're waiting on one more Ascendant. Until then, I suggest you relax."

Evy exhaled and sank into her chair as Kaelen unfurled a scroll beside her and proceeded to read in silence.

Relax? An impossible task.

With Kaelen now occupied, she had the freedom to study those in the room. Kaelen had said they were anticipating an additional Ascendant, which meant two others, besides herself, should be present.

Evy's attention landed on a man standing by a window across from her.

He stood with his arms crossed, his broad frame draped in black and deep crimson garments.

Loose waves of inky-black hair fell past his shoulders, framing a bearded visage.

And then there were his eyes.

A burning red-gold, glowing like embers beneath dark brows, stood out vividly against his earth-toned skin.

"King Zafir Soltris," Kaelen whispered, noticing her gaze.

Of course, Evy knew of him. Zafir Soltris, the Elemental King of Zarokan. A Djinn.

The strongest warriors in Aeltheon, a Djinn's strength was as legendary as their resilience. They didn't simply wield fire—they *were* fire.

Zafir turned his head, his glowing gaze locking onto hers.

Evy dipped her head in respect, her posture instinctively formal.

Slowly, he returned her nod.

Without a word, he faced the window, resuming his observation of the city beyond.

Across the lounge, another man, perhaps around her age, sat in a black leather chair, one leg crossed over the other in an effortless display of poise. His long fingers tapped against his chin, hazel eyes distant.

His chestnut hair, slightly tousled, fell over his forehead. A nearby lamp brought a warm glow against his pale skin. Angular features gave him an air of refinement: high cheekbones, a straight nose, and a well-defined jawline, striking in a way that was unmistakably Shifter.

She knew who he had to be.

"Royen Veyn," Kaelen whispered again. "The Young Master of Theribane."

Evy knew of his reputation, of course. A Veyn by blood, third in line of succession to the most powerful family in Aeltheon. Yet compared to his famous relatives, he was mostly an enigma. Little was spoken about him beyond his sharp mind, upbringing, and family's unyielding grip on the Hierarch's seat.

She studied him for a moment longer, curiosity stirring.

Royen looked up. Their eyes met.

Whatever thoughts had occupied his mind vanished. Royen's once-distant expression tightened.

The contemplative ease he'd held moments ago was gone, replaced by a rigid discomfort. He held her gaze only a moment longer before looking away, as though the mere sight of her had unsettled him.

This was who she was supposed to concede to?

"Don't take it too personally, Your Majesty."

A woman stood nearby, dressed in the same black robes as the other members of the Council.

Her dark brown hair was pulled into a tight braid over one shoulder, her features soft.

Beige, gossamer wings jutted from her back, their buttery sheen reflecting the light.

A Sylph.

An Ethereal.

"The Young Master of Theribane isn't much friendlier to anyone else either." A sly smirk tugged at her lips.

Evy followed her gaze back to Royen Veyn. He carried himself with careful detachment, as if keeping the world at arm's length.

The woman beside her sighed. "I do hope Orianna warned you about him. He is your greatest competition, after all."

The Magister's name caught her attention. The Sylph's presence felt familiar now that Evy studied her. Before Evy could ask, Kaelen greeted the woman with a quick glance.

"Good day to you, Councilor Varos."

"Varos? Lilian Varos?" Evy straightened. "You're the Second Councilor of Reyland, right?"

Lilian's lips pressed together. "I *was* the Second Councilor of Reyland." She took a seat next to Evy and leaned in close.

"Lawrence didn't like the fact that I had a hand in securing your townhouse in Ruitheon." Lilian offered a slight shrug. "So he had my position moved."

Evy's fingers curled against the folds of her robe.

"As grateful as I am for our lodgings, I'm just as sorry."

"Oh, don't be." Lilian waved a dismissive hand. "I thought I was doing my job, looking out for the domain I'm supposed to represent."

Evy sighed. She *had* done her job. The injustice was painfully clear.

"Where did they place you?"

"Second Adjunct Councilor of the Outer Islands."

Evy frowned. "That's not exactly a desirable post, is it?"

Even less desirable than Reyland, she thought. *She wasn't even in a First or Second Councilor seat anymore.*

"Let's just say it's a convenient place to send anyone who doesn't show unwavering loyalty to the Veyns." Lilian leaned in close to Evy's ear. "Being an Adjunct Councilor to the Outer Islands always felt more symbolic than functional."

Evy scanned the chamber. "So, who replaced you as Second Councilor of Reyland?"

Lilian nodded across the room. "Rita Tenzi."

A Harpy sat slouched in her seat, her heavy, slate-gray wings tucked tightly against her back. She was unusually short for her kind, with flushed cheeks and a vacant stare that drifted just off-center.

"A drunk Ethereal traitor," Lilian muttered. "And a Veyn loyalist through and through."

Evy opened her mouth to speak when a sudden breeze stirred through the chamber, carrying the scent of jasmine and fresh morning dew.

"Apologies for being fashionably late!"

The voice rang through the space, bright and musical, carrying an effortless lilt.

A figure swept into the room in a blur of color and motion.

A young woman. A Sylph, like Lilian.

Her warm bronze skin held a golden undertone, and a crown of tight, spiraling pink curls, as vibrant as the first blush of dawn, bounced around her face.

But it was her wings that left Evy breathless.

Radiant and weightless, they refracted light into a thousand tiny prisms, scattering rainbows around her like living jewels. Their delicate, gossamer-thin texture shifted between crystal and mist, never quite solid, never quite transparent.

"Celeste DuVent, Princess of Virenna," Lawrence announced as he stepped into the room behind her.

Celeste gave a playful salute. "At your service!"

She swept farther into the room, gaze flitting across the gathered figures until it landed on Zafir. Her almond-shaped eyes twinkled like emeralds, and her face brightened, a delicate flush dusting her button nose and full, high cheeks. Without hesitation, she strode toward him.

"King Zafir Soltris! The famous Elemental King himself. It's about time we met."

Zafir extended a hand for her to shake. "It's an honor, Princess."

Celeste ignored his hand.

Before he could react, she threw her arms around him and pulled him into a hug.

Evy stiffened, uncertain how Zafir would respond. But to her surprise, he remained still for a moment before patting Celeste lightly on the shoulder.

Celeste pulled away. "I knew you were a big softie."

Zafir arched an eyebrow. "That is a dangerous assumption, Princess. Best keep these thoughts to ourselves."

Celeste offered a light and unbothered laugh.

She turned toward Royen, who, at some point, had gotten out of his seat and moved closer to a window.

It almost looked like he was trying to hide behind the curtain.

Her smile widened as she set her sights on him next.

Royen recoiled and took a sharp step back as she approached.

Celeste huffed. "Oh, come on, Royen. After all these years, you're still like this?"

Royen scowled, shifting his weight as if trying to distance himself from the very concept of physical affection.

"You're insufferable, DuVent," he muttered.

"And yet, here I am, still waiting for you to take me on a date."

Royen scoffed and rolled his eyes, the faintest hint of pink spreading across his sharp cheekbones.

"That will never happen."

Celeste gasped. "You wound me." She pressed a hand dramatically to her chest. "One day, you will admit your undying love for me, and I will be there to accept it graciously."

Royen pinched the bridge of his nose.

Evy watched the exchange with mild fascination.

Until then, Royen Veyn had been the picture of composure—distant and utterly detached.

Yet somehow Celeste had cracked him.

Even if it was only a blush.

Celeste, still grinning at Royen's exasperation, turned her head and froze.

"Oh, my word. It's true! My Reylandic neighbor is here!"

Celeste flew at her, arms wide.

Evy barely had time to brace herself before the Sylph princess wrapped her in a tight embrace.

"You're even prettier in person, Queen Evalene!" she gushed, then drew back to study her face. "Those eyes! That hair! You're otherworldly."

"Thank you?"

"I've always wanted to meet you. The youngest ruler in Aeltheon! Meanwhile, I'm a couple of years older than you and still merely a princess," Celeste said, her full lips forming into a pout. "Not that I'm complaining. I'd be a terrible queen right now. Way too much work. Thank the Gods my mother is still ruling. I need my youth to have fun, you know?" She winked at Evy.

"Though I'm still not sure why my mother decided to send *me* as the Ascendant instead of coming herself. I'm going to miss all the summer revelries back home," Celeste said, crossing her arms.

An Elven woman in black robes strode toward Celeste. Her dark hair was in a neat bun and silver rings of various sizes lined her pointed ears. "It's because you're the fastest Sylph in all of Virennese history and the most skilled with air magic, Your Grace," she said. "It was a wise decision by Queen Talia."

Celeste sized her up. "You're Eliza Blanche, Second Councilor of Virenna, are you not?"

Eliza nodded.

Celeste groaned. "I really hope it wasn't *you* who convinced my mother to send me. If it was, I'll have a personal vendetta against you."

Eliza's expression dropped. Evy urged herself to stifle her own amused grin.

Before the Elf could respond, a deep voice cut through the chamber.

"If I could have everyone's attention."

Lawrence stepped forward, his imposing presence rippling tension through the room. Conversations died beneath the commanding grip of his voice.

"The time for pleasantries is over. The Ascendants will now offer their essence to the Heart," he continued. "From this moment on, the Heart itself will oversee the trials, thus initiating the Hierarch Wars."

THIRTEEN

The lounge's warm light faded as the group walked deeper through the Aurethium's halls. The farther they walked, the more the light faded, swallowed by the windowless walls ahead.

Lawrence led the way, his tall, broad frame still visible at the front of the group.

Behind him was Zafir. The ember embroidery woven through his cloak caught the lantern light and glowed like banked coals. Beside him, Celeste spoke with airy enthusiasm, her pink curls swaying as she gestured. Zafir nodded absently, but every so often, a small, fleeting smile tugged at his lips, amusement at whatever Celeste had said.

A few steps behind them, Royen moved at his own pace, hands clasped behind his back. His posture was straight, almost too straight to look natural, making him appear tall and commanding despite his slender frame.

He turned, looking past Lilian and Kaelen, who walked slightly ahead of Evy. His hazel eyes met hers before he quickly turned forward again, shoulders tensing.

Both Kaelen and Lilian looked back at Evy, arching their brows.

Evy offered a small shrug, silently returning the confusion.

As they continued, she saw obsidian doors ahead, as tall and wide as the corridor itself, looming beneath the raging torches.

Paintings lined the wall to the right in neat rows leading to them.

Evy slowed as they neared the first few portraits. The frames held the likenesses of past Hierarchs, each painted in stunning, lifelike detail, their watchful gazes fixed forward, frozen in time.

The name beneath the painting farthest from the door read: *Thylarion Veyn, Fourteenth Hierarch of Aeltheon.*

Evy studied his features. He looked young, far younger than she'd expected for someone who once ruled all of Aeltheon. His chestnut-brown hair was neatly combed back, his hazel eyes stern and calculating. He carried the classic, refined, angular facial structure of Shifters.

She scanned the next portraits. Each Hierarch wore nearly identical gold and sapphire ceremonial robes. Upon their heads sat the same towering crown: thick, twisting gold vines embedded with precious blue gems.

They all looked so young. These paintings must have been created at their inauguration, immortalizing them at the start of their power.

As they neared the grand doors, Evy caught sight of a painter perched atop a ladder, carefully touching up the portrait closest to the entrance.

The artist stepped back, allowing the regal figure in the portrait to emerge into view. Silver hair cascaded past the subject's shoulders, framing a face that was sharp, elegant, and hauntingly feminine. His smoldering lilac eyes stared straight into her soul. Various colored gemstones adorned his long, thin, pointed ears, and a tattoo of a sun had been etched onto his forehead.

He couldn't have been much older than Evy.

Beneath the portrait, the nameplate read: *Lutharion Skye, First Hierarch of Aeltheon.*

Despite his monumental role in Aeltheon's history, Lutharion Skye's story remained largely undocumented. The most enduring tale spoke of how, after Goddess Rui imbued Lumesphere with mana and taught its people the ways of magic, she left behind a fragment of herself through the Heart.

Before ascending back to the celestial plane, Rui had entrusted a single Aeltherian to wield the Heart and govern the realm's power—Lutharion Skye.

She had deemed him worthy of carrying her strength, wise enough to govern the flow of mana, and pure enough to resist the corruption of power.

Because the Heart's power was finite, mana had to be allocated with care, distributed where it was needed most.

Lutharion Skye's virtues of strength, wisdom, and resilience became the foundation for future Hierarchs, traits that marked one as worthy to govern mana in his place.

Evy heard a whisper brush against her ear.

"Most people don't know Lutharion Skye was a Lumiel."

She jolted slightly at the unexpected presence, then turned to find Lilian standing beside her.

"A Lumiel." Evy recalled what she knew of the extinct species. "Light Elves."

Lilian nodded. "Once, they were likely the strongest beings in the realm. No wonder Lutharion was chosen by Rui."

Kaelen cleared his throat. "We should keep moving."

Their steps carried them to the end of the corridor.

Carved from dark stone, the doors stood before them, their weathered surface threaded with shining blue veins that pulsed with the energy sealed beyond.

The very air was heavier, charged with invisible power.

Above the entrance, words were etched deep into the stone: *To Wield is to Serve, to Serve is to Sacrifice.*

"You are about to enter the Heart's Chamber." Lawrence came to an abrupt halt and turned to face the Ascendants. "Here, you will complete the ritual that will bond you to the Heart."

Evy swallowed against the tension creeping up her throat. The massive doors groaned as they shifted under their own weight, while four Councilors—two on each side—strained to pull them open.

An overwhelming pressure thrummed in the air like an invisible current.

Her spirits sensed it too.

They wavered in and out of sight, their forms restless. A wisp of light zipped past her shoulder. Another darted erratically above before dissolving into the shadows. Their whispers grew deafening, their agitation near-unbearable.

Lawrence spoke again, guiding them through the history of the Heart and the Hierarch.

"By law, only the Hierarch can wield and maneuver the power of the Heart, as is decreed by the sacred bond—"

Let me inside. I want to see.

The spirits wouldn't stop. Their frantic voices overlapped. Evy struggled to focus.

Power. I feel it. Delicious power.

"It wouldn't matter if it weren't law." Lawrence's words echoed through the chamber. "The Hierarch undergoes a sacred bonding ritual, making them the sole wielder of the Heart's power."

I'm hungry. Let me taste the power inside.

Evy clenched her fists.

Keep calm. She reached for the spirits with her mind, trying to soothe them.

"If anyone aside from the Hierarch tried to wield the Heart's power, they would be disintegrated. Destroyed completely."

The spirits wouldn't listen to her. The Heart's presence had thrown them into chaos, and the more she tried to ground them, the more their panic bled into her own.

"But do not mistake the bonding ritual the Council will perform on the Heart for wielding its power. Casting a spell upon it is one thing. Drawing from it, augmenting our own strength, is another."

She exhaled and did the only thing she could. *Stay silent,* she commanded. The spirits slowed immediately, one by one they withered away from her mind's eye, deflated.

She despised being overly authoritative with the spirits, and their somber reactions left an ache in her chest.

But right then, she had no choice.

Evy and the others moved on, bathed in blue light as they stepped into the Heart's Chamber.

The room was circular, its golden dome stretching high above them. Along the walls, twelve golden statues of Rui stood in formation. Each bore the same serene expression, arms outstretched in front of her.

Beneath Evy's feet, the floor was alive with constant motion. A shifting, liquid sheen of deep azure coursed above the stone floor and flowed in slow, rhythmic currents—its motion eerily reminiscent of blood running through veins.

At the room's center, a swirling orb of gold and blue hovered above the ground, its glow expanding and contracting, beating in a steady rhythm. Raw mana, pure and uncontained, radiated from its core, flooding across the chamber.

Encasing the orb, which Evy gathered must have been the Heart, was a lattice with golden vines, twisting in gnarled patterns, their edges lined with delicate thorns. They curved inward, barbs clinging to the Heart with an unyielding grip. Some of the metal thorns were broken, as expected of a relic as old as Aeltheon itself. What unsettled her was that it looked less like a reliquary and more like a trap. Like a snare meant to catch an animal.

She wasn't sure what she had expected, but those thorns seemed out of place. Menacing, in fact.

Along the wall, the Councilors were taking their places, each standing before a Rui statue.

At the center of the chamber, Lawrence turned to the Ascendants.

"The Heart carries the blood of this realm. To enter its trials, you must offer a drop of your own."

He gave Kaelen a curt nod. Kaelen returned the gesture and slipped out of the room.

"When the offering is made, we, the Council, will cast a spell that links your essence to the Heart, binding you to the Hierarch Wars," Lawrence continued. "Though the Council shapes the trials and places the obstacles, it is the Heart itself that will pass judgment on your performance."

Kaelen stepped back into the room, carrying a small silver platter. Resting atop it were four sapphire-bladed knives.

Lawrence took one without hesitation and turned toward the Ascendants.

Zafir was already stepping forward.

As he approached, Lawrence extended the jeweled blade.

Zafir took it without pause.

With a swift, clean motion, he dragged the blade across his palm. A thin line of dark blood welled against his copper skin.

Lawrence motioned him toward the Heart.

Zafir stepped closer and extended his bleeding hand. The moment his palm hovered near the orb, the Heart reacted. A sudden pull drew the droplets in, swallowing them into the light.

A red flash surged through the Heart.

Then, just as quickly, the glow returned to swirling gold and blue.

Zafir remained still briefly before stepping back, measuring the Heart's response.

Celeste stepped forward next.

She accepted the sapphire knife with delicate fingers and drew the blade across her palm. Her wings refracted light in a dazzling array of color as she extended her bleeding hand toward the Heart.

The orb reacted instantly, drinking in the drops of blood. A faint red glow pulsed, then returned to normal.

As Celeste stepped back, Evy's focus shifted to Royen.

He shifted on his feet, and his fingers absentmindedly picked at his cuticle as he scanned the Heart from left to right.

Evy watched as he took the knife and sliced his palm, flinching at the sting.

As he offered his blood, the Heart drank it in, its glow flashing red before fading back to gold once more.

A muscle ticked in his cheek. What was lurking beneath his passive demeanor—apprehension?

But before she knew it, Lawrence was in front of her, the final sapphire knife resting on the silver platter. Evy hesitated only for a second before picking it up. She drew the blade across her skin—a sharp sting followed, then the slow warmth of blood.

As she approached the Heart, incomprehensible noises stirred the air.

At first, it was just a faint sound, so distant she almost didn't register it. But as she neared the Heart, the sound grew clearer.

Whispers. They curled at the edges of her hearing, barely brushing against her consciousness. She slowed.

She thought the sound came from the Councilors, chanting some incantation under their breath, but when she glanced at them, their mouths remained still.

The whispers weren't coming from them.

Were her spirits speaking again? No, these voices were coming from everywhere, outside her mind, from the very air itself.

My children.

Why?

Fragmented words surfaced through the noise.

Love me.

The whispers sounded sorrowful and desperate. She strained to listen, to make sense of them, but just as she started piecing them together—

"Ahem."

Lawrence snapped her back.

Evy pushed the unease aside and stretched her bleeding palm toward the Heart.

The whispers vanished all at once.

The Heart turned red, the glow flaring before fading back to gold.

Evy flexed her fingers as she rejoined the other Ascendants.

But her heart was still pounding.

She wondered if the others had heard the whispers. But before she could dwell on it, a sudden burst of light flared ahead.

The Heart was strobing.

No longer a rhythmic blue and gold swirl, its colors shifted: gold to red, red to blue, blue to purple, then red again. The shifts came faster. The pool of mana beneath it surged and withdrew, pumping like blood.

A dull thrumming pressed against Evy's skull, and she lifted a hand to her temple.

Then, as suddenly as it had begun, the Heart's arrhythmia slowed, settling back into its usual swirl of gold.

Awkward silence permeated the chamber. Every gaze bore

into Evy, awaiting an explanation. But Evy, none the wiser, turned to Lawrence.

For the first time, his composure faltered. His mouth parted as he stared at the Heart.

"That must be a reaction to new blood." A faint tremor rippled through his voice. "The Heart has never... tasted a Witch before."

The others exchanged glances and nodded, accepting his words as truth.

Except Royen. His attention flitted suspiciously between the Heart and Evy.

"There doesn't seem to be anything wrong with the Heart." Lawrence scanned the orb a final time. "Let us proceed."

He strode toward one of the golden Rui statues, taking his place among the Councilors.

Questions raced through Evy's thoughts, but she forced herself to remain still. If Lawrence said all was well, so be it. Now wasn't the time to draw attention to herself, not when even the smallest doubt could threaten her place in the Hierarch Wars.

Ahead, the Councilors raised their arms, mirroring the statues that lined the chamber.

They began to chant.

"Let Rui herself place judgment on the worthiness of our Ascendants. Let her choose the wielder of her Heart," the Council intoned in unison.

Lawrence lowered his arms. "It is done. To allow time for preparation, the Trial of Wit will take place in three days."

Without another word, he and the rest of the Council filed out of the chamber in an orderly line.

Celeste huffed. "Well, that was efficient. And a little weird."

Royen shook his head and headed for the door. Zafir followed.

Celeste winked at Evy before slipping out after them.

Evy remained alone in the Heart's Chamber, feet cemented to the ground.

It was now official. The Hierarch Wars had truly begun.

And Evy was a part of it.

A sudden wave of nausea swept over her. She forced down the acid in her throat and willed herself to follow the Ascendants, but then she heard the voice again.

My child.

She turned to the Heart and felt a strange tether between her and the orb.

"What?" Evy whispered as she felt herself being pulled toward the Heart against her will.

"Queen Lovejoy?" A gentle voice broke her from her trance. Lilian stood at the doorway. "Is everything alright?"

Evy nodded.

She pulled herself back to reality and followed the Councilor out of the room. As the doors closed behind her, the pulse of the Heart echoed in her bones.

FOURTEEN

The next morning, Evy sat curled in an armchair, a steaming cup of tea left untouched beside her. Her desk was cluttered with books and parchment brought from Reyland, filled with notes on Aeltheon's history, geography, and politics—but for the past hour she hadn't touched any of them.

Instead, her full focus remained on the letter that had arrived the night before.

The messy, slanted handwriting was unmistakably Aeric's, and Evy found herself rereading the final lines again and again.

I don't fully understand what you're about to face out there, but I know you. And I know that whatever it is, you'll meet it with courage. I believe in you, Evy, more than you know.

I can't wait until you're finished with it all and can come home to me.

Write to me when you can.

—Aeric

Evy pressed the letter to her chest, her cheeks warming. A foolish grin tugged at her lips, and she was grateful no one was there to see it.

The door swung open to her left, and she flinched.

Irma stood in the doorway, her lower teeth pressed against her lips, stifling a smile.

Evy straightened. "Is everything alright?"

"You have a visitor." She sounded far too pleased.

Evy set the letter aside and followed Irma into the parlor.

The moment she stepped inside, a blur of pink shot up from one of the velvet chairs.

Before Evy could say a word, Celeste DuVent rushed forward and wrapped her in a tight, exuberant hug.

"Queen Evalene!" Celeste squeezed Evy so tightly she could hardly breathe.

Evy's hands hovered awkwardly before she patted Celeste's back. "Princess Celeste?"

Beside her, Irma let out a muffled squeak, failing to contain her laughter. Evy turned her head and glowered at her handmaid. Irma pressed a hand to her mouth and nodded, shoulders shaking as she obeyed the unspoken command.

"Please, drop the 'Princess' nonsense and just call me Celeste. All my friends do." She pulled away. "I was thinking perhaps we should have fun before the trials begin."

She rocked on her heels. "Come into town with me! We'll hit the market stalls, go sightseeing, whatever we want to do!"

"You... want to go shopping?"

Celeste nodded enthusiastically. "Come on, say yes! Let's have a little fun before we're stuck solving riddles and fighting monsters or whatever."

Evy hesitated, thinking of the books and scrolls waiting upstairs. With only two days until the first trial, she faced a daunting amount of review. She considered declining.

"Please, Evalene!" Celeste clasped her hands dramatically. "I can't go alone, and the boys are no fun." She flipped a strand of hair over her shoulder. "Zafir just grunts at everything, and Royen... Well, he's like talking to a brick wall, except I think a brick wall might be more entertaining."

A small laugh escaped Evy before she could stop it.

Celeste perked up. "See? You're already more fun than they are. And besides"—her full red lips curved upward—"we are neighbors, after all. We should get to know each other better."

Evy let out a small hum as she considered.

A friendly relationship with Virennese royalty, the Princess herself, would be invaluable for Reyland. Celeste didn't strike her as the political type, but alliances could take many forms, and this one might prove useful.

And, Evy had to admit, she liked Celeste's energy.

Since Orianna had told her not to worry about winning the trials, maybe she didn't need to push herself so relentlessly. A small reprieve might do her good.

Evy exhaled. "Only for a little while."

Celeste beamed.

"And call me Evy. All my friends do."

Celeste squealed as she grabbed Evy's hands. "This is going to be so much fun!" She linked arms with her and dragged her toward the door.

Celeste halted abruptly. "Oh! Before we go any further, we should disguise ourselves."

"Disguise?"

Celeste nodded, lowering her tone. "It's impossible to enjoy the city when everyone is watching you like you're some rare bird in a gilded cage. Trust me, I know."

She sighed. "So, we must go unnoticed. Luckily for you, I happen to be quite talented at illusion magic. Excellent for sneaking out to party."

Evy gave her a pointed look. "Of course."

Celeste winked, then lifted her hands. She whispered an incantation—a soft glow curled around her fingers before it migrated over their bodies, sweeping around them both like a gentle breeze.

Evy felt the magic drape over her like a veil. Next to her,

Celeste's signature pink waves had deepened to a rich auburn, her striking emerald eyes now a muted gray. Even her wings had vanished, dissolving into the air.

"Spells and enchantments are what the Ethereals are known for," Celeste said, inspecting her handiwork. "And I'm no exception."

Evy studied her reflection in a nearby mirror, amazed at the seamlessness of the illusion. Her pale hair had darkened to a warm brown, and her features had become rounder.

They both had long, pointed ears reminiscent of Elves, and their clothing transformed as well. Elegant royal attire melted into the flowing robes and layered tunics typically worn by Ruitheon's citizens.

Evy's lips parted in awe, but before she could comment, Irma appeared in the hallway. "Did they leave already?"

Irma took note of them and frowned.

"And who are you two? How'd you get in?"

Celeste let out a muffled giggle while Evy cleared her throat. "It's me, Evy. Celeste used illusion magic on us."

Irma's face cycled through three different expressions before she flushed with embarrassment. "Oh! Forgive me, Your Majesty! Your Highness! I didn't—"

Celeste doubled over laughing, waving her off. "No, no, it's perfect! See? It's working already. But despite the mana grid being so dense here, the spell only lasts for a few hours."

Evy nodded. "We should get going."

They stepped out onto the cobbled streets, their disguises allowing them to blend in with the crowd. Just two ordinary girls amid the late morning rush.

The marketplace stretched before them, stalls overflowing with fresh produce, bejeweled fabrics, delicate trinkets, and spiced pastries. The scents of roasted almonds and honeyed bread curled through the air as merchants called out their goods and wares.

Celeste dragged Evy from stall to stall, admiring silk scarves, laughing over gaudy jewelry, and holding up peculiar-looking fruit like rare treasures.

They stopped at a food stall and tried a delicate, coil-shaped dessert that looked like molten gold, its crisp edges glistening with syrup. A gentle bite sent a burst of richness over Evy's tongue. The shell gave way to a soft, honeyed center that dissolved almost instantly into pure sweetness.

"My goodness, this is the best thing I've ever eaten." Celeste licked the syrup from her fingers.

Evy agreed, savoring the sticky remnants on her fingertips.

"Celeste, I've been meaning to ask." Evy glanced over. "How do you know Royen?"

Celeste rolled her eyes. "My mother used to drag me to Ruitheon to have diplomatic talks with the Veyns. Thought I could charm them into an alliance or something."

Evy remembered how Royen kept trying to put space between them. "I'm assuming it didn't work?"

"Not even a little," Celeste said as she took another bite of her dessert. "But he's fun to annoy, isn't he?" They shared a laugh.

As they continued to meander through the marketplace, a growing crowd gathered around a makeshift podium. A robed figure stood at its center, his voice carrying over the hum of the city.

Then she heard the words:

"Witches."

"Outsiders."

Her steps slowed. Without thinking, she drifted toward the crowd.

The figure stood tall, his red skin gleaming under his blue hood, thick horns curving from his brow. An Ogre. His voice rang with conviction as he proclaimed, "From the Planar Astra, home of the Gods, Goddess Rui descended and gifted us mana, tearing out a piece of her own heart to breathe magic into the world."

The Ogre stretched out his arms. "But not to all. The Witches were excluded from her gift. And it was not without reason. We, the Children of Rui, know the truth—it is because they do not belong here."

Evy's mouth pressed into a thin line. She already knew where this was headed.

"They are not of Lumesphere, not of Rui's grace! The Witches are *Gaians*, invaders from another realm, and yet they are given the same privileges as the chosen of Aeltheon?"

Murmurs of agreement rippled through the gathered citizens.

"It is an abomination that they walk the streets of our holy city, that they have been welcomed into the sacred trials of the Hierarch Wars. The Council has turned a blind eye to tradition, to purity. But Rui does not forget. She does not forgive."

The murmurs swelled into chants.

"They do not belong!"

The speaker pressed on, his voice laced with cruel satisfaction. "But fear not! Witches will meet their reckoning in the trials. They dare believe they can stand beside Ascendants born under Rui's favor? We will laugh when the little Witch girl from Reyland, the one they call *queen,* crumbles to dust beneath Rui's judgment, proving once and for all the Witches were not meant for this world."

Evy's fingers curled into fists, anger simmering beneath her skin. She wanted to speak out, to make them see how wrong they were.

She opened her mouth—

A hand grasped her shoulder.

Celeste gently pulled her away, guiding her back through the marketplace.

"They won't listen," Celeste murmured once they reached a safe distance. "Words won't change their minds, Evy."

Her expression softened. "You'll have to show them they're wrong. Save your energy for the trials."

Show them? Evy gritted her teeth. *But are they willing to see?*

Celeste squeezed her shoulder. "Not everyone believes that kind of backward hogwash."

Evy met Celeste's earnest smile and slowly unclenched her jaw.

Despite Orianna's warnings about the realm's prejudice, it was comforting to know she had allies. But as they walked away, her heart continued to sink.

The crowd was still growing, their voices only getting louder. The hatred, the fervor, the belief that Witches didn't belong was so deeply rooted in them.

She had to shatter this system of prejudice. Dismantle it from its core.

No matter what it took.

Celeste suddenly straightened. "Oh, stars— I just remembered! I was supposed to meet with Eliza Blanche today."

"Councilor of Virenna?" Evy asked, recalling the Elf with silver rings adorning her pointed ears.

Celeste waved a hand. "Yes, yes. She wanted to check in before the first trial. Something about my performance reflecting on Virenna, blah, blah."

"Do you need to go now?"

Celeste nodded quickly. "Yes! But it won't take long. Just a boring little meeting. Come with me? Then we can grab dinner right after! Maybe a sweet treat and a goblet or two of wine."

Evy considered, then nodded. "Alright. Let's go."

Celeste beamed and looped her arm through Evy's as they headed toward the Aurethium.

As they neared the gates, Celeste raised a hand, dissolving their illusions.

The guards at the entrance bowed, then stepped aside as they entered the courtyard, and into the halls.

Celeste spotted Eliza near a marble archway. "I won't be long. Don't miss me too much."

Evy crinkled her nose but couldn't help a small smile as Celeste disappeared down the corridor, her voice light and melodic as she greeted the Councilor.

Left alone, Evy leaned against a pillar, arms crossed as she took in the ornate architecture around her.

Suddenly, she heard a voice from the far end of the corridor.

It was Lawrence.

He stood near an open doorway, speaking in low tones to someone inside. He clutched a scroll in his hand.

Careful not to make a sound, Evy slipped behind a statue, pressing into the shadows as she strained to listen.

"If you memorize this, you'll pass through the trial easily. Just don't let anyone see you with it."

Lawrence extended the scroll, and the figure inside took it. Without another word, the Arch Councilor turned on his heel and strode away.

For a long moment, the figure remained still, concealed within the doorway.

Then they stepped into the light, and she recognized his chestnut hair and hazel eyes immediately.

Royen Veyn stood alone in the corridor, staring down at the scroll, his brows drawn together.

After a sharp exhale, he tucked the scroll into his coat and walked away.

Evy remained frozen behind the statue.

The Council wanted another Veyn rule. And they planned to make sure Royen won by any means necessary.

An icy chill ran down her spine.

One thing was obvious.

As she had been warned, the Hierarch Wars were rigged.

FIFTEEN

The coliseum behind the Aurethium buzzed with commotion. Thousands of spectators filled the stands, their cheers rolling through the arena. Evy's skin prickled in the cool morning air, though the sun was climbing fast, offering solace in its warmth.

In the middle of the arena, the Ascendants stood before four identical clay structures, each featureless except for a single wooden door at the front. They were no larger than broom closets, and Evy couldn't understand how the Trial of Wit would take place in such tight quarters.

Lawrence stepped toward the structures. His scowl deepened at the sight of Evy.

A hush fell over the crowd as Lawrence raised a hand. His lips moved in a silent incantation as mist gathered at his throat.

"The time has come." His voice rang clear across the arena, amplified by a spell. "The first trial of the Hierarch Wars is upon us."

The spectators erupted, a deafening roar surging through the arena. Amid the cheers, Evy caught a few shouts of "Go home, Witch!"

A cluster of blue-robed figures occupied a section near the front of the stands, banners raised high. *Children of Rui. We Stand with Purity.*

She recognized the Ogre at the center—the same speaker from the marketplace. His red face was twisted with zeal, jagged teeth bared as he led the vicious chant.

"The Witch will taint us all!"

Lawrence turned toward the blue hoods and offered a brief, knowing smirk.

He had always peddled anti-Witch rhetoric, but as a member of the Council, he was bound to neutrality—at least the appearance of it. He couldn't openly condemn her during the Trials.

So he let others do it for him.

Evy dragged her attention to her feet, where mana thrummed thick.

For one reckless moment, she considered reaching for every spirit bound to her. She could show them what real power looked like.

Not part of Rui's plan?

She could show them exactly how much Witches belonged to this realm.

"If you show them your full power, you'll be deemed as dangerous." Orianna's voice threaded through her mind. *"They'll slam the door shut behind you. Maybe even bolt it."*

It took nearly all of her strength to swallow the simmering rage and feign indifference.

"This is the Trial of Wit—a test of strategy, logic, and knowledge," Lawrence continued, looking away from the Children of Rui and addressing the wider arena. "For the one who will govern Aeltheon, power alone is not enough. A true Hierarch must possess wisdom, the ability to see beyond obstacles, to solve what others cannot."

From the far end of the arena, the Councilors brought the Heart forward. The orb hovered weightlessly as they guided it ahead. Thick streams of mana spilled from the Heart's core, cascading like water, seeping into the earth, and dissolving into the arena floor.

A soft hum filled the air, and a slow pulse of light emanated from the Heart as it lifted higher above the four structures.

The Councilors began to chant.

"Seeing Heart of Rui, Giver of Mana, we are unworthy to judge what only you may understand. Witness the merit of those who stand before you. Weigh their wisdom. Find among them the one most worthy to hold your power and speak your will."

The Heart responded, its glow intensifying as tendrils of light unraveled from its center, streams of pure mana twisting through the air.

One by one, the tendrils stretched downward, latching on to each structure, embedding themselves into the clay. The moment the last tendril fused with its square, the ground trembled.

Evy glanced at the other Ascendants.

On her left, Celeste was playing to the crowd. She waved enthusiastically, blowing flirtatious kisses, basking in the spectators' adoration. The audience roared for her, swept up in her effortless charisma. Her crystalline wings caught the sunlight and surrounded her in illustrious prisms.

Beside the princess, Zafir rolled his neck. His focus remained locked on the trial ahead.

Royen stood to her right.

She hadn't forgotten what she had seen at the Aurethium.

Now, ahead of the first trial, he seemed composed.

Too composed.

He was the very picture of self-assurance.

Orianna had warned her the trials were designed to favor the Veyn heir, and the scroll Lawrence had slipped Royen was proof enough. But Orianna had also prepared her for this—for years, whether she'd known it or not.

Her goal may not be to win, but the knowledge Orianna had given her would have to be enough to keep her from falling desperately behind an opponent who had every trick up his sleeve. She refused to bring shame to Witch-kind.

"Each Ascendant will enter their assigned chamber," Lawrence said, "where they must solve a series of puzzles and challenges."

Evy studied the four structures, each now aglow with tendrils of light pulsing from the Heart.

For a fleeting moment, she thought she heard a whisper.

Why?

The voice hadn't sounded external, but more like a thought that wasn't hers. And it definitely didn't sound like any of her bonded spirits.

Where had it come from?

Lawrence's voice cut through her thoughts. "This trial is timed."

He turned to face the four competitors. "Though we in the arena cannot bear witness, the Heart shall be your judge. The faster you solve the challenges and escape, the more points the Heart will award. The first Ascendant to exit will earn the highest score, the second slightly fewer, and so on." Lawrence lifted a hand. "But there is more."

From the side of the arena, an attendant wheeled a pedestal forward, draped in royal-blue velvet. With a flick of Lawrence's wrist, the cloth vanished, revealing the prize.

A pair of golden gauntlets rested on the stand, their polished surface reflecting the sun. Delicate wing engravings adorned the sides.

"These," Lawrence said, gesturing to the artifacts, "are Celestial Gauntlets, a magical artifact that grants its wearer enhanced speed and strength. Whoever finishes first will claim them as an advantage in the Trial of Strength."

Evy's mind raced.

The Celestial Gauntlets.

That kind of assistance could guarantee victory in the next trial.

Too bad she already knew who they were meant for.

Royen stood motionless, his hands clasped behind his back, expression devoid of awe or ambition.

As if he already knew the gauntlets would be his.

Evy gritted her teeth.

She'd known the trials were rigged in favor of another Veyn rule, but she hadn't expected it to be so blatant.

If Royen won this trial and claimed the gauntlets, it would tip the next challenge in his favor.

Orianna had told her to do her best, that her goal wasn't to win, but to prove that Witches could stand among the Ascendants as equals.

But was she really expected to stand here and accept flagrant injustice?

Lawrence lifted his hand once more. Above the other Ascendants, a clock projection appeared, misty silver hands frozen at the starting mark. One materialized over her own head as well.

At Lawrence's gesture, the doors to the structures swung open, and the clocks above their heads ticked to life.

Beyond the entrance was only darkness.

The Ascendants met one another's gaze for a fleeting second.

Then they bolted.

SIXTEEN

The roar of the crowd faded into a distant hum as Evy surged through the threshold of the chamber.

The door slammed shut behind her, and she flinched. Her heart hammered in her ears as she scanned the space around her.

A few torches burned along the stone walls, casting dim light in the windowless room. Straight across was another wooden door.

Shelves lined the walls, crammed with an eclectic assortment of objects: statues, trinkets, rocks, even jars of food.

A massive stone table dominated the center space. Intricate etchings sprawled across its surface, forming a map of Lumesphere.

Aeltheon was sprawled at the center, its four domains carved into its body. Beyond its borders, the Outer Islands were scattered along the edges, flanking the continent like drifting debris.

Above the map, an inscription was engraved on the stone:

The Heart is contained in the center of our body.

Veins flow outward toward the realm.

The flow of blood goes both ways.

What is the blood flowing in traded for when blood flows out?

Evy reread the words.

"What is the blood flowing in traded for?"

It didn't make sense. The Heart only gave. It didn't take. How would the flow go both ways?

Evy tapped her chin, thinking. No, the keyword in the passage wasn't "Heart." It was "center," and at the very center of Aeltheon, of the entire realm of Lumesphere, was Ruitheon.

She returned to the words carved into the table.

The center's veins… The flow of blood…

Then it clicked.

Another keyword was *trade*.

The resources flowing into Ruitheon from the domains of Aeltheon and the Outer Islands. In return for the wealth that sustained the city's power, the realm is offered mana from the Heart.

Blood flowing in, traded for blood flowing out.

The rows of objects on the shelves took on new meaning—they were symbols of Aeltheon's trade.

Her thoughts drifted to a memory from years ago, when Orianna had her poring over trade routes, memorizing exports, tracking the flow of resources across Aeltheon.

"Who cares?" she'd grumbled. *"What do the other domains' trades have to do with us? It's not like we deal with them much."*

"For a leader, diplomacy is a powerful weapon," Orianna had replied. *"And the more you learn, the more you sharpen your weapon."*

Evy's entire upbringing had probably been part of Orianna's grand scheme, shaping her to become an Ascendant.

Her attention drifted back to the map—to Zarokan, the southernmost domain of Aeltheon. The largest of the four, it stretched wide across the continent, covering an array of shifting landscapes.

Etched into its territory were markings of diverse biomes: mountains, deserts, volcanic fields, jungles, forests, tropical beaches. A land shaped by Elemental beings and beasts, each adapted to their own unique environment.

Zarokan contributed a variety of resources to Ruitheon, but the real wealth of the domain was in what lay beneath them.

Minerals.

Zarokan's veins ran deep with ore, a crucial resource for Aeltheon's infrastructure and weaponry.

She surveyed the objects on the shelves until she landed on a lump of raw copper ore streaked with veins of teal and red.

Carefully, Evy lifted it and carried it to the stone table. With quivering hands, she placed the copper over Zarokan's position on the map.

Then the territory of Zarokan glowed gold.

It seemed her answer had been accepted.

She let out a slow breath, the tension in her jaw easing.

"Okay, focus. It's too early to celebrate."

She returned to the map, moving her attention northeast to Virenna, the second-largest domain of Aeltheon.

A land of dense forests and glimmering rivers, home to the Ethereals. Though Virenna's primary exports to Ruitheon were lumber and fertilizer, those weren't what made the domain indispensable.

Their true wealth lay in beauty.

Ethereals were artisans above all else.

Across Aeltheon, many desired their precious jewels, silks, and intricate works of art. Virenna's craftsmanship was unmatched, their creations symbols of status and luxury within the halls of Ruitheon's elite.

Back on the shelves was an ornate, gold-embroidered jewel box, its surface glistening in the dim light. She lifted the lid, revealing a delicate diamond ring nestled inside.

She carried the jewel box to the stone table and placed it over Virenna's position on the map.

A soft glow pulsed through the carved land, the golden light settling into the stone.

The puzzle had accepted her answer.

Evy smiled, murmuring a hushed *thank you* to Orianna for her mentorship.

To the west lay Theribane—smaller than Virenna and Zarokan, but still larger than Reyland. This answer came easily.

Among the rolling hills etched into the map, stood factories, workshops, and laboratories.

Theribane, home to the Shifters, did not have a reputation for magical strength like the other domains. But what they lacked in raw magic, they made up for in ingenuity.

For centuries, Theribane had received the largest share of mana from the Hierarch, a legacy of the Veyn dynasty's dominance in Ruitheon. But instead of using mana for spells and enchantments, the Shifters had forged it into a power source, fueling their machines, industries, and relentless cycles of innovation.

Evy returned to the shelves and spotted a miniature clockwork device, its tiny gears whirring. She picked it up and placed it on Theribane's position on the stone table.

A golden pulse blazed across the carved land.

Next came the Outer Islands, scattered along Aeltheon's edges. Though they had their own government, separate from the Hierarch and the Council, their divide had always been a facade. They still relied on mana from the Heart and had to support Aeltheon's economy by exporting food and crops.

Evy grabbed jars of sardines, dried fruits, and other preserved goods from the shelves. One by one, she placed them over five of the six islands, each glowing gold in acceptance.

Her hand hovered over Casper Island.

She left it blank. The island was abandoned, mana cut off. Nothing flowed in or out.

Above her head, the clock ticked away. Only twenty minutes had passed since the start of this puzzle. Evy allowed herself a small smile.

She was making good time. At least, she hoped she was.

She paused in front of the shelves. Should she slow down?

No. She couldn't afford to. If Royen had the answers to this puzzle, he might have completed it already. With her competitors' superior schooling and access to resources she'd never had, Evy could only hope she wasn't falling too far behind.

Only one place remained open on the map—the smallest domain tucked at the northernmost tip of Aeltheon.

Reyland.

Confident in her answer, she reached for a small stalk of wheat and placed it on the map.

The moment it touched the surface, Reyland's territory flashed red.

A sharp hissing noise filled the chamber.

Steam poured in from a crevice above the door.

Acrid fumes stung her nose. Her throat burned, her eyes watered. She coughed, then staggered back as the edges of her vision blurred, darkening until all she saw was black.

The next thing she knew, she was on the floor.

Evy awoke. She scrambled upright, gasping for air.

Dizziness washed over her. She looked up to the silver projection of the clock above her head.

Fifteen minutes lost.

A sharp cough escaped her lips. She wiped her mouth, and a streak of blood stained her hand when she pulled it away.

Had she been poisoned?

Evy summoned a light and air spirit and wove a healing spell into her lungs.

She shook her head and forced herself to concentrate.

Her body still felt weak, and she had no idea if she could survive another dose of the steam.

She couldn't afford another mistake.

But how had she gotten the answer wrong in the first place?

Evy noticed a string of dried fish. Reyland did trade fish, though not nearly as much as wheat. But maybe this wasn't about Reyland's main export. More like her answer for Virenna, maybe it was about what Ruitheon most valued, and perhaps fish was more important to the capital.

She didn't have time to waste. She had to try it.

Evy removed the wheat stalk and placed the string of fish on the table over Reyland.

Red flashed through the map.

Evy prepared herself for the mistake and urged her air spirits to circulate clean air around her to avoid the impact of the gas.

A low hum vibrated through the chamber.

Then a searing ball of fire erupted from the stone table and hovered midair before streaking toward her.

Evy barely had time to react before it slammed into her arm, scorching through her cloak sleeve. A hot, blinding pain lanced through her skin.

She gasped and stumbled back as the burn flared.

Pressing a hand to the wound, she tried to think through the sting.

What was it Orianna said about the first trial? Something about it not being too harmful?

"So much for that." Evy shook out her burning sleeve. "Poison gas, and now I'm getting hit with fire."

She called upon a light and water spirit and soon felt the

cool, soothing magic seep into her skin. The pain faded as the burned skin knitted itself back together.

She turned back to the shelves, frustration creeping in.

"Focus. This has to be a trick." She forced the words through clenched teeth.

If the correct answer wasn't wheat or fish, then what?

She examined the objects again, racing through possibilities.

Her attention caught on a small statue of an arch, its obsidian center gleaming under the dim torchlight.

It looked like a portal to Hollowrift.

Orianna's words came rushing back in a dizzying wave of realization.

"I brokered a deal with Kaelen Reed."

Reyland's main trade *used* to be wheat. Until Orianna negotiated for their right to compete in the Hierarch Wars. The price? Closing Hollowrift portals.

That deal had become Reyland's greatest contribution.

Heart pounding, Evy removed the string of fish from the map and replaced it with the obsidian portal statue.

The entire stone table glowed, a golden pulse rippling across the map.

With a deep, mechanical groan, the door ahead of her swung open.

Evy was overcome with relief. She rolled her shoulder as a faint ghost of pain tingled beneath her skin.

If this was the Trial of Wit, what chaos awaited her in the Trial of Strength?

Or worse, the dreaded Trial of Resilience?

She shoved the thought aside and refocused on the task at hand.

After a quick glance at the clock above her head, she stepped forward, her back straightening as she crossed into whatever lay ahead.

SEVENTEEN

She expected another small, dark chamber like the first.

Instead, Evy entered a vast hall, its sheer size striking after the cramped room she was in before. The ceiling arched high above her, polished stone floors stretching beneath her feet. At the center of the hall, raised up on a platform, sat a golden throne. Its intricate sapphire inlays glistened like stars.

Encircling it were twelve towering high-backed chairs arranged in a ring.

Figures were seated in the twelve chairs.

Each one was a translucent projection, their forms ghostlike. They were draped in heavy, dark robes, their hoods drawn low, concealing everything but the void where their faces should have been.

Who they were representing was painfully clear.

The Council.

The surrounding air shifted. An invisible force pressed in, wrapping around her like mist.

Her violet robes had vanished, replaced by a heavy foreign garment.

Deep blue fabric lined with silver-and-gold embroidery cascaded over her form.

She lifted a hand to her head, and cool material met her fingertips. A crown rested there, twisted gold metalwork adorned with sapphires.

She had seen this exact regalia before, lining the halls outside the Heart Chamber. It was painted in the portraits of all the past Hierarchs.

It dawned on her then.

Evy was about to play the role of the Hierarch.

She hesitated before stepping forward and lowering herself onto the empty, center throne.

The instant she sat, the twelve faceless Councilors rose in unison.

They bowed.

This was just a simulation, a carefully crafted illusion within the trial. Yet the display sent a chill through her.

This was a taste of absolute power, the kind held by only one person in all of Aeltheon.

Evy licked her lips. For a delicious, savory moment, she embodied that person.

The Councilors straightened and sat back down, their movements synchronized.

A single hooded figure remained standing, a scroll in hand. When they spoke, their voice echoed mechanically, neither male nor female, as if it belonged to no one and everyone all the same.

"To maintain peace throughout the realm, the Hierarch must navigate the will of the Council. Present your case, sway the room, and seal your decree."

Twelve floating orbs sparked to life above each Councilor's head, glowing a warm yellow.

The Councilor unfurled the scroll and read. "We are gathered to deliberate the Firesteel Highlands dispute between Theribane and Zarokan."

Evy stilled, listening.

"Theribane claims rightful ownership," the Councilor explained. "Ancient border records confirm the region fell under Shifter rule centuries ago."

Across the room, an orb shifted from yellow to blue.

"But Zarokan argues that the land remains unclaimed."

Another orb shifted to red.

The Councilor continued, "Theribane never enforced its control. They never built, never settled, never mined. Therefore, Zarokan deems it free for the taking."

The orbs above the remaining Councilors shifted, some from yellow to red, others to blue.

Sides were forming.

"The situation has escalated," the Councilor pressed. "Recently, Zarokan's miners and warriors moved into the Highlands, establishing camps. Theribane now demands that the Council recognize their authority and remove Zarokan's presence.

"If no ruling is made, this dispute will escalate into an open war between Theribane and Zarokan, a war that could destabilize Aeltheon as a whole." The Councilor lowered the scroll and sat.

Another figure rose, the orb above their head glowing blue. "The Firesteel Highlands have always been Theribane's," they said, their tone clipped and dismissive. "The maps prove it. Zarokan is violating international borders, and if the Council refuses to act, Theribane will enforce their claim themselves."

Evy's fingers tapped against the armrest, her mind working fast.

Blue means they side with Theribane.

A second Councilor stood, their orb also glowing blue.

"Theribane has the technological expertise to make use of

the Highlands," they said. "Zarokan is a land of warriors, not industrialists. If this Council is wise, it will remove Zarokan from the land so Theribane may make use of its resources."

Another Councilor stood, their orb glowing red.

"Theribane did nothing with the Highlands for centuries. They only value the land now that Zarokan put it to use. If you let the Elementals continue, it will benefit Aeltheon. Give in to the Shifters, and they will abandon it again, just as they always have."

Evy barely had time to process it before another Councilor with a red orb stood.

"Theribane is throwing a tantrum." They waved an arm in the air. "They've always used politics to take what they do not earn. The Council should not reward their greed."

Murmurs stirred through the chamber, the air thick with tension.

They grew louder until the room erupted into thunderous chatter.

Evy caught fragments of the conversation.

"Which side will bring greater trade benefits?" a neutral Councilor asked.

"If the Council rules in favor of one, how do we stop the other from retaliating?" another asked.

Evy sat still, absorbing everything—the shifting arguments, the power plays forming around her.

The chamber was unraveling into chaos.

Orbs flared as Councilors changed their stances, yellow turning to red, turning to blue. Voices overlapped, clashing in debate, the tension mounting as arguments flew from every corner of the room.

Evy straightened in her seat. She had to act. This was the first part of the test—she needed to take control.

"Order." Her voice cracked, drowned out by the deafening shouts around her.

She took a deep breath, letting air fill her diaphragm, then lifted her voice.

"Order."

Evy startled at the sound of her own voice. The word sliced through the noise.

The Councilors turned their faceless hoods toward her, the floating orbs still glowing. She could feel their attention now, bearing down on her, measuring her every move.

The true nature of the challenge was clear.

The Hierarch may be the grand authority over Aeltheon, but they do not rule alone.

The Council held the final vote on disputes between the domains and the Outer Islands, and they were the ones who carried out the Hierarch's will. To keep peace among the regions, the Council often voted on the policies and decrees the Hierarch proposed.

Though believed to be the most powerful figure in Aeltheon, the Hierarch still needed allies in government. Their power meant little if the Council refused to stand behind them.

And that was how she would win. She needed to sway the Council.

She took in the battlefield of opinions.

Eight blue. Four red.

Theribane already had the lead. The easiest path forward would be to side with them and reinforce their claim. With the majority already in their favor, she wouldn't need to convince anyone. Just agree, play along, and get through the challenge.

But doubt gnawed at her.

It felt too easy.

Just another cycle of surrendering to Theribane. Of validating their authority simply because they had always held it.

She knew deep in her gut that Zarokan's argument carried more weight.

Zarokan had been the ones to develop the Highlands. They

established mining infrastructure and used the land, unlike Theribane.

Theribane's claim had nothing to do with need or contribution. It was about control. About holding on because they could.

They were not miners. They did not care to be. Their argument was about power instead of progress.

Evy's fingers curled around the arms of the throne.

She had no desire to side with Theribane, even if it was convenient. And even though it was a simulation, she wanted to help Zarokan, because that meant helping Aeltheon.

She didn't know how much time she could afford to lose in this challenge, but she couldn't stomach taking the straightforward route. Not without at least trying to present her case.

She combed through everything she'd learned—her studies, her history lessons, Orianna's lectures—hunting for a strategy she could reshape. Then an idea struck.

"I propose…" She trailed off, weighing her words. "I believe there is a solution that benefits both parties."

The room fell still.

"The Firesteel Highlands will be officially recognized as Theribane's territory," she began. "However, the Council will mandate that Theribane lease mining rights to Zarokan for a period of fifty years."

A few Councilors leaned in. She pressed on.

"Zarokan will oversee the mining operations, utilizing the infrastructure they've already built. In return, they must pay a small share of resources to both Ruitheon and Theribane as compensation.

"This agreement will be legally enforced by the Council, preventing future disputes or sudden expulsions. Theribane retains political claim over the land, while Zarokan ensures its resources are used efficiently, a ruling that benefits all of Aeltheon."

Above her head, a glowing green orb appeared.

She hadn't realized she'd been assigned one.

Around the chamber, other orbs transitioned from yellow to green as murmurs passed among the Councilors. Some still held firm, red and blue glows unwavering in their stance.

A Councilor rose.

"All in favor of granting Zarokan full control over the Firesteel Highlands, revoking Theribane's claim," they said.

One red orb.

"All in favor of Theribane retaining full control, with Zarokan escorted out."

Five blue orbs.

"All in favor of Theribane retaining the Highlands while granting Zarokan protected mining rights."

Six orbs shone green. Evy's grip on the armrest eased. She had succeeded. She had shifted the Council to her side.

Evy had challenged herself. And she had won on her own terms.

As she sat on the Hierarch's throne, she felt a sensation far greater than victory.

Pride.

And power.

But before she could bask in the sensation, the Councilors flickered, their forms breaking apart like mist, unraveling into nothing.

The heavy robes faded from her shoulders. When she looked down, she was back in her own violet attire, the Hierarch's crown nothing more than a ghost on her head.

The chamber shifted. The grandeur of the throne room dissolved, melting away into plain, windowless stone walls.

At the far end of the room, the door swung open.

Evy looked around, letting the remnants of the simulation sink in.

She had played the Hierarch. And for a fleeting moment, it hadn't felt so far-fetched.

Maybe she wouldn't be terrible at it.

If she sat on the throne—the real one—she could fix all of it. Redirect the flow of mana. Give Reyland what it had always been denied.

"Don't try to win."

Like a hand against her shoulder, urging her to slow, Oriana's voice pressed into her thoughts. *"They'll slam the door shut behind you. Maybe even bolt it."*

Evy's shoulders sagged. She forced a deep, grounding breath.

There was no point in thinking so far ahead, not when she still had to survive the rest of the Hierarch Wars.

But as she turned toward the door, the taste of power was still fresh on her tongue. She only hoped she wasn't beginning to crave it.

EIGHTEEN

Evy emerged into a courtyard bathed in soft golden light. The sky stretched clear and blue, with only a few wisps of clouds drifting overhead.

At the center of the courtyard stood a low wooden table. Four children surrounded it, their projected forms almost lifelike. They sat, eyes wide and expectant, eerily silent.

Neatly stacked in front of them were biscuits, but the distribution was uneven.

One child had a towering pile. Two had a modest handful. The last had only two.

As she stepped closer, words materialized above the table: *Fairness must be found in a world imbalanced, but you hold no power beyond persuasion. No magic, force, or commands.*

Evy read the inscription twice, frowning. Her task wasn't immediately clear.

None of the children spoke, some looked smug, others nervous.

A sealed door stood across the courtyard. *It won't open until I do... what?*

The biscuits. The uneven distribution.

"Fairness must be found."

"Imbalance."

The children stared at her, waiting.

"No power beyond persuasion."

The pieces snapped into place, and she finally understood.

This challenge was about negotiation. She had to persuade the children to share. She couldn't use magic, force, or authority.

She let out a short laugh, shaking her head. Convince a group of children to share?

This had to be a joke.

But as she studied their small, expectant faces, her amusement faded.

Actually, this wouldn't be easy.

It was nothing like negotiating with nobles, warriors, or rulers. People who had something to gain and protect. Their motivations were typically clear: status, wealth, power, influence.

Children? They couldn't care less.

Titles didn't impress children. Nor did they care about who she was or what she wanted.

This challenge was about raw, bare-bones negotiation, stripped of politics and power.

And it may prove the most difficult challenge yet.

Evy took a step closer. She needed to understand what she was dealing with.

The boy on the far right had the biggest biscuit pile. He was older than the others, his arms locked around his hoard as he shoved a biscuit into his mouth, chewing aggressively. Even as he ate, he tracked the other children, like a predator guarding its kill.

When one of the younger children eyed his pile, he scowled.

"You can't take these from me!" he said, crumbs spilling from his mouth.

Evy crossed her arms. She decided to name him the Hoarder.

Beside him sat a larger boy with his own modest stack.

But his approach was different. Instead of hoarding, he was taking.

Without hesitation, he reached toward the Hoarder's pile and snatched a biscuit, ignoring the other boy's outrage.

Then he turned to the smallest child next to him, the girl with only two biscuits, and stole one.

"If they wanted biscuits, they should have stopped me," he said, then bit into it with slow satisfaction.

The Bully.

The smallest child didn't complain. Instead, she smiled. A warm, genuine smile that tugged at Evy's heart.

"They can have mine," she said.

Evy offered a soft nod in return. The Giver.

The last child, an older girl with a fair share of biscuits, sat at the table's end. She had watched everything—the Bully stealing, the Hoarder mocking, the Giver sacrificing.

The older girl's hands tightened in her lap. Her shoulders hunched. But she never spoke up.

Evy leaned closer when she saw the girl hesitate.

"If I say something, they'll get mad at me." The girl's voice trembled. "I don't know if I should get involved."

The Hoarder, the Bully, the Giver, the Bystander. The personalities presented seemed intentional, part of the puzzle.

She had to understand each archetype and negotiate. Convince them to share. Without magic, authority, or force.

Great.

The Bully reached over and snatched the last biscuit straight off the Giver's plate.

The little girl stiffened, her fingers twitching. But then, just as quickly, she forced a smile.

The Bully bit into the biscuit he stole, chewing slowly.

"What a pushover," he taunted, his voice dripping with mockery. "You'll let anyone take from you, huh?"

"That's enough," Evy snapped, stepping toward the table. "Give it back."

The boy leaned back lazily, chewing louder, mocking her too.

"Make me." His eyes gleamed with amusement.

A harsh, sputtering cough tore through the moment.

The Hoarder's face turned red, and his body heaved as he choked, desperately trying to shove another biscuit into his mouth.

Crumbs spilled from his lips. His eyes widened with panic. Even so, he kept going.

"Stop!" Evy shouted, stepping toward him.

But the boy shook his head violently, swallowing the dry biscuits so fast it looked painful.

The clock hovering above her ticked on, carving away the seconds. Her pulse quickened and her frustration flared. What if the other Ascendants had already finished? What if they were waiting for her? She'd look like a fool if she took much longer.

She was here representing all of Reyland. All of the Witches. Would she disappoint them over a few kids and some biscuits?

Stop. Focus.

She exhaled slowly through her mouth. She couldn't let her thoughts spiral.

She turned back to the children, the plates in front of them. Telling them what to do wouldn't work. If she wanted a proper solution, she had to make them *want* to agree.

She closed her eyes and forced herself to think like a child.

Her childhood in Reyland had been different. She hadn't gone to school with the other village children. Orianna, the

Spirit Matron, and the Spirit Sisters had raised and mentored her, shaping her life with duty.

Her only true childhood interactions had been with Aeric.

She smiled at the thought of him, of their days spent together, running through the meadows, laughing until their stomachs hurt.

The best days were when she had him all to herself. But sometimes he brought his friends along, and Evy had to share.

She searched through her memories. Something, a clue, an insight, must have existed. She had to understand each child's perspective. She had to understand their thoughts, their mindsets.

Her eyes snapped open. The Hoarder was still stuffing biscuits into his mouth.

He wouldn't stop if she told him to. That would only make him double down.

But what if she made him stop himself?

She thought back to Aeric and his friends, games turning to scuffles, tears shed over petty fights, threats exchanged in the heat of the moment. Children weren't inherently cruel or selfish, just as they weren't inherently kind or brave. They tested limits, pushed boundaries, seeing how far they could go before someone pushed back.

They were shaped by their environment, molded by what they could get away with, or what they were taught to value. Once you understood what they were testing, you could use it to guide them.

And that might have been the key.

She wasn't sure, but she had to try.

Her gaze drifted to the towering pile of biscuits before him. For the Hoarder, this was a game of pride. She could use that. First, she needed him to pay attention and shake him out of his frantic hoarding.

"Hm." Evy watched him slowly bite into another biscuit. "That really doesn't seem like the smartest thing to do."

The Hoarder froze mid-bite, cheeks still stuffed full.

"Everyone's going to laugh when you're doubled over with a stomachache," Evy said, feigning concern.

A few giggles rippled through the group.

The Hoarder's eyes darted around, reassessing the impact of his achievement.

"Do you want to be the fool who eats so much he throws up everywhere?" She leaned in. "No one will forget that."

The smug confidence in his expression cracked ever so slightly.

"Listen," Evy said. "I know you're the cleverest one here. I mean, look at how many biscuits you've collected!"

The boy's posture straightened.

"Can I tell you something?" Evy lowered her voice and leaned in conspiratorially.

"You see, the truth is… this challenge might be too tough to solve myself."

The Hoarder chewed more slowly now, listening.

Evy kept going. "Having the most biscuits? That was the first part of the game. But now, we have to figure out how to divide them so everyone has an equal amount. And…"

She trailed off and sighed. "I'm afraid I may not be smart enough to do the math on my own."

The Hoarder's fingers twitched against the edge of the table.

"I'm good at math," he said, crumbs spilling out of his mouth. He chewed quickly and swallowed the last of his biscuit. "I can do it."

"Really?" Evy clasped her hands together. "You'd be my hero!"

The Hoarder smirked, his pride instantly redirected. He picked up a few biscuits from his plate and set them on the Giver's.

"Wow! Thank you!" She beamed.

Evy gave the Hoarder a wink, and his lips stretched into a smug smile.

The older girl at the end of the table watched silently.

The Bystander had the fewest biscuits after the Hoarder and the Bully, but unlike the Giver, she hadn't offered to share.

She also hadn't protested when the Bully took more. She sat there, arms tucked close, watching it all unfold.

Evy recognized her type; it was probably the most common. She was the kind of person who didn't need to be challenged. She just needed a nudge.

The Bystander furrowed her brows as the Bully took another biscuit from the Giver's plate.

Evy took a slow step closer, keeping her tone light.

"Earlier, you told me that if you spoke up, you were afraid the others would get mad."

The Bystander crossed her arms over her chest.

"If someone else spoke up, would you agree with them?" Evy asked.

After a moment, the girl offered a slight nod.

"You already know what's right. You're just waiting for someone else to say it first."

The girl fidgeted.

Evy softened her voice, careful not to push. "What if you were the first? Maybe someone else is waiting for you."

The Bystander's lips parted, like she hadn't considered that before.

Evy didn't press further. Instead, she offered her another safe option.

"Can you help count the biscuits when we start dividing them?" Evy asked. "That way, no one gets cheated?"

Slowly, the girl nodded again, then picked up one of her biscuits and placed it on the Giver's plate.

Without being asked again, she started counting. She

surveyed the plates, ensuring everyone's portion was appropriate.

A hand darted forward.

The Bully had reached out again and swiped another biscuit from the Giver's plate.

But this time, before Evy could step in, the Bystander spoke up.

"Stop it."

The Bully turned to her with a grin, unbothered. "Oh? You gonna stop me?"

The girl stood her ground, fists clenched at her sides.

"I'm going to tell your mom."

Evy felt a spark of satisfaction. Now that she had a direct responsibility, the Bystander wasn't a bystander anymore.

The Bully only laughed, then tossed the biscuit back on the plate like it had never mattered to him.

"Relax," he said. "I was testing you."

She considered her strategy with the Bully. He seemed afraid of his mother, but this challenge was about persuasion. The inscription had said no force. Would threatening to tell his mom count as force?

She didn't want to risk it.

Instead of challenging him, she kept her tone calm, agreeing at first.

"You're right, the world isn't fair. And powerful people take what they can, right?"

The Bully puffed his chest. "Exactly."

Evy nodded, making it seem like she accepted his logic.

"But taking is easy." She reached forward and plucked a biscuit straight from his plate. "See?"

"Hey!" The boy jolted forward, reaching to snatch it back.

Evy leaned away, holding the biscuit out of his reach.

"Anyone can take from the weak. That doesn't make you the

strongest. It just means you're slightly stronger than the person you took it from."

She placed the biscuit on the Giver's plate.

The Bully scowled, his brows drawing together.

"You know what's harder than taking?" Evy asked, then took another biscuit from his plate. The boy folded his arms, glaring at her.

She let the question hang for several seconds before answering. "Protecting."

The Bully reached for the biscuit, but Evy blocked him, shifting her arm enough to keep him from grabbing it.

She pressed on. "Protecting someone is harder because other powerful people will come after them. And when they do"—she met his gaze—"they'll have to get through you."

The boy's fingers twitched.

"Taking from the weak?" Evy waved the biscuit in the air. "That's a piece of cake."

In one smooth motion, she handed the biscuit back to him.

"But protecting against the strong?" Her words rang with certainty. "That makes you the strongest of them all."

Evy leaned in, making eye contact with the Bully. "Right now, you're just another kid grabbing biscuits."

The Bully's attention dropped to his pile of stolen biscuits.

"If you become a protector, everyone will look up to you," Evy continued. "They'll remember you as the strongest because you kept everyone safe. They'll feel like they owe you."

The children nodded, watching the Bully with expectation.

"And your mother," Evy whispered. "Think about how proud she'd be to know what you did."

The Bully's eyes widened.

Then, with a half-hearted scoff, he placed the stolen biscuits back on the plates.

"Fine. Whatever."

As Evy had assumed, the Bully acted as though he didn't care about optics, but he did. Maybe his role came from a long trail of misbehavior, but underneath, he was a boy who wanted to make his mother proud and to have something he could be proud of too.

As the children distributed the biscuits among themselves, she felt the tension ease.

But then she noticed the Giver, still pushing biscuits away from her own plate, subtly sliding them toward others when no one was looking. She still didn't believe she deserved as much as the rest.

"That's really kind of you."

Evy gave the girl a small smile. "But you know, being fair and kind doesn't always mean giving everything away. Fairness means you should have just as much as everyone else."

The girl hesitated and looked down at the biscuits in front of her.

Evy nudged one back on her plate. "You need to take care of yourself too."

The girl's brows lifted.

After a pause, she nodded.

Instead of pushing her biscuits away, she straightened up and started checking the plates, making sure her own share matched the rest.

Evy scanned the table, counting carefully. It looked right. But the door didn't open.

She frowned. Did she count incorrectly?

Her gaze swept over the plates again—four neat, equal piles.

Then she drifted toward the Hoarder's side of the table. And there it was.

A single biscuit, resting beside his plate. He must've dropped it while inhaling them earlier.

Evy picked it up and turned it over in her fingers.

One extra biscuit.

If she added it to any of the plates, the balance would be

broken again. But if she didn't distribute it, the challenge wouldn't be complete.

She hesitated. What's the right choice?

Her gaze landed on the Giver, the one who had been willing to sacrifice the most.

Evy placed the biscuit on her plate. Maybe the most generous should decide. Would that make the result more just?

The girl blinked at her plate.

Evy wasn't sure what to expect. Perhaps the Giver would pass it to the Bystander, who hadn't been purposefully mean to her.

Instead, the girl beamed and pushed the biscuit back toward Evy.

"Are you hungry?" she asked. "You should have it."

Evy's brows furrowed. She almost refused, but the Giver shook her head.

"You need to take care of yourself too." She echoed Evy's own words.

Evy smiled. How do you argue with that?

She took the biscuit and ate it.

The moment she finished chewing, the children shimmered, their forms breaking apart into golden light.

Evy barely had time to process what was happening before the courtyard dissolved into a simple windowless chamber.

Ahead, the door swung open.

Her heart pounded. The arena lay just beyond the threshold.

She took off running toward the exit, hoping desperately she didn't fall embarrassingly behind the other Ascendants.

The moment she stepped through, the roar of the crowd slammed into her ears.

But the cheers weren't for her.

They were for Royen.

He was already in the arena, standing ahead of her, waving to the spectators.

Evy stumbled to a stop, and silence permeated the crowd.

She frowned.

Were they upset at how long it took her to finish the trial? Did she truly fall too far behind?

Lawrence had been approaching Royen.

But now he wasn't moving. His eyes were wide, frozen in shock, as if he were staring at a ghost.

Royen had turned toward her as well, his usual mask of composure dropped.

She mirrored his confusion and scanned the arena. There was no sign of Celeste or Zafir. The doors to their clay structures were still sealed shut.

Royen being the only one present meant he had finished first, just as everyone expected.

But then... had she come in second? How?

Above his head, Royen's time hovered in golden numbers.

She looked at her own.

Five minutes.

She had only been five minutes behind him.

Even with his advantage. Even with the scroll Lawrence had slipped him. Even with every disadvantage she carried from her upbringing.

She had still nearly beaten him.

The realization spread across the arena.

The Council. The spectators. Royen himself. They had all reacted with shock and silence because they had underestimated her. Evy didn't blame them. It appeared she had underestimated herself.

From the way Lawrence glowered, fire burning behind his gaze, Evy knew her placement was no cause for celebration. In fact, she shuddered, fear running like ice through her veins.

Orianna had told her not to intimidate them—not to stir the Council's ire—by coming too close.

And that was the first thing she had done.

Suddenly, a door flew open behind her.

Celeste stumbled out, her pink hair a tangled mess, her clothes singed at the edges. She looked like she had barely survived a battlefield, her emerald eyes blazing with fury.

She took one look at Evy and threw her hands up.

"I am *never* having kids."

NINETEEN

Royen had won.

Barely.

Evy still couldn't fathom how close she'd come to his finishing time, especially with the advantage the Council had given him.

She stood before her designated clay structure. Beside her, Celeste muttered under her breath, inspecting the tattered edges of her dress with exasperation.

Now, only one remained.

A final cheer erupted from the crowd as the last door reopened, and Zafir stepped into the arena, scowling.

Celeste was the first to speak, placing her hands on her hips. "Took you long enough."

"I let my pride take over." His voice held a rough edge as he rubbed a hand over his bearded jaw. "The mock Council hearing." His gaze dropped to the ground. "I wasted too much time trying to get them to vote in favor of Zarokan."

Evy instantly understood. Naturally, that challenge had been difficult for him. The Firesteel Highlands scenario wasn't a random dispute for Zafir. It was an actual fight, one his people had struggled with in reality.

And it had cost him time.

"I thought Reyland's major trade was wheat," Zafir said, his glowing eyes narrowing. "If I weren't made of fire itself, I would've been incinerated in that first puzzle."

Celeste lifted the singed hem of her dress. "Tell me about it."

She turned toward Evy, shaking her head. "I figured out I could dodge the fire once it came hurtling toward me, but I still had to go through every single item on those shelves before I found the right one. It was awful."

They didn't know.

Neither of them understood why Reyland's trade answer had changed.

Why it had almost cost them the trial.

Was it meant to be a secret? Surely, not.

"I'll explain later," Evy said in a low tone.

Awareness prickled at the edge of her mind. Someone was watching her. Her spine tensed.

Royen stood a few feet away. His mouth, usually a thin line against his tensed jaw, was relaxed. He studied her quietly.

In turn, she took him in. Not a single wrinkle in his coat. No scorch marks on his sleeves. Not even a scuff on his boots. He showed no signs of struggle.

Of course, he hadn't struggled. He had likely gotten every answer right on the first try. The Council had given him the answers beforehand, so he wouldn't have wasted a single second.

Royen hadn't looked away.

If anything, he was inspecting her more closely now, his gaze trailing over her, scrutinizing every detail.

A bead of sweat traced down Evy's temple—uncomfortable under his attention.

At last, Royen broke away and faced ahead toward Lawrence and the Council.

Mana pooled at Lawrence's feet before he spoke. "It is time for the Heart to judge the progress of the Ascendants." His announcement carried effortlessly through the arena, voice projected with a spell. "The one who stands at the top of this challenge shall claim the Celestial Gauntlets."

Evy couldn't stop herself from rolling her eyes. There was no suspense. The trial was based on time, and Royen had finished first. It was clear he'd be receiving yet another advantage heading into the Trial of Strength.

Lawrence smirked at Royen.

And Royen, ever composed, gave a small, almost imperceptible nod.

Evy expected nothing less. Orianna had warned her the Council would do whatever was necessary to secure another Veyn on the throne. Another victory for the Shifters.

From its place across the Ascendants, the Heart pulsed, a deep, rhythmic glow of gold and blue.

Above Royen's head, a golden orb appeared. It hovered like a halo, its glow illuminating the sharp lines of his face.

Celeste and Zafir had similar orbs above them. Evy's own glowed overhead.

The Heart continued to thrum with light, and the orbs shifted, changing in size and intensity.

The pulsing stopped.

The arena fell silent, anticipation thick in the air.

Evy studied the results. Royen's orb was the largest, the brightest. Zafir's was the smallest and dimmest. Celeste's orb hovered above her, larger than Zafir's, but not by much.

Celeste's emerald eyes widened at the sight of Evy's orb. It was slightly smaller than Royen's. Evy was right behind him.

A low rumble began in the stands, then the heckles rolled in.

The Children of Rui became more vitriolic in their chants. "Cheating Witch! Condemn her to death!"

Evy pressed her teeth into her lower lip to keep from laughing. *Cheating?*

She had earned every inch of that placement.

Despite being raised at the edge of the continent. Despite the odds stacked against her.

Evy had stood just behind the Council's chosen Ascendant.

Her gaze flicked toward Lawrence just in time to catch the sneer curling his lips. He hadn't expected this, for the gap between her and Royen to be this narrow.

Evy hardened herself, waiting for him to turn his disdain on her. Instead, his expression darkened toward Royen.

Evy didn't need to hear a single word to understand what was being silently said.

Why weren't you faster?

Why didn't you dominate the trial with the advantage I gave you?

Evy found herself wondering the same. If Royen had answers to the puzzles beforehand, he should have walked out of the challenge far ahead of her. But he hadn't.

It was almost as if—

As if he didn't use the advantage.

Evy released a small, audible breath.

Royen finally lifted his head and turned straight to her.

She immediately looked away, cheeks warm.

Lawrence turned to the crowd. A cool, practiced expression replaced his sneer.

"The Heart has placed its judgment." Lawrence clasped his hands behind his back. "Royen Veyn is the winner of this challenge, placing him in the lead of the Hierarch Wars."

The arena erupted, applause thundering from the stands.

"The Heart will judge each trial," Lawrence continued, raising a hand for silence. "But points will compound throughout the competition. The Hierarch will be determined by the Ascendant with the highest total at the end."

The difference between Evy's and Royen's orbs was nearly insignificant.

In that moment, a small, stubborn question crept into her thoughts: *If I hadn't made that mistake in the first puzzle, if I hadn't lost those fifteen minutes, could I have won?*

Lawrence approached Royen, holding up the Celestial Gauntlets for all to see.

"As the winner of the first trial," he said, "Royen Veyn will receive the Celestial Gauntlets, an advantage that will serve him well in the Trial of Strength."

The crowd continued to cheer.

But Evy was no longer paying attention to her surroundings. Her thoughts were on the next challenge.

Could she close the gap? Was she capable of winning, despite his advantage?

The thought flared, but then Orianna's warning came back to her:

"If you come too close to taking it all, they'll panic."

Evy inhaled slowly, biting back the stirring frustration.

The cheers quieted as Lawrence raised a hand.

"The second trial will take place in just over a month. Before that, as per tradition, the Ascendants will embark on the Procession in two days."

Evy's ears perked.

"The Procession will allow the people of Aeltheon to meet their potential Hierarch," Lawrence continued, "and give the Ascendants an opportunity to experience the lands they may one day rule."

Lawrence turned toward the Ascendants. "It will also give the Council time to prepare for the second trial.

"Please note that this year's tour will travel in the following order: Zarokan, Virenna, and Theribane. To preserve the traditional route and maintain the timing of the second trial, Reyland will host the final leg of the Procession after that trial, replacing the Ascendant Ball."

With that, Lawrence dismissed the Council, the crowd, and the Ascendants. The audience filed out of the stands, their exhilaration still crackling in the air.

As Evy made her way toward the coliseum's exit, she caught sight of Celeste and Zafir ahead of her, chatting easily as they walked.

She chewed on her nail. After what she'd just survived in that chamber, a month without proper training no longer felt wise.

In a way, she was grateful that Reyland's turn in the Procession would come after the second trial; otherwise, the gap between trials would have stretched on for weeks.

The others had likely been preparing for the trials their entire lives. If she wanted to keep pace, she would have to train on the road.

A voice cut through her thoughts.

"Miss Lovejoy."

Evy started at the interruption. Royen had fallen behind the others and stood a few paces away.

"May I have a word?" he asked.

She watched Celeste and Zafir disappear into the distance.

Then Evy turned and lifted her chin. "It's *Queen* Lovejoy."

Royen's lips quirked.

She frowned. "How can I help you, Young Lord?"

To her surprise, he chuckled.

"No need to call me that. I'm not the heir to Theribane. Call me Royen. Or Mister Veyn, if you prefer."

He spoke slowly. "The Lord of Theribane is my uncle. The title of Young Lord belongs to my cousin, Marq. Because his father is the Lord of Theri—"

"Yes, I gathered. I know how succession works, thank you,"

Evy cut in, her cheeks flushing with embarrassment. "I'm comfortable calling you Young Master."

"That's not even a real title. They made it up for me." Royen shook his head.

She studied him, momentarily caught off guard by the direction of their conversation. "Why would they do that?"

"Pageantry, I suppose."

His voice was deeper than she'd expected, each word spoken with the precision of a gentleman, like nothing left his lips without careful consideration.

"I suppose it's best practice for an Ascendant to be of importance, but Marq couldn't come because of his... condition, so my family decided I'm close enough."

Evy caught a hint of bitterness in his tone, but she didn't want to unpack the Veyn family dynamics.

Not now, at least, when her mind and bones were still weary from the trial.

She pressed her lips together, searching for a way to divert the topic. "You can call me Evalene, if that's easier. But don't call me *Miss*." Mostly because Leo might take his head, but she didn't say that part out loud.

Royen hummed, contemplating. "Celeste calls you Evy."

She crossed her arms. "My *friends* call me Evy."

Several seconds passed. His expression remained stoic before he inclined his head, his mouth lifting in one corner.

"Evalene, then."

His eyes dropped to her mouth before he finally spoke again.

"How did you come so close to me at the trial?"

She couldn't help the icy edge beneath her voice. "What are you trying to imply?"

Royen drew back, startled by her tone.

Evy's gaze sharpened. "Are you, of all people, suggesting I had an advantage in this trial?" Then, just loud enough for him to hear, "Because there's only one person here who had any sort of advantage, and it definitely wasn't me."

She refused to look away.

Slowly, the corners of Royen's mouth lifted.

"I thought I saw a flash of white hair at the Aurethium that day."

Royen exhaled, shifting his stance. "No. That's not what I meant. I didn't think you had help. Actually, I think I underestimated you."

Evy remained skeptical.

He went on. "I assumed the Reylandic were too secluded, too far removed from the rest of Aeltheon. I didn't expect to be neck and neck with someone raised so far from the capital."

Evy let out an incredulous laugh.

"So you thought I was some uneducated country girl? Did you forget I'm a queen? It might not be the same as yours, but we have access to education too."

Royen flinched, then sighed.

"Perhaps I'm the one too far removed."

She faltered, words dying in her throat. She had expected arrogance from him and, against her better judgment, had been ready to fight back.

"I threw the scroll away," Royen said.

His expression was no longer guarded, his usual cool detachment replaced by uncertainty. Or maybe shame.

"The one Lawrence gave me before the trial—I was meant to study it. That part's true. But I didn't. I wanted to test myself."

He didn't deny the advantage.

But he was admitting he'd refused it.

She didn't know if she believed him. Not fully. But what did he gain by explaining himself to her? It seemed he wanted to justify it to himself.

She stayed silent, anticipating his next words.

Royen exhaled, almost like a laugh, but stripped of any humor.

"You don't have to believe me," he said, quieter now. "I wouldn't either. Not with the history that comes with the Veyn name."

Before she could form a cohesive thought, before she could decide whether she wanted to respond, he transformed.

Mana pooled at his feet, then rose to blanket him in cerulean light. There was a blur of movement as his body warped and twisted. A small sparrow stood where the young man had been. The bird gave a single chirp, wings fluttering, then took to the air.

Evy watched in silence as Royen vanished into the sky, a speck of brown and beige consumed by the soft gray clouds.

She stood there for a long moment, his words echoing through her mind.

She *should* have inherently disliked Royen Veyn. She should have distrusted every Shifter for the centuries of corruption they'd sown. The realm called them liars, cheaters, manipulators.

And yet, she felt she might believe him.

Because for a fleeting moment, she saw his mask break. And what advantage could there be in *that*?

Evy knew what it felt like to be dismissed because of who you were. The realm thought Witches were incapable, their magic borrowed, their presence a mistake. She wouldn't fall into the same trap, judging someone else by the legacy of their bloodline.

Maybe Royen wanted to prove himself, just like she did.

And that was what bothered her most—the realization that even without studying the scroll, he had won.

His education and upbringing had placed him ahead before the trials even began.

And yet, she had come so close.

Even though it went against how she should have felt in that moment, she allowed herself a small sense of pride.

TWENTY

The sun hung low over Reylandic waters, casting the docks in deep gold and violet hues. The tide rolled in gently, lapping against the wooden piers as fishermen finished their day's work.

Yorik hauled a heavy net of fish from his boat, briny water spilling onto the worn planks beneath his feet. His hands moved easily, muscles shifting beneath the coarse linen of his tunic.

He passed a young fisherman along the dock, head bent as he mended a torn net. The man glanced up at Yorik and inclined his head.

Another Acolyte.

The Gods had a way of leading the broken to him. And once Yorik cleansed the world, he would heal them all.

"Whitlock!"

An older fisherman approached, wiping his hands on a stained cloth.

"How's your mother doing?" the man asked.

"She's had a good morning," Yorik said as he slung the net into a barrel. "And today's haul will make it even better."

The fisherman chuckled. "You always manage to bring home the best catch."

Yorik smiled as the man walked away.

Beneath the surface, the mention of his mother twisted his heart. Like him, she had been a victim of the world's cruelty. But his expression gave none of that darkness away.

Among the docks, he was just a fisherman. The world was not ready to accept its evolution, though change was the only remedy for its injustices. So he and his Acolytes would remain hidden in plain sight until the world had no choice but to accept him as its Herald of Chaos.

Cleanse the world.

Ever since Evalene left for Ruitheon two weeks ago, the voices of the Gods had been constant. They whispered one simple message, again and again.

Cleanse.

Yorik observed the other fishermen bringing in their daily catch. They couldn't see past the filth. That was fine. Yorik saw the world not as it was, but as it could be.

And soon, he would cleanse them.

Remember?

Yorik smiled. He did remember.

He remembered the night his father died, the night he killed the bastard to protect Aeric. His brother had been so little, and the monster, in another drunken rage, was about to beat him. Yorik made sure he never got the chance.

That was when he first heard the Gods' voices, whispering that he'd done a noble act.

They promised him a purpose.

Over time, they taught him to sever his spirit bond and unlock a new power. They led him to his father's grave, where he performed the Shadow Rites for the first time.

"Aeric, where were you today?" a fisherman shouted in the

distance. "You missed Barry getting drunk and flipping his boat!"

His younger brother walked toward him, a folded piece of parchment in hand.

"I went into town to check the post," Aeric called over his shoulder. "I'm sure Barry will get drunk on the job again and give us another reason to laugh."

He tucked the letter into his pocket and began helping with the nets.

"I got a letter from Evy," Aeric said quietly.

Yorik kept his hands busy with the tangled netting.

"Why don't you head home for the day, little brother," Yorik said. "Make sure Mother's alright. I'll take this haul to the market, and I'll be home soon after. We can talk more then."

Aeric nodded and headed inland.

Later that evening, coins jingled in Yorik's pocket as he walked the familiar path home, the scent of brine and sweat still clinging to his clothes. The voices followed.

Cleanse the world.

They wound around him, pressing against his thoughts. But as the cottage came into view, the murmurs faded into silence.

Lydia Whitlock sat by the window, motionless, her hands resting in her lap. Her stare drifted beyond the window, fixed on the fields beyond. The dull glow from a nearby lamp framed her frail form.

Yorik stepped inside and carefully closed the door before crossing the room. He leaned over and pressed a gentle kiss to her graying hair.

"Hello, Mother." His voice softened. "It was nice out today. I hope you got to enjoy some sunshine."

Lydia only just noticed him.

She offered her son a small smile. "You're a good boy, Yorik." Her nose crinkled. "But you smell like fish."

Yorik chuckled, the sound genuine, and lifted the small leather pouch at his belt.

"Worked the docks today, remember? Made good money from the haul."

Lydia's brows drew together.

"You work too much," she muttered. "You should be playing like the other boys."

A lump formed in Yorik's throat.

He reached out and gently took her hand, then rubbed his thumb over her thin fingers.

"I'm not a boy anymore." He placed her hand on his cheek. "See? I've grown."

Lydia studied his face, and recognition struck through her clouded gaze.

"Oh," she said in a whisper. "I'm so happy you didn't grow to look like him."

Yorik swallowed. She didn't need to say his name. The name of his father.

And she never would. Ever again.

Yorik grabbed a blanket and placed it over her shoulders.

The front door creaked open, and Aeric stepped inside, balancing two bowls and a steaming parcel in his hands. The scent of fresh bread filled the small cottage.

"Look what I got." He set the bowls on the wooden table. "The Lovejoys baked these and sent some over. Figured we could use a good meal."

Aeric turned toward them. "Lydia, are you hungry? We have delicious bread tonight."

She shrugged. "I want to sleep. I have a terrible headache."

Aeric's smile dimmed a little as he walked over and helped her to her feet. "I'll take you to bed."

Yorik watched as Aeric guided their mother to her room. The door clicked shut behind them, leaving only the quiet creak of the house.

A few minutes later, Aeric returned, massaging the back of his neck.

"At least she got out of bed this morning," he said in a low voice.

Yorik nodded once and took a seat at the table. The parcel of bread was hot, fragrant with butter and herbs, but he had no appetite.

"Aeric, why have you been calling our mother by name lately?"

Aeric pondered before he dropped into a chair. "I don't think she remembers who I am. I call her Lydia because if I call her 'Mother,' she gets confused and flustered."

Their mother was declining; there was no denying it.

The day Yorik saved Aeric from Marlin's wrath, he had been too late for their mother. He found her crumpled on the floor, blood trailing from her temple—she hadn't been the same since.

I'll cleanse this world for you, Mother, so you can wash yourself of the filth that has spread through you.

"Anyway." Aeric patted his pocket where he'd tucked away the letter earlier. "I had something to share."

Yorik leaned back against the chair, crossing his arms.

"Go on."

Aeric pulled the letter out and smoothed open the folded parchment.

"It's from Evy," he said, glancing up. "She wrote to me after the first trial."

Yorik raised his brow, signaling for Aeric to continue.

"She didn't give too many details, but she said she came in second." His lips curved up with pride. "She mentioned her competitors. Apparently, she's grown close to the Virennese Princess."

He squinted at the letter. "Celeste DuVent."

Yorik tapped a finger against the table. "The Sylph Princess. Interesting," he murmured.

Aeric frowned. "You know about her?"

Yorik didn't answer right away. He leaned back farther, his thoughts drifting.

"Did she say anything about the Heart?" he asked.

Aeric scanned the parchment. "Nope."

His fingers stilled against the table. "Keep writing to her and see if you can get more details."

"Evy actually mentioned she may not be getting my letters for a while," Aeric said. "She's leaving for the Procession and will be traveling all over Aeltheon."

"Did she say anything about the route?"

Aeric read through the letter again in silence. "Yeah, she said they're going to Zarokan first, then Virenna, then Theribane. After that, they'll circle back to Ruitheon for the second trial. Reyland won't get its turn on the tour until after that."

Yorik turned the information over in his mind.

"Did she mention any dates?" he asked. "Specifically for Virenna?"

"Why?" Aeric asked.

Yorik held his brother's gaze, waiting.

Aeric exhaled and refolded the letter. "She wrote this the day the first trial ended, so I'm guessing she posted it the next day." He tapped the parchment. "With how fast the post travels, it probably took a week to get here."

"And the Procession?"

"She said they were leaving for Zarokan in a couple of days," Aeric replied. "So by now, she's probably already on the road. Likely close to arriving."

Yorik leaned forward. "And they spend a few days in each domain."

"Exactly." Aeric set the letter on the table and shifted his weight against the chair. "If we work from when she sent this, we can estimate when she'll be in Theribane and Virenna."

Yorik was already calculating the days in his head.

"Well, if you want me to keep writing to Evy, I'm going to need some extra coin for express post." A foolish grin spread across Aeric's face as he rose from the chair. "I might even catch her before she gets to Zarokan."

Yorik frowned. "You really do love her, don't you?"

Color flooded Aeric's face. "That's none of your business," he muttered.

"Do you think she could ever truly love you the same way?" Yorik's voice remained gentle and curious. "When her duty demands everything?"

Aeric's shoulders tensed. "You don't know what you're talking about."

"Don't I?"

"Forget it. I'm not having this conversation." He headed for his room. "I need a quill."

The door shut harder than necessary.

With Aeric gone, Yorik leaned back in his chair and closed his eyes.

The whispers returned, overlapping as they spoke.

Ingredients.

Three ingredients.

The second.

Wings.

A vision unfurled in his mind. The wings were not made of feathers. They were unlike any wings he had ever seen, shifting between mist and solid crystal.

The voices stirred.

Breakable. Beautiful.

Aeric stepped back into the room, a quill in hand, and took a seat at the table. His movement woke Yorik from his trance.

"I'll be traveling to Virenna," he announced. "About the same time the Procession stops there."

Aeric stilled. "What?"

"You'll need to take care of Mother while I'm gone," Yorik said. "And pick up a few extra shifts at the docks."

"But how are you getting to Virenna? You don't have a permit to leave Reyland."

Yorik sighed and picked at his nails. "Don't worry about me, little brother. Just do as I say."

Aeric sat forward. "What are you planning, Yorik?"

"Just something that needs to be done."

Aeric waited for more, but Yorik didn't elaborate.

He didn't need to.

Whatever awaited him in Virenna, the Gods had given Yorik the right to claim.

TWENTY-ONE

Night had settled over the Ascendants' camp on the outskirts of Zarokan—three days out from Ruitheon, with two more still ahead in their journey.

Beige linen tents were pitched on dry, cracked earth. From the outside, the tents looked small and uniform. But within, they expanded into spacious living quarters, enhanced by magic and large enough to accommodate an entire household. They even provided a kitchen, which had delighted Irma, a bath, and a study.

Thin, singed trees stood still against the darkness, their blackened, leafless trunks swaying gently in the quiet wind. At first, Evy had thought the trees were dead, blasted by a mysterious explosion. Zafir had corrected her, explaining they were cinderbarks, native to the warm, dry regions of Zarokan. Though they looked burnt, they were actually fire resistant. The cinderbark forest thickened as they neared the volcanic region of Zarokan.

Inside her tent, a pair of folded letters sat on her cot. Evy recognized Orianna's neat handwriting on the first parchment immediately. The letter was brief. Orianna had evidently decided not to waste ink on pleasantries.

It was announced in Reyland that you came in second in the Trial of Wit. While the streets of Moonveil are filled with Witches rejoicing at the news, I must remind you to be wary.

Don't let them expel you like they did me.

I believe in you.

—Magister Gale

Evy sighed as she folded the letter. Orianna's expulsion—what had truly happened? Perhaps that missing piece would help her understand why she had to shrink herself in this competition while Reyland celebrated her as a symbol of hope.

But some walls, even she couldn't break down.

She unfolded the second letter. She would know that messy, slanted handwriting anywhere.

My Evy,

I'm so proud of you, though of course I knew you were capable. Orianna was kind enough to let me tuck my letter in with hers for express post, but she said I had to keep it short. The Harpies charge per page to fly it out. Surely one extra page won't break a Harpy's wings.

Evy gave a silent chuckle.

You know I'm no good with words. I can't tell you what's really inside my heart.

But I will waste no time showing you when you're back home. Every moment I can spare, I'll be at your side. Perhaps I'll quit being a fisherman and become a Spirit Sister, so I can stay in the temple with you. Is that allowed? I'll make them allow it. Even when you're off closing portals, I'll find a way to be there for you.

I realized something in your absence... Without you, my world is dark.

I can't wait to have you back. I swear I'm going to hold you tight and never let go.

Keep writing to me while I wait. Give me all the exciting details like what the Heart is like up close and if the other domains are as spectacular as they sound. I'll share them with all the bored Witches stuck in Reyland.

—Aeric

Evy, once again, was grateful no one was there to see the foolish grin plastered on her face. But her smile slowly faded as she traced Aeric's words with her thumb.

I will waste no time showing you when you're back home.

Aeric expected her back.

Back to Reyland.

Back without the Hierarch's crown.

Even he understood Evy's place in these trials.

Perhaps it was time she accepted it too.

She stood and tucked her loose tunic into her britches. A soft snore came from the armchair by the hearth. Irma had fallen asleep.

Evy crossed the room and slung an arm around Irma's shoulders, then gently guided her groggy companion to bed.

"Thank you, Evy," Irma murmured, still half asleep. "Wait, *I'm* supposed to put *you* to bed. Are you trying to steal my job?" She was snoring softly again a moment later.

Evy stifled a laugh and made her way over to the exit.

Just beyond the tent flap, Leo sat cross-legged in the dust. They exchanged a quiet nod.

Evy rolled her shoulder, trying to ease the stiffness from hours of sitting upright. The Ascendants had come in earlier that evening in a grand carriage with tall windows, clear on all sides so onlookers could glimpse the contenders.

There had been no resting. Her posture had to be perfect. Her expression had to be serene. A performance, mile after mile.

Now that the sun had dipped below the horizon, fatigue pressed into her bones.

She had felt this way every night since the Procession began. But it hadn't stopped her from training. Not once.

The second trial demanded strength. And with travel leaving her no time during the day, she trained at night, no matter how exhausted she felt.

Evy wasn't sure what form the second trial would take, which meant she had to be ready for anything.

Her temples throbbed with fatigue. Part of her questioned if there was any point in training so hard.

Royen would dominate the Second Trial. That much she already knew. Oddly, the certainty comforted her. She would never outmatch him there.

She had heard rumors of Celeste's wind magic and how quickly she could take to the air. And Zafir had a reputation as a fierce warrior. If she didn't push herself, if she didn't have the discipline to train, she would fall behind.

And if she fell behind too noticeably, she wouldn't be the only one who looked weak. Her efforts would reflect on the Witches.

She stepped beyond the boundary of camp and broke into a light jog, her boots crunching against the brittle earth. She moved among the cinderbarks, weaving through their slender trunks and soon picked up her pace, letting the rhythm of her breath clear her thoughts.

A sharp rustle cut through the trees behind her.

Evy slowed and strained to listen.

At first, she assumed it might be a guard or paladin checking on her. They had watched her on a few nights.

The sound came again. It didn't match the heavy, armored footfalls of the guards.

Her heart skipped. The forest was still. There was no wind, and yet somewhere out there, something moved.

Muffled steps like those of a hunter stalking its prey.

Zarokan was not a tame land. The farther one traveled from the settlements and cities, the wilder the territory became.

Phoenixes were said to nest near volcanic veins, their flames hot enough to cauterize her very soul. Salamanders, slower but far more aggressive, could swim through magma like water, their impenetrable bodies sheathed in molten scales.

Or worse yet—Lawrence's scowl after the first trial flashed through her mind. Would the Council move against her?

Evy instinctively called for her spirits. She had no desire to challenge any of the beasts or assassins that might be lurking in the dark.

But whatever was behind her, she'd rather meet it face to face than have it at her back. A spell began to form at her fingertips, and the figure emerged into view.

It was Zafir.

He moved with the confidence of someone who'd known these lands his entire life, his boots nearly silent against the cracked earth. His sleeveless tunic clung to his chest, and a faint sheen of sweat glistened on his brow.

"You move too quietly for someone your size," Evy said, clutching her chest.

Zafir gave a half smile. "And you move quickly. Like a mouse."

Her shoulders relaxed, the last of her fear slipping away.

"Training again tonight?" Zafir asked.

Evy cocked her head. "You knew I was out here training?"

"Queen Lovejoy, you're hard to miss. The first night you slipped out, at least three guards trailed you. Poor souls lost their breath trying to keep pace."

Evy laughed. "I remember that."

"I was curious," Zafir said. "I decided to trail you myself. Mind if I join you in your training?"

"You want to train with *me*?" A request Evy would have never expected from the Djinn King. Why would he want to train with her? She would probably slow him down.

"I came in last in the Trial of Wit," Zafir said. "I can't afford to fall behind again. I need to train and find a way to get ahead."

Evy searched for the right words. Perhaps this was an opportunity to learn from him. "I'd be delighted," she said at last.

Zafir grinned.

They took off again, side by side, keeping pace as they moved deeper into the cinderbark forest. The trees thinned, giving way to a wide clearing, the ground sloping gently into a bed of soft, scorched sand.

The moon hung overhead, illuminating the space.

Evy slowed to a stop. This would do.

"What's next in your training plan, Your Majesty?" Zafir asked, scanning the land around them.

"Call me Evy. We're training partners, after all." She stepped into the center of the clearing, her boots kicking up a soft cloud of blackened dust. "Since you're here, I was hoping I could train my fire magic."

"Sounds like a good plan."

Mana began to concentrate at his feet, glowing faintly beneath the ground. He raised his arm, heat pulsed from his skin, and in the next instant, a stream of fire burst from his palm, arced across the clearing, and struck one of the tall cinderbarks with a roar.

The heat hit Evy like a crashing wave. She instinctively stepped back, bracing herself against the sudden force.

"Not bad." Evy glanced at Zafir.

He motioned to the cinderbark. "Your turn."

Evy focused and called for her spirits. Five appeared, the red-and-orange wisps circled her. She glanced warily at Zafir and dismissed three of them.

She dug her feet into the ground. Mana stirred beneath her, drawn up through the earth and pooling at her core. Her spirits seized the energy and shaped it into a ball of fire in her outstretched palm.

A moment later, the fireball shot forward, streaking toward

the same tree Zafir had struck. The blast hit with a deafening crack, splitting the trunk clean in two. The cinderbark collapsed to the ground in a rush of ash and steam.

Evy scowled. Still unused to more mana, she didn't mean to strike as hard as she did.

Orianna's words came back.

"You'll be deemed dangerous, and they'll slam the door shut behind you."

Zafir watched her with narrowed, assessing eyes. Then his expression shifted.

"That was impressive," he said, brows raising. "Most impressive indeed."

Zafir walked over to the cleaved tree. "Your magic." He traced a finger along the bark. "It doesn't come from within you like the fire in my own veins. But I saw the mana seeping into you, like it does with any spellcaster."

Evy flexed her fingers as mana coursed through her. "I can't shape mana into magic like you can, but the spirits draw it from my body and perform magic for me."

Zafir crossed his arms, studying her more intently now. "So the spirits do your bidding? Just like that?"

"It's more of a partnership," she said as she wiped the sweat from her brow. "They don't serve me. They choose to help and carry out my will."

"And these spirits... they know your will? I didn't see you mutter any spells either, like the Ethereals or the Shifters do."

Fire spirits darted in and out of view. "We're bonded through our rites. The ritual connects us so deeply that they can sense my intentions. No incantations are needed, though speaking aloud to the spirits can help us focus."

"Strange kind of power," Zafir said.

Evy smirked. "Strange, but it works."

"It sure does." He turned his attention back to the splintered tree. "And it's strong."

Zafir pivoted and strode toward a nearby cinderbark. He planted his feet, gripped the trunk, and with a guttural grunt, heaved. The ground trembled. Roots tore loose. In one explosive motion, he ripped the tree from the earth and hurled it through the air like a javelin. It slammed into another tree with a deafening crack, splintering both trunks and sending shards of bark flying.

Evy gaped.

Zafir exhaled and turned to her. "Strength isn't always about the magic you use. Power comes in many forms."

A rustle sounded behind them, followed by boots crunching against gravel.

Celeste stepped into the clearing, moonlight reflecting on the shiny pink strands of her loose braid. She wore a creamy green shift that flowed to her ankles, the kind of gown meant for sleep, not wandering through a forest at night.

Royen trailed her, arms crossed, his expression caught somewhere between irritation and exhaustion. He, too, was dressed more casually than Evy had ever seen him: a loose tunic, open at the chest, and baggy britches tucked into worn boots.

"Look who I found." Celeste planted her hands on her hips. "I caught Royen sneaking after the two of you, so naturally, I followed him."

Royen scoffed. "That's not what happened."

Celeste placed a hand over her chest. "Oh? Then what do you call dragging me out of my tent because you thought Zafir and Evy were up to something?"

"You're the one who barged into *my* tent and said that. I was halfway through a chapter of my book."

Zafir shook his head. "You two are loud enough to wake the Sand Striders halfway across the desert."

"I hate Sand Striders." Celeste shuddered.

A wry smile tugged at Evy's lips as she looked between Celeste and Royen. "We weren't up to anything. Just training."

Celeste clasped her hands together. "Can I join?" she asked, then approached Evy without waiting for an answer. "I need to work off that stew Irma made. It was incredible, but I'm ninety percent sure it had a full pound of butter in it."

Moments later, the clearing was alive with bursts of light and energy as the three trained together. Royen sat off to the side, leaning back against a tree. His arms were folded behind his head, eyes shut.

Celeste lifted her arms and muttered a brief incantation summoning wind. A small stone near her feet shot into the air and spun rapidly, suspended mid-flight. Without hesitation, Zafir launched a bolt of fire, grazing the stone's edge. Evy followed with a focused stream of flame and struck it dead center. Celeste finished it off with a sharp gust of wind, scattering the crumbled shards into the dirt.

After a few rounds, Celeste turned toward Royen.

"Are you really going to sit there brooding or actually join us?" she called out.

Royen gave a faint shrug, eyes still closed. "I'm happy to stay here and rest."

Zafir huffed, rolling a small flame between his fingertips. "Of course you are. Why bother training when you've got the Celestial Gauntlets?"

Royen met Zafir's gaze. "Some of us train with our minds," he said evenly. "But if throwing fire at rocks brings you joy, don't let me stop you."

Zafir's jaw tensed. He glowered but said nothing more.

Celeste shook her head. "Boys."

Royen had already gone back to feigning sleep. His typical cold detachment didn't surprise Evy, but she thought back to the moment they'd shared after the first trial. For a moment, it had seemed like his icy demeanor was melting, like he wanted to let her in.

And then he'd taken flight, quite literally, vanishing into the sky as a sparrow.

During the carriage ride, he'd barely looked at her. As if their conversation had never happened.

Celeste tossed another stone into the air, sending it spinning high above the clearing.

Before anyone could react, a streak of blue-white light zipped through the darkness.

The stone shattered midair.

Evy tracked the falling fragments. One landed near her feet. She crouched to inspect it and found a perfectly round hole pierced at its center.

She turned.

Royen was still reclining against the cinderbark, one leg bent. His hands had only just begun to lower, a small metallic orb hovering over his palm. As Evy watched, the faint outline of a bow collapsed back into it. The weapon folded in on itself until only the orb remained, no larger than a marble. A gadget from Theribane, Evy surmised—one that drew mana directly from the grid and shaped it into a bow and arrows.

He smiled lazily. "Maybe I don't need the gauntlets after all."

"Show off." Celeste rolled her eyes.

Evy studied his effortless confidence, and a smile flitted across her face. Even she had to admit, it was pretty impressive.

TWENTY-TWO

The land grew more violent beneath them the deeper they traveled into Zarokan.

The last two days of travel had worn Evy down to the bone, but she still found herself pressed to the carriage window, marveling at the charred ridges carving deep, jagged lines through the earth. Veins of molten rock pulsed just under the surface, magma glowing through fractures in the blackened stone, casting a faint, hellish light across the redbrick path.

The air undulated with heat, bending the horizon like a warped mirror. The scent of sulfur clung to her nostrils, and the wind carried the faint hiss of steam rising from fissures where magma met groundwater.

Inside the glass carriage, the heat was trapped and suffocating. Every bump in the road rattled Evy's spine. Hovering at the edge of her vision, her spirits moved slower than usual. All except the fire spirits, who darted around inside the carriage, whispering eagerly and asking if they could slip outside to play in the magma.

Evy hushed them with a firm push of her will.

"It's so hot in here! I can't bear it," Celeste wailed, wiping sweat from her brow. "Can't we ride on horseback like Zafir?"

"King Soltris is outside to guard us." Royen shrugged off his coat. "This territory's riddled with feral Ifreeti tribes. They might try to attack the caravan."

"*Feral* is a harsh word," Evy said, frowning. "Zafir told us they're rival Ifreeti clans who've contested the Soltris line for generations. If they see the King of Zarokan traveling without his army, they might see it as an opportunity to attack."

"What's your point, *Evalene*?" Royen asked.

"My point, *Royen,* is that just because their families have been feuding doesn't make the rival clans feral."

Royen narrowed his eyes at her. Then, slowly, the corner of his mouth curved into a smug smile. "Sounds like you're projecting."

"What?"

"Have you ever met an Ifreet?"

She shook her head.

"Then how would you know they aren't feral?" He leaned back and folded his arms. "They're cousins to the Djinn, except more primitive. More volatile. Most of them are wildlings or mercenaries who refuse to follow the rule of law. They've got a taste for bloodshed, always one spark away from berserking—"

"Oh, by the Gods, if we don't get out of this carriage in the next second, I might actually melt." Celeste pressed her forehead to the glass.

Evy grimaced at Royen, then turned to Celeste. "Can you circulate air through the carriage?"

Celeste was still fanning herself. "Yes, but it'll just be hot air."

"Cast it anyway. I want to try something."

With a sigh, Celeste muttered an incantation and flicked her finger. A warm breeze began to spiral through the cabin.

Evy summoned a water spirit and focused on the motion of

the air. Magic pulsed through the space as the spirit cooled the current, scattering tiny ice particles into the stream.

The temperature dropped instantly.

Celeste groaned in delight and slumped back into her seat. "Evy, I absolutely adore you."

Even Royen let out a quiet sigh of relief.

"Can't you do air magic?" he asked, his attention on Evy.

She shrugged. "It's not my strongest area of expertise."

The Spirit Matron had once explained that every Witch had incompatibilities with spirits, and though Evy was bonded to a few air spirits, they never cooperated well with her. So she was grateful that her experiment with Celeste's magic proved successful—otherwise she might have melted away entirely.

Evy turned her head toward the window, the cooled air whispering across her cheek. She took in the landscape. Even here, at the edge of a volcanic frontier, Zarokan was more than just fire.

From the hours she'd spent poring over maps, she'd learned it was a land of extremes. Sprawling jungles and winding rivers carved through obsidian canyons. Snow-kissed mountains loomed beyond scorched valleys. Coastal winds carried salt from oceans so warm they steamed.

Zarokan was wild, *Elemental* in every sense of the word.

And it struggled to bow to a single kind of order.

Unlike the centralized courts of Virenna or the mechanical hierarchy of Theribane, Zarokan was tribal, and fiercely so. Territory was fought for instead of inherited.

The Elemental clans who called this land home lived by that truth. The fact that Zarokan hadn't torn itself apart was a testament to its rulers—to the Soltris line. A sign of sheer, unrelenting strength.

In the distance, volcanic peaks loomed higher, and nestled between them, partially embedded in a gargantuan mountain, stood the Infernal Citadel.

It jutted from the heart of the volcano, its upper spires piercing the orange-streaked sky. They rose in sharp angles, structures forged from obsidian and blackened steel.

Lava veins pulsed through the fortress's base like glowing threads, and thin plumes of smoke drifted lazily from its many balconies and battlements.

The citadel was so close to the volcano's bubbling mouth that Evy could only imagine what it must feel like to stand within it. Unless a being was made of fire itself, like the Djinn or Ifreet, she suspected they'd need to cloak themselves in powerful heat wards just to survive the air.

Royen's voice pulled her from her thoughts. "We're testing a mana-powered device in Theribane," he said. "A small enchantment-driven unit that draws heat from the air and channels it into a cooling core. We're installing them in homes first, then carriages."

"That's boring." Celeste waved a hand. "Evy, tell me more about your spirit magic."

Evy tilted her head, trying to figure out where to even start. "What do you want to know?"

"Well, everything," Celeste replied. "What does it mean to bond with a spirit? Are they like pets? Can you actually see them? What do they look like? Oh, and can you really see ghosts?"

Evy opened her mouth, but a voice outside of the carriage cut her off.

Zafir appeared on horseback beside the window. "You'll have to save the ghost stories." He nodded toward the road. "We're arriving in Ashgate."

Celeste leaned forward to peer past Evy and gasped as jagged rooftops and glowing vents came into view, backlit by the towering volcano above.

The carriage soon rattled into town, and the world outside their windows erupted with life.

Rickshaws weaved through the crowds, their wheels kicking up red dust as they swerved between pedestrians. Open-air stalls lined the roads, pressed shoulder to shoulder, their roofs patched with canvas and thin sheets of metal.

Elementals of all shapes and sizes cooked over natural lava streams, flames licking at cast-iron pots suspended by stone hooks. The air was thick with spice and smoke, the scents of seared meat and something sweet and unfamiliar filling the air.

Shops had no doors, only wide, open thresholds that invited customers in to wander freely. A Gnome boy waved from a crowded corner stall, shouting prices over the din as he held up a cage of tiny golden chicks. One chirped, and a puff of embers flared from its beak.

Ashgate reminded her, strangely, of Moonveil.

But this place was louder, hotter, and faster-paced.

Definitely more overwhelming.

The crowd turned as the carriage rolled past, whispers rippling through the street as townspeople leaned in for a better look.

Then the cheers began.

Evidently for Zafir.

He rode ahead of the carriage on horseback. Cries of "Soltris!" echoed through the streets. Some raised their fists in salute, others pressed hands over their hearts or bowed low as he passed.

The carriage slowed to a halt near the town center, its wheels grinding softly against scorched stone. The door swung open, and heat rushed in all over again.

Evy stepped out, her boots crunching against the sunbaked path. She quickly summoned a water spirit and cast a cooling spell over her garments. When she spotted the thin veins of lava weaving through the glowing mana grid beneath her feet, she reached for a light and fire spirit to protect her from burns.

Up ahead, Zafir was already off his horse, surrounded by a

small gathering. He stood beside a towering Stone Golem. Its body was stacked with slabs of granite, thick-limbed and slow-moving. Amber light pulsed behind its uneven, blinking eyes.

Beside it stood an Undine. Her translucent form undulated like a stream of water, her features delicate and ever shifting. Instead of speaking, she used graceful hand gestures, each movement sending ripples through her body.

Zafir laughed, loud and warm, and clapped the Golem on the shoulder.

"I need that necklace," Celeste gasped beside her.

The Sylph took off in a flutter of iridescent wings, her feet lifting from the ground. She glided effortlessly across the street toward a merchant's stand where trays of glittering jewels were on display.

And just like that, Evy was left standing next to Royen. Alone.

The two hesitated, then began walking, unintentionally in the same direction, at the same pace.

"This town is... lively," Evy said, trying to break the silence.

Royen gave a noncommittal hum, clasping his hands behind his back as he surveyed the crowded market. "That's one word for it. Maybe *chaotic* is more fitting."

They walked a few more paces in silence, the space between them taut.

"Is this your first time in Ashgate?" she asked.

He didn't look at her. "It is."

"Do you enjoy traveling?"

He paused at a stall displaying curved knives carved from volcanic glass and considered the items before replying. "Not particularly."

"So you don't leave home much?"

"That would be correct," he said, then glanced at her, as if waiting for judgment. "Not unless I have to."

She had no room to judge, especially when she'd never left Reyland before the Hierarch Wars.

"What do you do back home in Theribane?"

He released a short, unexpected breath of laughter. "I do what I'm told. Mostly."

He paused. "When I'm not doing that, I read. I study the city's designs. I like seeing how things work. How people build solutions."

Evy's brows lifted slightly.

"And your cousin Marq? What does he like?"

"Puzzles. We solve mechanical ones together." Royen glanced down at his boots. "And pretty girls. He's always talking about them, it's impossible sometimes."

It was the first time he hadn't sounded like a polished statesman, making the distance between them seem smaller—the conversation easier.

"Do you share similar interests?" Evy's mouth quirked in amusement. "Do you like pretty girls too?" She couldn't help herself.

Royen's eyes went wide, and a delicate bloom spread through his cheeks.

"I'm sorry. I'm only joking." Evy laughed into her hand. "You're fond of your cousin, aren't you?"

"He's the only one in that house who makes it feel like home. He's like a brother to me."

Royen gave a faint smile, carving a dimple into his angular face. Evy let herself enjoy his unexpected softness. Perhaps an alliance was possible after all.

"Oi! You two!" Zafir's voice rang out over the noise of the market.

Evy and Royen turned to see him striding toward them.

"You're not leaving Ashgate without trying this first." He jerked a thumb toward a street cart nestled between two stone columns. Steam billowed from metal trays, and the aroma hit Evy first—tangy and spicy enough to sting her eyes.

The vendor was an Ifreet, and though not every tribe rivaled the Soltris reign, his presence still surprised Evy. His crimson-toned skin glowed faintly. His eyes were astonishing—glassy, almost translucent, with slitted pupils that flickered like candle flame. They looked like lanterns containing the fire within.

The vendor handed her a clay plate of bite-sized, hollow, crisp golden shells, each split at the top and brimming with spiced potatoes, green chili, fresh herbs, and a generous drizzle of fragrant sauce.

Zafir grinned as he popped one into his mouth and gestured for the others to do the same.

Royen regarded the plate with barely concealed skepticism. "It's wet."

"That's the best part." Zafir reached for another.

Evy shrugged and tossed one into her mouth.

It exploded with flavor—crunch, tang, and fire all at once. Her eyes watered instantly.

Royen ate his whole, then went still. His face flushed pink. Then red.

Then he started coughing. Loudly.

Zafir doubled over with laughter as the Ifreeti vendor clapped Royen on the back hard enough to rattle bone.

"Not bad," Evy said. "But I think my lips just disintegrated."

Royen couldn't respond. He was too busy trying to breathe.

And Evy burst out laughing.

TWENTY-THREE

Evy stood before the tall, obsidian-framed mirror as Irma draped a glittering accessory around her waist.

Her quarters in the Infernal Citadel were far more lavish than she'd expected: black stone walls veined with glowing threads of red-orange light, ceilings high enough to echo, and a wide window that overlooked a river of molten lava cutting through the mountainside far below. Despite the volcanic aesthetic, the room had been magically cooled. A soft breeze whispered through hidden vents, and the stone floors stayed pleasantly chilled beneath her bare feet.

She'd slept better than she had in days.

And yet, guilt tugged at her.

She hadn't trained.

After they arrived the day prior, exhaustion had swallowed her whole. Following dinner and a quick bath, she'd collapsed into bed without a second thought. But before they'd retired, Zafir had informed the Ascendants that his court would host a grand party in their honor the following evening and that attendance was expected.

And this morning, Celeste had waltzed into her room at dawn.

"You're not wearing that to tonight's party, are you?" Celeste had asked, scandalized, when Evy pulled out her usual violet robes.

An hour later, Evy was back in Ashgate as Celeste dragged her from stall to stall, declaring it her personal mission to liberate Evy from her "mundane fashion prison."

Irma tightened the last of the silver cords and stepped back.

"Are you sure about this, Evy?" she asked, giving her a once-over. "Where did you even get these?"

"A few Ifreeti merchants in Ashgate." Evy sighed at her reflection. "Celeste picked out my entire outfit. We were being followed by guards from Ruitheon and wanted to shake them off, so we rushed."

She adjusted the thin straps on her shoulders. "I was trying to go for something a bit more… modest."

The cropped lavender bodice was embroidered with dozens of tiny mirrors, each one catching the light and scattering like sparks. It hugged her chest, leaving her midriff completely bare. A long, deep violet satin skirt was tied at her waist with a silver tassel, the fabric falling in flowing panels that split high on both sides, revealing her legs nearly to the hip. Fitted, knee-length undergarments kept her modest beneath the skirt. Strappy leather sandals wound up her calves, their laces stopping just below her knees.

A silver chain draped loosely around her waist with delicate coins clinking softly at every motion. More matching chains circled her wrists and trailed across her forehead, contrasting vividly against her tawny skin.

Her eyes were lined with thick bands of kohl, making her pale-blue irises glow like crystals, and her lips were smudged with rose-colored paint.

"At least the outfit is purple," Evy said, smoothing the fabric. "Reya's shade."

Irma raised a brow, skeptical.

Evy winced. "Celeste said it would be impolite not to wear local attire."

"She said it would be rude not to match," Irma said while brushing rouge on Evy's cheeks. "And that she'd never forgive you if you showed up to a party looking like a librarian."

Evy tried to laugh, but her fingers were already tugging nervously at the waistband again.

Celeste's emerald-green version was equally revealing and impossible to walk in without jingling like a wind chime. But she had insisted, claiming the Zarokan customs were bold, expressive, and sensual. Dressing up was a sign of respect.

And Evy, hesitant but too tired to argue, had gone along with it.

Now she wasn't so sure.

She swept her loose, snowy hair back as she considered herself in the mirror.

Clink.

She sighed again.

Irma walked around Evy, finger tapping her chin. "If Aeric could see you now, his heart would stop from happiness." She paused. "And a few other emotions."

Evy groaned and playfully shoved her.

Irma laughed, ducking out of reach with her hands raised in mock surrender. "I'm just saying, the poor boy wouldn't know where to look."

Evy shook her head, fighting a smile. "Are you coming to the celebration tonight? Zafir said the entire household's invited."

Irma started folding the clothes scattered on the floor. "Some of the kitchen staff told me there's a party in the cellars and enough wine to forget we're living on a volcano." She smirked. "They invited me."

"Are you going?"

"I was planning to stop by the courtyard first, in case you need me. But if you're alright, I'd love to go make a few friends. The Elementals seem genuine enough."

"Go." Evy took Irma's hand. "Enjoy yourself. I'll be fine."

Irma returned the gesture with a gentle squeeze. "You'll tell me if you're not?"

"I promise."

With that, Irma gathered her things and headed for the door, pausing at the threshold. "You look beautiful, but you should walk slowly. All that jingling might give you away to enemies."

Evy snorted. "Out."

Irma's laughter echoed as she disappeared down the hall, leaving Evy alone with her reflection.

She studied herself a moment longer, then let out a defeated sigh and turned for the door.

There was no time like the present. And she didn't want to be late.

Evy traversed through the dim halls of the Citadel, the coins at her waist and wrists chiming with every step. From somewhere ahead came a slow, thrumming rhythm that guided her forward.

The corridor opened into a vast courtyard, and the scenery unfolded.

Lava channels framed the perimeter in glowing lines, casting molten light across the black stone. Silken banners fluttered from balconies above, embroidered in gold and crimson. Floating lanterns drifted through the air.

At the far end, a band played lively, percussive music. On a raised platform, Undine dancers moved like enchanted fountains, their silver chains swaying, veils rippling with every roll of their hips and bend of their spines.

Banquet tables lined the courtyard, filled with plates of

roasted meats, spiced rice, baskets of flatbread, bowls of stewed vegetables, and goblets of ruby-red wine.

But no one was eating. Or dancing.

The crowd had gathered in a loose circle around a wide clearing in the center, voices humming with anticipation.

Curious, Evy wove through the crowd. Royen stood just behind the front ring of onlookers, arms loosely crossed. She made her way toward him.

"What's going on?" she asked, stopping beside him and trying to see over the crowd.

Without glancing her way, he answered, "Zafir's sparring. One of the young Stone Golems challenged him. Must be a ceremonial thing."

Then he faced her.

And froze.

For a full two seconds, Royen Veyn, typically unshakable and composed, seemed to have completely forgotten how to speak.

His mouth opened. Closed. Opened again.

Evy shifted, suddenly self-conscious. "Is it too much?"

"I— No! No." He straightened. "It's… You look… You're… You look—" He coughed into his hand. "Dressed."

"Dressed?"

"I mean, appropriately! As in, for the culture. Respectful. Very…" He was clearly grasping for a lifeline. "Traditional."

Evy fought a laugh.

His gaze darted briefly to the coins at her waist, then snapped back up as he caught himself. "It's hot out." He shrugged off his coat, looking anywhere but at her.

She hummed. "Well, thank the Gods I'm dressed for the weather."

Royen muttered something under his breath that sounded suspiciously like a prayer for mercy and turned stiffly back to the sparring ring.

Evy smiled to herself, watching his ears turn red.

The crowd erupted in cheers and stumbled back as a massive figure crashed onto the floor. A blur of stone and dust struck the scorched ground with a thunderous thud.

The young Stone Golem groaned, shards of gravel skittering across the ground as his heavy form collapsed. He tried to rise but staggered.

Zafir walked over and offered a hand to pull him up. His chest was bare, slick with sweat, a massive hammer of flame gripped tightly in one hand. The weapon glowed like molten metal, waves of heat radiating from its surface, embers drifting lazily from its edges. As the fight ended, the hammer dissolved into smoke.

The Golem grasped Zafir's forearm. Zafir hauled him upright with ease as the crowd roared around them.

Zafir scanned the crowd and landed on the two Ascendants.

His face lit up.

"Evy! Royen!" he called as he strode over. The crowd parted for him.

"I want you to meet someone." Zafir threw an arm around a young man walking at his side.

The resemblance was immediate—leaner than Zafir, but with the same striking, red-gold eyes and proud bearing. His inky-black hair was cropped close on the sides, and he wore a sleeveless black tunic embroidered with solar emblems along the collar.

"This is my son, Juleen."

Royen gave a polite nod. "An honor to meet you."

Juleen returned the gesture with a graceful bow. "The Young Master Veyn."

Then he turned to Evy. "Queen Lovejoy."

He reached for her hand and lifted it delicately, then brushed a kiss against her knuckles.

"I've heard you're quite the warrior," he said, voice as smooth as polished obsidian. "My father says you held your own during a night of training. I'd be honored to witness your skills firsthand."

Zafir clapped his son on the back and let out a booming laugh. "She's got fire, that one. You should spar with her, Juleen!"

Royen glanced between them. "Here? Now?"

Zafir waved a hand, his movements a little too loose for him to be entirely sober. "Why not? Nothing bonds domains like a friendly fight!"

Evy looked between the father and son, the glint in Juleen's eyes, the open clearing, the crowd already buzzing with anticipation.

She hesitated, then heard the murmurs threading through the courtyard.

"Is that the Queen of Reyland? The short one?"

"She's barely taller than his boot."

"There's no way a Witch beat our king in the first trial. She must've cheated."

Every sneer struck like a spear.

Then someone snorted, loud enough for all to hear. "Had to be luck. She won't last in a real fight."

"What's she going to do? Summon a ghost into battle?" another called out. "She can spook her opponents!"

Laughter scattered through the crowd.

Evy's ears began to burn.

Juleen stood in the clearing, calm and waiting, lips curled in a smirk.

Zafir leaned in, the scent of wine clinging to him. "He's good," he muttered. "But he's cocky. Wouldn't hurt to remind him fire doesn't make you invincible."

Evy arched a brow.

Zafir grinned. "Teach him a lesson."

"Alright." The coins at her waist jingled as she stepped into the ring. "I accept the challenge."

Juleen's grin widened. "As you wish, Queen Lovejoy."

As they strode toward the center of the ring, he leaned in slightly.

"I'll try not to burn your outfit." He winked. "You do look very pretty in it."

Evy scoffed, then called her spirits to the edge of her mind.

She and Juleen circled each other, and the crowd quieted.

Juleen made the first move.

Flames surged along his arm, spiraling upward before hardening into the shape of a long, gleaming spear.

He twirled the weapon, fire trailing behind him.

"Ready?" he asked.

Evy didn't answer.

She raised her hand, and the air around her hummed.

Juleen lunged.

The fire-spear sliced through the air with blistering speed. Evy ducked beneath the arc, the heat grazing her shoulder. Sparks erupted behind her as the spear struck the ground, carving a scorched scar into the stone.

She moved on instinct. Light on her feet, she drew on air spirits to boost her speed, grateful the wisps had answered.

Juleen spun a new spear in both hands and drove forward again, faster this time.

Evy backstepped twice, then planted her heel.

Her palm lit with magic, and a shield of water rose just in time. The spear struck it head-on. Steam exploded outward in a hiss.

Juleen staggered back, coughing in the mist.

Her other hand shot out. An arrow of stone took shape midair, and she let it fly.

The arrow struck the ground at Juleen's feet with a bone-rattling *crack*, knocking him off balance. He hit the ground hard, flames vanishing from his limbs as his back slammed into the stone.

He lay there, unmoving.

Evy stood at the center of the courtyard, hair tousled, violet skirts billowing.

Then came realization.

She had just beaten the prince of Zarokan in his own home, in front of his own people.

Too much, too fast. "They'll slam the door shut."

For a horrible, breathless moment, she braced for the crowd to turn on her.

Juleen blinked up at the sky, then he let out a low, hearty laugh.

He pushed himself upright and dropped to one knee before her.

Zafir followed.

And like a wave, the crowd of Elementals bowed in unison.

Evy staggered back in surprise. Across from her, Royen stood still, his head tilted as he watched her intently.

"This is how you earn respect in Zarokan," Juleen said, still kneeling.

Zafir clapped his son hard on the back. "What did I tell you?" he boomed. "She could probably take down an entire flock of Phoenixes on her own."

Juleen rose. "I wouldn't bet against her."

"Maybe I should marry you off to her, Juleen!" Zafir stood and placed a hand on Evy's shoulder. "What say you, Shaman Queen? You and my son, now that would be a powerful alliance. Spirit and flame. Brain and brawn. Diplomacy and chaos."

"I wouldn't mind," Juleen said, his expression softening.

Evy opened her mouth, whether to object or laugh, she wasn't sure.

Another voice interrupted their conversation.

"I'll spar with her."

All heads turned.

Royen stepped forward, jaw set.

Evy paused. "You want to spar?"

He gave a slight shrug. "Why not?"

Zafir snorted. "You sure, Veyn? She just flattened my son like naan."

"I'm aware." Royen turned to her. "Don't underestimate me, Evalene."

Before Evy could respond, Royen was rolling up his sleeves and striding toward the center of the clearing.

She followed without a word.

The courtyard stirred again, this time with a quieter, more curious energy.

Royen took his place across from her. His expression remained composed, but his fingers rolled a metallic marble—his bow-and-arrow gadget.

Mana pooled at his feet. The moment the signal was given, he moved.

Evy barely had time to think. He was faster, more fluid than she expected, even in Zarokan, where the mana ran thinner than what he was likely used to. In one seamless motion, he summoned a bow. The arrow followed in the same movement, let loose with uncanny precision.

Evy conjured a fire barrier just in time. The arrow burst into harmless sparks against it.

Another shot.

She dodged it and deflected the next with a shield of water. Royen was fast. Every movement looked effortless and calculated.

Then he vanished.

No.

Shifted.

His form rippled into a silver fox that darted around her with dazzling speed. Mid-lunge, he shifted again, this time into a falcon, wings slicing the air overhead, loosing another mana arrow as he reformed into his own body mid-flight.

Evy matched his volley with her own—arrows of fire, ice, and stone erupting from her palms.

The courtyard blurred around them in a storm of light and motion, but movement at the edge of the crowd caught her eye.

Two figures in golden cloaks—Ruitheon's guards. The same ones who had followed her and Celeste through the markets in Ashgate. Even beneath their glinting helmets, she could feel their attention on her.

The exhilaration drained from her immediately, her steps faltering.

She sent her next shot wide on purpose. Her fire spirit hissed in confusion, whispering questions about why she had missed.

She let a volley of Royen's arrows graze her barrier, shattering the spell before she raised it again. Her movements slowed, just enough to resemble fatigue instead of restraint.

They both froze, breathless, standing paces apart at the center of the ring. Royen tilted his head, observing her.

As if he could see right through her.

As if he knew she was holding back.

Before either could make another move, a voice rang out from the crowd.

"Enough!"

Celeste stood with her hands on her hips, wings flared. "By the Gods, did I come here for a brawl or a ball? Someone bring me wine. Or a dance floor."

Laughter surged through the courtyard, breaking the tension. The gathering broke apart in twos and threes, drifting beyond the courtyard.

Royen approached. "You're not what I expected." He exhaled softly and stepped closer, leaning toward her ear. "But you were holding back."

The warmth of his breath brushed her skin.

Evy jerked away. "I'm not sure what you're talking about."

A corner of his mouth lifted. "Next time, I'd like you to give it your all. I enjoyed the practice."

They stilled, a new current of understanding passing between them.

Then Zafir and Juleen approached, both wearing mischievous grins.

"You should seriously consider my offer," Zafir said. "A union between the Prince of Zarokan and the Shaman Queen of Reyland? Do you think your offspring would be more Djinn or more Witch?"

Evy's face went hot. "I—"

"My word," Celeste cut in. "I'm sure Evy's hand is already claimed by her own group of suitors."

"Group?" Royen repeated, brow furrowing. "Plural?"

Celeste beamed. "Of course. Have you seen her? I'd be shocked if someone back home hasn't already staked a claim. Right, Evy?"

Evy hesitated as Aeric's face flashed behind her eyes, but her silence said enough.

Royen's expression shifted. "Excuse me," he muttered, then turned and disappeared into the crowd.

Celeste faced Juleen with a theatrical sigh. "See? She's spoken for. But I, on the other hand, am tragically single. No one's fighting over my hand."

Juleen's eyes raked over her. "Hard to believe." He offered his arm.

She took it, and the two slipped off into the festivities.

Evy searched for Royen in the courtyard, hoping to talk about their spar, but he was already gone.

TWENTY-FOUR

The Virennese forest seemed to breathe around them.

Sunlight streamed through the emerald canopy, filtering in soft golden shafts that danced across the moss-covered ground. The glass carriage rocked gently beneath the Ascendants as it followed the winding path, wheels muffled by a thick layer of fallen leaves.

It had taken a week to travel through Zarokan's harsh terrain and Ruitheon's scorching desert sun before finally making it through Virenna's borders. Evy had welcomed the rich, cool scent of earth when they first crossed in. The kiss of shade from the trees above was a quiet relief.

After another week of travel, the forest opened without warning.

The carriage rolled through a vast meadow. Soft grass blanketed the ground like strands of silk, dewdrops glittering like stars along each blade.

And at the heart of it all stood the Crystal Court. As they passed the metal gates, the carriage creaked to a halt.

"Finally," Evy muttered, relieved that their longest stretch of travel had come to an end.

The Crystal Court was a palace that could have blossomed from the earth itself.

Its towers stretched skyward, sculpted from glimmering emerald glass and silver-veined gems. Under the high noon sun, the palace refracted the light, breaking it into brilliant, spectral shards across the ground. Curved balconies bloomed outward like petals, making the building resemble a glass lotus. The entire structure gleamed above the mana-charged ground.

Celeste leaned out the window beside her and beamed. "Welcome to my home."

The carriage doors swung open, and Evy stepped out into a dream.

Music drifted through the air like a sweet perfume, light and effervescent. Her gaze followed the sound to the courtyard, already alive with celebration.

Celeste's head tilted toward the music. She started toward the source of the revelry, and Evy, Royen, and Zafir followed close behind.

The palace gardens were a kaleidoscope of color and sound. Rose-shaped lanterns floated overhead, their light glowing in shades of magenta, turquoise, and gold, casting shifting mosaics across mossy stone paths and flowering hedges. Overhead, Sylphs soared in elegant arcs, their wings reflecting a milky sheen.

Fairies in all shapes and colors twirled in spirals, laughing as they flew over tables heaped with fruits and glazed pastries, floral wines, and candied blossoms. Evy's stomach grumbled as a group of Goblins, several flutes past sober, stumbled arm in arm, sloshing wine and howling an off-key love ballad. She was grateful the riot of noise swallowed the sound of her increasingly insistent stomach.

Near the stage, a band of Elves played a melody so lush it felt as if the forest itself were singing. The harp shimmered, its azure mana strings releasing notes like falling rain. The cello purred, grounding the airy trills of enchanted flutes.

Evy's mouth parted in awe. A thousand textures of sound and motion wove together into a celebration that could only belong to Virenna. She tried to take everything in at once.

Celeste's steps slowed as the laughter and music swelled around them. Her brows drew together before she let out a quiet, frustrated sigh.

"Celeste?" Evy asked. "Is everything alright?" Celeste didn't answer.

She scanned the crowd and landed on someone across the courtyard. Without a word, she strode toward her target. Evy followed closely, careful not to trip on the trailing edge of Celeste's green skirt. She sensed Royen and Zafir keeping pace behind her as they approached the heart of the celebration.

Celeste stopped in front of a long banquet table overflowing with towering cakes dusted in edible glitter, rose-custard pastries, goblets of sparkling nectar, and a unicorn sculpture made entirely of spun sugar, its horn already missing.

At the center of it all, lounging in a nest of velvet cushions, was a radiant, disheveled Sylph, laughing loudly as the goblet in her hand tipped and splashed wine across the table.

"Mother?" Celeste called out.

Queen Talia DuVent looked like a painting brought to life. Her silver gown glittered like starlight against her bronze skin, while soft pink hair cascaded in waves, barely tamed by jeweled pins. Her crystalline crown had slipped askew, dangling near one ear.

But the Queen paid no attention to her daughter. Instead, she stepped onto the table, her gossamer wings flaring as she threw her head back in continued laughter. Mid-twirl, she lost her balance, then caught herself and landed neatly in the lap of a nearby Elf.

The Queen traced his jaw with a red-lacquered nail. "You've saved me twice today, my hero," she purred into his ear.

Evy felt Celeste stiffen beside her. She stepped forward, voice deceptively calm. "Are we late for the welcome party or something?"

Queen Talia startled. "Celeste! Stars above, what are you doing here?"

"We're here for the Procession, Mother."

"Oh." Talia paused. "Are you here early?"

"No."

"Late, then?"

"We're here on time. I wrote to you and told you the exact date."

The Queen fluttered her lashes, then sighed. "Fine, I forgot." She flung her arms in the air. "But if it's a party you want, darling, I'll conjure one by moonrise. You know I can throw a fabulous midnight banquet."

Celeste pressed her fingers to her temple. "Then what's all this?" She gestured around them.

Talia waved her off and plucked a grape from a floating tray. "Oh, this? Just a small celebration for the gardener who found my crown earlier today."

She patted the Elf's cheek fondly. "This sweet thing right here. Isn't he precious?"

The Elf gave a sloppy bow while still seated.

A finely dressed Dwarf in silver livery stepped forward and bowed low, his long gray beard brushing the floor as he did.

"Your Majesty, the royal kitchen confirms preparations for the official welcome banquet are underway. Everything will be ready by dusk."

Talia clapped her hands together. "See? I didn't forget. I merely misaligned my priorities."

Celeste stared at her.

The Queen rose, wings fanning slightly as she adjusted her

crooked crown. "You'll have time to rest and freshen up before the real party begins," she said, then rested a hand on Celeste's shoulder. "But before you flit off, I need a moment with you."

Celeste tensed but let herself be guided a few steps away from the others.

Talia lowered her voice just enough to pretend discretion, though Evy still heard every word.

"Darling, wonderful news. I've secured an engagement for you with Marquis Pearce. A Sylph of excellent breeding, exquisite bone structure, and very well-aligned wing symmetry. The Pearce family was thrilled by the news."

Celeste's mouth dropped open.

Talia continued, undeterred. "So I thought, why not combine the festivities? A welcome banquet for the Ascendants and an engagement ceremony is efficient, don't you think?"

"You... What?"

Talia beamed. "You're welcome."

Celeste stood frozen. "I can't get engaged to someone I've never even met and know nothing about."

Talia frowned, genuinely puzzled. "Of course you can. His name is Alanis Pearce. He's very rich and powerful. You'll adore him. What more do you need to know?"

Celeste paled. "Wait, isn't he the widower? The one with a limp? He's nearly triple my age."

The Queen picked at her cuticle, entirely unbothered. "And? He's a wealthy marquis with impeccable breeding. And you are the most powerful Sylph born in three centuries. It's a perfect match. What more could you hope for?"

Celeste's voice dropped low, her hands trembling. "I was hoping to marry for love," Celeste said. "Or at least someone I actually like." Evy's arms shook as she resisted the urge to reach for Celeste. Royen and Zafir exchanged a glance, their expressions tightening.

Talia burst into high and musical laughter. "Oh, sweetheart. Love?" She waved a hand toward the Elf still lounging beside the banquet table. "As you said, the Marquis is older. He probably won't live too long if you're lucky. You'll have plenty of time for love after you bear a strong heir, and once you're a widow."

Celeste flinched.

Talia turned back to her. "You are what you are, Celeste. The strongest Sylph in generations. Do you think that's a coincidence? No. I married the finest mate I could find—an old, no-name Sylph with rumored Lumiel heritage. And my bet paid off. It gave me you."

Talia grazed Celeste's cheek with the back of her finger. "Now it's your turn. Marquis Pearce's bloodline is unmatched. This is your duty as Princess of Virenna. Just as it was mine."

Evy's fingers curled at her sides. She knew what it was like to feel trapped by expectation. To suffocate beneath a legacy she never chose. But when Evy studied Queen Talia's hollow expression, unmoved by her daughter's pain, she realized she had something Celeste did not—the unadulterated love of her parents.

She didn't want to interfere, but seeing her friend bereft of support, she couldn't stop herself. She reached out gently and placed a hand on Celeste's shoulder. The muscles beneath her palm were tense, shaking slightly under the pressure of forced composure. Celeste didn't react to Evy's touch. Her eyes were distant, as if in a trance.

Queen Talia's gaze drifted lazily toward them and landed on Evy.

"My, aren't you a pretty little thing," she cooed. "Are you one of Celeste's little friends?"

Evy opened her mouth, unsure how to answer, but the Queen barreled on.

"I'm always looking for good help at the palace. You'd look

darling in one of the lilac maid gowns. Would you like to work here?"

Pride flared hot in Evy's veins, but she paused as she assessed the Queen. There was no cruelty in her tone, no smugness in her expression.

Talia hadn't meant to insult her. A position in the palace, close to her daughter. In her eyes, it was a gift. A favor to Celeste.

Perhaps even an attempt at apology, softening the blow after stripping her daughter of choice and dignity.

The wrong reaction, any hint of offense, wouldn't reflect solely on Evy.

It would reflect on Reyland.

On Witches.

She straightened her posture. Just as she'd been warned, this was a kind of trial. One of diplomacy.

"I'm honored by the offer, Your Majesty," Evy said. "But—"

"She's the Shaman Queen of Reyland," Celeste cut in, mortified. "And an Ascendant in the Hierarch Wars."

Talia's eyes narrowed into slits, as if trying to reframe what she was seeing. "Oh! Well then… Welcome, little Witch!" She laughed into her hand. "My mistake. Someone once told me Witches were hideous wildlings, but you're actually quite pretty."

She looked to the crowd of revelers and threw her hands up in the air. "I was confused!" They all burst into laughter.

Evy swallowed her frustration. Royen shifted uncomfortably behind her, and Zafir gave a rough, disapproving cough.

With a clumsy flick of her wrist, Talia raised her goblet, sloshing nectar over the rim. "Ascendants! Yes, yes, delightful. Enjoy the garden."

Zafir and Royen bowed respectfully. Evy dipped into a controlled curtsy, her composure intact despite the sting of pride burning faintly beneath her skin.

"I'm so sorry about her," Celeste said as she turned away and looped her arm through Evy's. "We're going inside now before she tries to hire you as a chambermaid or betroth me to an ancient Gnome. This way."

Wings twitching with restrained frustration, she led them away from the gathering.

Behind them, Queen Talia continued laughing, her attention returned to the Elf she had been flirting with.

Celeste escorted the Ascendants through the crystal halls of the palace, her usual sparkle dimmed just enough for Evy to notice.

After showing Royen and Zafir to their accommodations across the hall, she led Evy to her room. Celeste stalled in the doorway, hands fidgeting with a ribbon at her wrist.

Evy took in her surroundings. The chamber's walls were laced with flowering crystal vines. Furniture carved from pale wood hummed faintly with magic. Her focus shifted to Celeste, whose gaze flicked from mirror to ceiling to nowhere at all.

"Are you okay?" Evy asked gently.

Celeste smiled a little too quickly. "I mean, my mother just offered me up to a man who probably uses a cane carved from his late wife's femur and basically called me a walking womb, but sure! I'm thriving."

"Celeste..."

"Before I left for Ruitheon, she told me she chose me as the Ascendant instead of herself to show off her creation, and because she didn't want to miss the Summer Ball. She actually said that."

Evy pressed her lips together, unsure what to say. She had always assumed Celeste had prepared to become an Ascendant. It never occurred to her that Celeste might have been thrown into the trials the same way she was.

Celeste jumped back in, quickly changing the subject.

"But I'm not here to talk about that." She waved a hand. "I brought you something."

She crossed the room, opened the wardrobe, and pulled out a lavender-and-silver gown, the color of dusk and moonlight. The bodice was corset-style, with tulle drop sleeves connecting the edge of the bust to the back. The skirt fell from the waist in soft layers, the train trailing behind it. The fabric twinkled like stars, studded with crystals that winked in the light. Evy had never seen anything so gorgeous.

"I had this made for you." Celeste held it up with both hands. "I saw the design in a book before we parted from Zarokan and thought, 'That's her. That's Evy Lovejoy.' You *have* to wear it to the banquet."

Evy stepped closer, her voice soft. "It's beautiful."

"I know." Celeste smiled again, though it withered at the edges. "Look, I know Royen's probably going to win the Hierarch Wars. He's got everything lined up: the name, the schooling, the gauntlets, the… glower. But if anyone could beat him, it's probably you."

She looked at Evy. Really looked at her.

"And if you did," Celeste added, quieter, "maybe I could be your royal dress attendant in Ruitheon. Wouldn't that be something? You, running the realm. Me, your scandalous shadow, trailing behind in silk and drama. We could change everything."

Her voice wavered. She laughed to cover it.

"Not that it would ever happen," she said, brushing a curl behind her ear. "Mother would drag me back by my wings before I made it to the capital. Marry me off before I could even pack."

She hugged the gown to her chest for a moment, then set it gently on the edge of the bed.

Evy watched her. "Celeste—"

But Celeste was already halfway to the door. "Anyway." She

brightened just a bit too much. "Try it on later. If you don't wear it, I will."

She flashed a playful smile, desperate to stay intact, and slipped out before Evy could say another word.

Left in the silence, Evy turned toward the gown. It glimmered in the last of the sunlight.

She touched the fabric and thought not of the trials or the Procession, but of the girl who had just left her. Celeste carried her own burdens, separate from Evy's. She might have been raised in a gilded palace surrounded by precious jewels, but it didn't matter.

There was always something missing in everyone's lives.

Everyone had their hardships.

And Evy wasn't the only one learning how to face them.

TWENTY-FIVE

The Crystal Court ballroom was unlike anything Evy had ever seen.

Its vaulted glass ceiling had been enchanted to make it appear as though the half moon hung impossibly close overhead. It was so vivid, so luminous that she could trace the silver ridges of its craters. Its glow bathed the room in pale light, softening the sharp lines of crystal pillars and glass archways.

Evy stood near the entrance, smoothing the fabric of her gown for the fourth time.

She had worn the dress Celeste gave her. Refusing would have felt cruel after the quiet vulnerability with which Celeste had offered it.

When Irma helped her slip into it, Evy had stared at herself in the mirror, eyes wide in disbelief. The dress complemented her deep olive complexion, drawing out its gold undertones and blending seamlessly with the softness of her snowy waves. For a fleeting moment, she felt as if she had stepped straight from Planar Astra itself—like Reya descended into Lumesphere to attend this banquet.

Which was precisely the problem.

From the moment she entered the ballroom, heads turned. A cluster of Elven men stopped mid-toast to stare. An older Harpy woman nudged her companion and whispered behind a jeweled fan.

Evy paced through the crowd, keeping her chin level, just as Orianna had taught her. But she couldn't shake the feeling that she had miscalculated. She was supposed to blend in among the Ascendants, not outshine them.

She spotted Zafir almost immediately. He sat at a curved banquet table upon a raised podium, a goblet resting untouched before him. Queen Talia occupied the seat beside him—far too close. She leaned into him, one finger tracing idle circles along his arm. Her lips moved slowly as she tilted her head, her rosy curls spilling over her bare shoulders.

Zafir was as rigid as stone. When Talia's fingers grazed him again, he flinched and shifted his weight away, ever so subtly.

Evy considered intervening—already rehearsing an excuse to pull him away. But she had barely taken two steps before he abruptly rose from his seat. He muttered something to the Queen, gave a stiff bow, and disappeared into the crowd with surprising speed for someone his size.

Talia merely shrugged as she watched him go, then reached for his abandoned goblet.

Evy exhaled, relieved she hadn't entangled herself.

She scanned the ballroom again, searching for Celeste, but instead found Royen. He stood near one of the crystalline pillars, deep in conversation with a stocky Dwarf whose thick fingers turned a small metallic orb—the bow-and-arrow device—over and over in his palm.

Royen's hands moved quickly as he spoke, tracing invisible blueprints in the air. His eyes were alight in a way she had never seen before. It was strange to see him so animated—almost boyish, like during their conversation in Ashgate.

Girlish giggles caught her attention. Across the ballroom,

Celeste stood within a circle of young Sylphs, their laughter bright as she twirled for them. They fawned over her sparkling green tulle dress, fingers brushing its delicate layers.

As Evy started toward her, the color drained from Celeste's bronze skin.

Evy followed her gaze.

An older Sylph man stood near the banquet table speaking with Queen Talia. His beard was long and white, trailing nearly to his chest. His wings—unusually large for a Sylph, nearly the span of a Harpy's—seemed to weigh on him. They pulled his shoulders into a permanent hunch, and he leaned heavily on an ivory cane to compensate.

Talia embraced the man, pressing her cheek to his before pulling back.

Evy pressed a hand to her mouth to stifle a gasp. Was that Marquis Pearce? The man Queen Talia intended to betroth Celeste to?

Oh, poor Celeste. When Evy turned back, the circle of Sylphs remained, still chattering and laughing, but Celeste was gone.

Evy wanted to go find her, to make sure she was alright. However, the ballroom had other plans.

The moment she turned, a pair of Sylphs swept into her path, their fingers reaching for the crystals on her sleeves.

"Is this Fairy silk?" one gasped, tugging the fabric toward the light. "It's exquisite."

Before Evy could answer, another reveler appeared at her shoulder, stroking a strand of her hair between his fingers.

"Remarkable," he murmured, wine heavy on his breath. "Is it natural?"

The crowd pressed closer. Hands grazed her waist, her arm, her skirts. Voices layered over one another—compliments, questions, laughter. The ballroom seemed to shrink, bodies hemming her in on every side. Her spirits stirred restlessly, their agitated whispers rising and layering over the voices around her until she couldn't tell which sounds were inside her mind and which were outside it.

She forced a smile and dipped her head. "If you'll excuse me."

Evy slipped between two laughing Goblins and made for the nearest corridor. The ballroom noise dulled behind her with each step, the crystal walls muting the revelry into a distant hum.

She ducked into the first quiet chamber she found and shut the door behind her.

When she finally gathered herself, she glanced around to see where she had stumbled.

It appeared to be an art gallery.

The paintings lining the walls were gargantuan, framed in silver and crystal, each rendered in astonishing detail.

Evy wandered deeper into the gallery. She passed ancient forest landscapes, grand scenes from Virennese history, portraits of Ethereal royalty draped in jewels and furs. But as she neared the far wall, a particular collection drew her attention.

At first glance, the figures in these paintings looked like Elves. But the longer she studied them, the more she noticed the differences. Their ears were longer and thinner, tapering into fine points. Their hair was pale, and each figure was painted with radiance flowing from their skin. On each of their foreheads was an etching of the sun.

Like Lutharion Skye, the first Hierarch.

Footsteps echoed behind her.

Evy turned, suddenly afraid the revelers had found her and came to drag her back into the ballroom.

Zafir stood in the doorway, one hand braced against the frame. "Evy." He offered a tired smile. "Mind if I hide in here with you?"

She almost laughed. "Hiding from the Queen?"

He grimaced as he entered and shut the door behind him.

"Someone spread a rumor that my wife had died, and the Queen seized on it." He dragged a hand through his hair. "I feel terrible for avoiding her, but that woman has no concept of personal boundaries."

Zafir's wife had died? When?

Evy's ears burned as she realized she hadn't seen the Queen of Zarokan at the Infernal Citadel. She had heard whispers that the King and Queen were estranged, but there had never been a moment that felt right to ask about his personal life.

"I know what you're thinking," Zafir said, watching her. "You didn't see my wife because she doesn't live with us. She prefers to spend her time with her tribe." His mouth twitched. "Juleen and I don't see her much."

Evy lowered her eyes, unable to form the right words. "I'm sorry," she finally managed.

"Don't be." Zafir waved a hand, though his attention drifted past her. "Such is life, sometimes." After several seconds, he looked around the room. "What were you doing in here?"

Grateful for the shift, she gestured to the gallery. "I was just admiring the artwork."

He drifted toward the collection she had been studying and leaned closer, eyes widening with recognition.

"Lumiels," he said quietly. "Their fate was a tragic one." He stepped closer to study a portrait of a Lumiel warrior mid-stride, a spear of light gripped in his fist.

"I still can't believe their pride drove them to extinction." Evy folded her arms. "Is it true they took on a Hydra along the Virennese coast without the rest of the army?"

Zafir remained silent for a moment.

"Pride was part of it, yes." His voice dropped. "But in Zarokan, the story is told differently. At first, the Lumiels didn't choose to face the Hydra alone. They were maneuvered into it."

Evy frowned. "What do you mean?"

Zafir crossed his arms over his broad chest.

"The Lumiels held two thrones. The Virennese crown and, more often than not, the Hierarch's seat. They were the most powerful beings in Aeltheon, and for a long time, no one came close to challenging them in the Hierarch Wars." He paused, seeming to consider his next words carefully. "The Sylphs wanted Virenna. The Shifters wanted the Hierarch's throne. So they aligned."

He moved to a portrait of a Lumiel king painted in full regalia, a white crystal crown resting on his brow.

"Their numbers had already been dwindling by then, birthrates low," Zafir continued. "But they were still formidable. So the Council didn't challenge them outright. They devised a more clever plan instead. One that appealed to their pride."

Zafir's attention remained on the painted king. "The Council went behind the Hierarch and convinced the Lumiels in Virenna that it was their duty to protect the realm—with power said to have been gifted by the Gods themselves."

The shadow beneath his brows gave his gaze an ominous glow. "They rode out together. Every able-bodied Lumiel, even those within the Council, convinced it was their bloodline's destiny. The Hydra slaughtered them." His tone hardened. "A few months later, the women and children left behind died of a so-called disease. The Council claimed it was genetic. And the last Lumiel Hierarch died knowing his race would die out with him."

Evy tried to swallow, but her throat had gone dry.

"They sent fellow Councilors to their doom?" she asked.

"Even within a single governing body, there are fractures. I'm sure you've noticed."

Evy thought of Councilor Lilian Varos and her demotion for refusing to share the Council's hostility toward Witches.

"But still—the murder of an entire species, and no one intervened?"

Zafir rubbed his beard. "No one disagreed," he said at last.

"The realm had grown afraid of their power, and it bred resentment toward the Lumiels. When the Council found a way to remove them, the realm looked the other way."

The gallery felt colder. The painted Lumiels stared down from their frames—phantoms of their former glory.

"If you show them your full power, they'll panic."

Perhaps Orianna hadn't been speaking from theory, after all.

Zafir must have seen her expression change. "Of course, this is all hearsay," he said, tone softening. "Stories told around fires in Zarokan. The history books say the Lumiels' pride was their undoing. That's the official account."

Evy met his eyes.

A quiet understanding passed between them. No matter how he tried to comfort her, he didn't believe the official version. And after hearing it from him, Evy wasn't sure she did either.

If the Council could orchestrate the extinction of the Lumiels, what would they do to the Witches?

Evy tucked the story away beside Orianna's warnings, Lawrence's menacing smirk, and the vicious chants from the Children of Rui.

She had yet another reason to be cautious.

And another reason to wonder if acting with caution would be enough.

TWENTY-SIX

Yorik navigated through the dense forest of Virenna. Though the canopy blocked the moonlight and cloaked the path in darkness, bioluminescent flowers lit his way in pulsing hues of blue and violet.

He had slipped past Reyland's borders and migrated into Virenna earlier that day. The Bound Blades hadn't seen him. He hadn't allowed them to.

He had studied the rhythm of their patrols, memorized the blind spots along the outer ridges. And he had used the spell the Gods taught him. One that let him become completely invisible to the mortal eye.

His head still pounded from the aftermath of the spell. No matter. He was close to where he needed to be.

The Gods whispered ferociously, threading through his mind as he wound between the pale, silver-barked trees.

This way.

The voices surged again, and Yorik took a sharp right.

They led him deeper.

Left at the fork. Down the slope. Past the split tree.

Each whisper tugged like a tether.

And then, he heard it.

A soft, wet sound. Sniffling.

Yorik stilled and took a breath before creeping forward.

Across a shallow ridge, bathed in the soft silvery glow of a nearby pond, sat a girl.

A Sylph.

She perched on a smooth stone, face buried in her hands as quiet sobs shook her tall, slender frame. Her rather expensive-looking gown was muddied at the hem. A crown of pink curls spilled around her shoulders like wilted petals.

But it wasn't her grief that caught Yorik's attention.

It was the wings.

They curled behind her like a shroud, shifting between mist and crystal. They were angular and refractive. Light scattered through them with every tremble of her body, casting broken rainbows across the moss.

Yorik's smile widened. He had found her. Celeste DuVent, Princess of Virenna. She was exactly as the Gods had described. Just as he had seen in his visions.

He had found what he needed.

It was time to move forward with his plan. Yorik took a step forward. Then another.

He could feel raw, unfiltered power rolling off her wings. The kind of power that only comes around once in a lifetime.

His foot snagged a twig, and the sound cracked like lightning.

The girl's head jerked up.

Before he could glimpse her face, she vanished into the air.

Yorik's head snapped upward.

There she was, suspended above the water, wings flared wide and radiant. The pond below mirrored her flight, iridescent fractals rippling across its surface.

"By the Gods," Yorik muttered.

The voices whispered urgently, but Yorik didn't notice them. He was lost in her silhouette.

"Who's there?" she called out. He caught a sliver of fear in her tone.

Yorik slowly stepped into the clearing, letting the soft green light from the glowing flora catch the edge of his face.

Celeste's body stayed tense, wings still fluttering above the pond, but her eyes softened.

"You're a Witch," she said. "Why are you all the way in Virenna? I don't remember you being in Evy's party."

Yorik blinked rapidly, feigning disorientation.

"I don't know," he said, making his voice sound hoarse. "I-I don't remember how I got here. I was just..." He rubbed the back of his neck, gaze darting to the side. "My mother's been ill. I was picking herbs by the riverbank, and then— I must've wandered too far."

He startled. "Wait. Did you say Virenna?"

She nodded.

He scrunched his face, attempting an expression of panic.

"I'm in Virenna?" He stepped back half a pace. "No, no, no. I wasn't even near the boundary. Gods, if I'm caught..." He pressed a hand to his mouth. "I'll be hanged. I didn't mean to cross, I swear, I wasn't trying to be here."

His shoulders slumped.

"Please don't tell anyone. I just need to get home."

He gathered tears in his eyes.

Celeste hovered a little closer. "Do you think you were enchanted?"

"Maybe."

He let a tremor ride his voice. "I remember a woman. Or something like one. She had butterfly wings. She was glowing and waved at me. I don't even know if she was real."

As he spoke, his fingers curled under his sleeve, initiating the summoning.

A soul, long bent to his will, twisted silently from the veil. Yorik shaped it into a vaguely feminine form, with delicate limbs and gossamer wings.

An otherworldly giggle echoed through the clearing.

The illusion materialized into existence beyond the far side of the pond. It hovered, pulsing with a faint bluish light, then darted between the trees, vanishing into the fog with a final laugh.

"Damn Fairies," Celeste said through gritted teeth.

Yorik kept his expression dazed, feigning confusion, hiding the pain that prickled through his fingers from the spell. "So I wasn't dreaming?"

She rubbed her temple. "No. You were probably enchanted. They do that sometimes. Especially to"—her gaze traveled slowly from his boots to his face—"handsome men."

A slow smile tugged at Yorik's lips.

She flushed, caught off guard. "Don't let it go to your head. It's probably just your cheekbones." She rolled her emerald eyes, but the hint of a smile betrayed her amusement.

With a soft rustle, she fluttered down, then folded her wings as she landed gracefully beside him.

"I'll escort you back to the Reylandic border." She brushed a strand of rose-colored hair behind her ear. "If someone catches you without a permit, they'll assume the worst. And since this mess was clearly an Ethereal's fault, I'll make sure you're protected."

Yorik looked at her with practiced innocence. "You'd really do that for me?"

She shrugged. "You were enchanted. It wouldn't be fair to punish you for that."

They started walking.

Celeste was a step ahead, leading the way.

"I'm Herald, by the way," he said. He faked the name so Celeste wouldn't ask Evy about him and expose his presence here. But he wasn't entirely dishonest. After all, he was the Herald of Chaos.

"I'm..." She paused. "I'm Rose."

She was lying, of course. He knew her name. She could pretend all she wanted, but she couldn't hide from him.

"Thank you, Rose." He played along anyway. "For not letting me hang."

She smiled. "Don't thank me yet. You've still got a ways to go."

They walked beneath the arching trees in silence, their steps muffled by the mossy earth. Fireflies drifted between branches, pulsing softly.

Yorik picked up his pace to walk beside her. "You seemed upset earlier." His voice was gentle but laced with just enough concern to sound sincere. "I didn't mean to intrude."

"You didn't." She cast him a sidelong glance. "You just happened to catch me running away from my engagement party."

"Oh. Should I apologize?" he asked sheepishly. "Won't you get in trouble for escorting a strange man through the woods when you're, you know... spoken for?"

She snorted. "I'm not spoken for. And I don't plan to be. Not to someone I don't love."

Yorik hummed in mock relief. "That's good to hear. I'd hate to think I was getting my savior into trouble." His mouth stretched into a roguish grin. "You've rescued me. I suppose that makes me the helpless damsel. How humiliating."

A soft burst of amusement slipped from Celeste. "Are we going to fall in love while I carry you to my castle, my sweet damsel?"

Yorik slowed.

"Only if we get to live happily ever after."

Celeste held his gaze a moment longer before turning away, her cheeks rosy. They walked on in silence.

Yorik studied the gentle slope of her shoulders. She was a hopeless romantic. He heard it in the softness of her voice when she spoke of love, in the bitterness folded behind her tone.

And he planned to use that against her.

He tugged on the pulse of darkness coursing through his veins. A thread of shadow curled from his fingertips and grazed the edge of her wing before dissolving against her skin.

Goose bumps rose on her skin as she shivered, and she looked around as if trying to find the source of the chill, then shrugged and moved on.

She didn't see that it came from him.

Good.

A sharp pain split through his chest. He swallowed the bloodied cough before it reached his throat, tasting iron.

The seed of the curse was planted.

"I get it, you know," he said, tongue coated in blood. "My mother's the same. Always dragging village girls into the cottage, pouring tea like it's a bride price. Says I'm too picky, and I'll die alone if I don't get it together."

That earned a laugh. Celeste turned toward him, expression brightening with delight.

Then she hesitated.

It would start small, an attraction like the one he saw in her eyes now. Soon it would engulf her entirely.

The pain returned to his chest, beads of sweat tracing down his jaw. He would pay dearly for this curse, but for now he had to endure the discomfort with all the strength he could muster.

"I must ask." Celeste's gaze traced his tall frame. "Why isn't a man like you already taken?"

"Why aren't *you*? A girl as breathtaking as you should be drowning in suitors."

She brushed a strand of hair behind her ear. "There were suitors. Just none worth the trouble."

"My sincerest apologies for speaking out of turn." His attention darted to her wings. "I can't help but speak honestly when I'm faced with something extraordinary."

"It's okay." Celeste's gaze dropped. "I appreciate your honesty. It's refreshing. But you still haven't answered my question. Why is someone like you not already taken?"

Yorik looked up at the dense canopy above. "Maybe I haven't met someone who truly stole my heart. Maybe I believe that kind of thing is worth waiting for. Like finding the perfect bloom in the garden."

He dropped his gaze to meet hers. "The one I'd clip and take home. A *rose* like no other. One I'd preserve in a jar and keep close. Forever."

Celeste didn't look away.

Yorik continued, "I think maybe you understand me in that."

Celeste nodded. "I guess I do. I've decided I won't give my heart to anyone unless they steal it."

His voice dropped, smooth as velvet. "I envy the thief."

TWENTY-SEVEN

The carriage rumbled westward, its wheels crunching over gravel. Three days since they'd left Virenna, and the forest had long since faded behind them. Ahead lay the foggy, rolling highlands of Theribane.

Evy sat beside Celeste, who traced idle hearts in the window's condensation. She couldn't help but notice the dark circles under Celeste's eyes, as if she hadn't been sleeping. But every time Evy asked if she was alright, she laughed and insisted she was fine—that she had avoided getting engaged to an old relic a few days ago, so she was more than fine.

Opposite them sat Zafir, half-dozing, and Royen, statuesque. He hadn't looked at her once since they left Zarokan, and he avoided her completely during the banquet in Virenna, always finding an excuse to be on the opposite side of the room.

It shouldn't have bothered her.

But it did.

"The Procession route doesn't make much sense," Zafir grumbled, breaking the silence. "Reyland sits just beyond Virenna's northern edge. It would've been the logical next stop."

Royen cast the Djinn a sidelong glance. "This path has been

followed for centuries: Zarokan first, then Virenna, then west to Theribane, before concluding in Ruitheon. My uncle insisted we follow Virenna to honor tradition."

"Stars forbid Theribane have to wait a few extra days for their turn," Celeste said, twirling a curl around her finger.

"I suspect the Council pushed for it too," Royen added. "Just to keep the second trial on schedule."

Celeste sighed. "Shame we have to skip the Ascendant's Ball to continue with the Procession. It would've happened after the second trial, right? I heard it's quite the party."

Evy arched a brow.

"Not that it won't be fun in Reyland." Celeste quickly shifted her tone. "I'm actually very excited to visit. To meet with some of the... people there."

"I can't wait," Evy said. She sighed heavily. "If I'm honest, I kind of miss home."

Royen glanced her way, his mouth set in a hard line. Maybe he saw homesickness as a kind of weakness.

Evy shrugged and turned back to the window.

Celeste leaned forward slightly. "Royen, what's Theribane like? Is Luxhaven as grand as they say?"

"It's fine."

After the first trial and then in Zarokan, Royen had softened. But now, he was stone again, back to his practiced aloofness.

Evy told herself it shouldn't matter. They were rivals in the Hierarch Wars. But some small, foolish part of her had begun to believe in the possibility of friendship. And a diplomatic relationship that might benefit them both.

If Royen became Hierarch, maybe their alliance would change circumstances for Witches.

Perhaps that was part of her purpose during the trials. Her true mission. So she had to try. Maybe she could break through to him again.

"Is it cold there?" Evy asked, folding her hands in her lap.

"It can be."

She turned back toward the window and sighed, the silence deflating her.

A sudden panicked shout cracked the air.

Then another cry, closer this time.

The carriage lurched to a stop so violently that Celeste slammed into Evy's shoulder and Zafir's boot collided with the opposite wall.

Royen flung the door open and leaped out before the wheels had fully stopped.

"What was that?" Evy asked.

The driver shouted, then screamed.

Zafir extended an arm. "Stay behind me."

But Evy jumped out, skirts hiked, energy bristling along her skin as she summoned her spirits.

The guards shouted in disarray, swords drawn but swinging wildly into the open air.

They were being attacked. Evy searched for the assailant, her pulse thudding painfully.

But there was nothing there.

"I don't see it!" Zafir shouted.

"Neither do I," Royen said, scanning the trees.

Celeste hovered slightly above the ground, wind swirling around her like a protective storm. "Is it hiding?"

Evy's spirits recoiled in unison, pressing inward against her like animals retreating from danger.

A guard was lifted off his feet, seemingly by nothing, and flung into a tree with bone-crunching force.

"Evy?" Irma called from one of the servant's carriages down the road. Her head stuck out the window, eyes wide with fear.

"Stay inside!" Evy yelled. "Whatever you do, don't come out!"

The injured guard staggered, clutching his skull. "My head!" he cried. "Stay out of my head!"

His eyes flashed red.

Then, with a sharp, inhuman cry, he turned his blade on himself and drove it into his own throat. Blood sprayed in the golden light of the day.

Evy gagged, bile rising as pure horror overtook her.

Movement between the trees caught her attention. Mist curled into a large and monstrous outline—a grotesque distortion of a body coalescing with dark vapor.

She'd seen one before in the Reylandic borderlands. That one had been caught in a trap by the Bound Blades. It was much smaller than this creature.

"Draemor," she whispered. Royen's brows drew in confusion.

"Draemor!" she shouted louder. "It's a Draemor!"

Evy squinted, trying to track its movement. The Draemor could cloak themselves, but her shamanistic powers let her glimpse their aura, just enough to follow.

"I can see it," she said. "It's invisible, but it can't hide from me."

Zafir was already moving toward the next fallen guard, flaming blades drawn. "Where?"

"There." She pointed. "By the oak, two strides left—"

Royen's arrow was nocked and fired before she finished. It passed clean through empty space.

Wisps of dark mist rippled with every step the creature took. The others couldn't see it, and they couldn't fight what they couldn't see.

Evy's fingers twitched at her sides. She could see the Draemor enough to strike it down herself. Within Theribane's borders, where the mana grid ran nearly as thick as Ruitheon's, her spirits were buzzing with power. A single blast of concentrated light magic would end this.

But that would expose *her*. Everyone around Evy would see a Witch take down a Draemor alone.

She bit her nail, heart hammering. Her spirits pressed

against her will. The fear from moments ago had burned away, replaced by restlessness, urging her to act.

Let's end it.

What are you waiting for?

"Evy?" Royen's voice cut through the noise. His eyes were sharp, scanning the empty air where she had pointed. "Where is it? We need to get this thing before it kills us all."

She flinched. The creature was heading toward them. They were running out of time.

A flash of memory. She and Celeste walking disguised through the markets of Ruitheon. Their combined magic that cooled the carriage in Zarokan.

"Celeste," she said quickly. "If I channel a light spirit, can you cast an illusion spell on it? Maybe we can neutralize the Draemor's invisibility."

Celeste's face lit with understanding. "Blend light with refracted glamour. I think I can manage that."

Evy extended her hand and summoned a spirit of light. It hovered just above her skin, illuminating her palm.

Celeste moved beside her and lifted her hand as she muttered an incantation. Thin green wisps flowed through her fingers, weaving into the spirit's glow.

The magic swelled.

Evy brought her hands together, cradling the spell. It pulsed with quiet force as light and illusion merged. She could feel the power thrumming in her bones.

Evy looked ahead as the Draemor closed in on them. She gave Celeste a nod, and together they cast the spell forward.

The air cracked. Light bent across the clearing and struck the dark mist. It hissed as the light met its skin. Steam rose where the magic touched it, weakening it.

The Draemor was revealed in full.

It towered nearly twice a man's height, its limbs grotesquely elongated, bent at unnatural angles. Gray skin hung in loose, rotting folds, slick with decay and carved open by deep gashes that pulsed with a sickly red glow. Its claws twitched as it moved, dragging through the dirt.

Its face was wrong.

A snarling mouth split high into one cheek, teeth like bone shards. One bulging eye rolled in its socket; the other had caved in, leaking dark fluid. It continued to convulse in short, sick bursts.

"Oh, no, no, no." Celeste recoiled at the sight of the creature. "There isn't a makeover spell in existence that could salvage that… that *thing*."

Zafir summoned a column of fire from his hands and hurled it. The Draemor screamed as the fire struck it, its voice a metallic shriek.

It charged.

A wild flurry of limbs and teeth launched at Zafir. He barely dodged the attack.

Royen fired again and again. Arrows struck deep but didn't slow it. The Draemor turned toward him, its protruding eye locking onto its next target.

"Royen!" Evy shouted. "Watch out!"

A blur of steel dropped from the trees.

Leo landed blade first, carving a clean line across the Draemor's back. His sword, powered by fire and earth spirits, burned like magma.

Dark blood gushed from where the blade struck.

The Draemor slashed wildly, but Leo was faster. He struck again, dismembering the creature's arm.

Leo slammed his palm to the ground. Molten rock erupted and trapped the Draemor in lava.

Royen fired an arrow through its jaw. Zafir's fire poured into the wound in its back.

The creature shrieked and went limp, smoke rising from its twisted form.

Zafir approached.

"Wait," Evy said. "It's not dead. Just incapacitated. You can't kill a Draemor, not truly."

For a moment, only ragged breaths filled the air.

The Ruithean paladins and guards gathered around the Draemor but kept their distance as they studied the creature.

Then they all broke into an argument.

"We need to chain it and send it to the Blighted Caves!"

"No cart can hold that—"

"We'll need mana restraints!"

"Enough!" Leo raised a hand. "You're wasting time arguing!"

Evy stepped forward. "There might be another option."

All eyes turned to her.

"The Draemor don't just appear. They need portals. If we find the one it came through, I can send it back to Hollowrift before it regains strength."

A few guards scoffed. "We can't take that risk. The Blighted Caves are secure—"

"If there's an open gate nearby," Leo cut in, "then the area's compromised. Let her check."

Zafir nodded. "Let's move."

They spread out through the trees.

"Here! Found something!" a guard called.

They rushed to join him in a clearing.

The portal floated between two oak trees. On the other side, a pitch-black sky stretched above a churning gray ocean, its waves heaving in a restless wind.

Celeste stepped forward, wide-eyed. "Is that… a portal?" She reached her hand out. "I've never seen one in person."

"Don't get too close," Evy said sharply.

"Why?"

"Hollowrift is a nexus where spirits and souls move between worlds. Some of those worlds may not have magic." Evy gently maneuvered Celeste away. "One wrong step and you could lose your power… or your way."

She gave Linius Wells a silent thank-you for recording his adventures. For his warnings.

Celeste stepped back and shivered. "Terrifying."

Zafir stepped past them, dragging the Draemor's limp body. With one solid heave, he flung it through the portal.

Evy lifted her hand. Spirits swirled around her, converging on her outstretched palm.

The portal shuddered as the air thickened. The rift began to collapse, threads of its strange light drawing inward like stitches.

One last flash, and the portal was gone. Evy's bones were weary beyond imagination. Her boots felt weighted with lead, and all she wanted was to retreat to the carriage and rest.

A hand caught her elbow, offering support.

"Evalene."

Royen stood behind her. The others had already started moving back toward the road, but he hadn't followed.

"Are you alright?" His other hand lifted toward her shoulder.

Evy recoiled before he could touch her again. "Y-yes. Of course I am." Blood rushed to the tip of her ears as she moved to meet with the others.

Why had she reacted so strangely to a simple act of kindness?

Or maybe it wasn't the gesture that mattered, but who it came from. She was certain she wouldn't have recoiled from Celeste's touch. Or even Zafir's.

But why? Cold as he could be, Royen was still a gentleman. A noble. He had likely been raised to act that way.

She needed to control her reactions before he mistook her behavior for disinterest in a diplomatic alliance.

"Wait."

His voice stopped her mid-step. "Can I speak with you?"

Evy faced him. His arms were crossed, one foot tapping impatiently against the ground.

He waited until the last of the guards had moved out of earshot.

"During the fight," he said, "you could see the Draemor, but you didn't attack it."

Her gaze immediately dropped to the ground.

"I revealed it."

"I watched you, Evalene. You were ready to attack. I saw it in your hands. And then you stopped yourself."

Evy opened her mouth, then closed it again, unsure how to respond.

"People died." His voice dropped. "*We* could have died. And you stood there."

She winced, the words hitting her like a slap to the face.

Because he wasn't wrong.

She had seen it. She could have ended the fight sooner. But while she hesitated, she had risked everyone's lives.

"In Zarokan, I knew you were holding back," Royen said. "I thought it was a form of diplomacy. That maybe you were trying not to offend me." He shook his head. "But this wasn't a spar. So what is it? What are you so afraid of?"

Evy swallowed against the lump in her throat.

For a moment, she thought about telling him everything. About Orianna's warnings. About the look on Arch Councilor Lawrence's face when she placed second. About how the Council likely had a part in the extinction of Lumiels and how they might easily do the same to the Witches if she stepped out of line.

But he was a Veyn. How could he bear the truth that he had been born into power, destined to claim it—with or without Lawrence's advantages? The ascension to power had never been a fair fight, at least not for certain groups. Royen would be disappointed to learn that even in wanting to run a fair race, he had been running alongside those in shackles.

"You wouldn't understand," she said.

Royen was silent for several seconds.

"If it's about restraint," he said quietly, "then I know a lot more than you could ever imagine."

He turned and walked away, leaving Evy in the stillness, alone with her weary bones and weighted conscience.

TWENTY-EIGHT

Celeste hung on to Evy's arm as the carriage hobbled forward. "I can't believe we'll have to go into the Blighted Caves for the third trial when it's filled with those horrendous monsters," she said, resting her cheek on Evy's head. "Why did they have to be *so* ugly? They make Sand Striders look adorable."

Zafir nodded slowly, arms crossed, his eyes closed in thought. "I have a very bad feeling about it, if I'm being honest. Fighting one Draemor was hard enough."

"It should be quite an easy task for Evalene," Royen muttered. Evy didn't think he'd meant for her to hear.

She glared at Royen and patted Celeste's hand. "Well, we still have to get through the second trial," she said, trying to divert the conversation. "And the Procession."

She offered Zafir a faint smile. "From what I've heard, the Draemor in the Blighted Caves are supposed to be weakened. I'm sure we'll all make it through just fine."

"Evalene's right," Royen said. His voice was quieter than usual. "There's no point worrying about it now. Besides, being home in Theribane will be a trial in itself."

He leaned slightly against the window, abandoning his usual rigid posture. He'd been silent for the past three days since the Draemor attack, clearly as shaken as the rest of them, though he'd done his best to hide it.

Then, unexpectedly, he looked at Evy.

His lips lifted in a shy smile.

It was small, but the way his hazel eyes glistened brought warmth to the gesture. Evy instinctively returned it.

For a heartbeat, the carriage seemed to go still. She wasn't sure what surprised her more—Royen's genuine, caring smile or the way it knocked the air from her lungs. Had he managed to let go of his prior frustration with her?

Celeste noticed too. Her gaze switched between them with open curiosity, but for once, she said nothing.

The moment passed quickly.

Royen shifted forward and said, "We're approaching Luxhaven now."

Evy leaned closer to the window to better observe the unfolding cityscape ahead.

Soon they entered the city. Horse-drawn carriages and mana-powered trams trundled past each other in a chaotic ballet. Towering redbrick buildings lined the paved streets, their facades accented with ornate wrought iron balconies and tall bay windows. Elaborately dressed citizens crossed wide intersections: lace gloves, cravats, layered satin gowns, and embroidered waistcoats on full display as if the entire city had dressed for a never-ending ball.

The air smelled of baked sweets and perfume, and the occasional spiral of coal smoke from a factory lifted into the sky.

Evy watched as a woman wearing a high-necked maroon gown giggled beside her companion. With a teasing glint in his eye, her partner stepped back.

And transformed.

One moment, he was a man in a silk cravat and emerald

waistcoat, and the next, a sleek brown stallion pawing at the cobblestones. The woman gathered her skirts and climbed onto his back. They galloped off between the alleys.

Celeste gaped. "Is that how they flirt here?"

Royen stayed focused on the window. "It's how they show off."

He paused, then added, "Animal forms are inherited. Passed down through bloodlines. The rarer or stronger the form, the more pride it brings a family."

"So turning into a horse is considered impressive?" Evy asked.

Royen gave a faint shrug. "Better than a squirrel."

She stifled a laugh. Royen's lips quirked, satisfied, it seemed, that Evy had caught on to his joke.

As they continued, Evy observed the smooth, paved roads. Thick, glowing bands of mana snaked through the ground, threading into and powering clock towers, lamps, glowing store signs, horseless carriages, and numerous other contraptions.

Her thoughts drifted to Moonveil. To its crumbling bridges and worn lanterns. To the way the Witches had to conserve and ration mana just to light their hearths or perform a healing spell.

If they had even a quarter of the power Luxhaven had, what would they be able to achieve?

The carriage jerked as they rolled off the cobbled path and onto gravel. The scenery changed around them as tall buildings gave way to rolling countryside, hills dotted with orchards and farmland. Shifters in animal form tilled the fields, shifting effortlessly between man and beast.

Then the land crested, and the sea came into view.

Perched on the cliff above the churning water stood Veyn Manor.

Its dark stone walls loomed against the pale sky, rising like a fortress from the cliff's edge. The sea pounded the rocks below with a constant roar, and the scent of salt filled the air.

They approached a tall iron guard tower. A man in the top compartment waved a hand, and with a hiss of pressure and the heavy clatter of chains, a drawbridge began to descend over the wide moat that encircled the manor.

The carriage crossed the bridge slowly, iron grating noisily under the wheels. They passed beneath the high stone archway and emerged onto the manor grounds.

Beyond the gates stretched a vast courtyard, manicured to geometric perfection. Polished paths split the grounds like measured grids on a map, bordered by hedges trimmed into flawless angles. There wasn't a petal or leaf out of place.

They came to a halt. Before them stood an immense manor house, stately and symmetrical, its limestone facade pale as moonlight. Ivy clung to its outer walls, climbing around tall, multi-paned windows. Twin towers flanked the main structure, capped with steep slate roofs. Delicate wrought iron balconies overlooked the courtyard. A shiver ran down Evy's spine. Though the manor was just as grand as the Crystal Court, she couldn't shake the cold, unfeeling presence of the estate.

Above the main entrance, the Veyn crest was carved into the stone—a wolf, a panther, and a hawk entwined. An expansive marble staircase unfurled from the front terrace like the hem of a gown, descending to a wide landing where three finely dressed nobles and a row of staff already stood waiting.

The tallest man, clad in a high-collared deep navy velvet coat embroidered with silver vines, stepped forward as Evy and her companions filed out of the carriage. His angular jaw was set tight, and his pale blond hair was swept back, not a strand out of line.

"Welcome to Theribane," he said. "I am Lord Aldrich Veyn, steward of this house and Lord of the domain."

His voice carried the clipped refinement of nobility, and

though he addressed all of them together, his hazel eyes stopped cold when they met Evy's. The faint lines at the corners of his mouth deepened with his scowl.

He moved on, gesturing to the man beside him. Slightly younger, with similar blond features but a softer bearing, tired hazel eyes, and a mouth set in a permanent line of disinterest.

"My younger brother," Aldrich said, "Mister Dominic Veyn."

Dominic stepped forward and addressed Royen directly. "Son."

Royen nodded back. "Father."

Dominic motioned toward a woman who walked up to stand next to him. Her rich brown curls were pinned into a precise coiffure, her sharp features complemented by the elegance of her attire. She wore an elaborate forest-green gown, and her jewelry glittered with rubies. Her blue eyes skimmed over the group with aristocratic detachment.

"My wife, Mistress Cara Ashcroft Veyn," Dominic said, his voice echoing the same clipped monotone as the Lord of Theribane.

Cara nodded at the Ascendants, a sneer-like smile plastered on her face.

Ashcroft? Evy thought. *Isn't there a Councilor of Theribane named Ashcroft?*

Suddenly, all three hosts fixated on Evy, their eyes boring into her. Her heart thumped harder as frowns carved upon their faces. It was obvious they didn't want her here. To them, she was likely a disease, ready to taint their stately manor. At that very moment, Evy felt as though she were a mouse standing in front of three very bored cats, ready to rip her apart for fun.

A soft creak of wheels on stone broke the tension in the courtyard. From a side entrance near the portico came a boy seated in a cushioned chair with large iron wheels. The contraption was enchanted, powered by mana, with a lever on one armrest that guided its motion.

He descended a shallow ramp.

Sunlight caught his golden-blond hair, casting it in warm halos. Dressed in a pale cream coat trimmed with gold embroidery and a soft maroon cravat, he looked like a prince out of a storybook. His hazel eyes sparkled as they landed on Royen, and his face lit up with an uncontainable smile.

"Royen!" he called cheerfully.

Royen's composure cracked. He stepped forward without hesitation, a smile tugging at the edges of his mouth. "Cousin. I didn't know you'd be out here to greet us."

"I had to see for myself and make sure you were alive." The boy lifted his brows. "You hadn't written in weeks. I was starting to think a Sand Strider had eaten you—"

He paused, tapping his chin. "Do Sand Striders eat people?"

He gave Royen a mock-serious look, then added, "Also, I had to escape Lawrence. He arrived a few days ago and keeps cornering me to talk politics. You know I don't talk politics."

Marq rolled up closer to his cousin, a conspiratorial glint in his eyes. "So? Was Zarokan full of shirtless Djinn warriors? Did the Undines flirt? Did you flirt? Please say yes." He leaned forward and pretended to whisper. "Give me something to live for in this mansion of endless gloom."

Royen stifled a laugh and cast a sideways glance at Evy.

A disapproving cough from Lord Aldrich demanded their attention.

Marq straightened ever so slightly.

"May I introduce my son," Aldrich said to the Ascendants, "Marq Veyn."

"The one and only." Marq brought two fingers to his temple and formed a salute.

Evy lifted a hand to her mouth, a grin breaking through before she could stop it. For a Veyn, Marq's presence felt strikingly different from the rest of his family, like sunlight piercing through a misty, gray morning. She understood at once why Royen was so fond of him.

Royen faced the group. "His proper title is Marq Veyn, the *Young Lord* of Theribane."

Aldrich glowered.

Royen's gaze dropped. The proud set of his shoulders wilted.

Aldrich returned his cool, detached expression as he addressed the group. "Ascendants, you may take the afternoon to rest. Dinner will be held in your honor this evening."

The household staff guided them into the manor.

Evy could only imagine what it was like to grow up in this hollow estate.

Even in the cold halls of the Reyani Temple, she was never without warmth.

The grandeur of Veyn Manor loomed around her when she stepped inside. Despite the glittering chandeliers and sculpted arches, it felt like stepping into the belly of an unfeeling monster.

TWENTY-NINE

Three chandeliers made of pure diamond hung like inverted gardens above a banquet table large enough to seat a small battalion. The ceilings arched high with painted frescos of winged beasts and crowned figures. Velvet drapes framed tall windows, and gilded statues stood in alcoves, watching silently like sentinels. Every surface gleamed, polished and perfect, and Evy imagined it was all impossibly expensive.

They were on the eleventh course.

Evy stared down at her plate. A delicate tower of cucumber ribbons and slivers of pink salmon rested on a wafer-thin cracker she was fairly sure had gold dust on it.

Her stomach protested. She was far too full to take another bite, but the idea of not finishing it, especially in front of the Veyns, made her break into a light sweat.

She sat a little straighter and carefully sliced a corner from the artful arrangement.

To her left, Royen sat, posture rigid as he took small sips of wine. Beside him was Marq, far more relaxed, occasionally nudging Royen under the table and whispering comments that made him suppress the tiniest smirk.

Across the table were the true wolves in the room: Lord Aldrich, Dominic, and Councilor Lawrence, along with several other impeccably dressed guests, all bearing the sharp cheekbones and cold smiles of the Shifter elite. Cara sat to her immediate right, her chair angled away as if trying to distance herself from Evy as much as possible.

The women glittered in jeweled gowns. The men wore tailored black coats with silver pins shaped like various beasts, signs of their houses. Their expressions hovered between idle curiosity and disdain.

Evy felt like a misplaced ink blot in a masterpiece painting.

She wished she'd been seated closer to Celeste and Zafir, who occupied the far end of the table. Celeste was chatting animatedly with one of the serving staff, enchanted by the silver-laced embroidery on their collar, while Zafir looked like he was planning a quiet escape with each passing course.

Evy lifted her fork, steeling herself to force down one more bite when a soft giggle sliced through the air.

She looked up.

Across the table, seated beside Lawrence, was a striking young woman, her bright green eyes watching Evy with thinly veiled amusement. Strands of copper ringlets slipped loose from her tidy updo, curling softly over one shoulder. Her features were exquisite, with high cheekbones, porcelain skin, and lips painted the softest shade of rose.

"I must apologize," she said with a wave of her gloved hand. Her gown shimmered with opalescent beadwork, the sheer sleeves drifting like mist when she moved. "It's just… I've never seen someone as petite as you eat more than five or six courses. Do they not feed you in Reyland?"

The silence that followed was as sharp as a blade.

Lawrence, seated beside her, offered a light chuckle. "Daphne," he said in a gently scolding tone, though the glint in his eyes betrayed amusement. "I'm sure Miss Lovejoy will forgive my daughter's lack of decorum. Won't you, Shaman Queen?"

Evy set down her fork, her fingers stiff. She could feel eyes turning toward her. But she lifted her chin and kept her voice even.

"I hope you'll excuse my poor manners, Lady Daphne." Evy folded her hands gently in her lap. "Where I come from, it's considered rude to refuse food that's been graciously served." She glanced down at her plate before continuing, "Reyland doesn't have the same food supplies as the other domains. Without a strong mana grid, our lands are harder to cultivate, and many of our people go hungry. We do what we can with what we have."

She looked up again, offering a polite, composed smile. "And we tend to be grateful for it."

Daphne ran a finger along the rim of her glass. "Oh, that must be terribly difficult. I truly can't imagine. Given what I've heard about Reyland, I wasn't expecting much." Her gaze moved over Evy. "But I did hope the Shaman Queen might manage something… decent to wear. Still, poverty is what it is, and to no fault of yours."

A few of the surrounding guests chuckled behind their wine glasses.

Evy's lavender silk gown was the finest Reyland had to offer. Magister Orianna had helped her choose it, and it had made her feel beautiful. But here, among the glittering Shifters in gowns threaded with gemstones and silks enchanted to shine like stars, she looked plain.

Evy sat up straighter and reached for her glass to keep her hands from trembling.

Before the silence could stretch further, Royen cut in. "I think Queen Evalene looks lovely." He gave her a sidelong glance, and blood ran to her face. She kept her head down, focusing on her plate before anyone noticed the flush.

“Not everyone needs embroidery and jewels to make an impression,” he continued. “Some people manage it with nothing more than being themselves.”

He added with a faint, sardonic smile, “Though I suppose that’s a kind of beauty you wouldn’t be familiar with, Lady Daphne.”

Daphne’s painted lips fell.

She turned toward Marq. “Are you going to let your cousin speak to your betrothed like that?”

Marq, unbothered, stabbed a piece of salmon with his fork. “Didn’t realize I was supposed to start policing compliments. Or fashion. Though if I do, I’d have to fine you for that lace monstrosity you wore the other day.”

Daphne went speechless. All she managed was a pout before huffing and turning her attention pointedly back to her plate.

“Also,” Marq continued, “Lawrence, why are you here? Don’t you have political conspiring to do in Ruitheon?”

“I’m here by personal invitation from your father. I couldn’t refuse.”

“A shame,” Marq said, taking a generous bite of food.

Evy stifled a laugh. Then her face dropped as she caught the scowl Lawrence directed at her.

As the eleventh course was cleared, silver trays were whisked away and replaced with delicate plates bearing glossy chocolate truffles. Cara Veyn’s high voice rang through the chatter.

“Royen, how could you be so cruel to Lady Daphne? Her family has stood beside ours for generations.” Her gaze settled coldly on Evy. “She was trying to be sympathetic.”

Royen let out a short laugh. “Well then, it seems Lady Daphne may need to go back to her governess and get a proper lesson on manners.”

Daphne crossed her arms.

Dominic Veyn let out a loud, humorless laugh and raised his crystal glass.

"Oh, come now," he drawled, his slur betraying just how deep into the wine he'd gone. "Daphne wasn't wrong. It's no mystery that Reyland's a wasteland. You're not offended, are you, *Miss* Lovejoy?" He waved his glass lazily in her direction. "Even you must admit, the pigs in Theribane live better than you do."

Evy's fingers tightened around her napkin.

"With respect, Mister Veyn," she said through gritted teeth, "may I ask what you know of Reyland and how we live?"

Dominic snorted. "I know it was generous of Aeltheon to let a bunch of *Gaians* plant their feet and call it a domain." He swirled the wine in his glass. "Letting you lot live. I thought it rather charitable, honestly." He leaned back in his chair, his voice laced with venom. "And what did the Witches do with that mercy? Turned fertile soil into a bog of starving villages and ghost-worshipping lunatics."

"Father." Royen set down his fork with a soft *clink*, but he said nothing more.

"Nice enough to let us live?" Evy repeated. She knew she should have stayed silent. She should have smiled and let it pass, like every other insult and jibe thrown her way that evening. But she could feel the cracks in her patience widening. "The Witches live, but barely."

The fine linen of her napkin bunched in her grip. "We survive in a domain intentionally cut off from the rest of Aeltheon. Our mana is the weakest by design. We're bound to our land, barred from leaving without written permission, as though we're criminals by birth. Our children grow up knowing hunger, our elders work themselves to death for crops that can barely feed their families.

"Reyland wasn't granted to us out of kindness. We were exiled there. And still, we endure. We're grateful for the gift bestowed by Goddess Reya. Grateful, because she saw us as worthy of survival."

Not a single breath stirred as Evy's voice faded, leaving behind a thick cloud of suffocating tension.

Waitstaff emerged, and porcelain clinked softly as the final plates were cleared.

Lord Aldrich rose from his seat. "I believe," he said smoothly, "we'll take our leave to the lounge now. There are still cocktails and brandy to be enjoyed, for those with the appetite."

Chairs scraped back. The room swelled with polite murmurs as guests departed for the lounge. But just as Evy relaxed her grip on the napkin, Dominic's voice rang out again.

"Well, maybe *your people* suffer because they never belonged here in the first place." He sounded almost bored. "You invited hardship the moment you claimed space in a realm that wasn't yours. Maybe Reya was simply amused when she handed your lot that joke of power."

Next to her, Royen threw his napkin onto the table. "Now, Father, don't you think—"

"Shut up, boy." Dominic pointed a finger at him. Royen flinched. "Don't forget who you're talking to."

The air grew taut once more. Evy remained seated, unmoving, but around her, the spirits stirred. They raced through the room, mirroring her agitation. A low vibration of invisible magic pulsed at her back and prickled the skin of those nearby.

Several guests stilled mid-step. One of the ladies near the hearth set her glass down with trembling fingers.

"You think we asked for this?"

Evy's voice cut through the soft rustle of movement.

"You think we suffer because we don't belong here?"

She looked up slowly, fury building behind her eyes.

"You say we're *Gaians*? Then riddle me this, Mister Veyn." Her words came faster. "Gaiasphere is a supposed realm with no magic.

Its people are said to be powerless. That part, I can almost understand. Witches, too, can't shape mana into magic on our own." She tilted her head. "But how could a powerless people survive crossing Hollowrift, a place of chaos? How could they be blessed by a Goddess of this world and still live to build a domain here?"

The room had gone deathly still. Only the low hum of her spirits remained. An eerie, invisible chorus of unrest.

"One would think," Evy continued, "that someone born into a family as high and mighty as yours, with access to every library, every scroll, and every drop of supposed wisdom, could spot the flaw in that logic."

She stood then, fixing on Dominic with open defiance.

A hand brushed her arm. It was Celeste. She whispered a word, but Evy couldn't hear her over her own fury.

"Or maybe," Evy said, voice quivering, "maybe it's not ignorance at all. Maybe you know exactly what we are. And maybe that's what terrifies you."

She stepped toward him.

"Because if we were *Gaians*, if we truly came here with nothing, no magic, no power, and *still* survived through Hollowrift… If we *still* carved a place from the dirt and made it our own, wouldn't that make us stronger than any of you? More powerful than you ever could be?"

She took another step.

"Because that would make us chosen by the Gods."

A chill wind swept through the room though no windows were open. Glasses chimed. The flames in the wall sconces flared then dimmed.

"Maybe that's why we were kept weak. Maybe you've all been afraid of what we'd become if we were ever allowed to stand on even ground.

"Maybe you weren't trying to keep us out at all. Maybe you were just trying to keep us down. But our time is coming,

Mister Veyn, and soon you won't be able to stop us, no matter how hard you try."

Silence.

Lord Aldrich's jaw clenched. Around him, faces stiffened, fury and fear simmering beneath their polished facades.

"What did you say?" Lawrence took a wary step forward. His scowl twisted into a knowing smile. Dominic, too, wore a sickeningly smug grin and gave Lawrence a quick nod.

It hit her then, what she had done.

What she had said.

She had allowed herself to break.

She'd insulted a Veyn. In a hall full of their loyalists.

She had teetered on the edge of open challenge, hinted that the Witches might pose a threat.

And Lawrence had caught her in the act. His cruel smile told her he meant to use this against her.

She didn't blame him—she had practically invited it.

Then, just as Aldrich opened his mouth to speak, a deep, hearty laugh tore through the room.

Zafir tossed his head back. "What nonsense is this little Witch spewing?" he said between chuckles. "Is she drunk?"

More laughter followed, lighter with a musical lilt.

Celeste leaned into Evy, hand gripping her shoulder. "Okay, okay," she said loud enough for the whole room to hear. "I'll admit it. Evy and I were sampling Fairy potions before dinner. Just a little sip, I swear. I didn't know her tolerance was that low."

Gasps and chuckles rippled down the table.

Celeste smiled as though the entire outburst had been a harmless joke. "Truly, my fault. Let me get her some air before she starts ranting about unfair lava quality in Zarokan."

Numb and stunned, Evy let herself be led away.

They slipped through a side door and out onto a balcony draped in ivy. The wind kissed Evy's face.

She gripped the stone railing, her nostrils flaring with every exhale.

"They would've torn me apart."

Celeste shrugged, the humor fading from her eyes. "As much as I want to reassure you, I agree. You weren't safe in there."

Evy stared out at the moonlit gardens, heart hammering.

She remembered the pride she'd felt after the biscuit challenge in the Trial of Wit. She had felt clever navigating each personality and getting them to do her bidding.

But this wasn't a trial moderated by the Heart.

This was the real world. Nothing was truly black and white.

And tonight, she hadn't passed the test.

She'd cracked.

Because her allies had protected her, the consequences may not come tonight.

But a deep, gnawing feeling told Evy they would catch up to her eventually.

As her pulse slowed, she was struck with a terrible realization.

If this had been part of the trials, they wouldn't have given her the mercy of being ranked last.

She knew without a doubt—they would've buried her.

THIRTY

Celeste hovered by the balcony doors, one hand resting lightly on the polished handle. "Stay out here. Let the night calm you. I'll go back in and smooth things over."

"Thank you. Truly," Evy said.

"Please." She waved a hand. "Someone's got to be the scandal buffer. Might as well be me."

Celeste stepped back inside. The doors shut behind her with a soft click, cutting off the muffled sounds of laughter and clinking glass.

Evy leaned against the cool stone railing and inhaled deeply. A storm of thoughts brewed within her.

Orianna would have been furious. No, not furious, but disappointed, which Evy considered so much worse. The Shaman Queen was supposed to embody grace, temperance, wisdom. Not rage or recklessness.

Evy imagined her words rippling outward, undoing the fragile opportunity for Reyland to earn respect.

Earn respect? The thought almost made her laugh. She'd have better luck asking a pack of wolves for it.

The salty breeze rolled in from the cliffs, stirring the hem of her gown and carrying with it the briny scent of the sea. For a moment, it took her back to the shores of Reyland, and she felt the aching gap in her heart. She missed home. She yearned to be somewhere she could let her guard down just once. To be free, if only for a moment.

For over a month now, she felt as though she'd worn a constant mask, and she was suffocating beneath it. Celeste was a friend. Even Royen, in his quiet, brooding way, might be becoming one. And Zafir had looked out for her tonight with his deflection. He and Celeste might have saved her from the worst of the Veyn family's wrath.

But still, measured words, diplomatic restraint, and the unrelenting weight of being the Shaman Queen and representing her people in the Hierarch Wars clung to her like a shroud.

Had she ever truly removed it?

In Reyland, she was the Shaman Queen first. Even to her parents, who had lost their daughter the day they took her to the Reyani Temple. She didn't belong to them anymore. She belonged to all Witches. Even Orianna, who had raised her with the love of a mother but the expectations of a leader, had never allowed her to just *be*.

Only one person had ever seen her as Evalene Lovejoy.

"You're not just the Shaman Queen. You're not just the Ascendant of Reyland. You're Evy—my Evy."

"Aeric," she whispered, the name escaping without permission.

She longed for him. For his comfort and familiarity.

She closed her eyes, remembering how close their lips had come just before her departure. His breath had brushed hers, the moon hanging above them a silent witness.

A soft whir of wheels broke through the silence.

Marq glided across the stone toward her, the moonlight

haloing his neatly combed blond hair. Royen followed, hands in his pockets.

"I hope we're not intruding." Marq's grin widened across his pale face.

Evy returned his smile. "Not at all."

Royen looked over the balcony, jaw tight.

"I should have said something. When my father started in on Reyland, I should've reminded him who you are. You're a *queen*. And who is he, next to you?"

Marq patted Royen's arm. Royen ignored the gesture and pressed on.

"I mean, you banished a Draemor to Hollowrift. You closed a portal in Theribane. The only other person with that kind of power is the Hierarch, and the past ones haven't done that for us. The way I see it, my family owes you."

His voice dipped, edged with bitterness. "But when my father drinks, he becomes worse than usual. Irreversibly odious. I—" His fingers curled into fists. "I should've defended you."

He was still afraid of them. Of his family. Too afraid to speak his piece when it mattered.

And it was eating him alive that he hadn't.

"You don't need to apologize," she said. "It was my outburst that pushed things too far."

Royen shook his head. "With the Trial of Strength coming up in less than a week, I think my family was trying to rattle you. They saw how close you came to winning the first trial. Maybe they thought if they got under your skin, they could throw you off your game."

He paused, his gaze drifting back toward the manor. "The best thing you could do now is prove them wrong."

The wind stirred again, brushing Evy's hair across her cheek. She idly pushed it back, her fingers grazing her lips. She didn't know what to say. She didn't know what to do. How could she prove them wrong when she was still trying to claw her way out of the grave she'd dug for herself?

"Well," Marq said, cutting through the tension. He leaned back in his chair with a small grin. "Now that we're no longer surrounded by our relatives, and I presume I can speak freely—I must say, Queen Evalene, you're just as pretty as Royen described in his letters."

Both Evy and Royen turned to him at once.

"What?" they said in unison.

"I didn't say that!" Royen snapped.

Marq looked innocent. "You said you didn't expect her to be so—"

Before he could finish, Royen clamped a hand over his cousin's mouth. "Shut up." His face flushed. "I'm never writing to you again."

Marq made a muffled noise behind Royen's hand, grinning all the while.

He threw up his hands in mock surrender. "Alright, alright! I give up!"

Royen yanked his hand away and groaned. "You licked me!"

Evy let out a soft laugh despite her nerves. She couldn't tell if Marq had been joking about Royen's letters, or if she was afraid to consider that he wasn't.

Pretty.

She kept her expression collected, but warmth permeated her cheeks. She prayed the moonlight wasn't bright enough to reveal it.

Aeric's crooked smile surfaced in her mind. He was waiting for her back home, missing her, writing to her, spending precious coin on postage just to make her feel supported.

And here she was flushing over an unverified compliment from a Veyn.

Besides, it was ridiculous and most definitely a joke. They

were rivals. The Hierarch Wars didn't leave room for anything else.

"I've got an idea," Marq said, eyes gleaming with mischief. "Let's sneak out of this dreadful manor and head down to the beach. A moonlit swim in the sea will do us all some good."

"It's nearly midnight," Royen said, unconvinced.

"And cold," Evy added, though admittedly intrigued.

"Exactly!" Marq said brightly. "That's the point. It's spontaneous and liberating. It'll be fun!"

The balcony doors creaked open behind them, and Celeste stepped out.

"Fun?" she echoed.

Marq turned toward her, his smile widening. "Care to join us for a late-night swim, Princess?"

"I'm in." She looked to Evy and winked. "It'll be just what you need."

Royen folded his arms, the familiar note of caution returning to his voice. "We're not supposed to leave the manor grounds. It might not be safe."

"Come on, we'll have two powerful Ascendants with us." He paused at Royen. "Fine, *three* if we include you. Who in their right mind would try anything?"

Royen rolled his eyes.

"We should do it," Evy said. "You're right, it'll be fun. It's just what I need to get my mind off tonight's disaster."

Marq clapped his hands together. "Yes! I knew I'd like you, Queen Evalene. So you, me, and Princess Celeste are in. Let's go!" He started to roll forward, his face bright with glee.

"Hold on." Royen grabbed the back of Marq's chair. "You're not going anywhere without me."

Together, they slipped through the neatly trimmed gardens. The path narrowed as it approached the cliff's edge where an old stone staircase curved down toward the beach. The waves crashed far below.

Evy took in the winding staircase. "Marq, how are you going to—?"

He gestured toward a thick bush near the cliff wall. "Mind tucking my chair in there for me?"

"What?"

Out of the blue, Marq's form rippled. Feathers burst forth where skin had been, and with a flap of wings, a brown sparrow soared into the night. A second joined him a moment later. Royen was sleek and as graceful as ever, even as a small bird in the sky.

"They never get tired of showing off," Celeste said with a fond sigh. She helped Evy wedge Marq's chair into the dense foliage, then looped their arms together. "Shall we take the slow way down?"

She and Celeste descended the steps together, the full moon illuminating their path.

At the bottom, the salty breeze hit stronger, tugging at Evy's hair as the waves rolled in. Overhead, the sparrows circled once before diving toward the sea. Midair, their forms rippled again, feathers became fins, beaks turned to snouts. With two mighty splashes, the sparrows were gone.

A couple of sleek sharks cut through the water, twisting and gliding with unmistakable joy.

"Fascinating, isn't it?" Celeste asked as the sharks cut through the surf. "All the strength of the Shifters seems to have settled into the Veyn bloodline."

Evy watched the boys. "How many forms do you think they're born with?"

"He refuses to confirm it, but I've heard Royen was born with at least a dozen," Celeste said. "A typical Veyn gets eight. Most Shifters only come into four."

Evy thought back to their spar in the Infernal Citadel and how Royen shifted between bodies as naturally as breathing.

Nudging a rock with her boot, Celeste mused, "All things considered, Royen is surprisingly humble."

"I guess," Evy murmured.

Celeste let out a slow sigh. "All that power, passed down like an heirloom. No wonder every influential family in Theribane tries to marry into them."

Daphne's voice echoed in Evy's mind. "*My betrothed.*"

And all at once, the pieces aligned. Lawrence's endless maneuvering, the reason behind his loyalties.

He wanted their blood in his line. In return, he'd do whatever necessary to keep the Veyns in power.

Evy thought back to Cara Veyn and how her place in the family had likely been sealed by Councilor Ashcroft's allegiance. Power traded for power. No wonder the Veyns had risen so quickly in Aeltheon. They held something others could not easily obtain, something they had been born with: influence. And anyone who managed to catch even a fraction of it only worked to shape and grow it until it reached far beyond their domain.

"I guess Royen and I have a lot in common," Celeste said dryly. "Who would have thought?"

Evy gripped her shoulder. "I'm truly sorry, Celeste."

"Don't be." Celeste's lips curved upward. "I believe in love. And I'll fight my mother. I'll fight all of Virenna if I have to before I let someone else decide who I spend the rest of my life with."

Suddenly, darkness slithered beneath Celeste's skin—a shadow along her wrist, thin as a vein, dark as ink. Evy blinked, and it was gone.

"What's wrong?" Celeste asked.

Evy rubbed her eyes. "Nothing. The moonlight's playing tricks on me."

Royen reappeared above the surf and shifted back into his human form. Marq followed, using his arms to stay afloat.

Royen looked down at himself, grimacing. "We really should've taken these off first. Our suits are going to be ruined."

Then his eyes found Evy. A flush rose immediately to his cheeks.

Marq caught the moment and grinned wickedly. "What are you two waiting for? Come on in!"

Without hesitation, Celeste unfastened her overdress and stripped down to her underthings before skipping into the waves with a laugh.

Evy hesitated, then glanced down at her own clothes.

"Irma's going to kill me if I ruin this dress with seawater." She peeled off her outer layers, not thinking too much of it. This was how girls swam in Reyland, in their undergarments beneath the stars. The moon was the only one watching now.

But when she glanced at Royen, he was as red as a beet and frozen in place.

Their eyes met.

He quickly shifted back into a shark and plunged beneath the waves, sending up an aggressive splash that sprayed Evy's eyes.

"Ah!" Evy cried out, rubbing her face.

Marq burst out laughing, one hand clutching his belly, the other pointing at Royen as he swam away. "Oh, you are so predictable, cousin."

THIRTY-ONE

The sun blazed overhead, its beams searing Evy's forearms as she stood in the center of the coliseum. It had been unseasonably hot since the Ascendants arrived in Ruitheon two nights ago, and to her dismay, the heat had refused to break. She'd spelled her linen pants and loose purple tunic with a cooling charm before leaving the townhome, but even that hadn't been enough. Sweat pooled along her hairline and traced a path down her jaw.

Beside her, Celeste fanned herself with one hand while a wind spell whispered through her fingers, offering short-lived bursts of air.

Royen stood on her other side in a similarly loose tunic, the front soaked through with sweat. The linen clung to his skin, outlining the lean muscle beneath.

She looked away quickly, blood rushing to her face.

It was the heat, she told herself. *Just the heat.*

Zafir sighed beside Celeste, eyes closed, face tilted toward the sun. The rest of them were sweating through their clothes, but he looked perfectly content. He was forged of fire, after all.

The crowd above them was almost as silent as the Ascendants themselves, the hush stretched taut with expectation. The only voices came from the Children of Rui, spewing their usual venom. Evy closed her eyes, trying to shut them out.

"I wish they'd just start already." Celeste fanned herself harder, wind ruffling her hair. "I'm going to be fried to a crisp at this rate."

The four towering structures from the Trial of Wit were no longer in the arena. Nothing remained but dirt.

She'd expected an obstacle course to be waiting for them, or some elaborate setup designed to display their strength or skill.

Instead, there was nothing.

The suspense of what lay ahead left a metallic taste in her mouth.

A fanfare of trumpets pierced the still air, and the crowd erupted, disrupting Evy's thoughts.

Cheers thundered through the coliseum as Lawrence stepped into view, flanked by the rest of the Council in their flowing black robes.

His eyes cut to Evy, and a grin flashed across his face. After her outburst in Veyn Manor, he should have been furious, yet he looked entertained. She felt like a trapped mouse, and he was the cat toying with her, drawing out the moment before the kill.

His grin vanished as Lawrence turned back to the crowd and raised a hand for silence.

He amplified his voice with a spell. "Welcome to the Trial of Strength!"

The crowd surged again with excitement. He let them settle before continuing.

"This trial is designed to test the physical and magical endurance of our future Hierarch. The one who wears the crown must prove they wield power worthy of this realm."

Another Councilor stepped forward with a tray draped in azure cloth. Resting atop it were a pair of gold gauntlets engraved with wings.

"As victor of the first trial, Royen Veyn has earned a boon." Lawrence tipped his chin toward Royen. "He will enter this challenge wearing the Celestial Gauntlets, an ancient relic gifted to the realm by the Gods themselves, said to enhance both speed and strength."

Lawrence lifted the gauntlets from the tray.

"But do not be fooled." His voice sharpened. "The advantage is slight. This trial demands more than relics. It demands the fullest measure of one's power."

He crossed the arena and fastened the gauntlets onto Royen's forearms. A faint glow pulsed from them.

Royen met Evy's eyes.

Then, slowly, he looked toward the dirt. His brows drew together.

Lawrence returned to his post and raised his hand. "Open the gate. Let it in."

A low rumble answered.

The massive gate groaned open at the far end of the coliseum. Metal scraped against stone, the sound shrill and jarring. A guttural growl echoed from the yawning blackness beyond—from a cage built into the coliseum wall. A cage so large Evy couldn't imagine what it was meant to hold.

Celeste gasped beside her. "Puppies?"

Then came the eyes. Six of them, colossal and glowing red, blinking against the sunlight.

Celeste leaped back. "Oh. Never mind."

The creature stepped forward. The ground shook.

Evy crouched, bracing herself, heart slamming against her ribs.

Dust and gravel scattered beneath the creature's weight as its form emerged from the shadows.

Lawrence's voice rang out above the tremors. "This is your challenge—strike down the beast born of nightmare."

Panicked shouts rippled through the crowd.

The earth continued to quake as the creature advanced, but Lawrence pressed on, his voice cutting through the rising noise.

"You may fight together," he continued. "But know this, the Heart will not measure teamwork. It will judge individual impact. Every blow you land, every wound you carve, will tip the scales in your favor."

Evy felt sudden pressure. Celeste's hand was gripping hers. Her face had gone pale as three massive, fur-covered maws crept into the light.

"And the one who fells the beast"—Lawrence's words were aimed squarely at Royen—"will earn the highest score. Victory in this trial belongs to the strongest among you."

The creature stepped fully into the arena, its entire form now visible.

It towered over them, fur coarse and black as pitch. From its hulking shoulders rose three snarling heads, each mouth lined with jagged teeth the size of boulders.

Zafir stepped forward, jaw set. "In the name of the Gods."

One of the monster's heads barked, a deafening boom that rattled the arena walls. Cries spread through the stands. Some of the crowd began to flee in panic.

Evy's pulse thundered in her ears. She had read about this in Linius Wells's diaries. About creatures that didn't belong in this world.

And she recognized this one from the description in some of his final entries.

"It's a Cerberus." The word was bitter on her tongue. "They must've dragged it out of Hollowrift."

"Astute observation." Lawrence's smile pulled tight. "Perhaps your Reylandic schooling wasn't entirely wasted, Miss Lovejoy."

Evy shook her head in disbelief. "Linius Wells, our former Shaman King, encountered this monster before." Her gaze remained locked on the beast's maw, slick with drool. "He said it nearly destroyed his entire scouting party. It's why he forbade Witches from ever entering Hollowrift again."

Royen turned from the beast to Lawrence. "This is reckless. Even for you, Daryn."

The Cerberus roared and lunged, but a massive, glowing chain snapped taut, yanking it back. The links coiled around its chest were alight with containment spells.

Lawrence snickered. "As you can see, we have it under control. Never underestimate the power of the Council."

The beast reared back and lunged again, claws tearing into the dirt as all three heads snapped forward with thunderous rage.

The crowd screamed. Sheer panic surged through the stands, and more onlookers fled.

Lawrence addressed the crowd. "Fear not. The creature cannot leave the arena."

The Cerberus strained against its glowing tether, muscles rippling beneath its matted fur, each head snarling in fury.

"While the beast remains dangerous," Lawrence continued, "it is confined to this space. And once the challenge begins, the bindings will loosen just enough to let it fight. But not enough to harm the audience."

Low growls rumbled from the creature's three throats as it dug its claws into the dirt.

The entry gate behind them creaked open.

The remaining eleven Councilors stepped forward in formation, hands raised. Suspended between them was the Heart, glowing in rhythmic pulses.

They moved carefully, guiding the relic into position at the arena's center. As it came to a halt, its glow deepened to a vibrant gold, and the Councilors began their incantation.

Thin tendrils of glowing blue mana unspooled from the Heart and drifted downward. They reached the ground and crept on, pulsing with power as they slithered toward the beast.

The Cerberus reared its heads and let out a deafening roar that shook the coliseum walls.

The Heart's tendrils twisted around its limbs, then sank into its hide, vanishing beneath the fur. The beast convulsed.

Evy couldn't look away. And then she heard it.

Evalene... my child.

She searched for the source of the voice.

Help me...

Softer now. It curled inside her mind like smoke. Evy stilled. Was she the only one who heard it?

Embrace me...

The words brushed her skull, and she felt a tug deep within her chest, as if an invisible force were pulling at her.

She looked to the others for any sign they'd heard the voice. Nothing. Just wide eyes and frozen stares locked on the Cerberus.

The Councilors finished their incantation and began to file out of the arena, the Heart drifting behind them. The whispers faded with every step.

Only Lawrence remained.

"The challenge begins the moment the Council clears the grounds," he announced, leaving Evy with no time to ruminate further.

His gaze slid to Royen, and a smile curled at his lips.

"Best of luck, Ascendants."

The Arch Councilor stepped out.

The Ascendants exchanged grave looks as the monster's chain groaned.

The Cerberus stiffened. Then, it began to stalk forward, each step heavy, its growl earth-shaking.

A metallic clang struck the floor.

The Celestial Gauntlets lay at Royen's feet. He had tossed them aside.

"What are you doing?"

"I don't need the Council's cheap tricks." He toed the gauntlets aside. "I can win on my own."

He shifted into a sleek cougar and darted toward the beast.

Zafir let out a thunderous war cry and summoned a massive fire-axe into his grip.

Celeste tapped Evy's shoulder. "Come on!" She launched into the air, wings slicing upward.

Evy stood frozen.

Zafir charged the leftmost head, fire exploding from his hands in blinding bursts. His axe swung wide, carving a path of flame across the creature's snout. The Cerberus roared, but Zafir pressed forward, relentless.

Celeste zipped through the air. She hurled blades of wind toward the middle head, each one slicing through its fur. The jaws snapped wildly, barely missing her as she twisted away with supernatural grace.

On the monster's other side, Royen moved like liquid. He shifted from panther to hawk to wolf in a blur, using each form to strike, evade, reposition. When he had the angle, he returned to human form and released a volley of glowing arrows, each one slamming into the beast's hide.

Evy watched, unable to move. Unable to breathe.

Move, something whispered. It was her own voice this time. *You cannot stand still. Move!*

And her body obeyed.

She raised her hand and summoned her spirits. She looked warily at the spectators and dismissed a few. Then ran into the chaos.

She slammed her palms into the earth. Vines erupted beneath the Cerberus's feet, twisting up its legs and locking tight. The beast snarled and yanked itself free with brute force.

A burst of fire surged from her fingertips and collided with the middle head. Flames danced across its fur, but the monster barely flinched, thrashing as Zafir's axe slammed down again.

Celeste dove from above, a gust of wind momentarily stunning one of the heads.

Royen, in panther form, leaped onto its back and shifted midair, firing a glowing arrow point-blank into its flank.

Still the beast kept coming.

Evy skidded back, dodging a claw that carved a crater where she'd stood seconds before.

It was too strong. They were barely slowing it down, even between fire, speed, magic, and strength.

One of the heads turned toward her, red eyes glowing in rage.

Her mind raced.

Evy summoned her water spirits, and they answered in frenzied waves, voices overlapping in both fear and exhilaration. Once again, she dismissed a few.

Ice bloomed at her feet and raced up her arms. A thin glacial spear formed in her grasp.

She threw it.

The ice missile soared through the air and pierced one of the Cerberus's eyes.

She winced at her accuracy and checked the stands, hoping no one had noticed.

The monster shrieked and reared back as its eye went white with frost. Blood and steam hissed from the ruined socket.

The ground quaked beneath Evy's feet as the beast thrashed, its heads snapping in every direction as it pulled on the chain with impossible force.

The air filled with the most dreadful sounds.

A groan.

A crack.

A shatter.

The glowing chain around the Cerberus's chest broke apart.

Evy froze.

The half-formed ice spear she'd begun to summon slipped from her grasp.

Realization dawned over the others as the Cerberus turned toward the stands.

Screams erupted.

"Run!" someone yelled.

One massive head lunged, its jaws closing around a cluster of spectators. The creature snapped them up like scraps. Blood sprayed across the stone as the crowd broke into chaos.

"No!" Evy lifted a trembling hand to her mouth.

Celeste landed beside her, shouting at the sight of the blood.

Zafir let out a string of curses while Royen stood frozen with his mouth agape.

The Cerberus raised its heads to the open sky.

It gave the shattered chains one last look before sniffing the air, leaping over the arena wall, and bounding into the city of Ruitheon.

THIRTY-TWO

The Council spilled back into the arena, expressions of pure dismay etched beneath their hoods. Most of the spectators had fled, scattering in fear after the horror that had just unfolded.

Lawrence stormed ahead of the others, his gaze sweeping the empty stands, the blood-spattered dirt, the enchanted chain he'd been so confident would hold an otherworldly monster.

Kaelen moved to his side and pulled down his hood as he took in the wreckage.

"We need to get the citizens to safety." Lawrence gestured to Kaelen. "Take the lead and get as many as you can into the Aurethium. Then raise a barrier."

Kaelen gave a curt nod and gathered a handful of Councilors. Before he turned to leave, he cast Lawrence a grim look. "I told you this was a terrible idea."

Around them, a few Councilors murmured agreement before rushing off into the chaos. Lawrence's lips tightened into a straight line, nose flaring from contained fury.

Another hooded figure stepped forward and lowered her cowl. Her soft, beige wings flickered with agitation.

"Should we lure the beast outside the city?" Lilian Varos asked. "We could ambush it. Attack it together—"

"No!" Lawrence snapped. "We can't lay a single hand on it."

Lilian opened her mouth to protest.

"The trial is still in motion," Lawrence cut her off. "The Heart is judging. If we cast even a single spell against that creature, it might register it as interference."

Lilian stared at him, stunned. "And what would that mean?"

Lawrence held her gaze. "We would be obliterated by the Heart itself."

He turned to the Ascendants. "This falls to you. The creature must be destroyed by your hands alone. Do whatever is necessary to end it."

He strode across the bloodied arena and bent to retrieve the Celestial Gauntlets from where Royen had cast them aside.

He straightened and marched back to Royen. "Pride is a luxury we can no longer afford." Lawrence thrust the gauntlets toward him. "You earned these. Now use them to save this city."

Lawrence took a step back. His form rippled and distorted—feathers erupted across his skin, bones cracked and realigned. In moments, the Arch Councilor was gone, replaced by a black vulture, wings spreading wide.

All around them, the Shifter Councilors followed suit. One became a sleek hawk, another a sharp-beaked raven, and even a brilliant parrot burst forth from a silver-haired woman's fading silhouette. A flurry of wings filled the air as they launched skyward and headed toward the Aurethium.

Royen considered the gauntlets for a long moment, then slipped them back on.

"Let's go." He turned toward the gate.

They followed him out of the arena and headed straight into chaos.

The city was in ruins. Dust plumes and smoke curled through the air as the Cerberus tore through the streets, each massive head snapping at the fleeing crowd. Buildings crumbled like sandcastles beneath its claws. Screams rang from every direction, some cut short as the beast devoured its victims whole.

Evy stumbled to a stop.

It was a massacre.

Zafir stepped beside her. "Of all the Council's mistakes, this has to be their worst." His voice dropped to a growl. "Summoning a Hollowrift beast into the realm and thinking they could control it, have they lost all of their senses?"

Celeste hovered just above the street, her wings fluttering. "What could they possibly have hoped to gain from this?"

"I think I know why they did this." Royen scoffed. "They wanted a spectacle. Something no mortal could kill alone, so they could parade these." He lifted his gauntleted hands. "The Celestial Gauntlets. Proof that their chosen one, their golden boy, was the only one strong enough to kill the Cerberus."

Evy quivered with frustration. The explanation made a sick sort of sense. The trial awarded points based on inflicted damage. If Royen monopolized the fight using the gauntlets while the rest of them barely left a mark, he'd be so far ahead no one could hope to catch up.

She turned to him. "It doesn't matter why they did this. Right now, we need to focus on stopping it."

The Cerberus let out another roar in the distance. The ground shuddered.

Royen hesitated, still watching, fists clenched at his sides.

"Royen." Evy's voice became more urgent. "Use the gauntlets. You might be the only one who can kill it before it harms more people."

He met her eyes. "Only if you promise not to hold back."

She opened her mouth to speak but was unable to find the words. He was right. They couldn't have a repeat of the Draemor attack in Theribane. Evy gave Royen a slow nod.

The four of them took off, racing through the broken streets toward the Cerberus. Dust and ash clouded the air as they closed in, the monster's gargantuan silhouette rising against the skyline.

The Cerberus turned, all three heads snarling as the Ascendants approached.

Royen was the first to strike.

He shifted, his form collapsing into the sleek shape of a hawk. Wings cut through the hazy air as he soared upward.

Mid-flight, just above the Cerberus's heads, his body twisted again, flesh reforming into human.

Momentum carried him downward, and he dropped from the sky like a meteor.

His fist slammed into one of the beast's heads, power surging through his arm from the Celestial Gauntlet.

Golden mana burst from the impact, the shockwave flinging rubble and debris in every direction. The creature staggered, snarling, but it didn't fall.

Royen didn't relent. He struck again. Then again. Each punch landed with thunderous force. For a moment, it looked like he was gaining ground.

Then the Cerberus bellowed.

Its center head lunged, fangs snapping. It rammed into Royen with its paw, an enormous swipe of brute force that sent him flying.

He crashed into the side of a stone building. The gauntlets flared with energy, softening the blow, but the fall was too great. As he slid down the wall and hit the ground, fine cracks spidered across the surface of the gauntlets.

Evy cried out and started toward him, but he lifted a hand, signaling her to stop.

The Cerberus charged again.

Royen raised both arms and a luminous mana shield bloomed into existence. Golden and radiant, the shield held fast as the beast slammed into it, its jaws crashing against the barrier.

The Cerberus snarled and bit again and again. Every strike sent deep shudders through the shield, pressing Royen farther into the ground.

Jagged cracks laced the gauntlets and continued spreading.

Evy's heart lurched in fear. "Zafir! Celeste! We have to help him!"

Zafir charged, summoning a vortex of flame and hurling it at the beast's flank. Celeste launched into the air and pelted the Cerberus with piercing blades of wind.

The monster barely flinched. Its three snarling heads remained locked on Royen.

The Cerberus lunged again, jaws slamming into the barrier. Cracks splintered across its surface like veins of shattered glass.

Royen braced himself, arms shaking, the gauntlets flaring wildly.

The Cerberus roared and sank its teeth into the shield again with brutal force.

The barrier disintegrated.

The shockwave knocked the monster off balance, but it blasted Royen backward too. He crashed through a crumbling stone wall, the sound of the impact deafening. The Celestial Gauntlets shattered, golden fragments scattering across the dirt.

Royen didn't get up.

"No!" Evy sprinted toward him.

He lay still. Unconscious.

She dropped to her knees and cradled his head in her lap. Blood streaked down his temple.

"No, no, no." She brushed his hair back with trembling fingers.

A booming growl reverberated painfully against her skull.

Her head snapped up.

The Cerberus was rising, steam curling from its nostrils. Its furious gazes locked onto her, and the beast charged.

Evy's mind raced.

She reached inward, calling on the deepest bond she had. "Reya, help..." With a desperate cry, she flung a hand outward.

A portal tore open behind her, swirling with dark mist.

With no time to think, she jumped up and dragged Royen's limp body into the void.

The Cerberus lunged.

Evy threw her hand back just as the creature's jaws snapped.

She sealed the portal shut and darkness swallowed them whole.

THIRTY-THREE

Crimson lightning flashed across a solid black sky, but the expected thunder never followed. The world around them was unnaturally silent. A blood-red crescent moon hung low in the sky, casting the world in an eerie scarlet glow.

Evy collapsed to the ground, her knees sinking into pale grass. She dragged Royen's limp body toward her and gently rested his head on her lap, then took in her surroundings.

They were in a meadow. If it could be called that. Every blade of tall grass appeared blurred and drained of color as if it had been inked in water.

"Royen?" she whispered.

He didn't stir.

She lowered her head to his chest and let out a breath of relief when she found his heartbeat.

Evy tore a strip of fabric from her sleeve and pressed it to the wound on his head, her hands trembling.

All around her, the meadow shifted in silent movement. Bright wisps zipped through the air, and shadows drifted between the distant trees.

She thought back to Linius Wells's journals.

"It is no place for the living."

They shouldn't be here.

He had strictly warned against the dangers of Hollowrift while detailing his many risky adventures.

Humanoid figures moved in the distance. Vague and shadowy, they drifted across the blurred meadow. They didn't seem to notice her and Royen and just wandered onward.

Souls, perhaps.

She had lost the ability to see souls as a child, long before she understood that she could, and she was struck by how clearly their forms appeared in this realm.

But beyond them, she saw others.

Monstrous creatures. Gargantuan, with multitudes of limbs crawling like octopuses. Their movements were unnaturally fluid like thick smoke rolling through the air.

She tightened her grip on Royen.

He groaned softly.

His eyes fluttered open, glassy with confusion and pain.

"Royen." Her expression lifted, then froze at the sound of whispers and rustling nearby. "You have to stand. We need to move. Now."

Royen blinked at the sky above them. "Where—?"

"Hollowrift." Evy looped her arm under his. "And we need to get out of here."

He staggered upright with her help.

Evy scanned the distance. Beyond the drifting blur of spirits, she spotted a faint ripple of pulsing light.

"There," she said. "We have to get to that portal."

Royen squinted at it. "Can't you just open one?"

"No." Evy tightened her grip on his wrist. "Not to Lumesphere. That kind of precision takes decades of training. I've only ever opened portals into Hollowrift, and even then, I haven't learned how to control where they go."

Royen just nodded, then winced and let her guide him.

They started toward the portal, the colorless grass whispering beneath their feet. Wispy orbs of spirits and shadows of souls drifted silently past.

"What are they?" Royen asked.

Evy turned to him. "You can see them?"

He nodded.

A blue spirit drifted inches from his face. He flinched.

"I guess you can." She watched as the wisp vanished into the sky. "That's a spirit."

Behind them, something large shifted in the darkness.

A low snarl cut through the silence.

A few feet away, an inky cougar composed of churning black smoke emerged from the tall grass. Its red eyes locked on her and Royen.

They froze.

"Can you see that too?" Evy asked.

Royen nodded again, slower this time.

The cougar crouched, then lunged.

"Run!" Evy gasped, yanking Royen forward.

They bolted. The cougar's footfalls thundered behind them, gaining fast. Evy's gaze locked on the portal ahead.

"Just a little farther!"

The beast's jaws snapped behind her.

With a desperate cry, Evy hauled Royen through the portal as the cougar's fangs closed on empty air.

They tumbled onto cracked earth. Dust billowed around them as they scrambled upright.

The ground was scorched and brittle, broken into jagged plates. The air tasted of ash. A barren wasteland stretched as far as she could see—no trees, water, or signs of life. Overhead, the sky was painted red, scattered with dense black clouds.

Evy turned toward the portal.

The shadow cougar stood just beyond the threshold. Its red eyes met hers across the divide.

But it just stared.

Then, without a sound, it turned and slipped back into the darkness, as though some invisible boundary warned it not to cross.

At the same time, Royen's body slumped beside her, his head lolling back.

Evy caught him before he collapsed. His weight made her knees buckle, and she lowered him gently to the floor.

When she touched his side, her hand came away slick with blood. She lifted the edge of his shirt and found a deep gash stretched across his ribs.

He groaned softly, and his eyes opened.

"Evalene." His voice was thick with pain. "I'm sorry… I'm being such a burden."

Evy swallowed hard and brushed a lock of blood-matted hair from his brow.

"You're not a burden." Her voice cracked. "You were really brave."

He gave the faintest shake of his head.

She blinked back the burn in her eyes. "You don't have to try so hard, Royen. Not with me." Her lips curved into a fragile smile. "And I think… you've more than earned the right to call me Evy."

A faint crease appeared between his brows. "I thought only your friends called you Evy."

She let out a soft laugh. "Exactly."

For a fleeting moment, his lips curved upward.

Then his eyes closed again, and the smile faded as unconsciousness pulled him under.

Evy pressed her hands over the deepest wound at his side and summoned her light spirits.

A gentle glow bloomed beneath her palms, warmth spilling into Royen's skin as the torn flesh began to mend.

Then all at once, the magic sputtered.

Evy gasped at the sensation. And then she understood.

There was no mana here. Worse, this place seemed to erase magical energy, no matter where it came from. Even in Hollowrift, she hadn't felt her strength fade this fast. This environment resisted magic.

The only power she had was what she brought with her, and it was quickly running out.

Still, she kept going. She poured everything she had into the healing spell, calling on her spirits, her last reserves, her final thread of strength. One by one, the spirits' presence slipped from her reach.

And the bleeding slowed. The wound knitted together.

Her vision swam. Her arms fell limp.

In the last few seconds before darkness took her, Royen's face blurred. The sharp angles softened. His chestnut hair deepened to auburn. His hazel eyes shifted to stormy gray.

And with one last breath, Evy collapsed onto his chest, her world dissolving into shadow.

Gentle fingers threaded through Evy's hair as her eyes blinked open.

"Aeric?"

The fingers stilled.

Her vision sharpened. She was lying on Royen's lap. He was awake, one hand tangled in her hair, the other wrapped around her fingers. Concern—or perhaps confusion—clouded his expression.

"You're awake," he said. "Good. I was starting to panic." He gave a sheepish smile. "Thanks for… saving me, *Evy*."

"Of course." She prayed her blush wasn't too obvious. She had given him permission, but hearing him address her so casually made her heart skip. "We're friends, after all."

"Where are we?" Royen asked, taking in his surroundings.

Evy sat up and rubbed her eyes. "I have no idea. I saw a portal and dragged us through. Getting eaten by a shadow cougar wasn't the ending I was hoping for, so I didn't have much choice."

Royen looked out at the cracked earth, the skyless void stretched above them like an empty canvas. "Feels like a graveyard for the Gods. Is this Gaiasphere?"

"No, I don't think so," she answered. "From the little we know of Gaiasphere, it would have at least some life to it. This place is so… empty."

"Perhaps we're the first to discover it."

Though it felt safer and less tumultuous than Hollowrift, it lacked any vibrancy, as if anything with life didn't belong. "It's a barren land," Evy said, not realizing the words had slipped from her mouth.

Royen nodded slowly. "Barrenland. A fitting name."

Evy turned toward the swirling portal. The cougar was gone. The entrance stood quiet and still.

"I think it's safe now," she said. "We should go. We need to find a way back to Lumesphere."

They stood and stepped through the portal, entering Hollowrift together. The landscape shifted around them like a fever dream. Skeletal forests melted into blackened fields, rivers flowed with red liquid, cliffs were formed from shadow instead of stone.

Souls drifted past, their faces blurred, their bodies only half shaped. Most simply watched as Evy and Royen passed, hollow gazes following them.

"I don't think they're hostile," Evy whispered, though the chill running down her spine said otherwise.

"There." He pointed suddenly. "A portal."

Far in the distance, a tear in the fabric of the realm pulsed with familiar golden and blue light.

She could feel the pull of its power even from afar.

Mana.

They ran.

As they neared, Evy recognized the silhouette beyond the portal. She could see Ruitheon's sand dunes and the city's spires rising on the horizon. A distant roar from the Cerberus echoed faintly across the threshold.

"This must be the portal the Council used to bring the Cerberus into Ruitheon," Evy said.

Royen peered through. "And it's still rampaging."

They crossed the threshold together. The moment her foot stepped back into Lumesphere, her magic surged to life.

Suffocating heat rushed over her, but she welcomed the familiarity.

The ground beneath them shuddered as another roar thundered. Black plumes of smoke rose from the cityscape.

Royen's jaw clenched. "What are we supposed to do about that monster when we can barely scratch it?"

Evy looked back at where the portal to the Barrenland still blinked behind them. The shadow cougar had stared after them but then turned away. It hadn't dared to cross the portal. As if it knew the Barrenland would neutralize its power and leave it defenseless.

That place didn't only affect Aeltheans; it changed the creatures of Hollowrift too.

At least, she hoped it did as she scoured for a solution.

A memory flashed through her mind. When they were in the cinderbark forest of Zarokan, she'd watched Zafir tear a tree from the scorched earth and hurl it like a spear.

"Strength isn't always about the magic you use. Power comes in many forms."

She turned to Royen, her lips curling into a conspiratorial smile.

"I have an idea."

THIRTY-FOUR

Evy told Royen her plan as they sprinted back into the chaos of Ruitheon, the Cerberus's roar echoing through the crumbling streets. Smoke curled into the air. Buildings lay in ruin. Terrified citizens fled in all directions.

Evy skidded to a halt as Leo Warring emerged from the haze, blade drawn, armor scorched but intact. Relief broke across his face when he saw her.

"I've been looking everywhere for you," he said, breathless. "Thank Reya you're safe."

Evy didn't waste a second. "Is Irma alright?"

Leo nodded. "She's safe. I got her to the Aurethium before the worst of it hit." His grip tightened around his sword. "Awaiting your command, Your Majesty." He lifted his blade. "We can take the beast down together."

Evy stepped forward and placed a hand on his arm. "You can't engage the Cerberus. If you strike it, you'll interfere with the trial, and the Heart will destroy you. I need you to return to the Aurethium and help the Council defend it."

Leo hesitated, then nodded.

As he turned to go, she caught his arm again. "Have you seen Celeste or Zafir?"

Leo looked down the street. "Celeste was by the collapsed tavern." Another pause. "She didn't look well."

A crease formed between Evy's brows.

"Thank you, Captain Warring."

He bowed and vanished into the smoke.

Evy and Royen hurried around the corner of a half-collapsed building, and there she was.

Celeste crouched low behind the rubble, arms wrapped around her knees, shoulders trembling.

"Celeste!" Evy rushed to her friend. "Are you hurt? Are you okay?"

She shook her head over and over, tears glinting at the corners of her eyes. "I can't do it. *I can't.* I tried, Evy, I really did. I hit it with everything, but it doesn't stop. It doesn't even flinch."

Celeste was spiraling. Her breaths came too fast.

"It's okay," Evy said gently, grabbing her shoulders. "You're okay. Look at me."

Celeste blinked up at her, eyes wide with panic.

"You're going to be alright." Evy's grip tightened. "But I need you to tell me where Zafir is."

A shudder passed through Celeste's frame. "He's out there," she whispered. "Trying to lure the Cerberus out of the city. He said if he could draw it toward the dunes, it'd be easier to fight without hurting people."

"Thank you," Evy said, then stood. "You've done enough. I need you to go to the Aurethium and stay safe."

Celeste wiped her nose and gave a small, shaky nod.

She launched into the sky, vanishing among the clouds.

Evy looked to Royen. "Let's go." They sprinted through the broken streets, dodging debris and leaping over shattered stones. The Cerberus's roar thundered closer.

"There it is!" Royen pointed through the smoke.

The great beast barreled down the boulevard, heads snapping in different directions, claws carving deep trenches into the stone. It moved with purpose, hunting something just out of reach.

It was Zafir.

He stood firm in the middle of the street, flames curling from his arms. He hurled another wave of fire at the Cerberus, shouting, baiting it.

"Come on, you overgrown mutt!"

The beast snarled and charged him, heads snapping at the air.

Evy's heart pounded. Zafir's flames were strong, but a noticeable quiver in his stance gave away his exhaustion.

He was running out of steam.

"We have to get to him," she said and grabbed Royen's arm.

They reached Zafir as he hurled another wave of fire. The Cerberus roared, its three heads flailing in different directions before it focused on him again.

Zafir's gruff voice cut through the chaos. "Where the hell have you been?"

"Hollowrift. It's a long story." Evy spoke quickly. She stepped forward, gaze locked on the towering beast. "But we're here now. I need you to trust me. There's a place outside the city. We have to lure it there."

Zafir glanced over, sweat streaking down his brow. "What are you planning?"

"I think I know how to weaken it," she said. "But I need you at full strength to pull it off." She looked over her shoulder. The Cerberus was tailing them, and quickly. "I don't have time to explain. Will you trust me?"

Zafir considered her, then gave a single nod.

"Take that." Evy pointed to a fallen spear. "Royen will lead you to the spot and tell you everything. In the meantime, I'll bring the beast to you."

Zafir grabbed the spear without hesitation. "Lead the way, Young Lord."

"For the love of the Gods, do not call me that," Royen said with a groan. The two sprinted off. Royen spoke quickly, tracing blueprints in the air as they gained distance.

Evy turned to face the Cerberus alone.

She raised both hands, summoning every spirit bonded to her. Mana pooled around her feet, light flared around her fingers, and heat swelled in her body.

"Come on," she whispered.

A barrage of spells erupted from her palms—blades of ice, bursts of wind, and crackling waves of fire. The Cerberus reeled, snarling, momentarily staggering under the force of her assault.

Then the beast bellowed. All three heads turned toward her, eyes blazing.

It charged.

She spun and ran.

Evy sprinted across the streets, her spells crackling through the air as she unleashed blast after blast at the monster behind her. The Cerberus tore through the wreckage in pursuit.

They reached the edge of Ruitheon where the portal to Hollowrift blinked in the distance.

The Cerberus suddenly slowed.

Its heads lifted, sniffing the air, claws digging into the ground. It rumbled low, hesitating.

Evy's chest heaved as she turned, hands trembling from exertion. "You don't want to go back, do you?" She bared her teeth. "You've tasted Aelthean blood. And now you want more."

She raised one hand and summoned all of her water spirits together.

An ice spear formed above her. With a cry, she flung it into the beast's eye. One of the heads howled, thrashing violently, blood and frost exploding from the wound.

The Cerberus shrieked, possessed with rage.

It charged again, blinded now in two eyes, with fury directing its path.

Royen and Zafir stood ready in front of the portal. She gave a sharp nod.

They gestured in return and slid through, vanishing into the shadows.

The Cerberus was nearly upon her.

Evy turned, leaped, and plunged through the portal as the beast's snarl followed close behind.

She hit the ground in Hollowrift. Cold, dark mist stretched in every direction.

Behind her, the Cerberus landed hard.

Evy didn't look back. She ran, weaving through Hollowrift's chaotic landscape, dodging the wandering souls and shifting shadows.

Each spell she cast chipped away at her strength. A shard of ice, and her water spirits evaporated, their voices fading to a whisper before going silent. Another burst of fire, and the fire spirits vanished from her mind like a candle snuffed out.

One by one, they slipped away from her.

Her vision blurred. Her limbs ached.

Just ahead, nestled between two jagged cliffs of shadowed stone, was the second portal. The one she had been searching for.

It pulsed with a dull emptiness that drained her energy the closer she got to it.

The entrance to Barrenland.

Evy turned sharply and fired another volley of spells into the beast. One hit its shoulder. Another singed the side of its face. The third struck one of its remaining eyes.

The Cerberus shrieked, rearing back, foam flying from its

jaws. It could barely see now, blinded by rage and pain. It thundered forward, no longer aware of the ground it trampled.

Evy crossed the threshold first.

And the Cerberus followed, unwittingly stepping into the magicless void.

Its massive paws stumbled on the cracked earth. The beast reeled, heads thrashing with ragged gasps as if the air itself had turned to poison. A deep wheeze rattled from its throats.

Evy stepped back.

It was working exactly as planned.

Exactly as she had hoped.

The monster's form began to shrink, muscle and mass collapsing in on itself as the magic sustaining it drained away. It staggered, whimpering. Its strength unraveled with each second.

Zafir emerged through a veil of fog, spear gripped tight in his hand. With a primal yell, he drove the weapon straight into the creature's side.

Again.

And again.

The Cerberus gave one final, shuddering howl.

And it finally collapsed, its body crumbling into stillness beneath Zafir's blade.

Evy exhaled, her shoulders sagging.

Royen stepped up beside her and reached an arm around her in an offer of support. She leaned into him as the last of her strength slipped away.

"There might not be any magic here," Royen said, "but it didn't change the fact that Zafir might be the strongest being in the realm."

Evy rested her head on his shoulder, the world spinning. "We needed him to finish it. No one else could have."

Zafir stood on top of the shriveled monster, eyes closed, face toward the sky, chest heaving.

"You know what this means?" Royen gave a faint, lopsided smile. "He dealt the killing blow. Zafir won the second trial."

They stared at the Cerberus in silence. The smoke from its mouths drifted upward into the void.

Zafir finally opened his red, fiery eyes, his chin lowering. The three of them exchanged a glance.

And said nothing.

For a moment, they allowed themselves to savor the quiet in the aftermath of chaos.

THIRTY-FIVE

Evy turned the knob on the lantern, and the bookshelves around them brightened as Royen brought over a handful of scrolls.

"Start looking through these." He set them beside her. "I'm going back to the shelves to grab a few more books."

She nodded, already unfurling one, but her thoughts drifted to a week ago.

Back to the moment she, Royen, and Zafir had stepped through the portal, returning to Ruitheon after their victory in Hollowrift. While she had been sealing the rift for good, the Council urged them to return to the coliseum so the Heart could render its judgment.

Celeste was already there, sitting on the ground with her knees drawn up, cheeks streaked with tears. The instant she saw them, she rushed over and pulled them all into a desperate embrace.

"Thank the stars," she'd managed to say between sobs. "I thought I left you all for dead. I never would have forgiven myself, knowing I did nothing while you were in danger. Oh, thank the stars."

They had murmured reassurances to Celeste as the Heart was carried into the arena.

Gasps echoed among the Councilors as the Heart placed its judgment.

The orb above Zafir's head blazed brightest, largest.

It was as Evy had expected.

Though the Cerberus had been destroyed because of her plan, the Heart gave more credit to the time he'd spent facing it alone in Ruitheon and to the killing blows he landed in the Barrenland. It was the Trial of Strength, after all, and his performance had put him in the lead.

Evy's and Royen's orbs were nearly identical at first glance until one leaned closer. Hers glowed slightly larger, placing her in second.

Royen had come in third.

Celeste had placed last.

She heard a faint, strange crunch and looked around, half expecting the coliseum's walls to begin crumbling. But it was Lawrence. Grinding his teeth.

His face was twisted in barely contained agitation as he glared at Zafir, who grinned back at him, taunting him.

Then Lawrence turned to her.

She couldn't hold back against the Cerberus, not if she wanted to avoid an even worse bloodbath. Not if she wanted her friends to survive.

And now Lawrence was really looking at her. At what she might be capable of. The fury in his eyes had been so raw it sent a chill down her spine.

Evy blinked out of the memory, the tingle of fear still present in her bones.

"One way or another, the Council will attempt to ensure a Shifter victory."

Two Ascendants now stood ahead of the Council's legacy. The Hierarch Wars were not going as planned.

If Zafir won the third trial and became the Hierarch, they knew he would likely gut the Council and rebuild it to benefit Zarokan.

The possibility of Evy winning was another scenario entirely, one full of unknowns and pure instability. The Council had to be growing desperate, and desperation bred dangerous thoughts.

Royen returned with two leather-bound books and placed them on the table among the scattered scrolls. "I'm sorry the Procession to Reyland was canceled." He took a seat across from her. "I was looking forward to seeing your home."

Evy shrugged. The Cerberus attack on Ruitheon had sent the Council scurrying, solely focused on repairs—delaying the start of the third trial by two weeks. They couldn't spare resources for the Procession. Or so they claimed.

"I understand." She absently scanned a scroll. "Bringing stability after the chaos of the Cerberus is a bigger priority."

But the truth hid beneath her words.

She was disappointed.

She had counted on the Procession to take her home, to allow her to debrief with Orianna and to hear something, anything, that might validate her progress as Reyland's Ascendant.

And more than anything, she'd wanted time with Aeric. A moment away from the scrutiny and pressure, where she could unfurl and just be herself.

Evy had a creeping suspicion this had been the Council's plan all along. Within the two-week delay, the Ascendants could have easily made it to and from Reyland, just as originally planned. Perhaps they never meant to expose Celeste, Zafir, and especially Royen to the conditions of Reyland. Gods forbid their future Hierarch garner sympathy for the Witches.

Royen opened one of the books and began flipping through

its pages. "At least it gives us more time to prepare for the third trial."

"Which reminds me," Evy said. "Thank you for coming to my rescue earlier."

Royen looked up and offered a small smile. In that moment, Evy was overcome with a quiet swell of emotions. They had been through so much together in such a short time—the Procession, the Draemor, the Cerberus, Hollowrift—and somewhere along the way, his icy demeanor had melted, and he had let her in. He had become a friend. A true ally.

And when he smiled at her, his sternness easing into brief, but more frequent, moments of warmth, she couldn't help but notice the softness of his lips, the way his features came together—handsome in a way she hadn't expected—

She glanced away, a rush of blood prickling the back of her neck.

His looks had nothing to do with it. She scolded herself for the thoughts and turned her attention to the towering shelves surrounding them, each lined with thousands of books and scrolls.

The Grand Library of Ruitheon was said to hold every piece of recorded knowledge in the realm. She was grateful that the Cerberus hadn't reached it.

She had tried to get inside earlier that afternoon to find literature on the Blighted Caves, but the scholars had barred her entry. Royen happened to be there with the same idea and stepped in, insisting they treat her, an Ascendant, with respect and reminding them the library was meant for the public.

"I figured it'd be easier if we tackled the research together." Royen set one of the books between them. "I suspect our greatest advantage will be knowing what we're up against."

Evy raised a brow. "Is that the only advantage you have?"

Royen leaned back in his chair, arms crossing tightly. "Yes." A scowl tugged at his mouth. "Although, if I'm being honest,

Lawrence tried to give me an enchanted ring. Said it would ward off the Draemor."

Evy smirked, unable to help herself.

Royen frowned. "What?"

Her smile widened.

"I'm obviously not going to use it." He scoffed.

A nearby scholar hissed a warning hush.

Evy lowered her voice. "Why not? We're allowed to take one object that might help us in the caves."

"If I take something, I want to obtain it myself."

"Then can you at least get those rings for the rest of us?" Evy asked. "I wouldn't mind avoiding the Draemor altogether."

"I wish I could." Royen shook his head. "Those rings are a Daryn family invention. Lawrence keeps them locked in the treasury and only issues them to paladins sent into the Blighted Caves."

Evy sighed. "Of course."

"Besides," Royen said, turning back to the scrolls, "we can't worry about objects or advantages when we don't know what we're walking into. Let's focus on why we're here."

They returned to their work and pored over the books and scrolls, looking for anything that mentioned the Draemor or the Blighted Caves, for the next hour.

At one point, they both reached for the same scroll. His fingers grazed hers.

"Sorry," he muttered, then pushed the scroll toward her.

"It's fine," she said, and meant it, though she didn't look up right away.

Royen angled an open book toward her. "Look at this. It's about the Draemlord. He's considered the king of the Draemor."

"The *king*? I don't like the sound of that." Evy leaned in and skimmed the passage. "It says the first Draemor ever imprisoned in the Blighted Caves still lives in the deepest lair. He's said to be as old as Ruitheon itself."

"Does it say anything about weaknesses?" Royen asked.

"Let's see." She spent a few minutes reading through the rest of the page. "Nothing specific. But there's something interesting here... It says he's forgotten his true name, so he's accepted the title of Draemlord completely. No one seems to know what his name used to be."

Her curiosity was piqued, and she glanced at the nearby scrolls. "Was there any mention of his name in those?"

When only silence answered, Evy glanced over. Royen was lost in thought, fidgeting, ripping at his cuticles.

"Royen?"

He inhaled. "Apologies. What were you saying?"

"Is everything alright?"

He hesitated, then let out a quiet sigh. "A letter came this morning. From Marq."

Evy's eyes widened. "He's not ill, is he?"

Royen shook his head. "He insists on traveling to Ruitheon for the final trial. He wants to be there for me." His mouth tightened. "I'm worried about him. About the dangers of travel in his state."

Evy imagined Lord Aldrich Veyn would never allow his only son to venture out of Theribane without proper protection.

"Marq will be fine," she said. "And having someone you care about here with you—well, it might help. Listen to this."

She unfurled the paper and read aloud. "The Draemor will first attack the mind before attempting to attack the body. They often target those with mental afflictions or acute melancholy, finding it easier to infest a vulnerable mind."

"'Infest' their mind," Royen repeated. "That sounds ominous."

"It's a metaphor for possession," Evy explained, her voice thinning as the memory of the guard in Theribane resurfaced. How he clutched his head, how his eyes flashed red before he turned the blade on himself.

She shuddered, pushed the thought aside, and kept reading.

"The Draemor should only be confronted by those with fortified minds and pure thoughts in order to avoid possession. Once a Draemor enters a weakened mind, curing the infection may prove futile. One *must* be mentally durable when facing a Draemor."

Royen huffed. "That must be why they call it the Trial of Resilience."

Evy nodded. "Exactly. You need a resilient mind to withstand the brutality of a trial like this." Royen's brows were still drawn together, expression distant.

"Don't you see? This passage explains that you have an advantage, after all." Evy reached for his hands. The feel of his skin beneath hers sent a tingling energy through her fingers. She willed herself not to withdraw. "And it's the advantage that matters most. If there's one thing I know, it's that Marq will help you stay strong. He'll help you stay resilient, 'mentally durable,' as the passage says."

She squeezed gently, truly happy for him, though she couldn't quite swallow the envy. She missed home more than she could express.

Royen was silent, his hazel eyes fixed on Evy's hands. "I guess you're about to have your own advantage."

He suddenly pulled back and started rummaging through his bag. "I meant to give you this earlier, but I couldn't find the right moment."

He took out a folded red sheet of paper. "I have a gift for you."

"A gift? For me?"

"Just a small thank-you for saving my life." He extended the paper toward her. "I remember before we arrived in Theribane, you mentioned you were homesick."

Evy leaned forward, squinting at the paper. "Is that—"

"A permit," Royen confirmed. "So you can bring someone special from Reyland. A piece of home."

"Royen." Her heart beat rapidly against her chest. "How?"

"I pulled some strings." He gave a faint, almost sheepish shrug. "You were right. Having Marq here is a big advantage. I figured you deserved something similar. It's only fair."

Unable to contain herself, Evy shot up from her chair, rushed around the table to him, and threw her arms around his neck.

He tensed at first, but then slowly, awkwardly, wrapped his arms around her waist. He had given her an advantage she desperately desired—one that could shape how they fared in the third trial. She let herself remain in his arms for a few blissful moments. He was truly her ally. There was no denying it.

"Thank you," Evy whispered. "You don't know how much I needed this."

At last, they let go of each other. His face was completely flushed, beads of sweat forming on his forehead. She must have held onto him too long, the heat between their bodies stifling him.

"Y-yes. Anyway." Royen coughed into his hand. "Who will you send for?"

She paused in thought. Summoning Orianna would be the practical choice. Her guidance would be invaluable in Ruitheon.

But would she bring the comfort Evy needed before the Trial of Resilience? As much as Evy loved her, she wasn't sure. She feared the Magister's presence would only add more pressure.

Either of her parents, then? No. She couldn't subject them to the harshness beyond Reyland's borders. And she didn't want them to see her like this, not while she was burdened and under intense scrutiny. She didn't want them to worry for her.

And only one other person came to mind. Someone strong enough to make the journey. Someone who would bring her some peace.

"Take me with you. I could protect you."

She remembered his words.

And maybe it wasn't his protection she needed, but the comfort only he could offer.

A smile touched her lips. "Aeric," she murmured.

Royen's expression puckered. "Aeric," he repeated. "That name again."

Evy paused. "What do you mean?"

"You've mentioned him before." He didn't elaborate. "Is he a… friend?"

Evy thought back to the moment she'd said goodbye, forehead to forehead, their lips almost touching.

"He's a very close friend. One of my oldest."

Royen glanced down at the scrolls. "I'm glad," he said after a moment. "You deserve comfort from such"—his jaw tightened—"companionship."

Then he gathered his things, avoiding her eyes. "Thank you for your time, Evy." He rose. "I need to write home and catch the post before it leaves the city."

Without waiting for her to respond, he gave a curt nod and walked away.

THIRTY-SIX

Yorik gripped the reins as he crested a low hill, the sun hovering above golden dunes. Ahead lay an arid stretch, a wasteland befitting the rot beneath it. He looked down at the thick, pulsing rivers of cerulean mana snaking through the land, and his lips curled in silent disgust.

The skyline of Ruitheon emerged in the distance.

Unholy, whispered the voice.

Yorik huffed in agreement. It was a city perched atop decay, draped in the facade of divinity.

Behind him, his brother leaned against the side of the open carriage, the wind tugging at his auburn hair.

"We're getting close," Aeric said, alight with anticipation. "Think Evy will be home when we get there?"

Yorik stayed silent, fixed on the road.

Aeric sighed. "You could at least pretend to be excited. I've never been outside of Reyland."

"I am excited, little brother," Yorik said, glancing back at him. "Everything is unfolding exactly as it should."

"Not this again." Aeric groaned. "Look, Yorik, I'm not here

for your divine plan or whatever. I gave you information. I brought you here. My part's done."

"Is it now?" He turned to face Aeric and was met with a glower.

"After you drop me off, leave us alone."

Yorik returned his gaze to the road, holding back an unexpected quiver in his lip.

After all he had sacrificed—the spells that had left his insides decimated. He had done it all for them—for Aeric and his mother. For them, he was willing to endure anything.

But there was no gratitude. No understanding.

Calm.

The voices wrapped around him, and he felt an instant warmth.

They'll appreciate all that you've done when you bring in the new world.

Yorik agreed.

They rode the rest of the way in silence.

As the gates neared, his grip on the reins tightened.

Aeric hopped down from the carriage as a guard approached. He pulled a red parchment from his satchel and held it up with a sheepish smile.

"I'm Queen Evalene Lovejoy's personal guest."

The guard examined the document. "You're cleared."

Yorik stepped down next and handed over a blue slip. As the guard studied it, the whispers in Yorik's mind turned frantic.

It's here.

The rot.

Yorik closed his eyes, savoring their fevered chorus.

"Temporary travel permit?"

The guard's question snapped him back. "That's correct," Yorik said calmly.

The guard gave it another look. "You have until the last light to leave the city." His hand rested meaningfully on the blade at his hip. "No detours. If you're not back and logged by sundown, there will be consequences."

Yorik offered a small, compliant smile. "Understood."

His expression darkened into a scowl as soon as the guard walked away.

The gates opened, and the brothers hopped back onto the carriage and rolled into the city.

Aeric leaned forward, eyes wide. "Gods, look at this place."

Yorik kept his gaze on the road. A woman on the street corner caught sight of them and glowered. Yorik's fingers tightened on the reins. He would level every one of them one day and they wouldn't see it coming. He clicked his tongue and drove on.

The carriage wheels clattered over smooth roads as they pulled into a quiet lane lined with palm trees and stopped in front of a large house.

Aeric leaped down before the carriage came to a full stop. Yorik climbed down after him, stretching his back as the front door creaked open.

"I wasn't expecting you until tomorrow morning," a maid said as she stepped out with a linen towel draped over her shoulder. She softened at the sight of Aeric.

"Irma!" Aeric grinned. "Surprise! We kept moving so we wouldn't waste time."

Irma opened the door wider. "Evy's at the library with the other Ascendants. She should be back soon, so why don't you both come in and rest?"

Yorik shook his head. "Can't. I need to be back at the gates by sundown."

Irma glanced at the sky. "There's still some time. You could at least get a bite to eat."

"I'd rather not test the guards' patience." Yorik turned to Aeric. "Enjoy yourself, little brother."

He winked, then climbed back on the carriage. Ignoring

wary glances from passersby, Yorik rode through the city. He found a narrow alley between two sandstone buildings and tucked the horse and carriage away.

Looking up, he noted Irma had been right. There was still light. Perhaps an hour, maybe two.

He stepped into the shadows, arms outstretched as he summoned a soul to power his spell. The air thickened with dark mist. A faint moan echoed behind him, and the sudden howl of wind drowned out its sorrow.

Cold numbness spread through him as the spell caught hold, drawing him inward and wrapping him in shadow. As long as he stayed in darkness, he would be invisible to the common eye.

Then came a sudden jolt of pain.

He collapsed to his knees, choking as blood spilled from his mouth. It splattered across dirt and stone. Another heave racked his body. His limbs trembled. His vision blurred.

The pain will pass, the Gods murmured in a soothing whisper. *When the spell is complete, when the last ingredient is ours, your body will no longer break. You will wield it all.*

He wiped the blood from his chin, drew a ragged breath, then smiled. His Acolytes were already en route to the outskirts of Theribane to gather the first ingredient.

"I will wield it all," he echoed.

The Gods spoke again, guiding him toward his next destination.

Yorik drew his hood tighter and stepped out of the alley, his spell still active, blending him into the city's dark edges as he moved toward the Grand Library.

He stopped at the edge of the plaza and slipped into the shadows between stacked crates.

There they were. On the library steps.

All four Ascendants trickled out of the marble doors, chatting as they descended into the evening light. Evy walked among them, smiling up at a tall young man Yorik guessed must be Royen Veyn.

Evy stilled, fingers pressing to the back of her neck. She looked around, wary. Yorik melted farther into the shadows. After a moment, she shrugged and continued walking.

Celeste trailed behind the others, arms wrapped around herself, her steps slow and unfocused. Her wings drooped behind her, trailing glittering mist. Her eyes were distant.

She was starting to crack.

It was plain as daylight.

And it was exactly what Yorik needed for the curse to take root faster.

He licked his lips, watching the soft flutter of her wings.

"Beautiful," he whispered.

She broke from the group, and Yorik followed her through the winding, lamplit streets until music and laughter drew her into a tavern.

He lurked outside, veiled in shadow, watching her through the window as she stepped inside.

The place was alive with sound, with pipes and drums and a bard shouting verses over a cracked lute. Celeste tossed a coin purse onto the bar and ordered a round of drinks for the house.

Cheers erupted. Men raised their cups and clapped her on the back.

She laughed, head thrown back, hair swaying like pink ribbons. She lifted her arms and danced, letting the rhythm carry her.

Yorik wiped fresh blood from the corner of his mouth. The shadow veil was breaking. He bled the magic away, then layered a thinner concealment. It would suffice.

The tavern door creaked open as he stepped inside.

No one glanced his way as he moved through the crowd.

He chose a table in the rear, close enough for a clear view and far enough to keep to the margins.

And he waited.

Eventually, Celeste returned to her seat a few tables away, breathless and rosy-cheeked, sipping from her cup.

She was facing him.

He let the veil fall.

Celeste tilted her head, squinting into the dim tavern light.

Then she raised delicate fingers to her lips. "Herald?" She gasped softly. "What are you doing here?"

Yorik leaned forward, letting the candlelight brighten his face.

"Hello, Rose."

THIRTY-SEVEN

The night air should have felt cool and welcome against Evy's cheeks after hours in the stifling heat of the Grand Library. Instead, her very bones shuddered with a chill she hadn't been able to shake since leaving with the other Ascendants. Her spirits had felt it too, restless and on edge, as though they sensed an unwanted presence. But when she had looked around, there was nothing.

She had blamed it on nerves.

Her boots crunched over the gravel walkway. She paused at the front door, hand resting on the knob, and let out a quiet sigh. Her thoughts shifted to the Draemlord.

After a week and a half of studying with the other Ascendants, they concluded they would have to face the king of Draemor to escape the Blighted Caves. It was the final challenge, the greatest obstacle, and the place where they believed many Ascendants had failed in past Hierarch Wars.

Royen had been convinced that the ring Lawrence offered him would have changed his outcome with the Draemlord. He believed the artifact would have weakened the creature just enough for an easy escape.

But he refused the advantage, wanting to prove his own worth.

The final trial was in two days, and Evy still wasn't sure she was ready. Wasn't sure she could face the Draemor or hold her mind against them. She only hoped Aeric would reach Ruitheon in time. Having a piece of home, even for a day, would help.

Evy turned the doorknob and stepped inside the townhouse.

"Irma, can you run a bath for me?" Evy called as she shut the door behind her. "And can you add strawberry tonic and almond oil? I need to get the smell of ink off me."

"Strawberry tonic and almond oil? Sounds delicious."

She froze.

That definitely wasn't Irma's voice. It was deeper. Familiar. Her heart fluttered with realization.

"Aeric?"

There he was, his auburn hair in wild tousles, a bit longer than when she'd last seen him. The summer had deepened his complexion, and the contrast made his stormy blue-gray eyes more vivid.

His mouth tugged into that sheepish grin she now realized she found irresistible.

Aeric shifted awkwardly. "Evy." His mouth opened, then closed. "Evy, I—"

But he never finished.

Evy crossed the room in a heartbeat and threw her arms around him, pressing her face to his chest.

Aeric held her tight.

Months of pressure and loneliness came crashing down like a wave.

She hadn't let herself fully feel it, even when she started to crack. Even when the Veyns circled her like lions in Theribane. Even when the Cerberus threatened their lives. She'd kept it all buried. What choice did she have, with the entire realm watching? When every judgment cast on her reflected on Reyland?

Evy's fingers tightened in the loose fabric of Aeric's shirt, and she inhaled. He smelled like pine. Like home.

Aeric held her closer, and Evy let go of her emotions.

Tears slipped down her cheeks, soaking his clothes as her body shook. Here, in his arms, she could unravel.

For the first time in what felt like forever, she truly felt safe.

And for just a moment, she could simply *be*.

Because the only person who had ever seen her, *really* seen her, was the boy who didn't think of her as the Queen.

Or the Shaman.

Or the Ascendant.

The boy who was holding her now, enveloping her in the warmth of his affection, had always seen her as Evy.

His Evy.

She pulled back just enough to look up at him.

"Thank you." Her voice trembled. "Thank you so much for coming."

Aeric said nothing, just looked at her with that quiet intensity she'd missed so desperately.

"I missed you," she said.

He leaned in until their foreheads touched. Just like that night in the field before she left Reyland. They had pulled away then. She couldn't remember why. She could only recall the regret of not seeing her feelings through.

This time, she wouldn't let him get away.

As naturally as the tide returning to shore, their lips met.

The kiss was warm, desperate, and filled with all the things they couldn't say in words. All the longing, the ache. It swallowed them whole, folding the world away until there was nothing left but the two of them.

When they finally broke apart, they were both flushed. Evy dropped her gaze to the floor, suddenly shy.

But Aeric lifted her chin with a finger, coaxing her to meet his eyes.

"I missed you too," he whispered.

She buried herself against his chest, arms wrapping tight around him once more. And she let herself melt away.

THIRTY-EIGHT

Celeste joined Yorik at the secluded table in the back, tucked far enough from the bustle to speak in private. She slid onto the wooden bench beside him, her hips shifting closer until their legs nearly touched.

"So how did you get that scar?" She pointed to the mark running down Yorik's brow.

He traced a finger along its ridges, thinking about the outcome of his late father's violent rages.

"A wayward fishing lure." He smiled.

"Really? How does that happen?" Celeste laughed. Yorik shrugged.

"Herald," she murmured as the tavern buzzed around them. "Meeting here... This has to be fate."

Yorik leaned in. "What are the odds?"

"But really..." Her arm brushed his. "What brings a Witch to Ruitheon? Not enchanted by another Fairy, I hope?"

Yorik lifted his mug, smirking over the rim. "I dropped off Queen Evalene's guest from Reyland." He kept it vague, omitting the details. If Celeste mentioned it to Evy, she might ask questions. Questions that could uncover far more than he wanted the Shaman Queen to know.

"Ah, yes. Her suitor from back home." Celeste rested her chin in her palm and let out a wistful sigh. "Poor Royen. His romantic gesture completely backfired."

He didn't comment, but a small, almost imperceptible frown tugged at the corner of his mouth.

Royen Veyn with the woman his brother supposedly loved.

He'd save that for later.

"How long are you in Ruitheon?" Celeste asked, lazily swirling the amber liquid in her glass.

"I have to be out before sunset," Yorik replied, then pulled the folded blue slip from his coat pocket. "Temporary permit. Figured I'd grab something to eat before heading off."

Celeste pouted, tucking a curl behind her ear. "Well, I'm glad I caught you before you vanished again. Ever since we met in the forest, I've been thinking about you."

Yorik smirked. "Can't lie, I've thought about you too. Didn't expect to run into you here, of all places." He leaned forward on his elbows, feigning innocent curiosity. "Are you in Ruitheon as a scholar?"

Celeste opened her mouth, then hesitated, reaching for an answer Yorik could already tell wasn't the truth. But before she could speak, a server appeared, balancing a tray piled high with warm bread and a fresh jug of ale.

"Let me know if there's anything else you need, Princess," the server said with a bow before vanishing into the crowd.

Celeste grimaced, staring at the space where he'd been.

"*Princess?*" Yorik echoed. "What does he mean by that? Are you some kind of royalty, Rose?"

Celeste turned to him slowly, lips pressed into a thin line.

Yorik tapped his chin. "I don't know much about this world, but I've heard Virenna only has one princess. And if I remember right, her name is Celeste DuVent."

She let out a groan.

"Okay, okay. My name's not Rose. I'm sorry I lied."

Yorik feigned confusion. "If you're not Rose, then..." His tone shifted. "Are you *actually* Princess Celeste DuVent?"

Celeste gave a reluctant nod.

Yorik began to rise. "Then I must sincerely apologize, Your Highness, for not addressing you properly—"

Before he could finish, Celeste grabbed his arm and yanked him back down.

"Please, don't do that." Her fingers fisted in the collar of his coat and she drew him close until their faces nearly touched. Her emerald eyes trembled with desperation and heat. "Don't get all courteous on me now."

"Princess," Yorik said, voice dropping, "someone like you shouldn't be seen with someone like me."

Celeste released his collar but didn't look away. "And why not? What exactly is wrong with you?"

"Well, for starters, I'm a Witch."

"And?" She crossed her arms. Yorik could see the faintest hint of a dark tendril flowing beneath her skin. The curse was rampaging within her. "That doesn't make you lesser."

"Your Highness, they'd flog me for this." He glanced around the tavern. "If the wrong person saw us—"

"I get to choose my own companions," Celeste cut in. "I should at least have that." Her gaze fell to the table. "And don't call me Your Highness or Princess. I hate it."

"Okay," Yorik said quietly. "I won't." His voice dropped to a murmur. "I hope I'm not being too forward. But... perhaps you could still be my Rose."

Celeste's cheeks flushed. "*Your* Rose?"

Yorik began to rise again. "Forgive me, I overstepped—"

"Relax." She tugged him back down and pulled him so close their bodies touched. "Maybe I could be yours." Her voice dipped lower. "Maybe just for tonight."

Yorik leaned in, his lips grazing the shell of her ear.

"Why just tonight?" he whispered and felt her shiver. "From the moment I met you in the forest, I wanted to pluck you from the garden and keep you tucked in my pocket forever."

They remained there, breath mingling.

But Yorik sighed and slid back. "Only, I do have to go soon. The sun's nearly down. I'll be in real trouble if I'm not back at the gate."

Celeste's smile fell. Then it returned, brighter. "I have an idea. I think I can buy you some time. Enough to stay the night."

He watched her carefully. "An idea?"

"Nothing my illusion magic and a small bribe can't fix." She leaned in again. "Will you stay with me, Herald? I could use a little distraction."

She licked her bottom lip and took a slow sip of her drink.

Yorik grinned. "I'd be honored to offer my companionship… in any way you require."

Celeste stood and grabbed his hand. "Follow me."

As they weaved through the tavern, the voices in Yorik's head began to whisper in a frenzy.

They're coming. Mark them. Follow them.

Confused by the sudden command, he quickly scanned the tavern. Two hooded men moved toward him, their skin like magma, their slitted eyes burning like fire.

Ifreet.

Them, the voices urged.

There was no room for hesitation. Yorik called upon the shadows and gathered a spell at his fingertips. As he passed one of the Ifreeti, he bumped shoulders with him.

"Watch it," the man growled.

"My apologies." Yorik placed a hand on his shoulder. His finger pressed just firmly enough to mark the Ifreet with a tracking spell.

A cold shiver ran through him. The spell would slowly wear

on his own mind and body, but he obeyed the Gods. They hadn't misled him yet.

He'd follow up with the marked Ifreet the next day.

There was another task to complete tonight.

He turned his gaze to Celeste's glittering wings ahead and caught up to her.

Together, they slipped out of the tavern and ducked into a narrow alley.

"Stay here." Her wings spread open. "I'm going to find someone I can pay to act as your decoy. Won't take long."

With a flutter of her wings, she hovered just high enough to press a kiss to Yorik's mouth.

He stumbled back, caught off guard, but then gave in completely. Her lips were soft, urgent, hungry. He kissed her back, just as ravenous, until all he wanted was to consume her entirely.

They finally pulled apart, but Celeste let her mouth linger along the edge of his jaw.

"I'll be right back," she whispered, and she was gone.

Yorik exhaled, letting the alley's cool air wrap around him.

A sudden haptic buzz needled in his ears. His expression shifted as pain lanced through his eyes.

A message from one of his Acolytes.

He stepped deeper into the shadows, away from the street's view, and let the spell unfold.

Dark mist curled in the air, swirling into symbols before solidifying into words.

Yorik let out a low, wicked laugh as he read:

We have the first ingredient.

THIRTY-NINE

"It's morning," Evy muttered.

She lay curled against Aeric's chest, one leg draped lazily over his. The swing rocked gently beneath them, its chains creaking softly.

A breeze slipped across the balcony, making her shiver. She instinctively pressed herself closer to the warm linen of Aeric's shirt. His heartbeat thrummed beneath her cheek as his fingers idly threaded through her hair.

As the sun rose, the world beyond the balcony began to stir. Birds called from the date trees below as hooves clattered faintly over distant cobblestone.

Evy let out a long, contented sigh.

They hadn't slept. Instead, they'd spent the night talking. Kissing. Then talking some more.

She inhaled, taking in the scents of sea salt and pine. If only she could bottle it.

"What a sight." Aeric looked beyond the grated metal railing.

The broken streets below looked almost peaceful. The jagged scars left by the Cerberus had already faded, swept away by the city's eagerness to rebuild and forget.

Evy lifted her head. "We should get some sleep soon," she said. "But maybe after that, we could walk around the city. Or what's left of it."

Aeric scanned the streets below as if searching for someone, though there weren't many people out at this hour. Before Evy could ask what he was looking for, he spoke again. "Do you think that's a good idea? Don't you need to prepare for the trial tomorrow?"

"Time with you is exactly what I need for the Trial of Resilience." Her nose brushed the line of his jaw. "If I'm going to survive whatever horrors await in the Blighted Caves, I need to stockpile on happiness."

He tilted his head until their noses touched.

"I wish you could skip the whole thing," he murmured. "Forget the trial. Forget all of it. Just stay here with me."

Their lips had just brushed when a sharp knock at the bedroom door startled them.

Evy sighed and pulled herself from the swing, limbs reluctant to leave the cocoon of Aeric's warmth.

Barefoot, she padded inside and crossed to the door. When she opened it, Irma stood on the other side, hands folded tightly in front of her apron.

"Someone's here to see you." Irma's voice carried a nervous edge.

Evy stiffened. "Who is it?"

Irma shook her head. "You should come down."

Evy glanced back. Aeric had slumped against the cushion, eyes closed, dozing.

She gathered her skirts, followed Irma into the hall, and descended the stairs.

At the base, she saw her visitor.

He stood near the front door with his back to her. His usually pristine collar was wrinkled, his hands limp at his sides.

"Royen?"

He turned at the sound of her voice.

Evy froze.

His face was twisted in sorrow, tears carving glistening paths down his pale cheeks. She rushed forward, hands finding his and gripping them tightly.

"Royen, what happened? Are you hurt?"

He shook his head, chest heaving violently. His lips parted, but no words came. Just ragged, gasping breaths, like a man drowning.

"Then what is it?" She pressed him, fighting the panic rising in her voice. "Please, tell me what's wrong."

It took him a moment before the words came.

"It's Marq." His voice cracked. "His caravan was attacked as they were leaving Theribane's southern border. They're saying it was the Draemor." He choked on his words. "Multiple, judging by the damage. They slaughtered everyone. Guards, drivers, his staff—" He broke off, sucking in a breath. "All dead."

He paused and lifted his gaze to hers. His hazel eyes were hollow.

"Except him. They didn't find Marq."

Evy stared, her pulse thrumming in her ears.

"Are you saying Marq is… missing?"

Royen nodded.

"The investigators said his carriage was torn open. There was blood everywhere. But no sign of him."

"Are they sure he's missing?" she whispered, fighting back tears. "They didn't find him anywhere?"

Royen dragged a sleeve across his face. "No. He was nowhere to be found. But they did find… a hint of him left behind."

"What was it?"

He swallowed hard.

"A sparrow feather."

With that, Royen's tears returned in a flood.

Evy pulled him into her arms. His body sagged against her, grief pouring out in broken gasps.

She held him tight, her own thoughts scattered with flashes of Marq's charismatic smile, the way he could dispel tension with an inappropriately timed joke, the way he always coaxed the best out of Royen.

She pulled back slightly, smoothing a hand over his trembling shoulder.

"Isn't it possible he escaped?" she asked gently. "Maybe he's hiding. Waiting for the danger to pass. Maybe he's just... lost."

"I need him to be alive," Royen rasped. "I *need* him, Evy. He's my family. My only *true* family. The only one who cared whether I lived or died. The only one who didn't see me as a political pawn."

His face crumpled again, and the sobs came harder. "He's the only one who gave a damn about me."

Evy's heart ached. She reached for his hand and squeezed it. "That's not true."

Royen didn't answer.

"Marq may be the one who's always stood beside you," she said, "but he's not the only one who cares."

His eyes were bloodshot, chest still rising and falling rapidly.

"I care about you, Royen. I don't care about the games this world makes us play. I care about *you*."

She held his hand tighter.

"And after saving your life, I think it's safe to say I give a damn whether you live or die."

He looked at her like he didn't know how to believe her.

But slowly, his hands curled around hers, grip tightening.

His breathing began to slow. He met her eyes, lashes still wet with tears. For a long moment, he just stared.

"I care for you too," he whispered at last. "More than I should, I think."

Royen lifted a quivering hand and brushed a strand of her

hair off her cheek, his fingers grazing her jaw with startling gentleness. His touch was featherlight as he tilted her chin upward.

And for some inexplicable reason, she found herself unable to move a muscle.

Is this a paralysis spell?

Another tear slipped down Royen's face and touched her lip, and her tongue grazed over it, tasting the salt.

No. This wasn't a spell.

Royen's face inched closer, and though her thoughts rebelled, her body stayed still.

What is he doing?

And then, before she could blink, before she could truly come to her senses—

Royen's lips hovered over hers.

She felt his breath warm against her skin, the faintest brush of his mouth almost touching hers.

Evy was still frozen. She didn't know why she couldn't pull away, even though her instincts screamed, ordering her to move.

He was going to kiss her, and she couldn't stop it.

Did she *want* to stop it?

Aeric's face flashed through her mind—the night she had just spent wrapped in his arms.

Aeric.

If Evy didn't act now, she would commit an unforgivable betrayal. One she could never walk away from.

The moment shattered. Her body jolted with clarity, and she pressed both hands to Royen's chest, pushing him back.

"I-I'm sorry. We shouldn't—" The words tumbled out, her cheeks burning with shame.

Royen's eyes widened. He looked down, as if the magnitude of what he'd almost done had finally hit him.

"Evy?"

The achingly familiar voice came from behind her.

She turned.

Aeric stood at the foot of the stairs, his gaze narrowing as it shifted between her and Royen.

Royen's transformation was swift. He wiped his face with the heel of his palm, dragging away any trace of tears. His mouth was set in a tight line. His eyes turned cold, giving him an uncanny similarity to his uncle, Lord Aldrich.

"Is everything okay?" Aeric's voice was tight with suspicion.

"I— Yes," Evy stammered.

Royen nodded once. "My apologies for the inconvenience, Queen Evalene." His tone was suddenly formal and clipped. "I simply wished to inform you that despite recent events, the Council has decided to proceed with the final trial tomorrow."

Evy nodded, barely registering the words.

"I'll see you there." Royen's gaze remained on her a moment too long. "Good day." He turned and walked out.

Aeric stepped to her side and wrapped an arm around her shoulders. "Who was that?"

She didn't answer. Her lips still tingled where his breath had touched them.

Stunned and tangled in guilt and confusion, she found herself unable to speak.

FORTY

Sunlight spilled through the arched glass windows, motes drifting lazily in the air. The scent of crushed rose petals perfumed the sour tang of spilled wine.

Yorik sat upright against the gilded headboard of Celeste's bed, a sheet of pale silk draped loosely across his lap. Her head rested there, rose-colored hair cascading over his thighs in soft waves.

Her breathing was slow and even.

His fingers threaded absently through her hair. He didn't realize he was stroking her until he caught himself. He scoffed and pulled his hand back.

The room was drenched in indulgence.

Crystal vases overflowed with exotic blooms. A chandelier glittered above, catching the light and throwing it in fractured bursts across the walls. Pillows embroidered with gold thread lay scattered across the bed and floor.

Yorik sneered.

While families in Reyland huddled in hovels and struggled to find food for their empty bellies, the elite drowned in comfort.

They were blissfully unaware that they were becoming fat with rot.

None of this would survive the cleansing. He would level it all. Scrape the world clean.

Yorik shut his eyes as the voices of the Gods closed in around him.

Heal the world.

Save them.

“I will,” he whispered. “I'll save them all.”

Celeste stirred at the sound of his voice. His gaze drifted across the curve of her bare back to the wings rising from her shoulder blades, quivering faintly from a residual dream.

So fragile.

And yet, so powerful.

A slow, hungry smile curved his lips. He hovered his hand over one wing and imagined the sound of tendons tearing, snapping beneath his grip.

He pictured unmaking her, piece by delicate piece, until she was no more an angel than he was.

But the Gods whispered again, firmer this time.

Not yet.

Yorik exhaled through his nose. They were right.

Celeste was far more dangerous than she let on. And she wasn't stupid, even if she liked to play the part. Striking now would be suicide. A waste of all he'd endured, and all he was becoming.

His finger traced the edge of her wing.

Celeste startled awake with a soft gasp. Seeing Yorik, her lips spread into a slow, sleep-heavy smile.

“Gods.” Her voice cracked. “What a night.” She nuzzled against his chest before looking up again. “It's been ages since I've had that much fun.”

“I hope I didn't pressure you,” he said. “I don't want you to regret last night.”

"Gods, no. I wasn't pressured. At all. I just…" She trailed off, fingertips tracing idle circles across his chest. "I don't know how to explain it." Her gaze dropped to his collarbone. "There's something about you that makes me feel… different."

She looked up again, emerald eyes glinting like jewels.

"With you, I can be Rose. I don't have to be Celeste. I'm tired of being her. I'm tired of everything that comes with her."

Yorik brushed his lips to her temple.

"You can be whoever you want with me."

And he meant it. Because it didn't matter who she thought she was. Soon enough, she'd be what he needed her to be.

But to get her there, he needed to act. He needed her in a place of irrevocable devotion.

"What is it?" she asked. "You're frowning."

Yorik let out a frustrated sigh. "You *are* my Rose, but you're also the Princess of Virenna. Pretending doesn't change that. And no matter how much you want to forget it, that's not a fate you can escape."

Celeste sat up and turned away from him.

Yorik reached for her hand, but she pulled back.

"Last night wasn't just a moment for me," he explained. "Whatever this is between us is starting to grow into emotions I can't ignore." He let out a short, self-deprecating laugh. "Maybe that's foolish. But the more my feelings grow, the more I worry what they'll cost."

She didn't speak.

He pressed on. "You can be whoever you want with me. Be Rose if you'd like. But the world won't see it that way. They'll only see Princess Celeste DuVent, heir to the Virennese throne. I doubt your mother or the rest of the realm would take kindly to a Witch in your bed."

When she finally turned to face him, her expression shifted from anger to sorrow and finally what he thought was desperation. He'd seen that look before in his own Acolytes, lost and searching for answers. She chewed her lip, her gaze distant, as if considering every gilded chain that bound her.

He'd found her soft spot. It was raw and exposed.

The voices curled close to his ear.

She's choking on the life they built for her.

She wants out. She wants to fly.

Celeste was a caged bird aching for the sky, desperate to taste the wind. But she didn't see what waited in the clouds. Didn't see the talons reaching toward her.

Fly to us, little bird, the Gods whispered.

We will catch you.

And never let you go.

"And never let you go," Yorik repeated.

"What?" Celeste asked, puzzled.

He shook his head, clearing the voices away. "I don't want to let you go."

Celeste gave him a half smile. "I don't want to let you go either." The hurt was gone, replaced by a look of determination.

"You're right. I don't have governance over my heart as a Princess. Not with my mother watching my every move." Her lips curved into a daring smile. "But if I become Hierarch? That changes everything. Hierarchs are untouchable. They can take any lover they want, no questions asked."

Her hand pressed against his chest.

"If I wanted a Witch lover, then I would have one. And I'd like to see anyone try to stop me." She leaned forward, eyes bright. "I'd cut the mana right out from under their feet."

Yorik just stared at her. Then his lips twisted. A scowl broke through before he could stop it. Of course that was her answer —to wield the rot itself, mistaking corruption for strength.

A piercing, cruel laugh burst from him, echoing against the painted walls.

The resolve in her expression withered into confusion, then offense.

"I'm so sorry." Yorik pressed a hand to his mouth. "Do you really believe you could win? I might be from the outside, but even I've heard how you've fared in the trials."

Her face flushed. She yanked the sheet around her chest.

"Get out," she snapped, voice shaking.

Yorik rose without protest and gathered his clothes from the floor.

He could feel her gaze on him as he dressed. They burned with fury but were tinged with a desperation she didn't bother to hide.

Once fully clothed, he made his way to the door. His thoughts drifted to the Ifreet he had marked the night before. This would be a good opportunity to slip away and track him, just as the Gods had commanded.

Before Yorik departed, his hand hovered at the frame.

He turned back. "For what it's worth, I meant what I said." His eyes hovered over her wings. "I never want to let you go."

Celeste said nothing, arms crossed tightly.

He turned again.

"Wait." Her voice was thin.

Yorik hesitated and looked back. The dark thread beneath her skin had spread into a thick web, branching toward her heart.

With feigned sorrow, he shook his head.

"I think it's better if I go. I shouldn't get my hopes up." He bit his lower lip, forcing a slight tremble. "Not if it means falling for someone I can't keep."

He stepped through the door. And he didn't stop.

Not even when she called after him.

Not even as the sound of her voice chased him down the corridor.

Yorik's strides quickened, echoing through the gilded hall.

Let her reach for him.

Because the more she reached, the easier it would be for her to tip.

And fall.

FORTY-ONE

A pale wash of gold spilled over the horizon, and shadows stretched across the looming dunes and hills beyond.

Ruitheon slumbered a few miles behind them, silent, still bruised from the aftermath of the Cerberus.

Evy rubbed her tired eyes as she took her place beside the other Ascendants. They had met before sunrise, and she was still trying to shake her exhaustion. The morning chill clung to her skin, but it wasn't the cold that raised goose bumps along her arms.

The Blighted Caves yawned before them, carved into the side of a jagged cliff. One gargantuan mouth split the stone at the center, wide enough to swallow a house, while over a dozen smaller openings dotted the surrounding rock face like the hollow, watching eyes of an insect.

Each entrance was shrouded with a thin veil of blue mist, a gossamer barrier that kept the vileness contained within.

A musty scent wafted from the openings, reminding Evy of death and rot.

She brought a hand to her mouth, willing herself not to gag.

They were surrounded by silence. There were no cheers or

trumpets, none of the fanfare that had marked the first two trials. Even the Children of Rui hadn't shown up. Evy didn't miss them.

A small cluster of citizens stood off to the side, brought in as witnesses. After the disaster of the Trial of Strength, there was no excitement in their faces. In its place were caution and fear.

The Council stood nearby in their dark robes. They had already set the incantation for the trial, and the Heart hovered above them with a thin tendril of blue mana stretching toward the rock face.

Evy squinted as a sliver of sunlight reflected off its golden, thorned cage. It wasn't whispering this time, but something stirred within it. She could hear a low, agitated hum, like the frantic wings of a disturbed beehive.

The sound vibrated in her skull.

Her spirits were equally restless, buzzing around her with jittery pulses. They didn't want to be here. She didn't either. This place felt wrong.

Lawrence stepped forward, the hem of his robes skimming the cracked earth.

"This is the final trial," he announced. "The Trial of Resilience."

The Ascendants turned to listen, and Lawrence scanned their faces before continuing.

"Each of you must choose one of the smaller entrances to the Blighted Caves. Not the center." He gestured to the largest mouth in the cliff. "That one is the exit."

He paced before them. "Every path will eventually lead to that central cavern. And beyond it lies freedom."

The wind shifted, carrying another waft of decay. Evy tried not to breathe it in, even though she knew she'd soon be engulfed by it.

"The goal of this trial is simple," Lawrence said. "You must exit the Blighted Caves before sundown. If you do not, a retrieval team will be sent in at dusk to extract you."

He paused and faced the Ascendants. "And if you require rescuing, you will be disqualified from the trials."

Evy clenched her fist. Disqualification would be a humiliating, public loss of dignity she couldn't bear to imagine.

"In addition to escaping," Lawrence said, "the Heart will judge how you survive. An Ascendant who emerges broken, spirit shattered, cannot be weighed equally with one who endures the horrors, barely scathed."

The Ascendants met each other's eyes.

"This trial will test one of the most sacred traits of the Hierarch. It measures the ability to withstand darkness and rise above evil."

His gaze settled on Evy.

"While you are allowed to take a single object inside with you, you are not permitted to harm each other."

Harm each other? Was the implication meant for her?

Evy gritted her teeth.

"This is not a test of sabotage," Lawrence continued. "Any attempt to interfere with another Ascendant's progress will result in immediate termination from the trials."

He lifted a hand toward the cliffs.

"Ascendants, choose your entrance."

For a moment, no one moved.

Then, slowly, the four of them exchanged glances, a hint of fear visible in their expressions.

Zafir moved first.

He cracked his knuckles and rolled his shoulders, then strode toward an opening near the far right.

He looked calm. Confident, even.

As he should. After the Trial of Strength, he was in the lead. He knew he was favored to win. During the study sessions in the library, he had said his fire would be enough to drive the vile creatures away. Evy looked him over. Sure enough, it seemed he had not brought an object to assist him in the caves. He would be relying solely on the power of his element.

Similarly, Evy had planned to rely on her light spirits alone, but now she wished she had brought a tonic to settle the discomfort in her toiling stomach.

Celeste hovered slightly above the ground, her wings fluttering. She tapped her chin in uncertainty, then selected a wide tunnel near the middle.

For the past few days, Celeste had insisted she was fine, but the light in her eyes, that spark Evy had come to admire, was gone. It had been that way since their encounter with the Cerberus. Evy wished she knew how to reach her friend, how to break through the facade and save her the way Celeste had saved Evy at Veyn Manor.

Then there was Royen.

He hadn't looked at her. Not once all morning.

He moved toward the far-left path, his expression blank. There was no hint of sorrow for Marq's disappearance, and that worried her.

But another worry tugged at her too.

The memory of Royen's lips hovering over hers. The faint tingle of his breath against her skin.

He had almost kissed her.

She shook her head, trying to banish the uninvited memory. *It didn't mean anything,* she told herself. Royen had been swept up in overwhelming fear and grief over Marq. A knee-jerk reaction. Nothing more.

Still, Evy wanted to talk to him, to make sure he knew nothing between them had changed. Their friendship mattered more than his slip of composure.

She turned to him as he passed. "Royen—"

But he didn't respond. Didn't even glance her way. His eyes were fixed on what looked like a wooden torch. It must have been his object, one he acquired on his own—still refusing the enchanted ring from Lawrence.

Evy swallowed hard.

Maybe it wasn't the best time to talk, not before the trial that awaited them. They needed to be in their best mental position for this challenge.

So she took a step toward a tunnel of her own. The mouth pulsed faintly with mana, a soft hum vibrating along the threshold.

Suddenly, out of the corner of her eye, she noticed movement.

Lawrence stood apart from the others, leaning close to a hooded Councilor and whispering. The other figure gave a single nod, then walked away.

Evy bit her lower lip as her intuition screamed.

But when had something *not* been wrong? Lawrence had slipped Royen the scroll before the first trial. Handed him the Celestial Gauntlets. And now, at the beginning of the final trial, with two Ascendants standing ahead of his chosen heir, he was likely scheming in corners. Maybe even working on moving against her.

Evy had done all she could to avoid the Council's ire. She had played Orianna's game. She had restrained herself, measured every step, calculated every display of power. She had shrunk for the sake of the realm's comfort. And all it had earned her was a target on her back that grew larger with every trial.

Was there ever any point in her performance?

Lawrence rejoined them, his cold gaze sweeping across the Ascendants one last time.

"The Ascendants may begin."

Zafir offered a slow, solemn nod, then stepped forward. His fiery eyes gleamed with purpose as he disappeared into the shadow of the cave.

Then Royen entered, fists clenched at his sides.

Celeste stood before her chosen entrance, adjusting a tiara she had claimed was enchanted with a protection spell. Her eyes were locked on something in the distance, just beyond a cluster of boulders.

Evy followed her gaze. A shadowed figure leaned against a rock. And just beneath the edge of their hood was a sliver of auburn hair.

Her heart skipped. *Aeric?*

No. He was still at the townhouse. She had told him to stay behind, to keep him safe after the chaos of the last trial. He'd promised her he would.

The figure turned and slipped behind the dunes, disappearing from sight.

Next to her, Celeste let out a soft, broken whimper.

"You don't have to do this," Evy said gently. "You can go in just a little, stay near the entrance, and wait for the rescue team."

Celeste let out a short, bitter laugh. "You think I'd let myself be carried out of this trial?"

"Celeste—"

"We all need to do this, Evy. Even if we pretend otherwise, all of us want that crown. You, Royen, Zafir…" She cast a look at the boulders. "And me."

She brushed a tear from her cheek and turned away. "Believe it or not, I have my reasons too."

Celeste stepped into her tunnel and vanished into the shadows.

A reason to want the Hierarch's crown.

Standing there alone at the mouth of the caves, Evy finally let herself name hers.

"Don't try to win," Orianna had said.

But Orianna wasn't here. She couldn't see that Evy had been marked by the Council from the beginning.

She thought of the Lumiels, of Casper Island, of all the untold stories the Council had erased through history. If they came for Evy, they wouldn't stop with her. They would come for all Witches.

Holding back wouldn't save her people. Not anymore.

It was glaringly obvious—the only thing that could protect the Witches was the throne itself.

She was done competing to belong. Now she was competing to rule. Because if she won, she would wipe the Council clean and turn their own threats against them.

And if the realm rebelled—her thoughts drifted back to the mock Council hearing during the first trial. She had navigated what was meant to be a realistic challenge. Perhaps she could do it again. Perhaps she could find a way to win the realm over.

Evy truly saw no other option.

She took one last look at the city in the distance. At the rising light of the sun.

Then she turned back toward the caves and stepped forward.

Shadows curled around her body, and the Blighted Caves swallowed her whole.

FORTY-TWO

Evy had lost all sense of time.

How long had she been walking? Minutes? Hours? It was impossible to tell within the constant darkness of the Blighted Caves.

She'd expected tunnels. Perhaps claustrophobic paths and narrow passageways carved into damp rock. But what she found beyond the mouth of the cave was a forest shrouded in eternal night.

Tall, ash-gray trees loomed all around, their black leaves rustling in an unknown source of wind. Delicate mist drifted along the mossy ground, and the cavern ceiling stretched so high above her that it gave a false sense of a starless sky.

The moment she entered the forest, she summoned her light spirits, and all fifteen answered, circling her in a slow, radiant orbit. She didn't send any away—she was done holding back. They immediately set to work, guarding her against the creatures that skittered between the trees.

She followed the marked path amid the forest. Her studies in the Grand Library promised that all routes led to the Draemlord's lair, and beyond that, the exit.

A deep, anguished bellow echoed from the distance. Evy looked up. *Was that... Zafir?* She nearly stepped off the path and into the forest but heard a hiss beside her. A thin, hollow-eyed Draemor tried to approach but was driven back by the glow of her spirits. It scurried away into the woods, its loose, decaying skin flapping as it moved.

The creature must have mimicked Zafir's scream to lure her into a trap.

A pulsing vibration hummed throughout the forest. The scrolls said it was a containment spell designed not just to trap the Draemor, but to keep them weak.

Weakened, she reminded herself. The spell had done enough to suppress the creatures but not so much that they weren't a threat. They would likely resort to more tricks than outward aggression in these caves.

Evy clenched her fist and kept walking.

Another noise broke through the silence. On the path ahead, voices spoke in hushed tones.

Evy froze mid-step, straining to listen.

Her heart lifted at the possibility of encountering another Ascendant. Maybe they could navigate the caves together, watch each other's backs.

But as she crept toward the sound, her hope began to fray. She didn't recognize the voices.

Her instincts flared, just as they had before she entered. Something felt very wrong. Whatever was up ahead, her body reacted before her mind caught up. She stepped off the path and hid behind a nearby tree, then whispered a command to her spirits, and one by one, they dimmed to the faintest glow.

As the light shrank, a low, guttural breathing filled the void.

A group of Draemor slowly approached, looking for an opportunity.

Sensing the danger, one of Evy's spirits flared. Immediately, the creatures twitched and retreated.

Evy swallowed hard, balancing on the razor's edge between concealment and survival. With her glow reduced to little more than a shimmer, she stole closer to the voices.

Their words grew louder and clearer as she approached. Up ahead, a dead tree lay collapsed across the ground, its bleached trunk split and rotting. Perched on one of its branches were two hooded figures.

Evy crouched and listened.

"What do you mean you couldn't find the body?" one of them snapped. "Kor, you damn idiot. I told you exactly where to go to find it."

"I swear it, Basi," Kor said through gritted teeth. "I went to the exact location, and neither Agni nor the Djinn's body was there. Maybe they both fled."

"Djinn's body?" They couldn't mean Zafir.

She thought back to the deep, thunderous shout she'd heard earlier. She had assumed it was a Draemor trap, but what if it wasn't?

Basi let out an irritated cluck and yanked back his hood.

Instantly, she recognized the copper skin and the glassy eyes with slitted pupils glowing like candle flame.

Ifreet.

"You had to have missed them," Basi continued. "Agni took care of the Djinn. They were slinging fire at each other until she hit him in the back. When I left, he was being mauled by the Draemor. He was practically dead."

"You sure? You should have stayed until he was actually dead."

Basi spat to the side. "It was a done deal. Agni ordered me to the second location to swap with you. She wanted *me* to handle the girl." He spun a dagger between his fingers, pointed teeth flashing in a grin.

"I could've handled a child on my own. It didn't need to be you," Kor muttered.

"You couldn't even handle finding a body. Agni made the right call."

Kor scoffed. "Maybe the Draemor got them both."

"Unlikely." Basi lifted a hand, fingers curled back to reveal a ring of sapphire and gold. "These will keep the Draemor off us. They've worked so far."

Evy's hand rose to her mouth.

Royen said Lawrence offered him a ring that repelled Draemor. Could this be the same kind of ring?

"Well," Kor growled, "they said if we don't produce a body, they won't help us. We need to complete this mission to get support to wage war on the Soltris line."

"Then go back and look for it," Basi commanded. "Pry his body from the Draemor's jaw if you have to." He shifted on the branch. "I'll wait here for the girl. We have to take care of both targets. That was the deal."

Evy didn't trust the Ifreet's motives—and she had no intention of staying to find out who the *"girl"* was.

She glanced toward the trees. Maybe she could avoid them if she left the path and went deeper into the forest.

She took a step back.

Snap.

Evy's boot cracked down on a twig.

She froze.

So did the voices. Both Ifreeti heads turned toward the noise.

"Who's there?" Basi barked and jumped to his feet.

She ducked lower, cursing under her breath, but it was too late.

A flare burst from Basi's palm and slammed into the tree trunk just inches from where she crouched.

"It's her," Kor snarled. "The Witch!"

Another fireball roared through the woods, and Evy rolled

behind a gnarled root just in time to avoid being scorched. She didn't stop to look back and bolted into the trees.

More fire crashed through the forest, igniting the underbrush in crackling bursts of heat. She kept running, branches whipping her face.

Eventually, the sounds of pursuit faded.

She slowed, chest heaving, and turned to check, hoping she'd lost them—

Dozens of figures, all grotesquely misshapen, stooped beyond the fog.

The Draemor slowly emerged, shifting and slinking, a wolf pack closing in.

Before Evy could remember to call on her halo of light, the voices came.

Weakest Shaman in history...

What a disgrace...

The taunts were laced with fury and disgust. Evy tried to cover her ears, only to realize they were speaking directly into her thoughts.

Should've picked someone else. Orianna's going to be so disappointed.

A vision of Orianna's angry scowl flickered across her mind unprompted.

You failed at Veyn Manor. There will be consequences.

You're the reason Reyland will stay forgotten.

An image flashed of Dominic Veyn gripping her neck, a twisted, menacing smile curling his lips. He mouthed the word *Gaian*.

She clutched her head, stumbling back. "No."

You betrayed Aeric.

Flashes of Royen's lips against hers—passionate and filled with hunger. Aeric stood behind them, mouth open in a silent scream, yet Evy still didn't pull back.

"No, that didn't happen."

You wanted it to happen. It is what you desire.

"That's not true."

You love Royen.

She wrapped her fingers in Royen's hair, pulling him closer, returning the kiss with full ferocity.

You'll break Aeric's heart. You'll break Royen's too.

You're wicked and don't deserve to love anyone.

Royen and Aeric stood side by side. Their skin cracked, then shattered like porcelain, leaving nothing behind.

"No, please."

You don't deserve to be here.

The world would be better off without you.

Evy stood at the edge of a cliff overlooking the sea in Reyland.

Reya will choose a better reincarnation.

Slowly, she raised one foot over the edge.

We can help you die peacefully. Come to us.

She gasped and squeezed her eyes shut. "Get out of my head."

She dropped to one knee, calling on her spirits. "Help me."

The wisps erupted outward in dazzling bursts. Beams of light shot through the air like lightning, searing into the Draemor with a high-pitched crackle.

The Draemor hissed and recoiled, scattering farther into the trees.

As she caught her breath, Kor's voice rang out from a distance. "There!"

A searing bolt of flame shot past her shoulder, missing by inches. Then Basi appeared ahead, cutting off her path with a wall of fire.

She was trapped.

Evy pivoted and raised her hand to the sky. A water spirit answered her call, but the lack of mana in the Blighted Caves dragged at her spell work. The spirit answered sluggishly, a spear of ice flickering in her hand before finally solidifying in her grip.

With a sharp cry, she hurled it at Basi.

He dodged, twisting his body with speed and power that made no sense in a place so starved of mana.

Evy narrowed her eyes as he came closer. A glowing glass vial hung at his throat. Kor wore one too.

Basi caught her staring. His grin tightened as he tapped the vial. "A gift from our benefactor. An extremely rare artifact that gives us added mana reserves. Without these, we wouldn't dare dream of attacking the Djinn."

Kor rushed her flank and hurled another burst of flame. "So you see why we can't fail. *They'll* give us more of these if we kill you, and we can finally take back Zarokan."

Evy dove and rolled across the forest floor, a tree trunk taking the blow behind her. She emerged on the other side, arms up, calling another shard of ice to her hand, but they were already circling.

They were too quick, their movements amplified by the surge of extra mana.

Her attacks slammed into bark, shattered on stone. Her breath was ragged, energy depleting. Her light shield was already draining her. Fighting the Ifreet on top of that was too much.

A sudden zipping noise cut the air beside her ear.

From the trees on her right, a glowing arrow sliced through the mist and slammed into Kor's shoulder.

He stumbled back with a grunt.

A second arrow flew. Then a third and a fourth. One pierced Basi's thigh; another slammed into Kor's chest, knocking him off his feet.

Kor hit the ground with a choked cry, writhing.

Evy spun toward the source, and Royen burst through the trees, a makeshift torch in one hand, his mana bow in the other.

The torch's enchanted white flames carved a ring of safety, forcing the Draemor to prowl just outside the light's reach.

Royen set the torch down and fired again. His arrow punched into Basi's shoulder, sending the Ifreet stumbling sideways.

Evy pressed forward, her next ice spear bursting through the air. Basi raised his other arm to shield himself, but he was too late. The spear shattered against his chest, and ice exploded across his torso.

He roared in pain.

Royen fired again, the arrow driving deep into Basi's side. The cord at his neck snapped, and the glass vial of mana tumbled free, landing at Evy's feet. She snatched it without thinking and felt energy surge through her.

She summoned another spell, channeling frost through her fingertips. She thrust both hands forward, and a pillar of icy light slammed into the Ifreet, piercing through him in a blinding flash.

"Behind you!" Royen shouted.

Evy whirled, lifting both palms.

A wall of ice burst upward just as Kor's fire struck, deflecting most of the blast, but the force still threw her to the ground. Sharp pain flared through her hand, and when she looked down, blood slicked her palm. The vial had shattered, and the energy faded from her body immediately.

Kor stepped through the smoke, fire curling around his fists.

Before Evy could cast again, Royen charged forward. With one hand, he hurled his torch at Kor's face.

The Ifreet screamed, clawing at his eyes as the splinters dug into his flesh. Kor staggered back, then fell to his knees. He looked at Evy with a single glassy eye, the other punctured with the splinters of Royen's torch.

Kor moved too quickly for Evy to react. He summoned a fireball and shot it at her. It hit Evy in the shoulder, and she cried out in pain. She lay on the ground and saw the Draemor waiting for her among the trees, their faint voices tugging at her mind.

Come to us, we'll give you a painless death...

"No!" Evy shouted, shaking her head violently.

Kor laughed as he summoned another fireball, ready to strike again. But then he froze.

It was as if he was trapped in time, unable to move a muscle.

Evy could only hear a whimper from his throat before Kor burst into millions of floating particles, the wind carrying him away.

At last, the forest fell still.

Evy turned to Royen, mouth agape. "Wh-what happened?"

He stared wide-eyed at the spot where Kor had been. "When he struck you, the Heart must have deemed him an interference in the trial. So... it got rid of him."

Maybe that was what happened to Agni, the one the other two Ifreet had spoken about. Maybe she hit Zafir and disintegrated as well. But if they hadn't found his body, perhaps Zafir had gotten away.

"The Ifreet back there..." Evy swallowed. "They mentioned attacking a Djinn. I think they meant Zafir. He could be in trouble."

Royen glanced at her. "Then that's all the more reason to find the exit as quickly as possible."

"But—"

"We should inform the Council of all this," Royen interrupted, raising a hand. "There's too much ground to cover, and they can send out a search party for Zafir."

Evy's shoulders slumped. But Royen was right—all she could do now was hope Zafir would still be safe when they made it out of the caves.

She watched Royen turn the torch in his hand. The wood had broken down to a nub.

"Thank you for coming to my rescue," she said softly.

He only gave a curt nod, avoiding her eyes.

"If you have trouble enchanting another torch, then we should stay together," Evy said. "My spirits can keep the Draemor at bay. It's safer."

He hesitated, then nodded again. "Fine."

They navigated through the trees and found the marked path.

He kept his attention on the trail, frowning as they walked. His coldness left a hollow ache. She desperately wanted to talk about the previous day, to make sure they were okay, but the words never came.

She didn't know how to bring it up.

So they continued to wander in silence until the forest thinned, and ahead of them rose a stone wall. A massive iron door was embedded in the side.

Runes circled the frame, glowing faintly with hazy light.

Royen stepped closer, inspecting the etchings. "This must be the gate to the Draemlord."

He reached forward.

The moment Royen's fingers brushed the iron, the door groaned and creaked open. It was as if it had been expecting him.

They exchanged a glance.

And stepped through the door to face their final challenge.

FORTY-THREE

Not here. Please.

Evy's spirits pleaded as she and Royen wandered through a narrow, dim hallway.

She felt their fear in her bones as one whispered in her mind.

We don't like it here.

They were nearing what looked like the end of the passage. The space opened into a vast, circular chamber. Evy squinted, trying to make out the details. It seemed empty, save for a single wooden door on the far side.

"That must be the exit," Royen said.

Evy nodded, then spoke reassuringly to her spirits.

We're getting out. And we're never coming back to this cursed place.

"Shall we?" she asked Royen.

"Let's go."

Together, they stepped into the chamber, scanning the shadows.

Royen lowered his voice. "We need a plan. This is supposed to be the Draemlord's lair. If we can spot him before he finds us, maybe we can—"

Well, well.

An unfamiliar voice slithered into Evy's mind.

If it isn't a new batch of Ascendants.

She stiffened. The voice was smooth yet vitriolic like poisoned honey. It definitely didn't belong to one of her spirits.

Royen froze beside her.

"You heard that too?" Evy asked.

Before he could answer, the voice echoed aloud from deeper within the chamber.

"What are you waiting for? Come on in."

Without warning, an invisible force tugged at them.

Evy staggered forward, Royen beside her. Their feet scraped across the stone as they were dragged toward the center.

From the far end of the chamber, a shadow peeled away from the wall.

The figure stepped into the light.

She wasn't sure what she expected the supposed Draemlord to look like, perhaps grotesque and gnarled like the creatures in the woods.

Instead, he appeared almost human.

His skin was a lifeless gray, the pallor of a corpse, stretched taut across jutted cheekbones. Blood-red eyes gleamed beneath heavy lids. Long, pointed ears poked through tangled strands of silver hair. His razor-sharp teeth glinted as he smiled.

There was something familiar about his striking, strangely youthful features.

His face held a feminine, haunting kind of beauty…

As she tried to place it, the figure stepped forward.

"It's been so long since I've had company." His voice was as soft as silk, nothing like what she imagined from the king of the Draemor. "I was starting to wonder if I'd ever eat again."

He looked them over slowly.

"But then, what a treat. A fresh batch of young Ascendants, delivered straight to my doorstep."

"Are you the Draemlord?" Evy asked, struggling to soothe the tightness in her throat.

He chuckled. "I suppose I am. That's what they've been calling me for... What is it now? Hundreds of years?"

Suddenly, a glowing arrow of mana zipped across the chamber.

Evy turned.

Royen stood with his mana bow drawn, already conjuring another arrow.

The Draemlord laughed as he flicked the shot aside with a single finger.

Royen fired again. And again. Each time, the Draemlord swatted the projectiles away like they were nothing more than bothersome insects.

"Is this truly the best Theribane can offer?" the Draemlord sneered. "How far the Shifters have fallen. The once-mighty Veyn bloodline, now thinned. Reduced to a fraction of its former strength."

Royen unleashed another barrage.

The Draemlord waved the arrows aside. "Just like that cousin of yours," he scoffed. "Frail boy. Shameful."

Evy and Royen exchanged confused glances.

"How could you possibly know that?" Royen growled. "You've been locked in here for centuries."

"I might be a prisoner," the Draemlord mused, "but I have eyes across the surface. Minions and spies who still answer to me."

He smiled sweetly.

"And they told me what happened to that Veyn boy," he said, stepping closer. "One of my own made a meal out of him... Didn't he?"

Royen snapped.

He let out a furious roar, mana crackling along his limbs, and charged forward.

"Royen, wait—!" Evy shouted.

But it was too late.

With a casual wave of his arm, the Draemlord sent him flying. Royen slammed into the far wall with a sickening thud and crumpled to the ground. He lay sprawled across the stone and groaned in pain.

The Draemlord turned toward him, a hungry glint in his eyes as he advanced.

But before he could reach Royen, a wall of radiant light burst between them.

Evy stood firm, arms outstretched, commanding her light spirits to form a protective shield. The Draemlord snarled, stumbling back.

She sprinted to Royen's side and dropped to her knees.

"Can you stand?" she asked, bracing him with one arm.

"No, my leg—" Royen muttered through gritted teeth.

Evy hiked up his pant leg. His shin was bloodied and swollen. It was broken at best.

She summoned more spirits and healed him. Beads of sweat formed on her forehead, and she shook her head as her vision blurred.

"You know," Evy whispered to Royen. "I really wish you had taken that ring from the Council. We might have had a chance to get out of here alive."

A booming slam echoed behind.

Then another.

The Draemlord had begun hurling himself at the barrier, each strike sending ripples through Evy's magic. Her spirits pulsed, struggling to hold the line.

"I've heard rumors," the Draemlord drawled between blows. "That Reya's vessel walks among the Ascendants. Why are you protecting your opponent, I wonder?"

His grin stretched wide. "Could you be lovers?"

He cackled at Evy's pinched reaction.

The Draemlord struck again. Silver light splintered across the shield.

"I can smell you, Witch," he hissed as he lifted his nose to the air. "I wonder what your reincarnated soul will taste like. Perhaps like a finely aged wine." The Draemlord licked his lips. "You'll pair well as I devour your *lover*."

Evy turned to Royen, panic rising. "We can't fight him. He's too strong," she whispered. "We need to get out. Can you manage that with your leg?"

Royen gave a faint nod. "I think so."

They both looked to the wooden door, only a few paces away.

But before they could move, a wall of twisting flame ignited around the exit. Their only escape now sealed behind a curtain of hellfire.

Evy spun toward it and summoned her water spirits, lashing the blaze with frost.

The fire persisted.

She tried again, pouring more mana into the spell.

Still, the flames held.

She gathered strength for a third strike, but a deafening crack split the air.

Evy turned, heart hammering, just in time to see her barrier shatter in a cascade of blinding light.

The Draemlord slowly circled them.

He was close enough that she could see the scar on his forehead, a raw-looking mark as though the skin had been ripped off.

Evy held Royen close, shielding him with her body.

"Tell me, vessel of Reya. What are you doing among Rui's little puppets?" His voice oozed amusement.

Her mind raced. She needed a way to stall him long enough for them to escape. Keeping him talking might buy them time.

"The Council voted on it," she said. "But if you have spies beyond the Blighted Caves, I'm sure you already knew."

"I did." He sighed, sounding almost bored. He stepped closer and bared his teeth.

Evy searched her memory. Anything from her studies at the Grand Library. Anything she could use.

Then she remembered a single line in an old scroll.

"You seem to know a great deal." She spoke carefully. "More than you let on. Except for one thing."

His brow arched.

"You don't know your name," she said. "You forgot it."

A low chuckle rumbled from him, closer to a growl. "I didn't forget. They stole it from me."

Evy paused. "Someone stole your name?"

"The Council," he snarled. "Not the sniveling weaklings you have now, but the Founding Council. The ones who built Aeltheon. Before they betrayed me and threw me into this pit, they stripped me of everything—my name, my identity, my memories… until all I had left was rage."

The way his voice crackled with unfiltered fury told her she had struck something raw inside him, a wound she could use to her advantage. "You were… *betrayed*?"

"Yes," he hissed. "By every person I ever knew. And they'll betray you too."

Evy hesitated. From what she'd studied, the Draemor were feral creatures driven by darkness. She hadn't expected one to feel emotions as human as betrayal.

His mouth was still, but his voice slid into her mind like a blade into flesh.

You already know the truth. You've seen their corruption for yourself.

Evy flinched.

You want to tear it down. To gut the Council and rebuild it. You want to cleanse the system.

A dull pain started to migrate behind her eyes, and she let out a strained sigh.

But you're thinking too small, Evalene. The Council is a symptom. The sickness runs deeper.

You need to cleanse the world.

You can save them all.

A light spirit grazed her temple, relieving Evy of the Draemlord's hold. "You didn't answer my question. Why would the Founding Council betray a Draemor?"

The Draemlord resumed his pacing. "They turned the Heart into a prison for an Egregore. Its rage festers the land and taints the world." He snarled, showing his pointed teeth. "And I tried to stop it."

Evy's head spun. "An… Egregore?" she echoed. "What are you talking about?"

Her thoughts flashed to the whispers she'd heard near the Heart.

My child.

Evy glanced at Royen, who gave a small shrug. "He's speaking nonsense," he muttered.

But the Draemlord's words tugged at her memory—the Heart's container, its golden thorns turned inward as if holding the Heart captive.

She looked up to question him again, but he was smiling eerily now. His voice slipped straight into her mind.

You've heard it speak, haven't you? You know I'm telling the truth.

She could almost feel him slithering through the folds of her brain.

Help me free it, Evalene. Help me free us all.

"Stop…" Evy whispered.

Together, we can cleanse the world.

"Cleanse…" she found herself repeating the words against

her will. "Cleanse the..." She tried to seal her lips shut. "Cleanse... the... world." A light spirit darted in front of her and sank into the side of her head, its magic breaking the Draemlord's hold again.

Evy shook her head violently. "Stay out of my head," she snapped.

"You see me as a monster," the Draemlord said aloud, slowly inching closer. "You think I'm a villain. I understand, look at me." He spread his arms, the sleeves of his dark cloak cascading in ragged heaps. "I've become abhorrent."

His face softened enough to give him a look of haunted gentleness. "But I'm trying to help you."

He began slowly pacing again.

"You think becoming the Hierarch means power. That you can force the world to change."

Evy's gaze darted to the door. The flames still curled around it, but the blaze had begun to flicker, like his hold was weakening. Royen had noticed too. His focus was locked on the exit.

"The Heart chooses you," the Draemlord continued, "but only to use you. Just like the Council. They're all leeches. And once you realize you're their pawn, it's already too late."

He turned to Royen.

"If you join me, I can offer real power. I can help you find your cousin... Marq, was it?"

Evy felt Royen's shoulders tense beside her.

"And you." The Draemlord turned back to Evy. "You shouldn't have to carry all this weight." He clucked his inky-black tongue. "Duty-bound to an entire race of people. You're just a girl."

He glided forward, extending a hand.

"You deserve to live a life free of the crushing expectations around you."

"I—" Evy's heart thudded against her chest.

Royen cut in. "You're just a Draemor. Why should we believe anything you say?"

The Draemlord's expression twisted.

"I am *not* lying," he growled. "The Founding Council took everything from me. They tore my name from my mind and cast me into the dark like a nameless abomination. And then—" His voice dropped to a bitter snarl. "They enshrined me. They twisted my image. Painted it as a symbol of peace and unity while I rotted in these infernal caves."

Evy and Royen exchanged a confused glance.

Enshrined him?

Before they could respond, the wall of fire over the exit flared in jagged bursts in rhythm with the Draemlord's emotions.

If she could rattle him further, maybe he'd lose control.

"So the Founding Council betrayed you… and misused your name?" she asked, speaking slowly. "I'm afraid I still don't understand."

The Draemlord scoffed.

"The Founding Council. The Councilors that followed. They're cut from the same cloth. Spreading the same pattern of deceit." He paced again, more agitated now.

His eyes burned like coals. "They've taken many names through time. But mine was the first. They stole my dignity, and they'll steal yours too." The corners of his mouth pulled into a gentle smile. "But it doesn't have to end that way. Join me. Together, we can burn it all down."

He extended his hand toward them.

"My minions are already out there, spreading the true divine mission. We can cleanse this world."

Evy's thoughts spun. Maybe Royen was right, and the Draemlord was just rambling. A stolen name. A false image worshiped for centuries. Why? What did any of it mean?

But then, memories began to resurface and a terrible, impossible idea began to form.

"Can't be..." she whispered.

"What was that, Little Witch?"

The Founding Council. An enshrined name.

The Draemlord's features struck her all at once. His long, thin pointed ears, silver hair, and sharp, feminine cheekbones. She had seen them before in a portrait in the Aurethium.

Features tied to an extinct race. To a renowned Lumiel.

And the scar on his forehead where a sun tattoo might have been.

Everything was aligning, but... It couldn't be. It was impossible.

"Your name..." Evy's voice barely carried above a whisper.

What if her wild guess was wrong? Would it send him into a blind rage? Would it drive him to kill them here and now?

"Speak up, girl," the Draemlord snarled, losing his patience.

The flame around the door flickered again.

Her instincts screamed at her to move, because if she didn't, they would be dead within seconds, swallowed whole by the Draemlord.

Evy had no choice. She had nothing to lose.

And so, no matter how impossible or absurd it felt, she had to try.

Evy rose. "Is your name Lutharion?" The words sounded absurd even as they left her mouth.

But the Draemlord stopped cold. "What did you say?"

Evy stepped forward, heart racing. "Is your name Lutharion? Or should I say, *was*?"

The chamber went still. The Draemlord stared through her, eyes distant.

"Lutharion..." His voice cracked. "Yes."

Evy staggered back a step. The chamber tilted around her,

the edges of her vision swimming. She pressed a hand to the wall as hundreds of questions flooded her.

Had she guessed right? The idea was impossible. It had to be a trick.

Because if it wasn't, then the Founding Council had stolen a name from a Draemor and given it to the first Hierarch.

Or had the creature taken Lutharion Skye's name for itself?

There was another possibility, one Evy didn't want to entertain—that perhaps the Draemlord's true identity *was*—

A sharp zip split the air.

A volley of mana-charged arrows struck the Draemlord, one slicing straight through the side of his face.

Evy looked up. Royen was now standing, his leg fully healed, a mana bow drawn in his hand.

The Draemlord staggered, momentarily stunned.

The wall of fire around the exit collapsed in a hiss of smoke.

"Now!" Royen shouted. He seized Evy's arm and pulled her forward. Together, they sprinted for the door.

As they reached it, Evy dared one last glance over her shoulder.

The Draemlord wasn't pursuing them. He stood motionless at the center of the chamber, blood trailing down his face, a strange, eerie smile etched across his lips.

His glittering eyes met Evy's.

Thank you for giving me my name back, Little Witch.

The words echoed in her mind.

Then she and Royen were gone.

FORTY-FOUR

Footsteps echoed through the long, damp tunnel.

"Cleanse the world."

Evy had summoned light spirits to illuminate the path, their glow casting a soft white radiance against the stone walls.

"Cleanse the world."

Still, there was no exit in sight.

How long had they been walking?

Royen's hand twitched in hers. Their fingers were still laced together. She didn't let go. She didn't want to.

If she let go, she might finally unravel. All the fear and pressure she'd buried might spill out, and Royen's hand was the only thing holding her together.

"Cleanse the world."

The Draemlord's words felt carved into her mind. Each time they surfaced again, she pushed them down and unintentionally squeezed Royen's hand.

To her surprise, he squeezed back.

As they walked, the silence left room for thoughts of the Draemlord—his words, his name—to creep back in uninvited.

"What do you think it all means?" she finally asked, her voice echoing through the tunnel.

"His name," she clarified. "The Draemlord said his name was Lutharion, the same as the first Hierarch. What does that mean?"

Royen's expression darkened.

"I don't think it means anything," he said flatly. "The Draemor lie. We read all about it, remember? They'll say anything to get inside your head."

"But what if—"

"For all we know he could've been prowling the surface during Lutharion Skye's reign, heard the name, and decided to adopt it. Maybe it was a joke to him.

"Once they locked him up, the Council most likely erased the name from his mind. I doubt they'd let some monster defile the name of the Hierarch."

Maybe Royen was right. It was all a trick.

Yet she couldn't stop seeing the Draemlord's face. The way he froze, and the wave of recognition behind his blood-red eyes. She couldn't shake the feeling that something had unlocked in him.

Had she done wrong by giving him his name? Was that why the Draemlord let them go? A warped kind of gratitude for what he believed she had returned?

"We need to focus on getting out of here and reporting the Ifreeti attack." Royen's voice cut through her thoughts. "If Zafir really is injured and at the mercy of the Draemor, the Council will need to send a rescue team."

"Agreed."

Evy squinted, then lifted her free hand. "Look."

A faint glow appeared far ahead.

Royen let out a sigh of relief. "The exit."

Their gazes met. His eyes glistened. A tingling sensation spread across Evy's palm as his thumb brushed lightly over it.

"We did it, Evy. We survived the Hierarch Wars."

Then together, still hand in hand, they ran toward the light.

Tears streamed down Evy's cheeks as her feet carried her forward. She was the first Witch in history to complete the trials.

But even as triumph swelled, the questions came faster.

Had she done enough? Would the Heart crown her? And if it did, would having the throne truly offer protection? Or would the Council hollow it out from beneath her, just as the Draemlord had warned?

Worse yet, what would happen if she didn't win? Would the Council truly let her go unscathed—let Reyland return to its place on the margins of the continent? Or, as Orianna had believed, would this open the door to a better life?

She swallowed the remaining questions. She could only take the outcome day by day.

"We're almost there!" Royen was breathless next to her, his chestnut-brown hair whipping back as they ran. "I don't think the sun has set yet. We should make it in time!"

Evy clutched his hand tighter and was overcome with bittersweet sorrow. They had entered this competition as rivals. But somewhere along the way, that changed. She had grown to care for all of them, Celeste and Zafir included.

Once this was all over, she would no longer be an Ascendant. Whether she became the next Hierarch or returned to her role as the Shaman Queen, she wondered if they would remain in each other's lives.

The only thing she was sure of was that no matter the outcome, everything would be different.

Her life was forever changed, the entirety of her being with it.

The light grew brighter.

Evy blinked against the brilliance, momentarily stunned.

Sunlight. Warm and golden, it poured through the mouth of the cave, shining like a beacon.

Her spirits vibrated with joy, zipping forward like shooting stars. They welcomed the light, the clean air, the release from the unholiness of the Blighted Caves.

And so did she as she emerged from the dark into the dawn of her new life.

FORTY-FIVE

The dry, sunbaked air of Ruitheon scratched at Evy's throat, but she welcomed it without complaint as they crossed the final threshold and left the gargantuan mouth of the cave humming behind them, Royen's hand still clasped in hers. Anything was better than the damp, moldy thickness of the Blighted Caves. She never wanted to return to them.

She should have let go of Royen's hand. There was no reason to hold on. But their hands remained, even as they stopped and stood blinking against the early evening sun.

The Heart hovered several paces ahead, pouring mana into the cracked earth. Upon their arrival, its surface pulsed once, then again, as if tallying them. The Council was scattered across the clearing, easily discernible among the sparse crowd by their dark ceremonial robes.

A faint whisper stirred the air.

My...

The voice trailed off into the wind before Evy could decipher what it was trying to say.

"They turned the Heart into a prison for an Egregore."

Could something truly be trapped inside? If she could steal a moment once the trial was over, she would return to the Grand Library and search for any mention of Egregores.

Movement caught her attention. She hoped it was Zafir, already out of the caves and waiting to greet them—unharmed and safe after all. Or Celeste, coming over to make some joke about the Draemor's beauty routine.

But it was only an onlooker, shifting across the clearing for a better view. There was no sign of the other two Ascendants. She frowned, desperately hoping they were okay.

Near the Heart, Lilian and Kaelen spoke in hushed tones. Their conversation broke as soon as they noticed her. Both offered warm smiles, relieved, it seemed, to see her emerge.

Evy glanced back toward the cave's gaping maw and saw Lawrence.

He stood apart from the other Councilors, hands clasped behind his back. His cold gray eyes widened when he saw her, his jaw going rigid. Then he noticed her hand still intertwined with Royen's. His expression hardened into a glower, his mouth curling into a sneer.

"Evy!"

She turned at the sound of her name, just in time to see a flash of auburn hair darting through the clearing.

Despite her warning, Aeric had come after all.

Relief surged through her. She let go of Royen's hand and ran forward to meet Aeric halfway, then melted into his embrace.

"You're safe," he whispered into her hair. "Thank the Gods. It's finally over."

Evy pulled back slightly, her arms still around him. "Not yet," she said quietly. "Not until the Heart declares a winner."

The sun was lower on the horizon, likely an hour from sundown. She glanced over her shoulder, scanning around the cave, hoping to see Celeste or Zafir emerge.

Instead, she found Royen.

He remained where she'd left him, lips drawn in a hard line as he watched her and Aeric. But the moment their eyes met, Royen's expression cooled into its usual stoic mask. He offered a curt nod, then turned away and strode toward Lawrence, likely to report the Ifreeti attack and Zafir's possible injury.

The sun had begun its final descent, painting the sky in shades of violet and orange.

Evy's heart dropped. There was still no sign of Zafir or Celeste. As soon as the sun set, they would be disqualified. But even so, what if they were hurt? Or worse? Evy shook the thought away. They were Ascendants, some of the strongest beings the realm had to offer. They would be fine. She was sure of it.

But the corners of her mouth still fell as she watched the Council gathering a rescue team of paladins. Lawrence handed a few of them familiar rings.

Even from a distance, she could see the sapphire and gold. They were the same ones the Ifreet wore in the caves—the ones they claimed would keep the Draemor away.

Royen had mentioned they were a Daryn family invention, so how would the Ifreet have gotten their hands on them? Had they stolen them?

As if sensing her unease, Lilian approached. Evy's ears rang with nervous static, barely catching the sound of the Councilor's words.

"They'll be okay. The crew will—"

But she didn't get a chance to finish. The Heart began to pulse as the sun finally bowed below the horizon.

Evy froze as a glowing orb formed above her, its surface shrinking then growing.

She turned to Royen, and the same orb hovered above him.

The moment had come. With or without Zafir and Celeste, the Heart had begun rendering its final judgment.

She tried to calculate the outcome in her head, desperate to anticipate the Heart's ruling.

Royen had been slightly behind her before the third trial began.

Lawrence said the Heart would judge their performance in the Blighted Caves, including how they endured. She had nearly succumbed to the Draemor. Nearly let herself fall. But she had saved herself.

Still, Royen saved her from the Ifreeti attackers. Probably saved her life. She had shielded him from the Draemlord's strike, thrown up her barrier just in time. And she had guessed his name, throwing the monster off-balance and buying them precious time through her conversation.

But Royen had landed the final blow. His arrows broke the Draemlord's concentration and shattered his spell. Royen had forced their escape.

Evy tried to weigh it all, his actions and hers. Who had shown more resilience? What did the Heart see when it looked at them? How did it measure their worth?

Then the Heart went still.

Gasps swept through the clearing.

Cold sweat collected at her temples. She was too afraid to look. Because when she did, her journey would be over in earnest. Her destiny cemented.

She gathered every ounce of her will and forced her eyes upward.

Whispers broke out around her. The Council argued in low, urgent tones.

Her thoughts tangled.

But there was no denying it.

The orbs were exactly the same size.

The Hierarch Wars had ended in a tie.

FORTY-SIX

The room was dark, save for a faint sliver of moonlight slipping through the curtain, casting a wavering line across Yorik's face.

He sat on the edge of the bed, eyes closed and head bowed, savoring the memories of his success earlier that day.

He had stood before the mouth of the Blighted Caves, his body racked with tremors as the last tendrils of the invisibility spell faded. Blood slicked his palm where he'd wiped his mouth. He was pushing himself too far, but the Gods had told him it was necessary. He had to enter the caves undetected. Once night had fallen and the area had cleared, he had successfully infiltrated the caves.

The tracker spell he'd slipped onto the Ifreet at the tavern had appeared as a thin, glowing thread, leading him through the forest within the caves. The Gods told him the second ingredient awaited deeper along the path, and Yorik hadn't hesitated.

He had heard faraway shouts from paladins still scouring the caves for the missing Ascendants. "I found her! I found the princess!"

He couldn't stop his grin. He would visit Celeste later in the evening.

A rustling among the dry foliage had drawn his attention.

A Draemor. It stood just beyond a dead bush. Yorik had frozen, observing the creature. Its pointed teeth jutted from a warped, gaping maw.

But the Draemor didn't attack. It simply stared, then slipped back into the woods.

They will not harm you, the Gods had whispered.

You are chosen. You are protected.

The tracking spell had led him to a body.

He recognized the man. He had seen him outside the Grand Library the night he first arrived in Ruitheon.

Collect what is owed.

Yorik had obeyed.

He was still replaying the moment when the door creaked open. Light flared as a lantern ignited, illuminating the room. A sharp gasp echoed.

Celeste stood frozen in the doorway, wrapped in a lush robe, her pink hair still damp and scented with flowers from her bath.

Her tired eyes widened.

Yorik slowly lifted a hand and placed a single finger to his lips.

Celeste nodded, her hand trembling as she set the lantern on the table.

"Where have you been?" she whispered. "I've been so worried about you."

Yorik only shrugged. "I convinced them to let me rent a room at the tavern." In reality, he had used a minor compulsion spell on the barkeeper, and the magic left him sick and retching for hours. "I wanted to stay somewhere you could find me easily."

Celeste nodded, then tears started to spill steadily down her cheeks.

Yorik was on his feet in an instant, crossing the room and pulling her into his arms.

"I'm glad you're okay," he murmured. "I was so afraid for you."

Celeste's sobs deepened, her body quaked in his arms.

"I'm so ashamed," she whispered, voice cracking. "They had to rescue me, Herald. I couldn't even make it out on my own."

Yorik gently guided her toward the bed and let her sink onto the mattress beside him.

"When they found me, a Draemor was so close to feasting on my mind that I could feel it taking hold of me." Her hands clenched into fists in her lap. "I didn't think I was going to come back. Not as myself, at least."

Yorik laced his fingers through hers.

"And Zafir..." Celeste trailed off and let out a shuddering breath. "They couldn't find him. Not a single trace. They think something terrible happened to him. Something... awful."

Yorik pressed his lips together, trying to hide a smile. He knew exactly what had happened to the Djinn King, and it truly was awful.

"And then when Evy and Royen started fussing over me..." Celeste trailed off, her mouth twisting into a grimace. "I just couldn't take it. I felt so weak. So helpless."

"I know. I heard," Yorik murmured, resting his chin on her head. "I also heard about the Heart's final judgment." He paused. "Is it true that Queen Evalene and Royen Veyn are tied?"

Celeste sniffled and wiped her eyes with the back of her sleeve. "It's never happened before. Not in any record we have. The Heart placed equal judgment on both of them." She drew her knees to her chest. "The Council called them to the Aurethium tomorrow to decide what happens next."

She shook her head. "But I don't know anything else. No one does. Everyone's scrambling."

Yorik stared into the darkness beyond the lantern's reach. The room fell into stillness. The Gods stirred.

Now. While she's open. Grief strips the soul bare. What you need must be given freely, and the broken give what the whole will not.

Yorik felt the dark thread pulse between them, stronger than ever. Her sorrow helped feed the curse, progressing it faster.

He needed to crack her open further.

"So." Yorik's voice turned cold. "You've been taken out of the running completely?"

"What?"

He watched her closely. Her eyes were swollen and red, no longer the glittering jewels they once resembled. "There's no hope of you ever becoming Hierarch now, is there?"

Celeste folded her arms across her chest and looked down at the floor.

"So that means," Yorik continued, each word laced with deliberate venom, "there's no possible chance of us ever being together."

The final thread holding Celeste together snapped. She let out a stream of shuddering sobs, her shoulders jerking violently.

Yorik squeezed her hand again.

"I came to say one last goodbye," he said softly. "I will never forget you. And though our time was brief, I don't think I'll ever love anyone the way I loved you, my Rose."

He brushed a tear from her cheek with the back of his fingers.

Celeste crumpled to the floor, her cries muffled as she buried her face in her hands.

For a moment, Yorik hesitated. Her grief and hopelessness reminded him of his mother, of how she had been after his father's torment. He shuddered at the thought of being compared to him. The image of his mother curled up the same way on the kitchen floor surfaced before he could stop it. Was this what his father had felt? That cold satisfaction of watching someone break beneath his hands?

The voices returned, tightening around his thoughts like a serpent.

You have her where you need her.

Let her marinate in her grief.

What you need from her will be freely given.

Yorik returned to clarity. He inhaled slowly, his expression hardening once more as he studied Celeste.

The web of dark threads beneath her skin was as thick and visible as her veins. The curse was ironic in this way—each wound he carved only made their bond harder to sever.

She was almost ready.

He turned from her, letting out a faint sigh. "Goodbye," he muttered. Then he crossed to the window, unlatched it, and slipped outside. As his boots touched the ground below, he jolted with every cry that echoed through the air.

He felt an odd sympathy for Celeste.

Because her sorrow wasn't for him. It went beyond the loss of a lover.

She mourned the loss of freedom. Of hope.

Many of the Acolytes had come to him carrying that same grief. And he had offered them a new beacon—the promise of a brighter world and a better life.

Perhaps when the world was remade, when he demolished the Heart, burned away the rot, he could give her what she always wanted. He was a savior, after all. A purifier.

The Herald of Chaos.

Yorik looked back and smiled at Celeste's window, her cries still audible from where he stood.

He wasn't wasteful. Like the Djinn King, he needed only a small part of her. But unlike Zafir Soltris, Celeste didn't have to die for him to obtain it. After he took what he needed, he would give whatever remained of her a better life.

If she could survive the cleanse, she deserved it. And Yorik would be happy to have her by his side.

FORTY-SEVEN

Constant chatter echoed off the marble dome of the hearing chamber. Evy assumed that under normal circumstances, the Councilors were meant to remain seated in the ornate, elevated chairs lining the curved back wall. But many were pacing, arguing, crossing the floor to whisper in tight clusters. Scribes worked in hushed urgency, their hands flying to keep pace with the chaos.

In the center of the chamber, Evy sat stiffly in her chair, the carved wooden arms cold beneath her fingertips. She glanced at Royen, seated beside her. His posture was rigid, his mouth drawn into a hard line. They'd been sitting and listening to the Council argue among themselves for what felt like hours.

He met her gaze and gave a curt, expressionless nod.

As if they were mere acquaintances passing by.

A memory from the Blighted Caves resurfaced, from when the Draemor had tried to take hold of her mind.

You don't love Aeric. You love Royen.

Evy looked away first, shifting uncomfortably in her seat.

No, the Draemor only twisted slivers of truth into lies.

She *did* love Royen in a way, but what she loved was their

friendship. She treasured it, just as she treasured her bond with Celeste and Zafir.

Right?

The single thread of doubt tugged loose the memory she'd tried so hard to bury. She licked her lips instinctively. She could still taste the phantom of Royen's tears on her lips from those few seconds when she hadn't wanted to pull away.

Why hadn't she? Was it shock? A desire not to hurt him? Evy pressed her lips together. Or had a part of her wanted it?

No. Not with Aeric waiting for her in the townhouse. Not after the journey he'd made, leaving his own duties behind just to support her.

A sharp cough from Kaelen jolted her from her thoughts.

He unfurled a brittle scroll and read aloud. "Ancient edicts state that in the event of a tie at the end of the three trials, the Council shall determine a suitable tiebreaker, one that tests another essential trait of the Hierarch. This process will repeat until the tie is broken."

That set off another wave of groans and arguments.

A stout, older man threw up his hands, bright copper hair shifting beneath his hood.

Second Councilor Marwin Ashcroft.

"Do you know how much setting up another trial would cost the treasury?" His voice was gruff. "Why not put it to a simple vote?"

Lilian responded swiftly. "How would that fairly judge any trait of the Hierarch? We need a legitimate new trial that reveals their worthiness."

And so it continued, back and forth, with no consensus in sight.

The Arch Councilor's seat, a little larger and more ornate than the others, was empty. She hadn't seen Lawrence leave.

"A vote makes the most sense," Marwin said with a shrug. "Gaining loyalty and making allies among the Council is just as important a trait in a Hierarch as anything else." He leaned back in his chair, smirking. "Wouldn't you agree?"

He winked at Royen, who scoffed.

Evy leaned toward him, searching for any excuse to speak. "He's your grandfather, isn't he?"

Royen sighed. "Unfortunately."

Kaelen shot Marwin a sharp look. "That may make sense once the Hierarch has chosen their own Council. But how does a vote among a former Hierarch's Council make any sense to—"

"He's a bit of an idiot," Royen whispered. "Ashcroft, that is. I'm embarrassed to share a bloodline with him."

Evy considered. "I suppose he just wants to see his grandson succeed. If my father were in that seat, he'd probably argue for whatever gave me the easiest win."

Royen shrugged. "They should take this more seriously." He tapped a finger against his armrest. "They're fools if they think the Heart will accept any tiebreaker designed to hand me the throne."

With every passing minute, every ridiculous debate, her dread mounted. The Hierarch Wars weren't over. Not really. And these deliberations were only dragging out the one thing she most wanted to know.

What happens next?

"Did you see where Lawrence went?" she asked, looking for a distraction.

Royen didn't look at her. "Messenger brought him a scroll about half an hour ago. He read it, then slipped out."

She sat straight. Could it be about Zafir?

They still hadn't found him in the Blighted Caves. The rescue team had gone back in earlier that day to search again.

She hoped he was okay.

The chamber doors slammed open with a thunderous crack, cutting through the Council's bickering. Even the scribes froze, pens suspended midair.

Lawrence stormed through the chamber, his boots thudding heavily against the marble floor. Behind him trailed an older man Evy didn't recognize. He was hunched and trembling, clutching a wrinkled hat in both hands.

Lawrence's mouth was curved downward, set and grim, while he scanned the chamber, ablaze with furious intent.

His attention locked on Evy.

He stopped just short of where she sat.

An immediate shiver ran down her spine. Lawrence's lips formed into a subtle, almost imperceptible smirk.

Something was wrong.

Very wrong.

Then he spoke.

"Evalene Lovejoy, Shaman Queen of Reyland, you are hereby accused of the kidnapping of Marq Veyn and the murder of Zafir Soltris."

FORTY-EIGHT

Silence permeated the chamber like dense, toxic fog, and all the air rushed from Evy's lungs.

Her head throbbed and thoughts scattered.

She was being accused of the kidnapping of Marq Veyn and the *murder* of Zafir Soltris? What in the name of the Gods was happening? This had to be a mistake. A test, maybe.

Yes. That was it. The Council had already decided the tiebreaker. This was all part of a new trial. A test to see how Evy would handle herself.

The Council will do whatever it takes to ensure a Veyn victory.

Evy shuddered. This couldn't be one of their blatantly corrupt schemes.

Could it?

Lilian spoke next, cutting through the silence. "Arch Councilor, with all due respect, on what grounds do you bring these ridiculous charges?"

Lawrence turned his glare on her, but before he could respond, Royen jolted from his seat.

"Evy was with me in the Grand Library when Marq's caravan was attacked. How could she have had anything to do with it?" Royen folded his arms. "Really, Daryn? If this is another one of your schemes, it's definitely the stupidest."

Lawrence chuckled. The sound was more growl than laugh.

"Well then," he said, his voice slick with satisfaction. "Perhaps we should hear from someone who was there and let the Council judge for themselves."

He gestured toward the man who had entered with him, and the man stepped forward hesitantly. His skin was weathered from years spent beneath the sun, his plain tunic and worn boots marking him as a laborer.

"This man," Lawrence said, turning to address the chamber, "was working a field near the southern ridge of Theribane. He claims to have witnessed the ambush on Marq Veyn's caravan with his own eyes."

Lawrence gave him a shallow nod. "Go on, sir. You may speak."

The man cleared his throat and wrung the brim of his hat between his calloused hands.

"I shifted into my crow form that morning," he began. "Droppin' seeds into the furrows of my field."

He paused and glanced at Lawrence, who nodded for him to continue.

"I heard a ruckus in the distance, shouting and screaming. So I flew toward it out of curiosity. I perched on a tree nearby, hidden in case there was danger."

He struggled to find his words and finally lifted his eyes to Lawrence again. "I'm so sorry, sir. It's a terrifying memory I've been trying to forget."

Lawrence set a hand on the man's shoulder. "I understand. Traveling all the way to the capital to speak before the Council takes real courage. But, for the sake of the realm, please continue."

The man nodded slowly. "That's when I saw the carriages marked with the Veyn crest, under attack by what I thought were Draemor." His voice trembled. "The vile, bloodthirsty things tore through the guards like paper."

Kaelen leaned forward. "Yes, we know of the Draemor. It's as the initial report stated."

The man shook his head. "That's what I thought they were, at first. I was about to fly back to town and warn folks. But then I saw something strange." He drew in a shaking breath. "A monster ripped out the throat of one of the guards. He was dead, there's no denying it. But..." His hands tightened around his hat. "A thick black smoke shrouded his body. And then he rose again."

Kaelen tilted his head. "You mean to say, sir, that the guard's corpse was reanimated?"

"Yes, Councilor," the man confirmed. "But he was all wrong. That's why I confused them with Draemor at first. When he stood, the guard was warped and monstrous. His flesh had already rotted, like he'd been dead and buried for years.

"I kept watching. Every time a guard fell, that same black smoke took them. They'd rise again and attack the others. And that's when I noticed them.

"Farther up the hill, there were red-hooded figures. I couldn't see their faces, but their arms were raised, and the same black smoke poured from their hands. I don't know what kind of magic it was, but it was them. They were the ones making it happen."

Evy's eyes widened—Leo Warring in the Sanctum—he spoke of bodies clawing up from their graves. He had believed it was Draemor activity, but this man seemed certain it was the work of others.

"And Marq?" Royen asked, his voice tight.

The man looked to the floor and gave a slow shake of his head.

"I'm sorry," he said. "I flew back to town to raise the alarm. When I returned with guards, only the bodies of a few staff and debris from the carriages remained. Whatever those things were, the undead, they were gone. And so was the Young Lord."

Evy sat quietly in her chair. She needed to understand, needed to know what thread they were spinning. What tenuous line could possibly tie her to this crime?

But as his story ended, she glanced around the chamber, still as bewildered as ever.

She tried to choose her next words carefully, but they spilled out too fast.

"I must apologize, but what does any of this have to do with me?"

Kaelen shifted uncomfortably in his seat, fingers drumming against the armrest.

Lilian nodded in agreement. "How does this implicate Queen Evalene?" she demanded.

Lawrence turned to Kaelen with a knowing smile, ignoring Lilian entirely.

"You understand, don't you?" the Arch Councilor asked him. "The connection?"

Kaelen slowly rose to his feet. He met Evy's eyes, frowning.

"Did Magister Gale ever tell you why she was banned from the College of Ruitheon?" he asked.

Evy shook her head. "She only said the College didn't agree with her research."

She bit back the rest.

"I was studying a way to empower Witches. And they didn't like that."

Kaelen rubbed his chin, then said, "It's because she was studying a peculiar and... dangerous kind of magic."

"Dangerous?" Evy's brows pulled together. "In what way?"

Kaelen's tone was careful. "Orianna believed this magic would strengthen Witches because they would no longer need to rely on mana." He stopped short, eyeing Evy's puzzled look before deciding to continue. "They would draw from an entirely different power source. She believed this power could free Reyland from dependence on the Heart, the Hierarch, or any ruling body.

"She called it necromancy. A power drawn from the souls of the dead."

He pursed his lips, throat bobbing as if trying to swallow against rising bile.

"When the dean discovered what she was experimenting with..." He paused and shuddered. "With *corpses*, she was immediately expelled from the College."

Evy's lips parted, but no words came. She stared, horrified, then finally found her voice. "I'm sorry, Councilor Reed. Did you say... *corpses*?"

"Yes. She had been trying to collect their souls and reanimate their bodies." Kaelen lowered his head. "That kind of practice felt unnatural. It couldn't be allowed within the sacred walls of Ruitheon, not in a city blessed by Rui herself."

Evy couldn't make sense of it. Why would Orianna commit such a horrid act? There had to be a misunderstanding.

Then another horrific thought struck her. The graves in Reyland. The bodies Leo had reported. What if it had never been Draemor at all?

Lawrence stepped forward again and spoke through the growing unease.

"You see it now, don't you?" His gaze swept across the Council. "The description of the attack and the magic used on corpses mirrors the very kind of spell work Magister Orianna Gale once studied. A magic she once tried to prove could be wielded by Witches."

He strode over to Evy and crouched before her, meeting her tearful eyes.

"A kind of magic that could only come from Reyland."

FORTY-NINE

Evy's mind went blank. She reached for fragments of thought, trying to piece them together, but nothing aligned. She couldn't tell which emotion struck first—horror, disbelief, or betrayal.

Did Kaelen say Orianna had been experimenting on... *corpses*? That couldn't be right. Orianna had been like a mother to her, her guardian. She had always been so righteous, always guided by her sense of duty. How could she have committed an act so awful?

But even so, how did it connect *Evy* to Marq's disappearance?

Royen cut in on cue. "But what does that have to do with Evy specifically? I don't understand her involvement."

"She's the Shaman Queen," Lawrence said, a smile sliding across his face. "Why would a battalion of Witches dare to attack a member of the Veyn family unless *she* commanded it?"

"Why would I order such a thing?" Evy burst out. Her hands had begun to tremble. She pressed them flat against her thighs to keep them calm. "I considered Marq a friend. What would I have to gain from this?"

"A friend?" Lawrence scoffed. "Is that so?" He turned to face her directly. "Evalene Lovejoy, did you have prior knowledge that Marq Veyn would be traveling to Ruitheon to support his cousin?"

Evy's mind spun. Royen had told her about Marq's travels in the Grand Library, just before he gifted her the permits. "Well, yes—"

"And were you not also aware," Lawrence pressed, not allowing her a moment to finish, "that the Draemor in the Blighted Caves prey on weakened minds, especially those who've experienced trauma?"

"What? Yes, but—"

"And we have motive," Lawrence announced to the chamber. "Evalene Lovejoy sought an advantage over Royen Veyn during the Trial of Resilience. She knew an attack on his family would shatter his resolve, which she learned from growing close to him."

He turned to her again. "She ordered her people to strike." He smiled wickedly.

"It's not true!" Evy shouted as she stood.

"Where is Marq Veyn?" Lawrence shouted over her. "At least give us that mercy. Are you looking for ransom? Or is he already dead?"

"This is ridiculous!" She turned to Royen, desperate. "You know me. You know I wouldn't do such a thing."

Royen kept his gaze toward the floor.

Say something. Please.

He didn't acknowledge her. Instead he looked at Lawrence. "The murder of Zafir?" His voice shook. "Is he dead, then?"

"I'm afraid so." Lawrence nodded solemnly. "His body was discovered deeper in the caves. He was brutally mutilated. Both of his eyes were missing."

"That wasn't me," Evy pleaded. "It was the Ifreet. They were the ones attacking. They came after me too."

"I've told you this, Daryn," Royen cut in. "The Ifreet were attacking her when I found her in the caves. They were out for her blood. I witnessed it myself."

Lawrence remained unmoved. "There were reports of Ifreeti mercenaries in the city and of Evalene speaking with several Ifreet during the Procession in Zarokan." He glared at Evy. "It's believed she hired them then and instructed them to meet her again in Ruitheon to work against King Zafir."

Evy racked her memory.

Speaking with Ifreet? It must have been when she and Celeste were shopping in Ashgate.

She was struck with sudden realization. The guards who had tailed them that day, the ones she and Celeste tried to shake, were likely spying and reporting everything to Lawrence.

This was all a misunderstanding.

"They were vendors," she said quickly. "Not mercenaries. We only spoke briefly while I bought clothes from them."

Lawrence scoffed.

Evy opened her mouth to say more, but the Council was already murmuring again, doubt spreading like wildfire.

"No, I assure you," Evy said, willing herself to stay composed. "Celeste can confirm it. She was with me."

"Princess Celeste is already on her way back to Virenna," someone called from the back. It was Eliza Blanche, Second Councilor of Virenna.

Despite the rising panic, Evy clung to hope. There had to be a hole in their logic, a crack she could wedge her truth through.

"If I hired the Ifreet, then why did they attack me too?"

"Because you ordered them to," Lawrence spoke quickly. "You gave instructions to attack you, to throw off suspicion in case anyone encountered you in the caves and saw you together."

She looked to Royen, and he shrugged.

Lawrence sighed. "I suppose it was a clever tactic, since the moment the Heart sensed outside interference, the mercenaries would be disintegrated on the spot. The perfect solution to get rid of the evidence of your involvement."

"No!" Evy pleaded, her voice cracking as she turned, scanning the chamber for a single face that believed her. "None of this is true."

The silence that followed was the loudest sound Evy had ever heard.

And in that silence, she understood that no one could save her. She was truly on her own.

Her voice thinned until she barely recognized it. "Please, you know I would never—"

Lawrence raised a hand, silencing her.

"I remember your outburst in Veyn Manor." Lawrence's voice grew dark. "'You've all been afraid of what we'd become if we were allowed to stand on even ground.' Was that your goal, Queen Evalene? To command fear? If so..." His eyes burned. "Congratulations. It worked."

Evy's legs stopped holding her, and her fingers found the edge of her chair to support her.

"We fear you because it is now evident—you are a *monster*." Lawrence's voice swelled. "And we cannot allow a monster to run free."

Evy stood frozen, her mind spiraling. She'd been so close.

Close to reaching the summit. To everything coming together.

She was on the brink of becoming Hierarch. How had it all unraveled?

Had she been building Orianna's dream—*her* dream—of a better future for Witches from straw instead of stone? Had the prospect ever been possible to begin with?

Her lips parted, but only a whisper escaped.

"But the Hierarch Wars. The tie..."

"There is no tie," Lawrence declared. "Not anymore. With

the evidence before us, it is clear you violated the rules of the third trial. The murder of another Ascendant disqualifies you from the Hierarch Wars."

"No..." Her legs completely buckled and she sank into the chair, hands gripping the armrests as the chamber narrowed to a pinpoint of light.

Lilian stepped forward. "The Heart hasn't disqualified her. How can you dismiss her so easily?"

Lawrence reached into his cloak and produced a bundle of aged scrolls, unfurling one.

"There is precedent," he said, lifting a finger. "During the Eighth Hierarch Wars, an Ascendant from Zarokan attempted to cheat beyond the Heart's view. He almost got away with it, but his deception was uncovered by the Council during a separate investigation. The Heart may be the final judge, but it can also be summoned to bear witness through memory." He rolled the scroll closed.

"There is a sanctioned spell that allows us to present the memories of key witnesses directly to the Heart. If the evidence is strong, the Heart will take it into account."

His eyes brightened as he looked at Evy. "And may change its prior judgment."

Lawrence tucked the scrolls beneath his arm and addressed the Council.

"The witnesses have already been gathered. They are here in the Aurethium now, fully prepared to share their visions with the Heart today."

Evy chewed her lower lip until she tasted blood. Witnesses? What witnesses?

Lawrence watched her like a predator watching the life drain from its prey.

"If their memories confirm what we suspect," he went on, "the Heart will be compelled to act. When it does, Evalene Lovejoy will be disqualified."

He strode toward Royen and placed a hand on his shoulder.

"Which will leave only one candidate remaining. Royen Veyn, the winner of the trials, and the rightful Hierarch of Aeltheon."

A numbness spread from Evy's fingers to her wrists, then through the rest of her body, until she could no longer feel the chair beneath her.

Lawrence had positioned everything exactly where he wanted it. He had engineered every piece of this, likely from the instant she placed second in the Trial of Wit and became a threat. No— She recalled the look of pure abhorrence the day they had met at the Aurethium. Evy wouldn't be surprised if he had begun his maneuvering from the very start.

These so-called witnesses were probably people he planted in the right places at the right times, twisting harmless moments into evidence. The guards who watched her speak to Ifreeti merchants. The Heart would see only the image of Evy speaking to Ifreet and connect it to Zafir's death and the mercenary attack.

Oh, Zafir. He's gone. The sorrow hit her all at once. She had been so consumed by the injustice of her own circumstances she hadn't been allowed a chance to mourn him.

Over the time they had shared as Ascendants, she had come to appreciate his steadfast presence. She had grown immense respect for him as a king. All his life, he had fought to earn his place, for his family, his line, his domain, and against those who told him he could never reach for more. In that, they were alike. And now he was gone.

He had fallen victim to Lawrence's schemes as well. The mercenaries had worn Draemor-repelling rings, just like the one Lawrence tried to give Royen. He had probably intended for Evy to die with Zafir, but the plan had not unfolded the way he wanted.

There were likely witnesses from Veyn Manor too, people

who had seen her anger at the dinner and twisted it into threats. She remembered Dominic's smug expression after her outburst. It must have been his goal all along to goad her. She had always known the consequences of that moment would return eventually, but she never imagined it would be used to accuse her of crimes she had not committed.

Who knew what else Lawrence had arranged or how far he had gone to twist the truth.

As Evy met his eyes, she felt as though she were staring down an infallible beast.

She felt cornered, with nowhere left to turn. What was she supposed to do? Accuse the Arch Councilor of killing Zafir, attempting to kill her, and twisting lies into charges? No one in this chamber would believe her. If she tried, they might even execute her on the spot.

Her mind spun, and the chamber, the crowd, the sound of her own breath all blurred into a hollow, ringing void.

Lilian shot to her feet.

"Are we just going to accept this? She hasn't been given the chance to prove her innocence!"

But this was never about the truth.

Orianna's voice surfaced as if she were standing right behind her.

"If you come too close to taking it all, they'll panic."

She had been right.

"You'll be deemed dangerous, and they'll slam the door shut behind you."

She had been right all along.

"Maybe even bolt it."

Lawrence had all the answers prepared, ready to dismantle every argument. Supposed witnesses ready and waiting in the Aurethium. This had all been orchestrated by him, and he wasn't going to let his plan fail.

"You're going to treat her like a criminal before her formal hearing?" Lilian's voice rose. "Is this what justice looks like in Aeltheon now?"

Lilian whirled on the rest of the Council. "And none of you are going to do anything about it, are you?" Her voice dripped with disgust. "Spineless fools."

She fixed her glare on one in particular. "Kaelen? Even you?"

Kaelen absently stared at the arm of his chair.

"Enough, Councilor Varos," Lawrence spat. "Or I will have the guards escort you out."

Lilian sank back into her chair with a huff, arms crossed in tight defiance but did not speak again.

Evy finally found the strength to speak. "What will become of me?"

For a moment, Lawrence remained silent. Then he slowly exhaled through his nose.

"Despite Councilor Varos's impassioned views on justice in Aeltheon," he said, shooting Lilian another look, "she's right—the Council must uphold the law. The Heart may disqualify you from the trials, but it is our job to prosecute criminals and keep this continent safe."

He adjusted the cuff of his robe and met Evy with a cold, appraising gaze. "And so, Evalene Lovejoy, though the evidence against you is overwhelming, you are entitled to a hearing if you choose to waste the Council's time."

He stepped closer, lowering his voice.

"Or you can spare us the performance and turn yourself in. Do that, and we'll ensure your punishment is... less painful."

Her vision swam. She blinked until the room came back into focus, then forced herself upright, one hand braced against the armrest.

And despite the world crashing down around her, she laughed. Soft, barely audible—from a distance, it probably looked like she was heaving for breath. But she couldn't help it. She no longer knew what to do with her grief, her desperation.

She pressed a hand to her mouth, but Lawrence had already noticed.

His mouth twisted with irritation.

He wanted to break her.

Eliminate her.

To crush her spirit until she regretted ever daring to step beyond Reyland.

But seeing her intact, refusing to crumble under his schemes, had vexed him. And it gave her new resolve. She would never give him the satisfaction. Not when there was still a sliver of hope. No matter how small. She would not give in.

Evy raised her chin. "Then I choose a hearing. I want to defend myself in a formal trial."

"Very well," Lawrence said. "Until a date is set for your hearing, you are banished from Ruitheon and must leave the city immediately."

"Banishment?" Lilian cried, arms still crossed. "I thought she wouldn't be punished until after her hearing!"

Lawrence shot her a look that warned she was dangerously close to sharing the same fate.

"Please try to understand." Kaelen raised a hand in front of Lilian. "The Arch Councilor is taking precautions for the safety of the realm." He glanced at Evy briefly. "If the Shaman Queen is involved in necromancy… if the Witches are… then we must ensure they're contained and observed somewhere secure until the hearing."

Lilian looked ready to argue, but Kaelen gave her a pointed look, silently urging her to stop.

Lawrence turned back to the Council, his voice firm with conviction.

"We will present evidence to the Heart today and will proceed with Royen Veyn's inauguration tomorrow. The realm cannot remain without a Hierarch any longer."

Evy glanced to her side, hoping one last time Royen might speak up.

But his head bowed in his hands, eyes fixed on the marble floor.

She thought back to the Blighted Caves when they'd clung to each other, hand in hand. His gentle squeeze. His quiet reassurance.

They were allies. Friends. And now? Did he think she was guilty too? Did he consider her a monster? That, perhaps, was what broke her heart most of all.

"Royen?" Evy called, voice hoarse.

He didn't hear her.

"Oh, Marq. What did they do?" he whispered repeatedly.

Lawrence glanced over his shoulder at Evy. She met his gaze with unfiltered contempt.

"Out of the goodness of our hearts, and in the spirit of justice, we gave the Witches a fair chance in the Hierarch Wars." His expression twisted between disgust and triumph. "But it seems our kindness was wasted on your people."

He turned and strode toward the door, then paused at the threshold.

"We're done here," he spat. "You're all dismissed."

FIFTY

Please, Herald. Meet me in Virenna. I'll find a way to get you there. I'll do anything. I love you.

Your Beloved,

Rose

Yorik chuckled. He sat hunched on an old crate in the shadow of a narrow alley, using the sliver of afternoon light to read a handful of letters that had been waiting for him at the tavern.

He unfurled another piece of parchment. The ink was smudged where a single teardrop had struck.

I can't stop thinking about you. I'll do whatever it takes to be with you. Even if that means running away.

Your Beloved,

Rose

Yorik leaned back, letting the scroll dangle between his fingers as a cruel smile spread across his lips. "Whatever it takes?" he murmured, amused.

Slow footsteps crunched over gravel, breaking the stillness.

"I can only spare a few minutes before Warring tracks me down," Aeric said sharply. "What do you want?"

"Little brother, you finally responded to my summons."

Aeric glanced at the cart just behind Yorik. It had been packed with supplies, horse tethered and ready. "You're finally leaving. Good," he said flatly. "I came to see you out. Make sure you're not staying to cause more trouble for Evy."

Yorik simply smirked.

"You ruined everything." A muscle ticked in Aeric's cheek. "Evy's been banished, charged with crimes she didn't commit. They've named Royen the next Hierarch, and the Heart's been sealed away again, far from your grasp."

Yorik stood slowly, brushing dust from his shirt. "You give me far too much credit."

"Don't lie to me," Aeric snapped. "It was you and the Chaos-bound. Marq Veyn's disappearance, the death of Zafir Soltris—it was all your doing, and now Evy is taking the fall."

He stepped closer, eyes burning. "And now what? How will you get to the Heart? How will you destroy it now? You've missed your chance, Yorik."

"Have I? Oh, Aeric. You still don't get it, do you?" He let out a low, mocking laugh. "I didn't come to Ruitheon to reach the Heart."

Yorik walked over until he stood towering above his brother. "I came to collect the ingredients."

"Ingredients," Aeric echoed. "What does that even mean?"

Yorik took another step forward, their bodies nearly touching. "I can't just walk up to the Heart and destroy it. First, I need to perform a spell taught to me by the Gods. And this spell requires three ingredients from the blood of the strong."

Aeric staggered away from Yorik's proximity, nearly losing his balance. Yorik laughed and returned to the crate.

"My Acolytes got the first ingredient. Though I must admit, they were sloppy. They weren't supposed to be seen." He sat down. "The second ingredient was practically handed to me." Yorik tapped the corner of his eye. "Zafir Soltris."

Aeric grimaced, his discomfort causing Yorik to grin. "Unlike the simpering Veyn boy and his caravan, the Djinn was a real threat. He would've decimated us in a second."

His smile widened.

"I didn't kill Zafir," Yorik said, voice lilting. "That wasn't me. All I did was take what I needed from the aftermath of his downfall."

He motioned Aeric closer with a finger. "And the third ingredient?" Yorik dropped his voice. "I have it right where I want it. I'll get what I need soon enough. And once I do..." Yorik hardened his expression. "They can seal the Heart away, bury it beneath a mountain. It won't matter. Nothing will matter once I complete the spell. Once I'm transformed."

Aeric shook his head. "I've had enough, Yorik. Leave me and Evy out of it."

Yorik raised his hands in mock surrender. "Don't worry. Evy's part is done, unless she decides to intervene. And your job now is to make sure she doesn't."

"I'm serious," Aeric snapped.

"So am I." Yorik shrugged. "Either way, I plan on disappearing for a while, so you don't have to worry. You'll have to look after Mother in the meantime."

"Where are you going?" Aeric demanded.

Yorik glanced at the letters in his hand. "I'm meeting with a friend. A special friend."

"Great," Aeric said. "I want nothing to do with any of this anymore. None of this Chaosbound business. Orianna will clear Evy's name, and once that's done, she and I can go back to normal."

Yorik stood and checked the reins on his horse. "Sure, if that's what you think."

Aeric scoffed and turned to leave, but Yorik called after him.

"It's not me you should be worried about, little brother." He frowned. "You might want to keep a closer eye on Royen Veyn.

The way he looks at her..." He whistled low. "It would even make me blush."

Aeric froze, then turned, glaring. "What did you just say?"

"I'm not your enemy. But Royen?" Yorik hesitated before deciding Aeric deserved the blunt truth. "He wants to steal Evy from you. There's no doubt. It's etched all over that boy's face."

He watched Aeric's fists clench, the fury barely held back. "Seems like you already knew that, didn't you?" Yorik asked. "How does Evy feel about it? Do you suppose she knows?"

"Shut up." Aeric barreled into him and fisted the collar of his coat. "Just shut up. You don't know anything."

His face was twisted in rage so pure that Yorik flinched. It was Marlin's face—a replica of his father in one of his drunken fits, hunting for some reason to unleash his fury. Aeric must have noticed his expression because he released the collar at once.

He exhaled through gritted teeth. "I'm done here." Aeric turned away. "I'm not worried about some Shifter. Evy is *mine*."

Yorik called after him. "Will you tell her?"

Aeric halted.

"About me?" Yorik clarified. "About what I've done. It could help her, you know. Might even save her in her upcoming hearing."

Aeric stood still for a moment. Then, without a word, he walked on.

Yorik watched until Aeric vanished, then turned to his horse. "Didn't think so."

He expected nothing less. They were Whitlocks, after all. Brothers.

And no matter how much Aeric tried to fight it, there was no bond more steadfast than brotherhood.

FIFTY-ONE

The sun sagged behind Ruitheon's skyline.

Evy paused in front of the townhouse, savoring the last bit of desert light as it warmed her face. She'd grown used to the arid heat and wasn't sure she was ready for the chill of Reyland's approaching autumn.

A letter from Lilian had arrived that morning. After Evy had left the Aurethium, the witnesses presented their visions to the Heart. Lilian had found it strange when the Heart didn't react, but when she tried to argue with Lawrence, she was dismissed. "All was going as expected," he had told her. The Council took the silence as confirmation, and Evy had been disqualified from the trials.

Lilian wrote that she refused to accept it, and the letter went on, but Evy crumpled the paper and tossed it aside. It didn't matter. She was already on her way out.

Her fingers curled around the strap of a trunk she'd already tightened three times. Behind her, Irma moved briskly through the house, double-checking that nothing had been left behind.

With Irma busy inside and Leo off to purchase supplies with Aeric, she had hoped solitude might quiet the storm within her.

But all it had done was make the silence louder.

Her arms hung limply at her sides. She couldn't bring herself to lift another bag. She had simply lost her will.

What was the point now? Who was she being strong for?

Her hands wouldn't stop trembling. The more she tried to keep them still, the worse it became.

Evy turned from the carriage and slipped into the small garden behind the townhouse. She found a palm tree near the edge of the path and sank against it, her back pressing into the rough bark.

For a long moment, she tried to hold it all in and swallow the ache in her throat. But her mind felt like a dam straining against a flood, cracks spreading faster than she could seal them.

And when it finally broke, she let it all out. Evy buried her face in her hands and sobbed.

How foolish she had been to think the Council would ever allow her to become the Hierarch.

Tears rushed down her cheeks as the truth settled in.

Orianna had warned her. She'd said the institution would never stand behind someone like her, a Witch. She'd warned that too much ambition might provoke powerful forces to act against her.

And still, Evy hadn't listened. How could she? When the Cerberus tore through the city, she had lost her sense of choice. How could she hold back, present a facade, while others paid the price?

She never imagined they would go so far as to frame her for crimes she hadn't committed. How naive she'd been to think the Council cared about truth or innocence.

She thought she would be done with trials after the Hierarch Wars. Yet here she was again, awaiting another, one that would decide not her worthiness as an Ascendant, but her very life.

"The evidence against you is overwhelming..."

If that were true, her sentence would likely be death.

Her sobs faded into ragged breaths. Lawrence's voice was replaced by the Draemor's whispers.

"Reya will choose a better reincarnation."

Maybe they were right. Maybe this was what she deserved for daring to hope beyond her place.

The soft thud of footsteps jarred her from her thoughts.

She expected to see Aeric returning from his errands. He had been trying to comfort her all night, confident that Orianna would help her find a way out of this. But his certainty felt suffocating.

After all, wasn't Orianna part of the reason she was in this situation? Because she had never told Evy, or perhaps anyone in Reyland, the full truth of what had happened during her years as a scholar. How could Evy trust her with her future? How could she trust anyone?

She lifted her head, already searching for an excuse to dismiss Aeric again.

But it wasn't him.

"Royen..." she breathed.

He sat beside her and drew his knees up, letting his arms rest loosely across them. As he looked to the sky, the fading light warmed his hazel eyes, making them appear golden.

For a few long moments, neither of them spoke.

Then Evy turned to him. "I had nothing to do with Marq's disappearance," she said, her voice hoarse. "I would never—"

Royen pulled her into a tight embrace, his arms wrapping around her like a shield.

"I know."

Evy exhaled against his shirt. For the first time since she'd left the Aurethium, she felt relief.

"I'm sorry," he said softly. "I should've done more. I should've spoken up against Lawrence. I was just... shocked by what they said about Marq."

Evy shook her head against his shoulder. "There was nothing you could've done."

Royen's grip tightened. "Still. You don't deserve this."

She let herself rest in his arms a little longer before pulling back to meet his eyes.

"You'll get through this... As Hierarch, I'll find a way to pardon you. I swear it."

Evy let out a dry laugh. "I doubt your Council would like that very much. Don't go making enemies on my behalf."

"Lawrence thinks he's untouchable, but I'm going to remove him and all his loyalists from the Council." His eyes burned with fury. "To keep you safe, I'll do it. I'd do anything for you."

She almost laughed again, but the way he looked at her, with such burning intensity, made her pause. For a moment, she was back in that hallway, the warmth of his lips hovering over hers...

Her cheeks flushed, and she turned away quickly, hands fidgeting with her robe.

"The coronation," she blurted, desperate to change the subject. "It's tonight, isn't it? Why aren't you getting ready?" She scanned his clothes: loose tunic, brown linen pants. The most casual she'd ever seen him. No one would guess he was about to become the most powerful figure in Aeltheon.

Royen leaned back. "I wanted to see you first. Say goodbye."

Her throat tightened as she realized she wasn't sure when she'd see him again.

He went on. "And I wanted to tell you that no matter what happens, I'll always be on your side."

Royen looked down at his hands. "When your name is cleared... maybe I could offer you a seat on the Council. You and more Witches. Maybe together, we could actually build a better world."

Evy studied him.

She believed him. She believed *in* him and truly felt that the realm might be in good hands.

"As much as I'd like that," she said, her smile faltering, "I don't think I'm ready for that kind of responsibility."

Royen frowned.

She sighed, watching the sun start its descent below taller rooftops. "There may be Witches practicing necromancy right under my nose," she said. "My own people. And I had no idea. What kind of Queen does that make me?"

Royen opened his mouth to protest, but she shook her head.

"No," she whispered. "Before I try to change the world, I need to do right by my own. I need to reclaim what it means to be Shaman Queen.

"Maybe everything that's happened was Reya guiding me back to my true purpose. Maybe Reyland needs me as a Queen, not a Hierarch." She traced circles in the dirt. "Or on a Council seat."

Royen looked down at his boots. "I'm going to miss you. Selfishly, I hoped you'd say yes to the Council... so I could see more of you."

He reached for her hand.

"I know you have your own path." He squeezed it gently and lifted his gaze to her face. "But if you ever need me, I'm there. That'll never change."

The sinking sun illuminated Royen's face, bathing him in gold.

She couldn't look away. The light caught his features, sharpening the angle of his jaw and softening the edges of his mouth. His hazel eyes sparkled like the sun itself. Evy had always thought Royen carried the refined traits of the Shifter bloodline. But in this light, after seeing not just his exterior but parts of his soul, she realized he transcended simple handsomeness.

He was beautiful. Magnificent. In every way.

Evy couldn't find the words to match the swarm of emotions

that stirred within her. So she nodded and laced her fingers with his.

Time slowed. She let herself savor the warmth of his hand and the comfort of his presence.

Until a voice cut through the stillness.

"Evy?"

They turned. Irma approached, then slowed when she spotted Royen.

"Oh," she said, startled. "Pardon me. I didn't mean to interrupt."

Evy pulled her hand away gently and stood. "It's alright, Irma. What is it?"

"The carriage is ready," Irma said. "Captain Warring's loaded the last of your things. Aeric said he'll meet us at the gate."

Evy nodded. "I'll be right there."

Irma frowned as she glanced between them, then disappeared behind the hedge.

Evy's gaze traced over Royen, memorizing the lines of his face. By the way he looked at her, he was doing the same.

She couldn't regret anything that had happened during this journey. Couldn't regret leaving Reyland and becoming an Ascendant. If she hadn't, she never would've met Royen.

Or Celeste.

Or Zafir.

Or Marq.

Or the many others who'd become her allies.

Her friends.

"Thank you," she said softly. "For everything. For believing in me when no one else would."

Royen gave a lopsided smile. "You don't need to thank me for that."

"I do." Evy returned his smile. "Your friendship means a lot to me."

They remained for one last breath, then Evy stepped forward and pulled him into a tight, heartfelt embrace.

"Bye, Royen," she whispered. "You're going to make such a good Hierarch."

Royen kissed the top of her head. "Goodbye, Evy."

She let go first.

They walked to the front of the townhouse, where her staff waited, ready to depart.

Evy climbed into the carriage, the effort heavier than it should have been. She settled on the seat across from Irma and smoothed her skirt with trembling fingers. The door creaked shut behind her.

Through the small window, she saw Royen standing alone.

He lifted one hand in a slow wave.

Evy pressed her palm to the glass.

Neither smiled.

As the carriage jolted forward, she remained fixed on him until the darkness swallowed him from view.

And her chest tore open in a way she hadn't expected for a man she had once considered a rival.

The carriage rolled through Ruitheon. Outside, townspeople swept rubble into piles and reconstructed broken storefronts. The city was still rebuilding after the chaos the Cerberus left behind. No one batted an eye toward her.

Life moved on.

By the time they reached the gates, the sun had nearly dipped below the low hills of the dunes, faint stars appearing in the sky.

Aeric waited there, just as Irma had said. He climbed into the carriage and sat beside Evy.

"Ready to go home?" He took her hand and brushed his thumb over her knuckles. "And don't worry, alright? Orianna will take care of everything. This will all be behind us soon. We can go back to normal."

He leaned in and kissed her. His lips were warm and familiar, carrying the comfort of home, of everything she had known before the trials reshaped her.

She kissed him back. Tried to lose herself in it.

But her mind betrayed her. It drifted to the salt of a teardrop that had landed on her lip and the way her tongue had moved to taste it before her thoughts had time to protest.

She pulled back from Aeric and turned toward the window.

"Yes, I'm ready," Evy said, even as a knot formed in her throat.

The carriage carried them into the desert dusk. She wasn't sure anything would ever truly return to normal.

How could it?

She had left Reyland as a girl who had never stepped beyond her domain. She had crossed the continent, survived the Hierarch Wars, faced the Council, and forged life-changing bonds. She was no longer the same Evy who first journeyed to Ruitheon.

And beneath the pain of failure, a strange resolve had begun to bloom.

Maybe this was her reckoning.

Reyland needed her. The Witches needed her.

If she could endure the impending hearing, she would devote every breath to lifting her people with the power she still had.

She would seal the portals across Aeltheon and use that task as a step toward redemption.

Even if it only softened the hatred the world bore for Witches, she would wear herself to the bone if it would make a difference. If it helped the realm see that they were not a threat.

And she would uncover the truth behind necromancy.

If the attack on Marq truly had ties to rogue Witches, she would be the one to stop it. She would not allow Reyland's name to be bound to evil ever again.

Evy rested her head on Aeric's shoulder and closed her eyes.

The road ahead would be steep. But she was wiser. Stronger. And she understood the truth behind her purpose.

As sleep began to tug at her, she forced herself to stay awake just long enough to peer once more out the window.

Somewhere beyond the horizon, Reyland waited for her.

Ready to reclaim its Shaman Queen.

EPILOGUE

Evy jolted awake as the carriage lurched violently to one side.

She threw out her arms and braced herself against the interior. A thunderous crack split the silence. The wheels skidded across the road as the driver fought for control. She crashed into Aeric and bumped her knees into Irma.

"What was that?" she shouted, then opened the window and shoved her head out. "Are we under attack? Is it the Draemor?"

They were deep in the desert now, Ruitheon a blur behind them.

Leo's voice reached her, tight with panic. "I don't think so, Your Majesty. It feels like an earthquake!"

Evy pulled back inside.

"That hurt," Irma muttered, rubbing her knees. "The Gods must be angry."

"That's just folklore," Aeric began. "It's actually—"

The ground rumbled again, more violently than before. In the distance, dunes collapsed, sand avalanching in waves. Sand Striders burst from their burrows and scattered across the road.

Then came the scream.

A piercing, inhuman shriek split through the sky like lightning.

"Where is she?"

Evy clutched her ears, folding inward from the sheer force of the sound. Irma whimpered beside her.

Another quake rippled through the land, shaking the carriage.

"Bring her back to me!"

The voice came again, ragged and full of unearthly rage. The carriage rocked dangerously on its wheels.

Where was it coming from? It didn't seem tied to any one direction.

"What's going on?" Aeric shouted.

Evy flung open the door and leaped out, desperate for air as her head throbbed in pain.

The moment her boots hit the ground, she saw it.

The thick bands of mana were thinning into erratic strands, lashing wildly. They snapped toward Ruitheon like a tide pulled inward, then surged back out like blood through a struggling heart.

The Heart.

Royen's coronation—wasn't it now?

In the distance, a handful of guards galloped toward them, golden cloaks whipping violently in the wind.

"Stop!" one of them shouted, his voice barely cutting through the rising storm. "By order of the Council, stop!"

Then the voice returned.

"Incomplete. Incompetent. Unworthy vessel."

The guards' horses shrieked and reared, tossing their riders as the land continued writhing.

Evy stared in astonishment.

"That voice," she whispered. "It couldn't be—"

"My child!" it screamed. *"Come back to me!"*

My child...

She had heard those words before in whispers. There was no longer any doubt. The Heart was speaking. It had been speaking to her all along.

And now it was screaming for her.

Evy scoffed.

Of course the Heart wasn't finished with her. She was still an Ascendant in its eyes. Lawrence had tried to manipulate the Heart, to bend it to his will. But it hadn't worked.

The Heart had rejected his judgment, and now it demanded her return.

Evy looked back at the guards, still struggling to rein in their horses and reach her.

The carriage horse was rearing too, the driver barely managing to hold on.

Then she spotted Leo. His battle-trained steed was jittery but mostly composed beneath him.

Evy ran to him and lifted her arm. "Help me up."

Without hesitation, he reached down and pulled her up onto the saddle behind him.

"Your command, Your Majesty?" Leo asked over the wind.

Evy glanced toward the distant chaos in Ruitheon. A sudden energy pulled at her before she could brace for it.

It started behind her ribs. A pressure, like a fist closing slowly around her lungs. Then it sank deeper, into her bones. She felt herself slipping off the horse, lurching back, gripped by an invisible force.

"Come back!"

She grabbed Leo's waist and held on tight. The Heart was trying to drag her back.

"Go, Leo."

Evy gave one last glance toward the storm brewing in the distance, at the chaos the Council had sown and now were forced to reap.

Let them face it. Let them get a taste of their own consequences.

The pressure returned to Evy's chest, the Heart pulling her toward Ruitheon.

"Don't leave me!"

She wasn't ready to return to the Heart's clutches. Not when her people still needed her. Not when she had to become the Shaman Queen she had promised to be.

"Leo, take me home!" she commanded.

Leo glanced back at the carriage, where the others still waited.

She needed to distance herself from the guards. There was no time to calm the other horse.

"They'll catch up," she said firmly.

Aeric leaned out the window, his face pale as he watched her. His mouth moved frantically, but Evy couldn't hear him above the wind.

Leo clicked his tongue, and the horse surged into a gallop as they headed toward Reyland.

The deafening wind howled violently around her, but Evy heard it one last time, the sound now mournful and desperate—

My child...

ACKNOWLEDGMENTS

Bringing *The Hierarch Wars* to life has been one of the most rewarding challenges I've ever taken on. My ultimate goal was to create an outstanding book, and there's no way I would have made it here alone.

Thank you to my editorial team: Katie Reed for her thoughtful developmental guidance that took this story to the next level, Jodi Hughes for her diligent and thorough line and copy editing, and Stephanie Taylor for her meticulous proofreading. Your insight, care, and attention to detail strengthened this story to the quality I envisioned, and I'm incredibly grateful for your work.

Thank you to Elias Prado for transforming my illustration into the final cover design. Your eye for composition and the care you put into hand-drawing the title brought this cover to life.

To my early readers and ARC team, thank you for your time, your honesty, and your excitement for this story. Your support meant more than you know, and when I felt like losing motivation, your words and feedback kept me going.

To my family, friends, and colleagues, thank you for your encouragement throughout this process. Your excitement was contagious and kept me energized. A special thank you to my husband, my biggest supporter in everything in life, who encouraged me to reach for my dreams every step of the way. But also thank you for making me take healthy breaks and forcing me to go outside once in a while.

A big thank you to my son who told me to finish my book so I could help him write a thousand-page book about "fun." I can't wait to take on that project with you one day. Maybe not a thousand pages, though.

To all my English teachers who have encouraged me to write —thank you. I wouldn't have had the courage and confidence if it weren't for you.

To my Papa, who instilled creativity and a love for the arts into my very being—I did it. I wrote a whole book. I know you're proud, watching from above.

And finally, to the readers, thank you for picking up this book and stepping into my world. I hope you enjoyed the journey. I hope your time with the characters felt like genuine friendships. Your support is what allows this world to exist. From the bottom of my heart, thank you.

— M.J. Badal

ABOUT THE AUTHOR

M.J. Badal is a Bangladeshi-American fantasy author who writes stories featuring complex magic systems, political conflict, and slow-burn romance. She earned a degree in sociology from UC Santa Barbara, which reflects her interest in power structures and group dynamics in her worlds. Raised in California and now living in Colorado with her family, she balances work, motherhood, and world-building.

instagram.com/m.j.badal_author
tiktok.com/@m.j.badal_author
goodreads.com/mjbadal

STAY CONNECTED WITH MOON BEAN PUBLISHING

Thank you for reading *The Hierarch Wars*.

Join the Moon Bean Publishing newsletter for updates on future releases, exclusive content, and more from the world of Lumesphere.

Subscribers get:

- Early access to releases and announcements
- Exclusive content—like a recipe from Zarokan!
- First access to limited promotions and collectibles

Join here: Moon Bean Publishing Newsletter (https://www.moonbeanpublishing.com/newsletter)

Thank you for being part of this journey.

GLOSSARY

Acolyte — A follower of the Chaosbound, sworn to the Herald and his mission to cleanse mana from the realm.

Arch Councilor — The presiding head of the Council, chosen from among the twelve sitting Councilors. Currently Lawrence Daryn.

Ascendant — A domain's chosen champion in the Hierarch Wars, bonded to the Heart for the duration of the sacred trials.

Ashgate — A city of Zarokan below the Infernal Citadel, built on volcanic earth. Known for its bustling open-air markets.

Aurethium, The — The palace at the heart of Ruitheon; a fortress of white marble crowned with a golden dome. Seat of the Hierarch and the Council, and the home of the Heart.

Barrenland — An empty realm beyond a portal in Hollowrift, named by Evy and Royen upon discovering it. Magic does not work there, and even creatures of Hollowrift lose their power within it.

Blighted Caves, The — A sealed prison holding imprisoned Draemor. The setting of the Hierarch Wars' third trial, in which Ascendants must find their way out alive.

Bonding Rites, The — The seasonal ceremony in which the Shaman bonds young Witch children to spirits, granting them access to magic.

Bound Blades, The — Reyland's border guards and peacekeeping force, led by Captain Leo Warring.

Celestial Gauntlets, The — An ancient relic said to have been gifted to the realm by the Gods, granting enhanced speed and strength. Awarded to the winner of the Trial of Wit as an advantage in the Trial of Strength.

Cerberus — A monstrous three-headed beast of Hollowrift, dragged from its realm by the Council and chained in the Ruitheon coliseum to serve as the challenge of the Trial of Strength.

Chaosbound, The — A hidden movement led by Yorik Whitlock that seeks to destroy the Heart and sever mana from the realm, believing it festers like a disease.

Cinderbark — A fire-resistant tree native to the warm, dry regions of Zarokan. Their thin, blackened, leafless trunks appear burnt, yet the trees thrive in volcanic terrain.

Council, The — The twelve-seat governing body beneath the Hierarch. Each of the four domains holds two seats, ranked First and Second Councilor. The remaining four seats belong to the Outer Islands: First and Second Councilor of the Outer Islands, and First and Second Adjunct Councilor of the Outer Islands.

Crystal Court, The — The palace of Virenna; home of Queen Talia DuVent and Princess Celeste. A glimmering structure that resembles a glass lotus, refracting sunlight into spectral shards across the surrounding meadow.

Djinn — A species of Elemental that resides in Zarokan. Legendary for their strength and resilience, they do not wield fire so much as they *are* fire.

Draemlord, The — The king of the Draemor, who long ago forgot his true name and accepted his title completely.

Draemor — Creatures of Hollowrift, born of malice, drawn to suffering, sustained by destruction. They slip through unsealed portals into the realm and can be imprisoned in the Blighted Caves.

Elemental — One of the four races; resides in Zarokan. Species include the Djinn and the Ifreet, among others.

Ethereal — One of the four races; resides in Virenna. Known for spells and enchantments. Species include Elves, Sylphs, Pixies, and the extinct Lumiels, among others.

Forgotten Folk, The — The ancestors of the Witches; a people left out when mana was given to the realm. Reya took pity on them and granted them the ability to bond with spirits.

Gaiasphere — A realm of myth and legend where neither magic nor mana exists. Some scholars at the College of Ruitheon believe the Forgotten Folk originated in Gaiasphere and crossed into Lumesphere through Hollowrift.

Heart, The — The sacred relic that binds mana to Lumesphere; a fragment of Goddess Rui herself. Wielded only by the Hierarch, through a sacred bonding ritual.

Herald of Chaos, The — The self-proclaimed title of Yorik Whitlock, leader of the Chaosbound.

Hierarch, The — The supreme ruler of Aeltheon and sole wielder of the Heart, chosen each generation through the Hierarch Wars. The line traces back to Lutharion Skye, entrusted by Goddess Rui.

Hierarch Wars, The — The sacred trials held upon each Hierarch's death, in which Ascendants from the four domains compete for the throne and the right to wield the Heart.

Hollowrift — The liminal realm beyond the portal, home to spirits, souls, and dark creatures like the Draemor. A passageway between portals that may lead to other realms.

Ifreet — A species of Elemental that resides in Zarokan, made of fire like the Djinn. Rival Ifreeti clans have contested the Soltris line for generations.

Infernal Citadel, The — The royal residence of Zarokan, partially embedded in a gargantuan mountain among the volcanic peaks. Black stone walls veined with glowing red-orange light, windows overlooking rivers of molten lava, chambers magically cooled against the heat. Home of King Zafir Soltris and his son Juleen.

Lumesphere — The world; the realm of mana and magic, imbued with mana by Goddess Rui. Contains the continent of Aeltheon and its four domains. It also included six Outer Islands.

Lumiel — Light Elves, an extinct Ethereal species once considered the most powerful beings in Aeltheon. Held the Virennese crown and the Hierarch's throne for generations before being maneuvered into extinction.

Luxhaven — A grand city of Theribane, where mana flows so freely it powers trams, clock towers, lamps, and more inventions.

Magister — An elected office of Reyland; a political and administrative leader who serves alongside the Shaman Queen. Currently held by Orianna Gale.

Mana — The magical essence Goddess Rui gifted to Lumesphere. It flows from the Heart, is drawn from the environment into living beings, and is required by all to work magic.

Moonveil — A coastal Reylandic town. Marked by mana-starved soil, crumbling bridges, and worn lanterns, its Witches must ration mana for even simple needs like hearths and healing.

Paladin — A holy guard of Ruitheon who works in service of the Council. Paladins are trained in combat against Draemor and are dispatched into the Blighted Caves on missions and rescues. They wear protective rings of Daryn family invention.

Planar Astra — The home of the Gods. Rui descended from the Planar Astra to imbue Lumesphere with mana, and ascended back to it after leaving a fragment of herself in the Heart.

Reya — Goddess of Spirits and daughter of Rui. She took pity on the Forgotten Folk and gave them the ability to bond with spirits, transforming them into the Witches. Her chosen vessel is the Shaman.

Reyani Temple — The temple of Reya in Reyland; home and seat of the Shaman Queen. Its cold halls are kept by the Spirit Matron and her Spirit Sisters, who raise the chosen Shaman from childhood.

Rui — Goddess of Mana and mother of Reya. She descended from the Planar Astra, imbued Lumesphere with mana, and left a fragment of herself in the Heart before ascending back.

Sanctum, The — The sacred chamber within the Reyani Temple, where the Shaman performs the Bonding Rites. A circular stone platform sits at its center. Sconces along the walls glow with light spirits, and powerful wards keep Draemor at bay.

Shadow Rites, The — A dark ritual performed by the Chaosbound that severs a Witch's spirit bonds and unlocks the power to command souls.

Shaman Queen / Shaman King — Reya's chosen vessel, reincarnated in a Witch each generation; the spiritual and political leader of Reyland. Performs the Bonding Rites and can close portals to Hollowrift.

Shifter — One of the four races; resides in Theribane. Shifters can transform into non-magical animals; animal forms are inherited through bloodlines, with rarer forms carrying more pride. The Veyn family has held the Hierarch's throne for generations.

Souls — Distinct from spirits; the lingering essences of the dead. Souls drift through Hollowrift, where the realm acts as a nexus between worlds. Some Shamans are born with the ability to see and hear them. Necromancy is the forbidden practice of drawing power from souls; Yorik claims the Shadow Rites grant him the power to command them.

Spirits — Entities from Hollowrift bonded to Witches through the Bonding Rites. Each serves as a conduit for drawing and shaping mana, manifesting as elemental wisps of light, fire, water, and more.

Spirit Matron — The elderly head keeper of the Reyani Temple, who oversees its order and trains the Shaman through her childhood. She wears a gossamer veil and a hooded lavender robe and carries a small silver bell that signals the start of ceremony. She and her Spirit Sisters take vows of solitude.

Spirit Sisters — The order of Witches who serve the Reyani Temple under the Spirit Matron. Sworn to solitude, they raise the chosen Shaman from childhood. During the Bonding Rites, they cleanse the Sanctum, and guide Witch families through the ceremony.

Sylph — A species of Ethereal that resides in Virenna, known for their skill with air magic.

Veyn Manor — The ancestral seat of House Veyn in Theribane, perched on a cliff above the sea and surrounded by a wide moat. Its symmetrical limestone facade and twin towers project grandeur, but a cold, unfeeling presence pervades the estate. The Veyn crest—a wolf, a panther, and a hawk entwined—is carved above the entrance.

Witch — One of the four races; resides in Reyland and descended from the Forgotten Folk. Witches can draw mana like all Aeltheans, but cannot shape it into magic on their own; they rely on their bonded spirits to work magic for them.

PRONUNCIATION GUIDE

Characters

- **Evalene** — ev-uh-LEEN
- **Evy** — eh-vee
- **Aeric** — AIR-ik
- **Yorik** — YOR-ik
- **Orianna** — or-ee-AH-nuh
- **Royen** — ROY-in
- **Veyn** — VAYN
- **Zafir** — zah-FEER
- **Soltris** — SOL-triss
- **Kaelen** — KAY-lin
- **Daryn** — DAR-in
- **Juleen** — joo-LEEN
- **Lutharion** — loo-THAR-ee-on
- **Linius** — LIN-ee-us

Goddesses

- **Reya** — RAY-uh
- **Rui** — ROO-ee

Realms & Places

- **Lumesphere** — LOO-mis-feer
- **Aeltheon** — AYL-thee-on
- **Reyland** — RAY-land
- **Virenna** — vur-REN-uh
- **Theribane** — THER-ih-bayn
- **Zarokan** — ZA-roh-kan
- **Ruitheon** — roo-EE-thee-on
- **Aurethium** — aw-REE-thee-um
- **Reyani** — ray-AH-nee
- **Gaiasphere** — GUY-uh-sfeer

Beings

- **Draemor** — DRAY-mor
- **Draemlord** — DRAYM-lord
- **Lumiel** — LOO-mee-el
- **Ifreet** — EEF-reet
- **Djinn** — JIN (silent D, like "gin")
- **Sylph** — SILF

www.ingramcontent.com/pod-product-compliance
Lightning Source LLC
LaVergne TN
LVHW091247150826
845673LV00006B/1349